Also by Sarah Willis

Some Things That Stay

The Rehearsal

The Rehearsal

Sarah Willis

Farrar, Straus and Giroux

New York

Farrar, Straus and Giroux
19 Union Square West, New York 10003

Distributed in Canada by Douglas & McIntyre Ltd.
Printed in the United States of America
First edition, 2001

Library of Congress Cataloging-in-Publication Data
Willis, Sarah.
The rehearsal / Sarah Willis.— 1st ed.
    p.   cm.
ISBN 0-374-24861-3 (hardcover : alk. paper)
1. Steinbeck, John, 1902–1968—Dramatic production—Fic-
tion.   2. Theatrical producers and directors—Fiction.   3. The-
ater rehearsals—Fiction.   4. Farm life—Fiction.   5. Actors—
Fiction.   I. Title.

PS3573.I4565557 R45 2001
813'.54—dc21

                                              2001023624

Designed by Jonathan D. Lippincott

In memory of my father, Kirk Willis

We are such stuff
as dreams are made on.

—William Shakespeare

Rehearsal: a private performance.

—*Webster's Ninth New Collegiate Dictionary*

The Rehearsal

Thursday

❧ ❧

As the station wagon reaches the crest of the hill, Will Bartlett catches sight of the house and the barn. He twitches, a blink moving through his body; suddenly he sees an answer to what's been nagging at him for months, just as if someone has been tapping on his shoulder and finally decides to shout in his ear. He's glad no other cars are on this narrow dirt road; his hands are a bit unsteady as an image overlays the barn: a set, an interior with bunks, wooden crates, and the scattered belongings of working men. "Damn!" he says.

"What now?" Myra looks at him from the passenger seat, but he doesn't glance her way. It's enough to have to concentrate on the road; there are two kids asleep in the backseat, and potholes the size of craters.

"I have an idea," he says, not so much to Myra as to himself, to move thoughts into action, test the sound of beginnings.

Myra shakes her head, and Will knows she is tired of his ideas, in spite of their merit. Just last night he wanted Myra and the kids to sit with him on the front porch with their eyes closed, staying silent for an hour, absorbing the sounds and scents of the city; memorizing them like a sonnet. Then tonight they would do the same thing here, sitting on a blanket in the front field; compare the busy street in Pittsburgh to the open expanse of their farm in Chautauqua. He loves doing stuff like this. The kids thought it was a great idea for about ten minutes. Myra had gone inside before they even started. She said she had to finish packing.

But most people do what Will asks them to. It's his voice: a commanding voice. All the reviews mention his voice—it gets old, or so he says. Secretly, he's worried that someday his voice might *not* get mentioned, and then what would that mean?

"Do I want to know about this idea?" Myra asks.

"It'll wait." He turns onto the pebbled lane bordered on each side by a soggy drainage ditch and overgrown weeds. About a quarter mile up, just before it reaches the house, the lane curves to the left and heads over to the barn. *The truck with the props and furniture can get to the barn easily*, Will thinks, already imagining the men unloading it. He'll have to make some phone calls tonight. He'll need the entire cast to make this work. They'll come, once he explains things; the actors enjoy being together; they are, in many ways, one big family. As he steps out of the car, he knocks a fist three times against the fake-wood paneling. It can't hurt.

The car stopping has woken Beth, who nudges Mac. Myra had laughed when, eighteen years ago, Will had told her about his plan to have a boy and a girl named Mac and Beth. Two years later, married and pregnant, she had gone along with naming their first child Beth. Eight years later, when they had a son, she hadn't thought the idea so funny. They had compromised on James MacArthur Bartlett, but everyone calls him Mac, and Will wonders if the boy even knows his first name. Mac isn't the quickest of kids. Sometimes he seems to be living on another planet altogether. It doesn't bother Will one bit. *Eccentric* is a word he's quite proud of.

"Are we there yet?" Mac asks.

"No, stupid," Beth says, rolling her eyes. "It's *another* house just like ours."

"Leave him alone, Beth," Myra says, with the same agitated tone Will has heard her use a hundred times when talking to Beth. Will wonders if Myra knows what her voice gives away. Maybe that's what makes Beth so angry all the time. Or maybe Beth's anger is what makes Myra so tense. The chicken or the egg? Even as he considers the conversation he might have with Myra, he discards it, knowing where it will go. She'll just tell him that he's not home enough to know what he's talking about.

He's not home enough, that's true. But he knows what he's talking about.

Still, it's easier just to do the things he needs to do. Like unpacking the car. Saving the theatre.

Unpacking will take some time. Myra can pack a car like no one else, filling every nook and cranny with the things they will need for the next three and a half months. Each spring they do this. The Mill Street Theatre in Pittsburgh closes in mid-May, and the summer season at the Chautauqua Institution—where The Mill Street Theatre performs eight of twelve plays from the past season—doesn't start until July. Will and Myra withdraw the kids early from school and move to their summer house, a ten-minute drive from popular Lake Chautauqua and the Institution. For six weeks Will can read plays, fix up the house, or just do nothing, although doing nothing is never as much fun as it sounds and usually ends up making him nervous as hell.

When they were young, the kids hadn't minded this back-and-forth living, but Mac, eight now, couldn't join the softball team, and dragging Beth, a stubborn sixteen-year-old, away from her crowd had been no mean feat. Luckily, she wanted to be an actress, and Will's carrot this year was to offer her a job with the company: property assistant, with pay. He'd even heard her bragging about it to a friend. The thing is, even though he's six foot four, sometimes the kids make him feel small, or even worse, like an old log in their way as they walk down some path he didn't even notice them turning on to. Then again, there are times—like Beth bragging about her job at the theatre, or the sight of Mac's tumbleweed head of hair bobbing up and down as he plays some imaginary game—that make Will feel as though it doesn't matter how big he is, there just isn't room enough inside him for all his love. When he feels like that, he gets anxious. The gods will know his weakness. Having children is like having fate take hostage of his heart.

As the kids climb out of the car, Will walks over to the barn. He has to be sure it can be what he needs it to be: a place to re-work *Of Mice and Men*. To *live* it. He's been the artistic director of the summer theatre for twenty years. Back in Pittsburgh, he's a director and an actor, but here at Chautauqua, he's *the* director. It's his baby. And the rumors he's been hearing lately are that this might be their last season here, that the Chautauqua Institution might not ask them back after the summer of '71. The elderly patrons and rich vacationers want something new. He's heard they want opera instead. Opera! My god! So he has to create a play so powerful that the Chautauqua Institution, and The Mill Street Theatre, will understand what only a resident company is capable of accomplishing. The true give-and-take of actors who work together year in and year out. The board of The Mill Street Theatre will not be happy if they lose their summer revenue. They have already been discussing laying off the actors, bringing in traveling productions of Broadway plays, an occasional big name like Tony Roberts. Who the hell is Tony Roberts? It's now or never. Will stands in front of the weather-beaten barn—which was once red but is now the

color of splinters, its doors propped open with cinder blocks—
and crosses his fingers. He walks inside.

There is a small narrow room in the front of the barn. Will
nods, thinking this room will be just right for Nate Johnson,
who plays Crooks, the black stable hand. In the play, Crooks is
not allowed in the bunkhouse, which will be the main part of
the barn. They should stick to that rule while living the play,
Will thinks, although Nate might not like that. Being the only
black actor in the company is already enough of a division. But
that is the reality of *Of Mice and Men*. They'd better go for it
all the way.

Passing through the narrow front room, Will enters the interior of the barn: a huge open area with a dirt floor, six square
posts, and a rusty rake. All around is the heady smell of mold
and damp wood. Pale thin mushrooms sprout in dark corners.
At least they won't have to clear out a lot of old junk. They
leave the barn empty since vandals or rot would destroy anything left behind. The kids use it as a playhouse sometimes,
bringing in chairs and tables and putting on skits that go on far
too long. Will always itches to show them how to make their
skits tighter, but Myra says she'll kill him if he does, and he understands. He probably expects too much from them. Still . . .

But now the barn will be put to good use. There was something deadening about performing *Of Mice and Men* last Octo-
ber inside the concrete walls of the theatre. All along he felt
something was missing. In this barn they can take *Of Mice and
Men* further—where, he isn't quite sure, but finding out will be
half the fun.

It can't hurt to try.

Beth's father comes out of the barn, rubbing his hands together
and nodding. Suddenly he shouts, "Hot damn!" A crow barks
and flies from the dead tree near the house. The crow is the

same color as her father's hair, a glossy black so dark it has a
purple sheen to it. For the first time, Beth wonders if her father
dyes his hair. She knows he's pretty old, fiftysomething, although he'll never say; it's like a family secret or something, a
family secret even she can't know. So typical. But the idea he
might dye his hair makes her feel embarrassed, and she doesn't
like that feeling. He's the coolest dad she knows. He's a director, and an actor, and she's going to be an actress, and he'll direct her, and she'll be great and maybe famous. Only, so far, he
hasn't let her act in anything, even though he's hired other kids
for children's roles. He says it would show favoritism if he used
her. He says she has to be a very great actress first, so people
won't make catty comments. But Beth has been taking acting
classes on Saturdays since she was six and spent years going to
the theatre after school to watch the rehearsals. She's listened to
her father's every word, played along with all his weird exercises, memorized monologues, gone to hundreds of performances, and put on dozens of skits. And now that she's ready,
he just hasn't noticed.

She'll be seventeen next April. The world seems both huge
and belonging to her. If someone would just give her the key.

Beth watches her father study the barn and knows he's up to
something. She imagines the barn becoming whatever he needs
it to be, widening or shrinking, growing stronger, straighter,
even proud. Her father can do anything, and she's going to be
part of it.

Mac watches his dad, who's looking at the barn and swearing.
Mac thinks his dad's happy now, but then why's he swearing?
It's hard to tell when his dad is mad, or happy, or excited, because all those times, he yells and moves his arms around like
he's drawing in the air. Mac's friends are all scared of his dad.

Mac's not really scared of him, but he does sometimes feel all his muscles pull in on him and get tight when his dad gets excited, or mad, or happy. Those times, Mac's not sure what his dad will want him to do. Sometimes when his dad gets ideas, he has Mac do strange things, like everybody has to walk around with a frown to see if that makes them mad, or walk around with a smile to see if that makes them happy, or talk with their face and no words, which Mac liked but Beth hated and said was stupid. But sometimes Mac's dad gets ideas and never tells Mac what they are, like painting the living room back home blue, and drawing leaves on the walls, and Mac has to figure out what's going on.

Lately, his dad has been telling him he's going to be a great actor someday. Mac's not sure he likes that idea at all.

Mac carries his pillow to the house and looks over his shoulder to see if his dad is going to call for him, tell him to walk like a monkey or talk like a bird—which Mac thinks is a good idea and might suggest it sometime, except Beth will say it's stupid. But his dad just stares at the barn and rubs his hands. Mac goes in the house and looks around. They have been coming here for five summers, and he always wonders if it might have changed while they were gone, but it's just like it was, and he likes that. Except for the spiders.

Will's hands are large and capable. He has built puppet theatres, fixed sink drains, and hooked together the tiny clasps on Myra's bracelet, but right now his hands move like wounded birds. At the beginning of each sentence they rise chest high, flutter, and drop. It's because they have no audience. Myra won't look at him. Won't answer him. He never imagined it was going to be this difficult to convince her, or that she would get so mad. He's completely unprepared for this fight. He's already said everything he can think of, so he begins to repeat himself.

"So the guys who play the ranch hands, and George and Lennie, will live right in the barn. Sleep on the bunks. The rest can stay in the house." Will follows Myra with his eyes as she unpacks a suitcase and places the folded clothes in the oak bureau they found on the side of the road last year. Myra had refinished it. She is good with her hands, too, but right now her hands are smoothing out the clothes a little too fastidiously. Will wants to grab those carefully folded socks and toss them across the room. He needs to get going. Make those calls.

"Beth and Mac can share Mac's room. And you and Melinda can sleep in Beth's room. You like her. It'd be like camp. Norton and Greg can sleep in our room, and I'll sleep on the couch."

Myra's lips tighten, and she picks up the empty suitcase to carry it to the hall closet. He steps in front of the door to block her way.

"It could be our last chance. . . . If the Institution doesn't ask us back, it will give the Mill Street board the excuse they need to send us packing. It's not just the summer season at risk here. You know that. Resident companies are falling right and left. Their boards think Broadway actors will bring in the bucks. By the time they realize that doesn't work, it will be too late! Think about it. We'll lose our livelihood to a trend. Frankly, Myra, I'm scared. We need to get their attention."

"How will they *bathe*?" Myra says, turning her face up, glaring at him. "Where the hell will everyone brush their teeth? Go to the bathroom? Are you going to hand out numbers? Who's going to feed them? The cook is offstage! Do I get that role? Oh, that'll be just great. The final stab. I get to be the unnamed, unseen cook. No problem memorizing my lines! Make it easy on you, huh? And whatever makes you think I like

Melinda? And what about Frank's wife? Where will she stay? You haven't thought this out. You want to take a flying leap into the wild blue yonder, and you expect me to close my eyes, hold your hand, and jump?"

"Yes," he says without thinking, then, "Kathryn won't be coming with Frank. She's going to stay with her mother in Texas. We'll build an outhouse, maybe a cabin. We'll need some kind of hard work. We can't ranch, but something to bring us closer to the play, the characters . . ."

"But—"

He takes the suitcase from her and puts it on the floor, then grabs her hands and kisses them. "I've done crazy things before. *Romeo and Juliet* in slang before anyone else tried it. You thought I was nuts, but it got great reviews! And I asked you out the day I met you, and even though you thought I was strange, you agreed to go out with me, and that turned out all right, didn't it?"

"This is different, Will. This is—"

Lowering his voice, speaking as softly as he can, Will looks Myra in the eyes. "This is my livelihood, Myra. It's all I know how to do. It's how I support this family. Please let me do it as best I can, for a little while longer."

"Oh, hell," Myra says. "Really, Will . . ."

Will knows he's won by the tone of her voice. She's not angry now, just resigned. He avoids smiling. Don't blow it now, he tells himself. "I promise we'll do all the cooking, and we'll clean up after ourselves."

Myra nods once, but her jaw is tight. Will is torn between pulling her close for a hug and dashing downstairs to the phone. He hugs her, but she stays rigid in his arms. "It'll work. You'll see."

"I don't see. And I don't see where I fit into this plan either, Will."

He doesn't have an answer for that, so he just holds her until she shrugs out of his embrace.

Myra sang her way through school: in the Meadville High School choir, and on the Meadville High School stage, she sang her heart out. In her senior year she played the lead, Gale Joy, in *Best Foot Forward*. In college she played Julie in *Carousel* and Laurey in *Oklahoma!* She sang in summer stock for two years before joining The Mill Street Theatre; they had decided to do more musicals that year. They produced *South Pacific* first and brought in a "name" from Broadway to play Nellie. But for the next musical they couldn't afford a "name," so Myra got the part of Fiona in *Brigadoon*. The audience loved her. The local paper assumed she was from Broadway, too, and said they hoped she'd come back for another role. Myra bought three dozen papers and mailed the reviews with her Christmas cards to everyone she knew.

Myra met Will at the theatre, and they were married two years later. A year after that, at four months' pregnant, Myra quit acting. It wasn't actually discussed as a choice, just discussed. When Beth was five, The Mill Street Theatre decided to do *Show Boat*, and at Will's suggestion, Myra auditioned and got the leading role of Kim. But Myra was scared. She hadn't been on the stage for almost six years. From the first rehearsal to the last dress rehearsal, she felt butterflies in her stomach. Each time she stepped onto the stage it felt like her heart might stop beating. Then, too soon, it was opening night.

That night, on cue, she stepped out onto the stage, looked out at the audience, and panic gripped her throat. To this day she can remember the trickle of sweat running down her cold, clammy skin. She stood for an eternity as everyone stared, as actors and audience went from anticipation to worry to whispers. She found she *could* move but not speak (or sing), so she walked off the stage. Three feet into the wings her legs quit working, and she tripped and fell into the ropes, banging her shin hard against a light. The pain was nothing. She was filled to bursting with a knowledge as hot and bright as any spotlight: she would never act again.

Everyone was kind. The understudy was dressed in less than five minutes. They were nice enough not to insist she take off her costume right there in the wings. The replacement wore something else until the next act. Will was supportive. Understanding. He said he'd heard of it happening to other actors. He didn't name names.

From that day on, Myra hated some part of herself. Some days it was a big part, like her heart, some days only a small part, hardly noticed, like a kidney or a lung.

Will still loved her. Forgave her. Almost forgot about it. He had a short affair a few years later. It lasted only months.

But Myra still sings. She sings when she is alone. She loves to be alone at their summer place: the kids at camp, Will at work, and she in the backyard, hanging laundry or pruning a fruit tree, and *singing*; the sound of her voice in the summer air, full and vibrant as it was years ago.

As Myra unpacks the kitchen things and rinses mice droppings off the stored pots and pans, three things occur to her. First: she will not be alone for a whole month; she will not have a moment to sing. Looking out the kitchen window at the backyard, she feels a deep loss, as if something has been taken from her that sits out there, waiting, just out of reach. Already she misses the sound of her own voice.

Her second thought is: Will wants to ask the actors here, to their farm, not just because he wants to put on a production so wonderful that it will save the theatre, but because he needs the actors to fill an empty place inside him, a space that needs constant validation—a place that Myra believed she once filled, but no longer does.

Which leads directly to her next thought. The theatre, which she has left behind (although she sees plays, talks about plays, invites actors over for dinner, goes to opening night parties; still, she has left behind her vision of ever being on the stage again, left behind, she thinks, the pain of failure), is moving in with her, and her husband has invited it in her door. A vision flashes through her mind. She sees herself in an airplane, looking out at the bright, blue, perfect sky, a passenger who was once a pilot. Where the hell is she going?

The water suddenly turns scalding, and Myra pulls back her hand, almost breaking the plate on the steel sink. Someone must have flushed the toilet. That will happen often in the next month. She will have to be careful.

Beth is dying to know what is going on. As she comes downstairs, she can hear her mom banging pots and pans around in the kitchen, which means she's pissed, probably at her dad and his new idea. He's standing over by the phone going through his big tan briefcase with a scowl on his face. Any minute now her mom's going to yell for Beth and tell her to scrub the floor or something. It always goes like that. Her mom gets pissed at her dad, so she takes it out on Beth, which pisses Beth off so much she'll do something like trip Mac, who never gets picked on 'cause he's so little, and Beth's mom will get *really* pissed at Beth, and Beth will get *really* pissed at her mom, and they'll have some big fight—like the time her mom told Beth she was a thorn in her side, and Beth told her mom to get a life—so that now when Beth sees her dad doing something that will piss off her mom, Beth just takes a shortcut and gets pissed at her mom. She kind of knows she should get pissed at her dad, who always starts this whole thing with his crazy ideas, but the idea of getting pissed at her dad makes her nervous. Also, she needs to be nice to her dad so he'll put her in a play.

"Damn it!" Orange scripts and yellow legal pads spew out of her dad's briefcase and fall onto the living-room floor.

"Do you need some help, Dad?" she asks softly, knowing sometimes it's not a good idea to interrupt him.

"My black phone book. It was in here. Goddamn it, I need it." He doesn't usually swear in front of her—actually, he does, but only when he's too occupied to even realize she's there, like now.

"You left it on the kitchen counter in Pittsburgh, and—"

"What?" He straightens up so quickly, the briefcase falls onto the floor, spitting the rest of the papers out in one solid heap as if throwing them all up. Beth knows how that feels. When her dad gets this mad it always makes her sick to her stomach. She hurries up with what she was saying.

"And I picked it up. It's in the box with the mail we brought."

His face changes from anger to gratitude so fast, it makes Beth dizzy. "That's my girl! Can you get it for me?"

"Sure." It's only in the kitchen. She's back in less than a minute. He claps, like he's applauding her. She bows.

"You're always there for me, you know that, don't you, Pumpkin?" He takes the thick black book from her and starts flipping through it.

He hasn't called her Pumpkin in a long time, which is okay, since she's really too old to be called by a childhood name, but she doesn't mind it so much this time. "What are you doing? You seem pretty excited."

He stops flipping the pages and looks at her for a while, obviously trying to decide if he should confide in her. She tilts her head sideways with the look that says, *I'm interested, please tell me.* She's seen it done in the movies, and she's practiced it in the mirror. It works real well with boys. Finally he nods.

"Yes," he says. "You could be a big help, actually." He glances toward the kitchen, where they can both hear her mother banging the cupboard doors. "I might need an ally on this one, until it gets going. She'll see I'm right, eventually." This last part is said to himself, but since he says everything loudly, that never really works. Beth's heard him say all sorts of things he didn't know she could hear. He talks to himself as he paces in the living room back in Pittsburgh. Once she heard him say, "The woman needs a good fuck." She *thinks* he was talking about a character. He usually is.

"Come and sit down. I'll explain." They sit on the couch, and he tells her how the theatre might change from a resident theatre to the kind that doesn't have the same actors all the time. He tells her that he needs to try something bold to get the board's attention, so he's going to invite the cast of *Of Mice and Men* to the farm, to "live the play." He is bound and determined to save his theatre. They must take this chance. Does she understand?

"Of course I do, Daddy. It's a great idea!" She can't believe it. It sounds like they are going to have a commune, right here, at her house. And *Of Mice and Men* is her favorite play in the whole world. The part of Curley's Wife is to die for. Melinda Holbrook played it in Pittsburgh, and she was so great. Someday Beth is going to play that role. Oh my god! The whole cast will be coming here for a month! Her father is so cool. "So what can I do?"

"Well," he says, looking toward the kitchen again, "just support me on this, could you? It'll take a lot of work, having all these people here. I could need you to do just about anything. We'll have to bring up the props, organize rehearsals, plan exercises. Make lists. You'll be my girl Friday. With your help, we can save the theatre." He taps her on the chin with his fist. She stops herself from thinking how corny that gesture is. "Can you do it? Be there for me?"

"Sure, Dad, you know I will." It's like being the stage manager, she thinks. "What can I do first?" she asks.

He's already gotten up and gone over to the phone table to get his black book and doesn't seem to have heard her. Beth gets worried, remembering last year when he said she could be in a play soon and then never mentioned it again. She tilts up her chin and smiles. To find an emotion, you can act it physically, and the emotion will come more easily. She's really been studying hard. Being his girl Friday will be her chance to show her dad how much she's learned. "What can I do?" she asks again, making sure her voice projects, even though her dad is only just across the room.

"Well, honey, could you pick up all those papers I spilled?" Her disappointment must show, because he adds, "You'll need paper to take notes for me. Make a list of the actors I call, and cross them off the list when they agree to come. Keep track of when they can get here. And Beth, thank you." Before she can even bend down to pick up a piece of paper, he's dialing the first number.

Will calls Ben Walton first, because Ben's his best friend and would agree to go to the North Pole if Will asked him. Ben says he'll come tomorrow. Will's glad Ben doesn't have a girlfriend right now. Otherwise he would have stalled for a few days. Sometimes Ben gets a little crazy over women. Ever since his divorce six years ago, the man falls in love on every first date. It never lasts. Women leave Ben behind like wet Kleenex, Will thinks. Like his character of Lennie in *Of Mice and Men*, Ben has the soul of a Saint Bernard. He's a nice guy but needs a backbone. He's a great actor, though.

Will loves directing Ben. Ben could go on to Broadway, but he's smart enough to know that without the right director, he could drown there. He chooses to stay at The Mill Street Theatre, a *resident* theatre, where he gets the best roles, delivers his best performances, and is a very large fish in a small pond. Will and Ben make a great team.

Will calls Norton Frye next. Norton plays The Boss. If Ben is a Saint Bernard, Norton is a peacock—a man who wears an ascot *and* a toupee. Oddly enough, Norton is a matinee idol at The Mill Street Theatre and receives fan mail from elderly ladies that makes even the actors blush. Norton has a cat he brings with him for the summer and who lives with him in the small boardinghouse in the nearby town.

Norton answers the phone on the first ring, glad no one is around to see him lunge for it the way he does. "Hey, Norton," the voice says. "How are you doing?"

Norton pauses. Not because he doesn't recognize Will's voice, since anyone would recognize Will's voice, but because Will has never called Norton at home for anything except dire emergencies, like blackouts at the theatre, or an ill actor that Norton will have to fill in for. Since no plays are being performed right now, it must be that someone has died. Norton is preparing his shocked and upset voice when Will just goes on, oblivious to Norton's nonanswer.

"I had this crazy idea here, Norton, and I need your input," Will says. "What I need, really, is you." Will pauses, and Norton is confused. No one is dead, and the "I need you" routine sounds familiar, but the timing is wrong.

"What?" Norton asks, just as Will starts again.

"See, Norton, as I drove up our lane, I saw the barn, and

somehow it became the set for *Of Mice and Men*. Boom, just like that. It was calling to me. And I thought, this is it! Rehearse it here! Not just for a few days, but live it, maybe do improvisations. Doesn't that sound great? You loved rehearsing *A Midsummer Night's Dream* in our field, didn't you? Remember how rehearsing it in the great outdoors gave birth to all sorts of new ideas? How it enhanced the production? Brought it new life? And then when we took it back inside, all that carried right with it. The audience felt it. You know they did. Well, this is the same idea, but bigger. This might be our last season if we don't pull something out of our hat. Let's show them what we're made of. What a resident company really means."

"What?" Norton says again, because he has no idea what Will is talking about. Norton wonders if Will is drunk, except Will is a sloppy drunk, and there is no slurring of words.

"What I'm saying here is, I want you, and the whole cast of *Of Mice and Men*, to come up here to the farm and live with us. We will rehearse the play here. You'd get a room in the house, since you play The Boss. The guys would sleep in the barn. We'll find its heart, its soul. We'll blow the audience away when we take it back to the theatre. I know this is what you believe theatre is all about. I need you to help me convince the rest."

Okay. *Now* Norton gets it. Here is Will at his best. Manipulative, enthusiastic, so full of himself, he believes every word he says, and—the scary part—convincing as hell. Norton can feel himself wanting everything Will envisions: the experience of immersion in play to the point of becoming the characters and, just as important, the adoration of the audience. But live at Will's farm? With all of them? Norton shudders.

"What time period are we talking here, Will? A week?"

"A month! Why not? We all have the time off. The farm is huge. There's a lake nearby. What else are you doing?"

"We've performed it already, Will. We only need a week to

refresh it. And frankly, I was going to do a commercial for WJKL and make a bit of money on the side."

"*Money?* You're thinking about *money*, Norton? How many commercials do you think you can do a year from now, when the board brings in the Show of the Month from Broadway? But I'll tell you what. I'll get you some money. Fifty a week, and all the food you can eat. That's a promise. And we aren't going to refresh this play, Norton. We're going to re-invent it. We'll have guaranteed jobs for the next decade. I don't know how much you've heard, Norton, but I've got wind of more than I like. I'm nervous. If you can think of a better plan to save our ass, I'll listen. But I'm not planning on doing commercials for the rest of my life. *This* is my life."

Norton laughs. He can see Will right now. The man must be having a fit trying to hold the phone to his ear and wave his arms about in the air like a bandleader conducting Beethoven's Ninth.

"Look, Will, it sounds interesting. Can I get back to you?"

"No. It's now or never. You say no, now, and I'll call the whole thing off."

Norton almost says it. *No, Will, you're nuts.* But the words don't come, because Norton thinks Will is a great director. And truthfully, Norton hasn't signed any papers for that commercial. It's more like a good possibility. But it's only a voice-over. It would take a day. The rest of the time Norton's planning on taking day trips, writing up his adventures in his diary. If Will could get them some money for this . . .

"What about my cat?" Norton asks. "I can't leave Betsy here."

"Bring her. She'll love it."

"But Lars will have to bring the dog."

"Norton, that dog is blind. He's no threat to your cat. Will you come? Can I count on you?"

"Look, Will, I'll come. But I need some money. You under-stand that, don't you? Something to make up for the commer-cial."

"Word of honor, Norton. I'll get you the money."

"When should I arrive?"

"Tomorrow."

Norton laughs again. "Listen, Will. I'll come, but I can't come tomorrow. I'll be there on Sunday."

"But—"

"No buts, Will. And I don't really suppose you need my as-sistance convincing anyone, do you?"

"Well, if I do, I'll give you a call."

"I'm bringing the cat. Tell Myra I said hello."

"Thanks, Norton. I owe you one."

"You'll owe me more than one, Will."

"You'll be begging me to do this again next year."

I don't think so, Norton thinks. He is pretty sure one month will be more than he'll ever want.

Beth watches her father with pride and fear. Her father is *the director*. He acts, too. He is the best Shakespearean actor of them all. His deep voice and tall height fit those roles perfectly. He would have loved to play Lennie in *Of Mice and Men*, but he's too thin—there would be no believing Will could buck bar-ley or break someone's neck. And he would have loved to play George, the man who travels with Lennie, but besides being way too tall for the part, Lars Lyman is so obviously perfect for the part of George, it would be a crime not to cast him. Beth knows all this because her father tells her, and her mother, and Mac, at the dinner table every night, talking about the after-noon's rehearsal before going back to the theatre for the evening. Beth ingests the theatre along with meat loaf and baked potatoes. She grows tall on her father's words. Her skin shines from his dreams. Her stomach aches with his disappointments.

So she listens with fear as he makes these calls, because she has just started to understand that her father may not be perfect. He may be a flawed god. Someone might say he's crazy. Someone might say no.

She can't believe the theatre could be disbanded, the actors cast out. These people are her family, and *actors*, and to Beth, there is nothing else in the world worth being. Except, recently, there are other things that seem almost as interesting. Like guys. Talking to guys. Being looked at by guys. Kissing them. Touching their bodies and watching them shudder. Being touched. It's pretty great.

Also, music: The Beatles, although she still can't believe they broke up—refuses to believe it. Simon and Garfunkel. Three Dog Night. Janis Joplin. Music makes Beth feel things more strongly. Sadder, happier, lonelier. Carole King's "It's Too Late" almost makes her cry, and Beth hardly ever cries unless she gets so mad tears come with anger like goose pimples with cold. The last time she cried really hard was last fall, when her mom ran over their cat who was sleeping in a leaf pile, and those tears came back for days without warning. She hasn't really forgiven her mom for running over the cat, but there are so many things she hasn't forgiven her mom for, it just fits right in with the rest of them, like not letting her go see *Five Easy Pieces* with Mike, and the way her mother got pissed out of her mind when Beth got caught cutting school, and grounded her for two weeks. But really, Beth doesn't *hate* her mom—it's just that when Beth is a mom, if she ever decides to have children, she is going to do things differently. Like not blaming them for every little thing.

Beth is going to be just like her father. If she had to be anything else in life, like a stewardess or a nurse, it would be like wearing the red A that that Pilgrim woman had to wear; it would show all the world she wasn't good enough to be an actress. She couldn't bear it. If Beth were her mother, she would be so embarrassed! Imagine walking off the stage right during the play! *I would move to Alaska and never show my face again*, Beth thinks. But she's nothing like her mom. People say she looks like her, but looks are deceiving.

Her father hangs up the phone after talking to Lars Lyman and gives Beth the thumbs-up sign. Then he knocks on the wood table three times and picks up the phone again. It's beginning to get dark.

Mac will not go to sleep until he completely searches his room for spiders. This takes a long time because even though he has looked under the bed with a flashlight six or seven times, a spider might have crawled under the bed while he was looking elsewhere. There was one on the ceiling when he first came in, but his mother got it. He made her open the paper towel and show him the smushed carcass. There are no curtains in his bedroom, because that's where he found a big black spider last year. Big, black, and hairy. Probably a tarantula. He has brought his own sheets and blankets from home. Spider eggs could be in the ones stored here. When he is as sure as he can be—which isn't all that sure, but his mom is beginning to get that very tense tone in her voice—he says good night and closes his door, stuffing a towel into the crack at the bottom of the door, which will do no good, he knows, because there is a crack at the top of the door. He sleeps with his light on, his socks on (tucked over his pajama bottoms), and a long-sleeved turtleneck shirt. And a red stocking cap. He has to concentrate on sleeping with his mouth closed. Once he read that the average

person swallows eighteen spiders in their sleep during their lifetime. The article had one of those blown-up pictures of some
kind of hairy spider. When he closes his eyes, he sees that picture plain as day, so he tries to go to sleep with his eyes open.
But he gets scared of what he might really see, and closes them.

Myra stands in the hall outside Mac's bedroom, waiting for
Beth to get out of the bathroom. She stands between her children, awkward, not much like a mother at all—as if she has
just faked it all along and might get caught, sent back to Go.
Once she had hoped to have another child; the relief that she
didn't is undeniable. Will used to say he wanted a third child,
but Myra thinks he meant it in an abstract way, as another
credit to his name. Myra wanted a child in a very physical
way—when Mac went off to kindergarten, Myra needed something to do. It was hard to get a job that she could leave each
May to follow her husband to the country, and being a mother
was a good job. Necessary. She believed in staying home with
her children when they were young, even if she hadn't done it
as well as the first flush of motherhood had inspired her to do.
She wanted to try it again, lose herself in the love of a baby,
wear herself out keeping up with a toddler, be even a better
mother than before, push her limits of love and patience. She
did better with Mac than with Beth; she has allowed him to be
more himself, whereas she has, *had*, expected of Beth, all she
had expected of herself: love, kindness, good morals, hard
work—all of which she herself has failed in to some degree, and
she sees those failings multiplied in Beth. Are her children's failings her own? She doesn't know, but just a few years ago she
had wanted to find out. But time makes a difference. Recently,
each day has seemed a test, not just with Beth but of herself.
She is uncomfortable in her own skin, and it's not because of

the wrinkles around her eyes, or even the lines around her wrists like the rings in tree trunks that mark time, but a need to be wiser and smarter along with the wrinkles. It's as if her body has matured but she has lagged behind, dulled by motherhood, and being a wife, and cleaning the same damn countertop three or four times a day for days, and months, and years, until it is as faded and dull as she. Myra is tired of being wed to a brilliant man. She would like to be brilliant in some way herself. She would like to be proud of something more than of her husband and her children.

Beth is the tough one, Myra thinks. It's good to have a daughter with a strong will, isn't it, in this day and age? Beth has never been a momma's girl. A daddy's girl, that she is. Sometimes it bothers Myra how Beth follows her father around like a puppy looking for affection, treating Will like he's God's gift to aspiring actors. Is that what Myra used to do, at the theatre? Is that why Will fell in love with her? Is that why he doesn't love her the same way now, because she doesn't fawn over him like everyone else? He told her once that it was hard to come home at night and be asked to take out the trash or change a lightbulb, when at work he tells everyone what to do and they admire him for it. He was drunk, and he denied it the next day, but she knows it's true, as well as she knows it's true that she's not the great mother everyone thinks she is. Her own daughter treats her like shit sometimes, and Myra lets her get away with it because it's easier to ignore it than deal with it. Or to decide who to blame.

What kind of role model is she, anyway? What has she taught Beth besides how to tuck in the sheets, how to make a tuna casserole? No wonder Beth dotes on her father. Still, Myra is tired of getting walked all over by her daughter—and her own husband. Carefully, Myra opens the door to Mac's room and peeks in. He's sound asleep, his mouth open like a little O.

He's delicate and soft and her baby, for now. She closes the door quietly until it clicks shut. Beth is still in the bathroom. Myra bangs on the door. She'd better get out of that bathroom before Myra goes crazy just standing here.

With her eyes closed, Beth wipes off the cold cream with a tissue to remove the last traces of mascara. The smell of cold cream brings back one of her earliest childhood memories. She must have been around six. She and her mom had gone into the men's dressing room after a play. She doesn't remember which play, only that from the audience it didn't look like her dad had on makeup, but up close it was a different matter. There was this beige stuff all over his face (which she now knows is called base), and he even had on eyeliner, blush, and lipstick. He had to use tons of cold cream to get the stuff off. So did the other men in the dressing room, all digging their fingers into the dark blue glass jars and tossing tissue after tissue into the garbage. The smell of cold cream makes her feel like she is surrounded by those actors; it excites her, and calms her. She is almost there. She is on her way.

When she was young, her dad would bring home his old makeup, the squeezed-up tubes of base, short stubby pencils, and oily crayons to use as lipstick, but her parents wouldn't let her out of the house with makeup on until her sixteenth birthday. Now she wouldn't walk down to the mailbox without wearing lipstick, blush, and mascara. But at least she is very careful about cleaning her face every night. Some of the actors have permanent blackheads and pockmarks from years of stage makeup. Beth is lucky. She's got good skin, and she's going to keep it that way.

When she's finished with her nightly routine, she opens the bathroom door and finds her mother just outside. It must have been her mom knocking before, when the water was running. Beth knows she was in the bathroom for a long time and is just about to say she's sorry when her mom jumps all over her.

"Jesus, Beth, didn't you hear me? Other people live here, you know."

"Yeah, I know," Beth says, crossing her arms and not moving out of the way. "You want me to get zits?"

"No, just be more considerate."

Beth shakes her head and starts to walk off, but her mother stops her. "Don't slam any doors. Mac is sleeping. And don't open his door."

"Yes, ma'am," Beth says.

Mac is her mom's favorite. It's so obvious. Beth knows the story about her mother freezing on the stage. She heard her talking to her friend, Mrs. Luoma, about it. Her mom told Mrs. Luoma that she had frozen onstage because she had taken off so much time after having Beth that she had lost her courage. Then she said, "But this makes it all worth it." Beth knew exactly what "this" was. Her mom was pregnant with Mac and rubbed her stomach all the time like it was some kind of stupid good luck charm. Beth was the reason Myra couldn't act, but Mac was her salvation.

Before she goes to bed, Beth sneaks over to her brother's door and opens it just a little bit. A little bit ought to be enough.

F r i d a y

๛ ๛

When Mac wakes, he sees right away that his door is open, just a crack. Tears well up in his eyes. In slow motion, he lifts the covers. No spiders, but they could be anywhere by now.

At breakfast his sister tells him that when she was going to bed, she saw the biggest spider of her whole life crawl into his bedroom. She says it was carrying a big, round, white egg sac. His mom says she is making up a big fat lie and makes Beth do all the breakfast dishes, then go to her room for an hour, but that's not going to fix anything. After breakfast Mac searches his room again. He begs his mom to get him a new door, with no gaps, but she's in a pretty bad mood and just tells him to grow up.

By ten o'clock Friday morning, Will has reached everyone except Melinda, who will play Curley's Wife, the only female character in *Of Mice and Men*. Melinda is the youngest and newest member of The Mill Street Theatre, and by far the prettiest. She's also quite social. She has friends who aren't even actors. No one knows where she is. She's probably asleep in some guy's bed, Will thinks, angry she's not home, where she belongs, to get his phone call.

Not knowing if she will come to the farm is driving him crazy. He feels unfinished, like he's not wearing his shoes or hasn't zipped his fly. His shoulders are so tense, he has to keep shrugging and rolling them in circles. He does this as he paces back and forth in the barn. Every ten minutes or so he goes into the house and calls Melinda's number, lets the phone ring fifteen times, then goes back out to the barn. He knows he should be doing something, but he can't figure out what to do. If Melinda would just answer her damn phone, he could get on with making plans.

He could rake out the barn, but he might as well wait until Ben gets here. Ben's a big guy, just like Lennie; his upper torso swells against his shirts, and Will knows he used to lift weights. His arms hold the shape of muscles, but Will doubts they have the strength they boast; still, he'll be a big help getting things ready. No one else can make it today. Most of the cast will arrive over the weekend, and two of them won't get here until Monday. They have other things to do first. Will rolls his eyes.

On his way into the house, Will passes Mac, who stands by the open door of the station wagon looking at the backseat like he's trying to figure something out.

"Lose something in there, son?" Will asks, because things do turn up in that car that have been lost for a long time, like Beth's favorite hairbrush, stuck like a hedgehog under her seat for years.

"I think I'm going to sleep in here tonight," Mac says. "Do me a favor, Dad. After I close the door, leave the windows rolled up, okay?"

Will nods. "Sure."

By the time he gets to the phone, Will knows he told Mac he'd do something, but he can't remember what it is. He hopes he didn't promise to drive the kid into town for a damn comic book or something. Myra could do that. She has to go get supplies anyway. Last night, around one in the morning, Will wrote a two-page list of some staples he figures they ought to have for the weekend. He stuck it to the fridge. Myra hasn't mentioned seeing it yet, but you can't really miss it. Will figures that since Myra hasn't said much of anything to him this morning, she's seen the list.

Melinda doesn't answer the phone. Will feels a headache coming on.

He thinks about having a drink, but his own rule is: no booze before or during work. Technically he's on vacation, but he's trying to get something together that deals with work, so he figures he's working.

Pacing in the barn again, Will thinks about alcohol. In the play, the field hands only go out drinking on weekend nights. The actors aren't going to like being told they can't drink. How can he stop them from going out to a bar at night? It's beginning to be obvious that they can't live the play every moment. Would a comedy have been a better choice? Has he acted impulsively, out of desperation rather than from true inspiration? He kicks at a barn post, and dust falls to the floor. This is a good idea, isn't it? He tries to find the excitement he first felt when he drove over the hill and saw the barn, but it's not quite there. It's tinged with doubt, like a tarnished brass ring. He wants to wash off these second thoughts. He wants to be sure again, so he closes his eyes and imagines the actors here, in the barn, playing their parts, enthusiastic, asking Will for advice, climbing new heights, breaking new ground. He fills himself with the belief that he's a great director. He opens his eyes. He's a middle-aged man standing in an empty barn.

Will's legs feel weak, and he leans against the barn post. This exercise has always worked before. Close your eyes, imagine you're a prince, or a mayor, or a salesman, then open your eyes, and you are. Something must be very wrong—he's only trying to be himself, the sure, confident man he was just a day ago. If this is so hard, is it at all possible to find the brilliance of a few years ago, when he was at his peak, winning awards, interviewed by the *Times*? He's embarrassed right now by the image of that interview framed above his desk at the theatre, fading, a vain boast of yesterday's glory, waiting to be quoted at his funeral.

Oh, hell, he's getting way too dramatic about all this. He directed three plays last year to great reviews! He's not dead yet, and neither is the theatre. If only Melinda would answer her phone, he could think straight. The quiet in this barn is driving him nuts. He heads to the house.

Myra stands on the edge of last summer's weed-covered garden. She looks at the brown lumps of earth that will need to be turned, but she keeps seeing the goddamn grocery list Will stuck on the fridge. Then she sees herself filling up two or three grocery carts with all that shit Will thinks they need, then unpacking it and putting it away in the cupboards. She sees herself giving Will the cold shoulder, and she sees him blatantly ignoring her, pretending everything is fine. She sees herself being nice to Ben Walton when he arrives—someone she genuinely likes—but can also see herself grinding her teeth behind his back. Finally, she sees herself going to bed alone, while Ben and Will stay up all night talking about Will's stupid idea. Standing by the garden, Myra has already lived this day, and didn't like it one bit.

But what is she to do? There really isn't anything to eat.

She'd better go to the store. What choice does she have? Make Will go? Betty Friedan never lived with Will. And maybe that's exactly her point.

Beth is getting really excited. Not only are nine actors coming to stay at her farm, but one of them is going to be Greg Henry! He's the guy who plays Curley, the Boss's son, who wants to be a boxer. Greg Henry is twenty-six and looks like an older version of Kurt Russell, except that Greg Henry's eyes are brown, not blue. But he does have that same square jaw and sexy smile, and he's always been really nice to her. He even flirted with her at a party last summer. She was probably a little too young for him last summer, but she's older this year.

She has just got to tell Deb, her best friend back in Pittsburgh, about Greg Henry coming to the farm. She'll be so jealous! No one's around right now—her mom's out staring at the garden like *that* might make it grow, and her dad's pacing in the barn, muttering, and Mac's setting up camp in the car like some moron—so it's the perfect time to call Deb. But just as Beth reaches for the phone, she is scared out of her mind by her dad yelling "No you don't!" at the top of his lungs, which makes her jump a foot in the air, and her ears ring.

"What?" Beth can hardly hear the sound of her own voice.

"Don't touch the phone, Beth. I told you that."

"But, Dad, I just want to—"

"No buts, Beth. I want that phone free in case Melinda calls."

"Dad, she's not home. You just called her. I just want—"

"Forget it. This is important. Leave the phone alone."

Beth can't believe how stupid this is, that she can't make one little phone call. It's not like she's going to ruin the whole rehearsal by making one phone call. Nothing's even happening yet. "Jesus!" she says, and looks at her dad. He looks at her.

Now they're having a staring contest. She can feel her face get hot and her eyes all tight. She swears she won't look away first, but she does, she can't help it. She can't stand him being mad at her. It's enough to have her mom always mad at her. Her dad's the nice guy. Most of the time.

"Don't say *Jesus*, Beth, and don't stand there sulking, and whatever you do, don't touch the phone." He says this all slow, like she's stupid or something. Well, she's not stupid.

"What if Melinda doesn't come? Are you going to get another actress? You'll need *someone*." Beth can't ask for the role. She's got to make it look like his idea. She stands up as straight as she can. She could look twenty-two, or whatever age Curley's Wife is in the play.

"She'll come, Beth. It's her role. She'll call. Trust me, she'll call."

Beth has a momentary vision of cutting the phone cord, but it would be no use. She'd get blamed without a glance Mac's way. Maybe she could gnaw the wire to shreds, make it look like the mice got it. She rolls her eyes at her own stupid idea.

"Isn't there something you should be doing, Beth?" her dad asks, walking by her and picking up the receiver, then dialing the phone.

"Like what?" Beth says. "Like memorizing lines I can't use?" She can't believe she said that, but it feels good, so she lets the words just hang there, see what they do.

This gets his attention. He looks up from the phone. Beth can hear the hollow echo of the ring, nothing, ring. "One step at a time, Beth. One step at a time."

"I'm not a baby!"

"I know you're not. But you're not ready to play the role of Curley's Wife either." He pauses, raising his eyebrows, so Beth understands he saw right through her. Oh, well, at least he has the idea now, and if Melinda *doesn't* come . . .

"Acting is a learning process, Beth," he says, waving his free hand around for emphasis, as if she were sitting ten rows back instead of standing right here in front of him. And it hits her, the déjà vu of having this conversation with her dad while he waits on the phone for someone else to talk to, stuck, unable to do anything else but fill in the time by talking to her—lecturing her, really, as if she were listening to him on the other end. Then, once he's had his say, he hangs up on her and moves on. Conversation over. Time to go do something adult. She is important only in the idle moments of his life, and there aren't that many, because he likes to keep busy. It's a weird thought, and it makes her think . . . but she can't, because he's talking louder and louder.

"You have to play the spear-holder first, then the maid with two lines. It can take years, even for an actress out of college, to get a decent role in professional theatre. You have to take what you can get and do the best you can. You'll get there. You have theatre blood in you, but you have to have patience."

Yeah, Beth thinks. I have *good* acting blood on one side, and *bad* acting blood on the other, and that makes me a big zero. Well, I'm not going to walk through life doing nothing.

"But what am I supposed to do right now?" Beth says, hating the whine in her voice. "I'm bored!"

"Good—you can come to the store with me," her mother says.

Her mom's standing in the doorway of the kitchen. There is no privacy here at all. Everything is heard by everyone else, because there's nothing else going on.

"I don't want—"

"You're coming," her mother says. "You're your father's right-hand man, I hear, and since *he's* apparently not going to the store, you get to. Right, Will?"

"Good idea. Beth, you assist your mother, and bring me the receipts. Then you can establish an accounting list of our expenditures."

Yeah, like using big words is going to make it seem like a cool job, Beth thinks.

"Go on now. I need to make a call."

Beth and her mom look at Will. He's still holding the receiver. They can hear the ring, nothing, then the ring, like the refrain of a sad song.

The grocery store is a big joke. It's a tenth the size of the grocery store back home. To get any kind of good selection, they have to drive forty-five minutes into Jamestown, which her mom hardly ever does, but watching her mom frown at the grocery list, Beth bets she'll have to go to Jamestown. God knows she won't ask Beth to go with her on that trip. Beth would pile up the cart with ten different sugar cereals and a dozen types of cookies. Beth has a real sweet tooth, especially now that she's discovered pot.

She's not stoned right now, even though she's brought a nickel bag with her this summer. She's very good at waiting for the right moment. The right moment is going to be when she and Greg Henry are alone.

"Get a dozen frozen orange juice," her mom says. "I have to find canned artichokes. Have you seen any?"

"Yeah, sure," Beth says. "Back in Pittsburgh. Give me the car keys, and I'll go get some." Beth walks away, toward the frozen foods, without waiting for her mom's reply. The car is a bone of contention. A big bone that Beth hopes her mom will choke on. Even though Beth is now sixteen and took driver's ed in school, she isn't allowed to go out for her license. There are more excuses for this than stones in the road, and they grow more numerous every time Beth complains. First, there was just no time to make the driver's test, because her dad needed the car for work. Then, when Beth pointed out a possible time, they decided the extra insurance would be too much. When

Beth found a part-time job at the drugstore near their house, they decided it was too chancy to risk their only car on a new driver. (No one mentioned risking Beth's life until about twenty excuses down the line.) They have agreed to allow Beth to drive down the lane to get the mail, but Beth won't let them imagine for a moment that something that moronic might appease her.

Beth finds a new treasure in the frozen food section. Chocolate éclairs. She piles three boxes into her arms, along with the orange juice, and puts them in the cart, which is now full, even though the list is not even half finished. The éclairs make her think that maybe she could smoke just a little of that pot today. She hasn't tried out this batch yet, and she better make sure it's good before she offers some to Greg.

"Well, if he wants artichokes," Beth's mom says, crumpling up the list, "then he'll have to go get them himself. I'm done."

The cashier at the check-out line is one of the townies whom Beth played with when she was younger. Bucktoothed and maybe six feet tall. She says hi to Beth with that look of *Don't I know you and aren't you a nobody?* This look, coming from a six-foot, bucktoothed, scraggly-haired townie, solidifies Beth's decision to try out that pot as soon as she gets back to the farmhouse.

The total is eighty-two dollars and forty-two cents. Her mom starts muttering under her breath, and Beth is so embarrassed. Her mom looks like a mental patient. What will people think of them?

When her mom starts the car, Led Zeppelin blasts out of the radio, and she turns the station to another channel, where some dumb, slow song is playing. Beth reaches over and turns the station back to Led Zeppelin. Her mom turns the car off, right there in the parking lot.

"What is your *problem*?" Beth asks.

"You really want to know?" her mom says.

No, Beth thinks, but she's not dumb enough to say it. "What?" That's neutral enough. It's not like saying, *Sure, tell me all your problems, Mom. I've got a few hours.*

"You."

Beth can't believe her mom said that. She can feel her eyes get hot.

Her mom closes her eyes in that pained way she always does, then shakes her head slowly. "I'm sorry, I didn't mean it like that. Look, Beth. I don't like your music. It sounds like noise to me. I know you like it. I can't believe you listen to it *just* to annoy me. But it gets on my nerves. I know you don't like my music. Frankly, I'm sick of it. It makes me feel old. I'm stuck here, in the middle, with no one playing the songs I want to hear. You know what?" She reaches over and touches Beth's cheek, and Beth tenses. Her mom takes her hand away. Beth feels kind of bad, but it's too late now.

"You don't know how lucky you are, to have everything ahead of you. You can do anything you like. You don't have to be an actress, just because your dad's a director. Sometimes when you do those monologues, you look so desperate. You can do anything, Beth. Find something you love, and just enjoy it. And try to be nice to people. Like me. I could use it."

Beth is embarrassed and fascinated. Her mom does this, sometimes, as some kind of lesson for Beth, a mother-daughter talk, spilling out emotion like a train wreck or something. And Beth is always drawn in, but then her mom will say something she thinks is all wise, that's really just putting Beth down.

"I don't have to be nice to someone who says I can't act!"

"I didn't say you can't act."

"You said I look desperate. That's not a compliment, is it?"

"I just mean you try too hard to—"

"Oh, thanks. Maybe I shouldn't try at all, like some people I know."

"Look, Beth, I made a home for us. That's nothing to scoff at. I'm your mother, and I'm going to tell you when I think you've got an attitude that's going to hurt you. And hurt me."

Beth knows her mom added that last bit for sympathy. But it won't work. "I'm doing just fine, so leave me alone. I'm not so bad."

"I didn't say you were."

"I know what you said, Mom. Maybe you should listen to yourself sometime."

Her mom stares at her for the longest time, with that look like she wants to say something that would make Beth a better person just by hearing it, but now she's just going to make Beth imagine what great words of wisdom she's missing out on.

"Some lady wants your spot," Beth says, pointing to the new red car waiting for them to pull out. Myra starts the car, and the radio comes on. Simon and Garfunkel are singing "Bridge over Troubled Water." As they drive away, Beth figures something out. Her dad lectures to her when he can't escape, and her mom lectures to her on car rides when Beth can't escape—which means her mom really wants to talk to her and her dad doesn't, but either way, what they really want is to hear themselves talk. So why don't they talk to each other and just leave her alone?

When they get home, Mac runs to the car shouting. "Don't leave the doors open! Just open and shut them real fast! Here, I'll do it for you. Why didn't you tell me you were going? Did you leave the windows down? Did you?"

"You're such a wimp," Beth says, leaving the side door open. Mac runs around the car and slams the door shut. Then he runs to the back of the station wagon and slams the rear door shut before their mom can even get out of the way. The door catches her elbow, and she yells, dropping the bag of groceries, which rips open and spills frozen orange juice cans across the yard.

"Oops," Mac says.

"Pick them up right now," Myra says, teeth clenched.

Beth is amazed at the way her mom can change words into slaps. Beth will have to try that sometime.

An hour later, out in the woods, flying high on half a joint, Beth grins at a bulbous growth on a tree. It looks like her Grampa Bartlett. He had a big nose with bumps all over it. He was pretty nice and kept peppermint candies in his pocket, but even with all that peppermint, he smelled like foot powder. Beth didn't know what it was he smelled like until after he was dead. By mistake, she walked in on her father in the bathroom while he was pouring this white powder all over his feet, and the whole bathroom smelled like Grampa, which made Beth suddenly sad, and afraid, since now her father smelled like foot powder, which reminded her of an old, dead man. If she ever gets married, she's going to make sure her husband never uses foot powder.

After looking at the knot on the tree for a while, she notices a fern nearby, just beginning to uncurl. It's so intricate, so completely far out. She kneels on the ground and watches to see if she can catch it opening. She stares at it for the longest time, and just as her head begins to nod and her eyes shut, she thinks she can hear the fern singing to her. Yes! It is. Her eyes open. Someone is moving through the woods, up near the top of the ridge. A woman with blond hair flowing around her face. Dancing. Arms moving about like wings. Singing? Jesus, it's her mother.

If she didn't know it was her mother, Beth would be interested in this vision. A woman alone in the woods, com-

muning with nature, just as Beth is doing. But it's just her
mother.

Myra thinks this land is like a person. It changes each year—
growing thicker in places, just as she has. It needs to be ad-
mired, and it needs to have some privacy. And it has secrets;
there are things Myra will never know about these woods no
matter how closely she looks, but there are also places in these
woods she knows as well as the faces of her children. There is
the top of the hill, where the maple and birch are spread out,
the ground covered in pressed brown leaves. A person can
move about freely yet stay snug in the deep of the woods,
where there is no view of a house or a road. This is the place
that listens to Myra, and for that she loves it most.

Last year, in those moments when everyone had gone off,
she would sing in the field behind the house, because there was
something special about the way her voice carried for miles on
a breeze. This place, on the hill, was where she came to think
quietly: to sit on the large humpbacked boulder, knees tucked
up, her head cupped in her hands. The woods listened—it was
just something she believed. But today Myra walked into the
woods, to this spot, and found that she could sing here too.
Her voice filled this space differently than the field; it echoed
off the trees, as if her notes were bright and colorful birds let
loose. It's a wonderful feeling, and she never wants to leave, but
after a while she feels she has overstayed her welcome, and she
says good-bye to the hill and heads back home.

When she arrives at the house, the kids want dinner, while
Will still paces between the barn and the house. Myra loses
whatever it was she found in the woods and becomes a mother
and a wife. She peels potatoes, and finds the silver hairclip for
Beth, and carries the blankets to the car for Mac, being sure to

shake them before placing them on the backseat of the station wagon. She does all these things well, as graciously as she can.

Through the kitchen window, Myra watches Ben climb out of his car, and it's like the curtain opening on the first act. The actors have begun to arrive and there is no going back. The two men vigorously shake hands, grinning. They're like two little boys with their first cap guns, going off to play cowboys and Indians. Myra has the urge to yell, "Oh, grow up!" and that's when she understands that for the next month she will be something like the mother of a Boy Scout troop. What is it about actors that they never grow up? With this thought, she realizes she has excluded herself from this group. There is a tug from somewhere under her rib cage, and she bends over slightly as if hit.

Only last month her best friend, Hattie Luoma, who was taking an oil painting class, asked Myra why she didn't try something *else* creative. Myra had retorted that she was an actress who couldn't act anymore, and she had no intention of being anything else. She didn't explain that after acting nothing else seemed important enough to bother with, that acting was the only credible art, and everything else seemed silly. Or that she still dreams of acting, that's it's hard to watch plays, that sometimes she thinks maybe, maybe she'll try it again. But right now, watching Will and Ben disappear into the weather-beaten barn as if it were some grand arena, Myra wonders what it was about acting that seemed so important. Surely other things are just as important, like being a doctor, or a scientist, or a teacher. Or maybe something she could do, really do: teach voice lessons, write theatre reviews. There must be something she could do that would fit their seasonal life. Will had suggested, only once, that she work backstage, maybe in the costume department. She had cried, and he never mentioned it again. But it doesn't sound so bad, now, does it?

These thoughts are so new, it's like opening up Pandora's box; the possibility of other careers frightening because it means that there are *more* things she might try and fail. Possibilities tease her with a sly meanness that makes Myra want to go upstairs and crawl into bed and maybe never get up again.

Screw that, she thinks fiercely, fighting off self-pity. It works. She nods to herself and goes outside to say hi to Ben.

While driving here, Ben had a long discussion with himself. Since he's alone much of the time, he puts his thoughts into different voices inside his head, just to keep himself company. All the voices agreed: Will's idea is a bit strange, but Ben will do everything in his ability to make it work. His biggest fear is that they will all get bored in the next month, or end up hating each other. He decides his job is to keep everyone happy. He doesn't mind seeming a bit foolish in order to make someone smile.

Will leads him into the barn, talking a mile a minute. Ben just listens. He doesn't have to do anything to make Will happy. It's Myra who will need to be cheered up today. Will must be driving her nuts with all this energy. Ben's always felt a little sorry for Myra having to put up with Will at times like this— which is damn well pretty much always. He's a great guy and all, but Will can be a bit overpowering. Even Ben can get exhausted by all that unbridled enthusiasm. The man can direct, though. Sees visions in his head unlike any other director, then gets the actors to bring them to life. Takes more talent than Ben has, that's for sure. Ben's just glad he can act.

Will's talking about the problem of getting the scenery and props sent up. "Trent says he'll take care of it, but you know what that's worth. We'll just have to hope. The real problem's the bunks might not arrive before the actors. I don't know where anyone will sleep." Will shrugs, then rubs his hands together. "Hell, we can sleep out on the lawn under the stars for a few nights. I haven't done that since I was a kid."

"I slept out on your lawn last summer, but I was dead drunk." Ben was pissed that no one had awakened him and driven him home. He'd sworn off drinking that day, and many days since then.

"Did I mention the creek?" Will says, changing the subject.

"Yeah, you told me about the creek, Will, and you're right, that'll be perfect, but let me tell you, there are limits to this reality stuff you're handing out. No loaded gun. Got that? Just *pretend* bullets, okay?"

Will laughs, and a funny thing happens. Will's laugh doesn't bounce off the old walls of the barn—it just dies, as if it got sucked into all that wood. It's nothing like the sound of voices on a stage, with concrete walls and a high ceiling. The lack of resonance is unnerving. Will's laugh has disappeared like a forgotten dream.

"Well, it's not Radio City Music Hall," Ben says, noticing the frown on Will's gaunt face. "But I sure wouldn't mind the Rockettes. This place needs some life."

With that, as if on cue, Myra walks into the barn.

During dinner, Beth is on her best behavior because this is it, the beginning of her career in the theatre. Tonight is, as her father says, the real start to the summer season, because Ben is here, and the rest are coming. He toasts it with a glass of bourbon. "To the summer of '71. To great theatre."

Beth pretends her grape juice is wine. It's good practice. Actors don't drink real alcohol on the stage, it's just colored water.

They recall the flavor of alcohol from memory, and the feeling it brings. And they act drunk wonderfully. They've had more practice at drinking than she has, but she's had her share of gin and whiskey from her parents' cabinet, so she has something to base her pretending on, and she's still a bit floaty from the pot. When she lowers the glass to the table, she feels a warm flush. She's going to be a great actress someday, with her father's help.

Beth is even nice to Mac. She offers him the bowl of cranberry sauce with a "Would you like some cranberry sauce, Mac?" Myra looks at her suspiciously, a crease in her forehead, and keeps looking at her until Mac has the cranberry sauce solidly in his hands. Beth knows she expected her to slide it onto his lap or something. Her mother is always expecting the worst from her.

"I'm working with the company this summer," Beth tells Ben, because he's looking at her and that makes it easier to talk to him. Her mom has told Beth to call him Mr. Walton, but her dad said to call him Ben. That discussion was ended in a stalemate of, Do whatever you think is right, so Beth never calls Ben anything at all. He's pretty cool, though. He's big and heavy, but he doesn't look fat. And he's got that kind of smile that's infectious, and Beth always finds she's smiling back at him, and then it feels like they've shared some secret or something, and it makes Beth blush, but feel good too. Beth decides that now that she's a company member, she'll call him Ben. She just hasn't gotten up the nerve to do it yet.

"I've heard. Prop girl, huh? Very cool." He does that smile thing, and she feels herself grin back and blush like an idiot.

"Yeah."

"*Marigolds* will keep you busy." He's talking about *The Effect of Gamma Rays on Man-in-the-Moon Marigolds*, which The Mill Street Theatre performed this past winter and which Beth saw a dozen times. It's like her favorite play in the whole world. The stage is filled with junk. There are hundreds of props. Even the skeleton of a dead cat.

"Here's to *Marigolds*," she says, raising her glass. She drinks the rest of her grape juice in one gulp.

"And here's to your mom for putting up with all of us," Ben says. "To Myra!"

Now Myra blushes. Beth doesn't toast her. Her glass is empty anyway.

"And here's to my girl Friday!" her dad says, and refills his glass from the bottle.

A little embarrassed but really happy, Beth lifts her empty glass up and clinks glasses with everyone except Mac, who's on the other end of the table spooning paths through his mashed potatoes. "Thanks, Dad," she says. Her eyes feel all hot, so she looks down at her plate. The cranberry sauce has run around the edge of her mashed potatoes. It looks like the mashed potatoes are bleeding, and she decides not to eat them. She offers them to Mac, and Myra's eyebrows go up. Shit, she may as well not even try to be nice to Mac, if her mother's going to treat her that way no matter what she does.

That night, when Mac goes out to the car with the flashlight to sleep for the night, Beth imagines all the things she can do to scare him. Throwing pebbles at the car. Creeping up and making animal noises. Sneaking up and opening the door and running away. But she knows she can't do that now. She's part of The Company, and they wouldn't do such things. Well, on second thought, they might, but she'd better not.

A floor lamp casts a circle of light over Will and the high-backed chair he sits in. On the other side of the low coffee table, Ben half-sits, half-lies, on the couch. It's one-fifteen a.m. and everyone else is asleep, but they have been talking and drinking for hours. Their voices are on the verge of being hoarse. Sometimes Ben closes his eyes while Will speaks, but he's listening all the same. This kind of talk is what he lives for. He's tired, but sleep, like being drunk, is just a way to pass time until the next play. Ben's ex-wife said the theatre was his mistress. It was corny, but true. Too true, now.

Will leans forward in his chair, his hands moving through the air as he speaks. "It all depends on the relationships we build in the first scene. A play is a series of reactions, from the first line to the last. The ending is, in effect, the result of these reactions. You, as an actor, know where the story goes, but the audience shouldn't. They should feel it's happening for the first time as they watch, yet—and here's the trick—when they get to the end, they should say *oh!* and see that they have been on a direct path here all along; that what they knew about Lennie and George right up front has led them to this end. You see that, don't you?"

Ben nods, and Will goes on; his voice grows louder, words explode in the air. "You two have to be in each other's skins, close as two people can be. Lennie and George are like two brothers. Two orphans. They *need* each other, they *love* each other. The tenderness George shows Lennie, even in this brutal world, should make us all ashamed. It's a love story. Plain and simple. Look what George does because he loves Lennie. He *kills* him. To save him from suffering in jail for the rest of his life. Think of how hard that has to be. The audience needs to feel, from the minute they leave that river bank, the dream dying. Even when they make plans, we must feel them falling apart as they speak. That's where the tension lies. But all that will work only if we set up these two characters and their relationship in that first scene by the creek."

"So," Ben says, "no pressure, but it's up to me and Lars. The success of this play depends on us."

"Well. Yes." Will shrugs and smiles.

"So why did you invite everyone else up? Maybe you should have just nailed Lars and me in the barn until we became best friends."

Will is silent for a minute, then nods. "Good point, Ben."

"Hey, Will. Lighten up. Don't get any crazy ideas."

"Where would I be without crazy ideas, Ben? I'd be a bank teller."

"Not a chance. You ever been in budget for a production yet?"

Will smiles. "Not yet, but I'm getting closer."

Ben puts out his cigarette and lights another. "The problem is, Lars is pretty hard to get to know. He's so damn quiet."

"I know," Will says, leaning forward in his chair. "I have an idea."

Ben grins. "What? You want us to hold hands for the next month?"

"Couldn't hurt. No, really what I want is for you to think about how these guys wear their hearts on their sleeves, even George, even though he's trying to be closed and tight, he can't help it. And Lennie is like a kid, he hasn't learned to hide his emotions yet. Let's go for that, that rawness, that openness. Spend the next month just opening yourself up to feeling things intensely. Let it all out. Go for broke."

Ben chokes on the smoke he has just inhaled. He can't help laughing. "Shit, Will, have I ever told you how fucking nuts you are? If anyone wears their heart on their sleeve, it's you."

Will stands up, puts his drink on the table, and paces back and forth like a tiger trapped in a cage. "It's because I love *this* theatre, Ben. This one. Nothing else will ever be the same to me. But we have to shake the old out of us. That's what the board's tired of, the same old inflections, the same old expectations. New York actors aren't *better*, but no one knows what to expect, so the audience will come just to find out. They'll have bigger houses for a while, and then they'll have to do something else, huge shows, and they'll never break even. Then they'll remember a show like *Marigolds*, with its small tight cast, and they'll wonder what happened to us. But we'll be gone. Norton will be doing voice-overs for carpet stores, Melinda will be a weather girl, Greg Henry will be on a daytime soap opera because of his smoldering good looks, you'll be in some theatre thousands of miles away, and I'll be dead. We have to make them understand *now!*"

Ben doesn't know where Will gets his energy. His own body is molded into the couch, his legs propped up on the table, his head resting against the couch's thick armrest. Myra has set up the bed in Mac's room for Ben, since Mac is sleeping in the car, but Ben thinks he'll just fall asleep here on the couch. First he has to say something he's been thinking since Will first called. It has to be said.

"Look, Will, the idea is great, really, but a month is just too long. We'll work it to death in a month. It'll dry up."

Will's nod freezes. Ben waits, worried how Will might take this slight betrayal. Ben has seen Will explode with anger, although never at Ben; at things usually, like a wobbly set or slow curtain, but these things were caused by people, people who don't quickly forget the look on Will's face, or the sharpness of his words. Once Ben saw Will lift a concrete block and throw it right through the canvas set. Ben is not expecting a physically violent reaction right now, but he does look to see what lies near Will's hand. A glass ashtray brimming with cigarette butts, a mostly empty bottle of bourbon, and two empty glasses. But instead of being angry, Will begins to nod.

"Yes, you're right," he says. "I thought of that. But I think I've found a solution. What if we did workshops, acting workshops, like in college? We could try new things, take chances. I feel such a need to break out of the old mold. We could even choose a play we love and work on it. Not something popular, just something we love. What do you think?"

Ben considers this. It's interesting. "But that means bringing the whole company here, Will. That's another, what, nine people at least. Myra will kill you."

Will leans back in his chair and smiles. "That's the truth. So we can't mention it to her yet. Let's get this thing going first, give it a few days. She'll grow to love it. Then when we suggest inviting the rest up, she'll be happy to go along with it. But it might help if someone else suggests it."

Ben shakes his head. "Jesus, Will, you take the cake, you know. And who might you be thinking of to bring up this grand idea?"

"My best buddy, Ben, of course." Will gets up and heads up to bed. He knows a good exit line, especially when it's his own. Ben laughs again and closes his eyes.

Saturday

❧ ❧

Mac wakes up Saturday morning before anyone else because it's hot and stuffy in the car, which makes him think of tombs and mummies, so he gets out quickly and shuts the door as fast as he can. He's standing up, outside, before he's really all awake. Picking up a handful of pebbles, he throws them at Beth's window, halfway between wanting to bother her and just wanting her to come out and play. The pebbles miss her window and rattle against the house. He'd try again but then imagines what Beth would do if he really did wake her.

He'll go look for crayfish in the creek. Maybe it's so early, they'll be sleeping and he can actually catch one. He walks to the creek still wearing his red plaid slippers.

Will wakes up impossibly thirsty, his tongue like a dead fish in his mouth. Careful not to wake Myra, he rolls out of bed to get a drink from the bathroom faucet. Out the window he sees a thread of footprints through a sea of green grass. They start at the gravel drive and lead down toward the creek. He grins at the beauty of the path his son has made for him to follow. Like a treasure map.

Downstairs, Will throws on a flannel shirt and slips into his shoes. The air outside is chilly with the promise of warmth. He knocks three times on the wood siding.

Will walks next to his son's prints, not on them, making his own path. At the bottom of the hill, Mac's prints disappear under the branches of one of the apple trees that border the creek. He knows where his son has gone: to the place where the creek bed is covered with broken shale. Last year Will showed Mac that this is where crayfish hide. Mac had been too afraid to try to catch them, and Will had gotten just a little peeved at his son's reluctance. Sometimes Mac's fears can be a bit exasperating—and the way Myra babies him is no help. Still, here he is, trying this all on his own.

Will crouches low and walks in a slow, careful squat. He doesn't want Mac to know he's here. Now Will sees him: Mac in his Spiderman pajamas, bent over the creek, one hand hovering over the water, getting lower inch by slow inch. Finally his hand enters the water and flips over a stone.

"Oh, shoot, shoot, shoot," Mac says.

Will wants to say, *Try again, son,* but doesn't. Mac needs to do this on his own. Will stays crouched down, more pressure on his knees than is comfortable, and watches as Mac tries another dozen times, and even says *shit* once, before Will has to straighten out his legs. Will thinks it's been about fifteen minutes. The length of an intermission.

"Hey, there," Will says. "Whatcha doing there, kid?"

Mac turns, startled. "Hey, Dad. I'm trying to catch a crayfish."

"Any luck?"

"Nope."

"Want a ride back to the house on my shoulders?"

Mac hesitates, and Will knows Mac's afraid to get up on his dad's shoulders. Admittedly, that's quite a height, but Mac should trust his dad not to drop him. Finally Mac says, "Sure," but Will sees the shrug all the same.

They have to go out into the open field before Will can bend over and let Mac climb onto his shoulders. Mac weighs just fifty pounds, still, he feels heavier than Will imagined he would. Will has to adjust Mac a few times until he's balanced just right. The walk up the hill to the house is filled with hope and stumbles.

Well, this is it, Myra thinks as she walks down the stairs to get the coffee started. This will be her last quiet morning for a long time to come. There is, though, this odd feeling of excitement, a whisper in her head that says it might be fun. She shakes her head, getting rid of the image of finger foods and chip dip. This is not going to be a party. A really long sleepover maybe. She shudders. What the hell did I let him talk me into this time?

Ben is in the kitchen, sitting at the table drinking a cup of coffee. He hasn't shaved, and he rubs his chin as soon as he sees her. "Morning, Myra," he says shyly, then fumbles up from the chair. "Want coffee? I think I made it a bit too strong."

"Sit down, Ben. I'll get it myself."

"Did you sleep well?" he asks, sitting back down at the table.

"Oh, sure. Just the normal nightmares. Nine men coming to my house for a month. Standard kind of stuff. Woke up in a sweat, then went right back to sleep." She's trying to joke around, but it comes out a little sarcastic. Still, Ben laughs.

"I've had that dream. Women though. Dozens of them.

They all turn out to be bill collectors." Myra smiles. Ben nods to the chair across from him. "Come on. Sit down."

She does. She takes a sip of her coffee, and her mouth puckers. Casually, she pours in two teaspoons of sugar and gives it a good stir. Now it's just plain undrinkable. She puts the cup down.

"That bad?" Ben asks.

"No, no, not at all."

He gives her a sheepish look. "Yes, it is."

"Well, maybe." She smiles. She wants him to know it doesn't matter, that it's better to have bad coffee made for her once in a while than always having to make it herself. But she can't say that. It's not something you say to your husband's best friend while you sit alone with him at the breakfast table. "So where is Will?"

"Thought he was still sleeping."

"Nope. Not in bed. He must be in the barn. You slept on the couch, Ben? There was a perfectly good bed upstairs for you."

"The couch was just fine. So, you okay with this, Myra? All these people?"

Myra looks at Ben. He looks like he really wants to know. She's as honest as she can be. "I don't know. I'm going back and forth on it. Back mostly. He steamrollered me, Ben, as always. Made me believe this was important for the theatre. Maybe it is. But it's more important to him. I can tell."

"Steamrollered me too. But I can't think of anywhere else I'd rather be." They're quiet for a while. It's a very comfortable quiet.

"Too bad he didn't think of doing this for *Waiting for Godot*," Myra says. "Just the two of you up here. I could handle that. God, you were good. What a team. Did I ever tell you how proud I was of both of you? What was that? Five years ago, and I still remember every minute of it. I cried every night during the curtain call."

"Thanks." He rubs at his face again. Myra could swear he was blushing. "You know, Myra," he says, looking down at his coffee, "I'm sorry I never got to see you act. I heard you were wonderful. And that you sang like an angel."

Now it's her turn to blush. No one ever mentions her acting. She is very touched that Ben has. That he doesn't pretend she never did. "Thank you."

It's awkward now. No one is drinking coffee.

"Tell you what, Myra. Before I go shave, show me how you like your coffee, and I'll make it every morning. Maybe that will help mask the odor of nine sweaty men."

"I don't think Norton sweats," Myra says automatically, trying not to show how touched she is by Ben's offer. "But thanks for reminding me how bad this place is going to smell. I think maybe I'd better buy a gas mask."

"Sorry. I was trying to cheer you up. Guess I'm as good at that as at making coffee."

"No, you did just fine. Thanks." She pats his hand. "I'll show you how to make the coffee. That would be very nice."

Before she can get up, Will comes into the house, Mac following. Their shoes, and slippers, are soaking wet and make squishing noises. "Up already?" Will says, crossing the kitchen to get to the coffeepot. Puddles follow him. He pours a cup of the black liquid and takes a large gulp. "Great coffee, Myra. Just the way I like it. Thanks."

Myra glances at Ben, who just smiles at her and shrugs. She smiles back.

"Hey Ben," Will continues. "I have this idea with the barn. Would you take a look?"

"Sure, Will." Ben puts his cup in the sink and waves good-bye to Myra. The two men go outside.

"Mom, I'm hungry," Mac says.

Myra is left with a hungry child, a wet floor, and a pot of bad coffee.

Chip Stark parks his white and rust Impala next to Jimmy McGovern's yellow Cyclone GT. A handmade sign is stuck in the ground: THEATRE PARKING. The sign looks like a joke next to the old barn, but Chip bets Will made that sign in all seriousness. Will's a great director, but his sense of humor is wanting, in Chip's opinion.

Jimmy got here first, even though they both left Pittsburgh at the same time, 'cause Jimmy is an asshole sometimes and probably drove ninety miles an hour. He's Chip's best friend, but the kid needs to grow up. He's only a year younger than Chip, who's twenty-six, but he acts like a teenager half the time, and dresses like one. He looks like an idiot with his red hair, his freckled round face, his damn ugly pink shirt, and his green Day-Glo pants. Chip can't help grinning, though. The guy's a barrel of laughs with his bad jokes, and a gold mine of weird headlines. Jimmy's Irish background shows in more than just his freckled face and red hair; he's full of blarney.

Chip gets out of his car and walks up to the two men. "Howdy, Will," Chip says. He has to practice his southern accent for the part of Whit. He and Jimmy play minor parts in *Of Mice and Men*, just ranch hands with a few lines, so his role needs that extra kick of an accent. He's already got a slow strut down real good, since that's the way he already walks. "Howdy, Jimmy. Kill any small animals on the way here?"

"Hello there, Chip," Will says. "Jimmy here tells me you two are going fishing? Today?"

Chip rubs the top of his bald head, a habit he picked up in college when he started losing his hair. What little hair he has left now, he wears in a tight ponytail. When he lost his hair so early, he quickly learned that the best defense is a good offense. He wears mirrored sunglasses, black jeans, a black T-shirt, a black leather jacket (unless it's just too damn hot), and an expensive pair of cowboy boots. Then he draws attention to his head by rubbing it with his palm to a high sheen—and just waits for some asshole to look his way. And he changed his name as soon as he joined Equity. John Blimpe was dead and gone.

"Well, Will, we told you we were going fishing today. We were on our way to Michigan when you called. You're the one reminded us we got a big lake full of muskie just ten minutes away. Remember? You weren't saying all that just to get us up here any old way you could, were you?"

"Well, no. But I thought we could get some things set up today."

Jimmy McGovern laughs, although Chip's not sure what strikes him funny. "There will be plenty of time for that, Will. You've got us captive here all night long. But the fish are jumping right now. And I had to drag this guy out of some woman's bed just to get here so early, and let me tell you she was . . . oh, hi kids, how you doing?"

Will's kids, Beth and Mac, have walked over from the house. Beth is a real hot babe. The little kid always looks like he just woke up.

"So the lake has muskie?" Jimmy says, changing the subject from women to fish, which Chip thinks Jimmy probably likes better anyway. Chip's never seen Jimmy with a woman, but he isn't going to make any judgments. Frankly, he doesn't want to know.

"I think so," Will says. He puts his hand on top of Mac's head. "We tried to catch crayfish in the creek this morning."

"Those little bitty things?" Jimmy says. "Mac, you got to think bigger than that. Want to come fishing with us in a real lake? We'll rent a motorboat. Maybe we can catch the Loch Ness monster."

Mac's face is blank, as if the question wasn't asked of him but of someone else. Will looks at his son. "Sure, Mac will go with you guys, won't you, son? You won't be gone too long, will you?"

Chip's worked with Will long enough to know how they have just been manipulated to come back early. Except it goes right over Jimmy's head.

"Heck, no, we'll be gone till dinnertime," Jimmy says. "But you'll love it, kid. We'll get pop and chips and sandwiches and make a day of it. Just what a kid like you needs. Fresh air and slippery fish. You get bored, I'll tell you some stories that will wake you right up. This will be fun. Good idea, Will! Tell Myra to stick some spuds in the oven, and we'll bring the rest of dinner home in a bucket. Come on Mac, climb in." He opens the car door and takes out a big black suitcase, handing it to Will. Mac looks up at his dad, who shrugs. Mac climbs in the backseat. Fishing rods are sticking out the windows.

"Oh, Beth!" Jimmy says, getting into his car. "Why don't you bake a cake! Let's celebrate. I hear you're part of the crew this year. Congratulations!" Beth grins ear to ear, beaming as if someone just crowned her Miss America. I'd vote for you, Chip thinks. The girl's got legs up to here. He watches as she runs off toward the house, then he goes to his car to get his rod and tackle box.

They drive off down the lane, pebbles spraying like popcorn. Will stands there holding the black suitcase like the bellhop in *Plaza Suite* waiting for a tip.

Myra watches Beth make the cake and offers no advice. She refuses to be drawn in by any of this party atmosphere. The truck with the scenery, which includes the bunks, won't arrive until

Monday. On Sunday night six grown men will be sleeping on her living-room floor. She is determined to hold on to the anger she feels every time she walks through that living room, even though she had a really sweet conversation with Ben this morning, and Jimmy and Chip have won her heart by asking Mac to go fishing, and the glow on Beth's face as she stirs the batter is priceless.

Around noon Ben insists on making everyone lunch and says they must eat on a blanket outside. He won't let Myra do a thing. He makes grilled ham and cheese sandwiches and carries them out on a platter with a jar of pickles and a bag of chips. Beth brings out a pitcher of cherry Kool-Aid and the *Flintstones* jelly glasses. As they sit on the ground, Ben tells stories about his ex-wife and her white poodle. Once, after a bad argument, he painted a red bull's-eye on the poodle's freshly groomed fur. She made him pay for that prank through the nose, he says, but it was worth the story.

The rest of the day is spent idly for Myra. There is nothing yet to do but relax and imagine what is to come.

At five o'clock Chip, Jimmy, and Mac come home with eight fish on a stringer. Bluegill and largemouth bass. Mac caught a fish himself and can't stop talking about it. His cheeks are red and shiny from the sun, and his curly light-brown hair has glints of gold. Jimmy cleans the fish outside, and Chip lights the grill. They tell Myra they'll take care of everything. She tries to remind herself this is simply the calm before the storm, that as soon as the rehearsal begins, she will be forgotten, but then Mac shows her exactly which fish he caught and asks her if she'll eat it.

"This one, Mom, I caught it for you. See that yellow stripe there? Jimmy says that's a special fish. Will you eat that one? I put the worm on the hook all by myself. It's really gross. Jimmy said he'd keep his eye on my fish so you can have it. He says you're the hostess with the mostess. I drank four Cokes, but I'm still pretty hungry. Jimmy and I are going to share that big one. It's a bass, and he caught it. He caught most the fish. He says a man in Michigan caught a fish with three gold rings inside. Maybe my fish'll have a gold ring. You can eat the fish, but I might want to keep the ring, okay?"

Myra kisses the soft top of Mac's head and tells him she can't wait to eat the fish he caught for her. Her eyes moisten, and she busies herself with setting the table.

At dinner Mac can't eat the fish. Myra can see his fear as soon as the plate is set in front of him. He cuts it up and moves it around and slides some under the potato skin. He's terrified someone will mention it, but no one does. Chip says, "Great fish, pardner," and Ben says, "Sure is," and Jimmy says, "Good job, doc," and nobody, not even Beth, says, "How come you're not eating any fish, Mac?" Myra says the fish Mac caught for her is the best-tasting fish she ever ate. And it is.

After dinner, when Beth brings out the cake, round with perfect swirls of white frosting, Myra thinks this dinner is the moment she will choose to come back to, if given a choice. She looks over at Will, needing to catch his eye, to be proud of what they have created together. He's talking to Ben about the play.

The sun begins to set, and amber light illuminates the back windows like a warm-hearted song. Myra hums "Let It Be" as everyone retires to the living room. On the coffee table is a bottle of Jack Daniel's and five glasses.

Ben tells the story about the time a row of lights fell during the first act of *Three Sisters* and missed every actor onstage. Will says they were saved by his talented blocking. Then Will tells about the time Ben's tights split wide open in the crotch during the swordfight scene in *Henry V*, and they improvised lines, in blank verse no less, to get him offstage. The stories shift back and forth between Ben and Will, with Jimmy and Chip adding the desired laughs and clever asides. Myra watches Beth, who listens to these stories with a show of bright anticipation, even though she has heard them at least a dozen times before. And Mac, her shy son, is grinning ear to ear, sitting between Jimmy and Chip. Myra is so exhausted by the up and down feelings of the day, she just listens. Finally, she closes her eyes and lets the sounds of the men's voices rumble across her face.

When she wakes up, Mac is asleep with his head resting on Jimmy's shoulder. Beth is asleep on the floor. Jimmy, Ben, and Will are talking about a production of *Wine and Roses*. Chip isn't talking, but he's awake. He smiles at Myra. No one else notices she has woken up. Getting up to go to bed, she thinks she hears Will say good night, but maybe he's just quoting a line from the play.

Chip watches Myra walk upstairs. She's a good-looking woman, kind of like a soft version of Gena Rowlands. Gena Rowlands is sexy, Chip thinks. He wouldn't mind a love scene with Gena, even if she's a little old. He's been thinking about going out to Hollywood. Well, who the hell isn't? But damn if he's going to wait tables. He needs to get some credits first. Get an agent. He's got plans.

Chip wonders if Will's going to go upstairs after Myra. Chip would, if she weren't Will's wife. He's never gone so low as to sleep with a married woman, not that he knows of, anyway.

That Beth, though, she's hot, with those long legs and full mouth. She must be almost eighteen. Not that he'd take it too far with Will's daughter—that wouldn't be smart. But hell, he's not brain dead. Funny thing, though, he can't get Will's daughter to look at him more than a second, even flashing his best grin her way. Well, she'll notice him. He'll make sure of that. The days of fat little John Blimpe are long gone. He feels sorry for that sad sap he used to be. *You turned out okay, kid*, he wants to say. *The girls like you*. And contrary to the jibes he used to hear, he likes the girls. Yes, he does.

All in all, it's been a damn good day. The fishing trip was a hell of a lot more fun than he expected (he laughs, remembering the look on Mac's face when Jimmy told the story about the kid who had been locked in a cage by his parents for six years), and that fish dinner was great, and now, listening to Will talk about the theatre, well, Will's one of Chip's idols. Still, he can't believe Will stays downstairs after Myra goes up.

Sunday

❧ ❧

Beth wakes at seven, the alarm sending shivers down her spine. Today's the day. Greg Henry is coming! To stay at her house. And there are no other women here, except her mother, who doesn't count.

Beth wants to be the first in the shower, just in case Greg comes early, say eight a.m., which he might, it could happen, and God forbid she be in her nightgown when he comes, because her nightgown is so drab. Now, if she had something slinky and low cut, then she might want to be caught off-guard, but not in this flannel thing with the ruffle on the bottom. He'd think she was some dorky kid.

Even though she knows there are a few extra people in the house this morning, and the hot-water heater takes an hour to heat back up, Beth takes a long shower, using lavender soap and strawberry-scented shampoo. Afterward, wrapped in a towel tucked tightly around her breasts—pretty decent-sized breasts she must admit, ample even—she combs out her chestnut-colored hair. If she had a driver's license, it would read "chestnut" for hair color and "dark almond" for eye color, even though Patsy Martin, who already got her license, says those aren't real choices, but what would she know, with her plain brown hair and plain brown eyes? Beth's hair is parted evenly down the center, falling to about five inches past her shoulders. Combing it out nice and smooth takes quite a while, during which time she imagines that Greg Henry has shown up, and when she walks out of the bathroom with only her towel tucked tightly around her ample chest, and barely covering her butt, she will bump into him as he comes upstairs to use the bathroom after his long trip, for which he woke up at four in the morning because he was just dying to get here quickly—for some vague reason that he only figures out when he is confronted by the nearly naked, and still slightly damp, Beth.

Coming out of the bathroom, Beth runs into her mother, who says, "Good morning, sweetheart." Beth rolls her eyes and goes into her room to change. If her mother calls her "sweetheart" in front of Greg Henry, she will just die.

Will wakes to the sound of the shower running and thinks he has been dreaming about the shower running all night. Why would he dream that? But now the dream is gone, and a headache takes its place, as if it were just waiting for a conscious mind to ravage. Bang, it's there, and there's little room for anything else. God damn Melinda, Will thinks. He'd be fine if he just knew where the hell she was.

Light strikes through the front window like a viper. Will closes his eyes. Only after his eyes are shut does he realize he's in his living room, and that there is someone on the couch, and someone else in a chair. Slight aches in his shoulders and knees become stiff dull pains. The shower stops running, and it's as if someone has turned off a jet airplane. Will's thankful the maddening sound is gone, but only for a second, because now all he can hear is his head pounding.

He could get up, move very slowly, and get coffee, which might help, but it's doubtful. Even moving slowly is a bad idea. He can't go back to sleep, not with this headache. He does the only thing that might really help. With his eyes closed, he thinks about the play. There are many plays Will loves, but none as much as the one he is about to direct, whatever play that might be. Only last month he was in love with *Summer and Smoke*. What a magnificent play that was! But now there is only *Of Mice and Men*. And even though they already produced this play eight months ago, he wants to look at it anew. He is ready to fall in love again.

Every play has its spine, a theme that holds the whole thing together, Will thinks, as if he's lecturing a class of young actors, something he loves to do when he has the time. In *Of Mice and Men*, the spine is: a dream of a better life. George and Lennie dream of owning their own farm. Curley dreams of being a pro boxer. Curley's Wife dreams of being a movie star. Candy, once he hears about George and Lennie's plan, dreams of joining them. The same for the black stable hand, Crooks. They all want in on the dream. Is Lennie's death, in the last act, the death of dreams? Of hope? Will doesn't think so. It's a sad and tragic ending for the play, but there is hope for a better life now for George. Can a man keep a promise forever? Should he?

He's read the play dozens of times and asked these and other questions over and over. The questions give him ideas, they get him excited. He feels "on." It's that "on" feeling that makes Will feel alive, a true part of the theatre. It's addictive. A week after the last good review, he needs another one. He needs to move men across the stage with purpose, find themes, come to great realizations, feel that eureka moment that startles and inspires him. And here he sits like an old potato. There are things to be done. He stretches his arms above his head. He stands up. The headache is gone.

Squinting, Will thinks it's going to be a very bright day. Myra walks down the stairs. She's smiling.

"Good morning!" she says. "Sleep well?"

She doesn't wait for his answer, just walks into the kitchen, hopefully to start the coffee. Will wants to sit at the table drinking coffee with Myra, discussing the play, as they used to do. He remembers holding her hand, struggling to understand Ionesco. Talking about Ibsen for hours. That hasn't happened for a while. It's not that she doesn't act that bothers him; he no longer dreams of being the next Bogart-Bacall team of the resident theatres. He did think that once, but it was his love for her that had been thinking, not his brain. She was a charming ingenue with a lovely voice. Never Bacall. He should never have suggested she go back to the stage. That it was his idea that failed still bothers him. All those people looking at him afterward . . . But it's not her *not* acting that distances them, or even the few affairs he did have. It's that she doesn't quite get his ideas anymore, his passions. He will tell her all about his plan to rework *Hedda Gabler*, and she will only ask him how he plans on getting the hot water tank fixed. But he still loves her. She must know that.

He imagines himself kissing Myra good morning, with a little tongue, like they used to during the first few years of their marriage. Maybe they'll go back upstairs to bed—well, figuratively speaking, since he didn't sleep in bed last night. Maybe after they make love, she'll listen to his ideas for the next few days. Maybe she'll get excited. Maybe she'll join in on the fun. Maybe he should brush his teeth first.

Myra has made a decision. It's going to be a gorgeous day. She will pack up a book, some fruit, some bread, and a bottle of wine, and go for a hike. A long hike. She's not going to sit around here all day as actors invade her house. She's going to leave now, while the going's good, before anyone asks her for anything. It takes two minutes to pack, and one more to write a note.

I'm going for a walk. Be back by before dinner. Have a nice day.

Me.

Nate Johnson, who plays Crooks, the black stable hand, arrives around one in the afternoon, after rising at seven to attend church. Nate's not thrilled with God, but old habits die hard—that, and the fact that his dead mother would roll over in her grave if he didn't go, an image that bothers him as much as God does. The only thing Nate is sure about is that God couldn't care less what Nate thinks of him, considering He hasn't struck Nate down dead yet for his suspicion that God's not all he's cracked up to be.

Will, Ben Walton, Jimmy McGovern, Chip Stark, and Will's son stand in the front yard watching Nate's car drive up like it's some great moment in history. He swears they've stopped breathing by the sheer excitement of it all. These people are all nuts, he thinks, but at least none of the actors are prejudiced—they're all too busy thinking they're so damn special to worry about someone else's skin color. Nate's just another actor to them. Means he's part of the club—probably just as nuts as the rest of them.

Will's daughter, Beth, comes dashing out of the house, stumbles on the top step, and almost does a back flip trying to straighten herself out before landing on her knees. By the time he's out of the car, Beth has gone back into the house. Nate wasn't who she was hoping to see. He wonders who she is waiting for. Nate hopes Will knows what he's doing.

There are hellos all around, people asking how the drive

was, if he's eaten, if he wants something to drink. He's got two bags, and there's actually some sportive fighting over who's going to carry them. Then they all head to the house; Nate follows, limping slightly. His knee has locked up on him after driving two and a half hours. He'd blame it on the weather, but it's a pretty nice day. Seems like his knee thinks it's gonna rain every day now.

Inside, he's offered a glass of lemonade, and his bags are placed in the living room. Mac follows Jimmy McGovern around like a baby duck. The kid's a bit odd, Nate thinks. Always looks at Nate like he's gonna pull a knife on him. Looks at everybody that way, except here he is, practically holding Jimmy's hand. God knows what happened here in the last two days. He's not gonna ask.

Will's explaining that Myra has gone hiking for the day, when Beth comes downstairs. Her shorts are so short, Nate can see the curve of her butt sticking out under the fringe of blue jean. Will looks like he wants to say something to his daughter, but he's still in the middle of his story about Myra, and before he can finish, the daughter's out the door and walking down the lane.

They make lunch, then go outside and stand around on the lawn, waiting for the next guy to show up. Nate's pretty sure the next one to pull up the lane is gonna get the same red-carpet treatment for about the same hour Nate got. Will's great with the charm, when he wants something. Doles out affection with a purpose in mind, then moves on. Nate doesn't mind that so much, long as he knows what to expect. Long as nobody expects too much.

By early afternoon, two more actors have arrived: Frank Tucker, who plays Slim and is so full of himself Will half-expects the man to swell up and float off on his own hot air, and Norton Frye with his cat. Norton hasn't quit complaining about the sleeping conditions yet. Will told him to come early. The bunks will come tomorrow, then Norton can have the room Ben's sleeping in.

"So where's the wife?" Frank asks, interrupting Will as he's trying to explain what he thinks was wrong with the production last winter of *Of Mice and Men*. "She must be ready to shoot you for inviting all these people here during your vacation."

"Taking a walk," Will says, his jaw tight.

"A long one, I bet." Frank tosses his head back in that way he does when he thinks he's said something funny, and smooths out the corner of his mustache, using his right index finger. He's so vain, he actually had the nerve to ask Will to reblock a scene so he could enter from stage left, to show his good side. Will told Frank he didn't have to enter at all. Frank just threw back his head, patted down his stupid mustache, and said, "Can't hurt to try." There must be a role he could cast Frank in that would require him to shave his mustache, but Will hasn't found it yet.

Will is about to get back to the subject at hand, the rehearsal, when he sees Jimmy McGovern getting in his car with Mac and Ben.

"What's going on?" he asks them.

"We're going fishing again!" Mac says, already in the backseat.

"Huh?"

"Yes sir!" Jimmy says. "Chip, Ben, Mac, and I are going to go out and catch us some dinner. Your food's all gone, Will. Tell Myra not to fuss, we'll bring some potato salad back with us. Think you can catch us some potato salad, Mac?" Jimmy says, tousling the kid's head. Mac laughs like it's the best joke in the world.

"But—" Will sputters. "But—"

"It's two-thirty," Jimmy says. "We'll be back by seven. Do we need beer?"

"No, we have plenty of beer," Will says.

"Then we'll get more," Jimmy says with a grin. "Hey Frank, stay out of the booze while we're gone."

"Screw you, McGovern," Frank says. Will shakes his head. Is this how it's going to be? The two of them argue in an almost genial way, night and day, the genial part getting thinner and thinner as time goes on, and it pisses off Will more and more. He's got sibling rivalry enough at home.

And this is his home.

"Think I'll go call the wife," Frank says, as Jimmy drives away.

"I should check on my cat," Norton says. They walk off.

Will throws up his hands. He had something important to say, and now his thoughts are left hanging in the air like laundry left to dry. He goes into the barn.

It's empty, which is a bit of a jolt; he's described the props and furniture so often, they have become real objects in his mind. He goes over to where one of the bunks will be and sits on the ground, trying to get a feel for what will come. It's idiotic, sitting here on the dirt floor, but damn it, he'll do anything to save this theatre. If he can. He feels like that kid with his finger in the dike. Except he's no kid anymore. He'll be sixty in a few months. He doesn't look sixty, not nearly, but he's been in the theatre long enough to know how flimsy an image can be, even when you're looking in the mirror. Makeup doesn't make him King Lear. Black hair dye doesn't make him young. But he's trying. Damn it, at least he's trying. Theatres all over are doing plays in the woods, rewriting scripts. Some of it sounds ridiculous to Will, but he admires their chutzpah. He wishes someone would acknowledge that he, too, is trying something brave (maybe a bit late in the game, but that doesn't mean it won't work). They're all off fishing, or fussing with a cat—or taking a walk in the woods. He's out here in the barn, believing it's a bunkhouse. For them. He does all this believing for them.

Beth stands at the end of the lane and counts to sixty. She's tried this counting trick already—she's tried all sorts of things, like reciting the monologue from *Our Town*, and walking up the lane without turning back. Nothing has worked. She's back to counting to sixty; she can't help it. There is nothing else to do to pass the time until Greg Henry gets here. Even if her father allowed them a TV, she couldn't sit still to watch it. Each time a car turns onto the lane, her heart pounds. She knows exactly where her heart is now; she can touch the ache in her chest.

And, her mother has walked off. Not that Beth cares, except that every now and then, when she's finished counting to sixty and there's no sign of Greg Henry, she thinks she'll go find her mom, for distraction. Her dad is around somewhere, but he's acting all edgy. He's not usually like that when they're here at the farm. Usually he's quieter and moves more slowly, and plays checkers with them. Well, sometimes. But right now he's just a director and not a dad. For one second Beth understands how that might upset her mom.

Fifty-nine. Sixty. No sign of Greg Henry. She kicks a stone, and it plops into the ditch on the side of the lane. She'll go crazy, waiting for Greg Henry to come. She can't help thinking that he must be thinking about her too. That they're meant to be. And if they are meant to be, what's another sixty seconds? She starts to count again. As soon as she sees his car, she's going to head back up the lane, as if she were just out for a walk. He'll see her glossy chestnut hair and her long legs, and wonder who the good-looking woman is. Then she'll turn, startled, and he'll think, *Beth*. That will be the moment they'll remind each other of, sometime in the future that is theirs.

Myra's lost in the woods, but she doesn't care. She has found this beautiful spot where a creek winds through an old pine grove, the forest floor a beautiful dun color of thick pine needles. In the air, golden-breasted birds flitter from branch to branch, and a lone monarch butterfly floats about like a musical note. She didn't eat any of the bread or cheese, but she drank all the wine. She left the backpack about a mile back, next to the huge old oak, which she can't possibly miss on the way home. She is free of encumbrances, at one with the woods.

Myra decides that if she sits very, very still, a deer will come to drink from the creek. If she were a deer, she certainly would. There is a special stillness to this place, even with the golden-breasted birds trilling out their song; a special glow from the sun that finds its way to the forest floor. One spot, right under the pine tree, has the exact shape of her bottom worn into the earth. She sits down and watches the creek bubble. In a few minutes, she is asleep.

Mac grins so widely he can feel the wind against his teeth. They have caught a dozen fish, cruised at high speeds, and pissed off the side of the boat. (Mac had to close his eyes when Ben Walton stood on the side of the boat, because Mac thought they'd tip over for sure.) He rubs his cheeks; they won't go back to their normal position, and his mouth aches. But he's not complaining, even though his forehead is hot from the sun, even though the guys teased him about drinking a beer, handing him one, then pulling it back, and even though Jimmy really scared him with the story about the boy who had a second head growing out of his chest—which will probably give Mac nightmares forever. It's such a good day, he's even sure he's going to eat the fish he caught.

They get home at eight. The sun has gone below the tops of the trees, and the shadows are long and sharp against the grass. Mac feels taller when he gets out of the car. His shadow is ten feet long. Beth comes out of the house as they pull up, but she walks right by the car and goes down the lane.

Mr. Johnson, the black guy, whom Mac doesn't know very well (and is a little bit scared of—his skin is that real dark color like the pictures of those tribes in Africa, and it makes Mac think of cannibals and men with bones through their noses), stands by the grill. The pasture behind ripples in the shadows, and Mac suddenly feels tired beyond belief. He wants to show his mom the fish he caught, and he wants to go to bed. His forehead is hot and it hurts.

"Hey, Nate!" Chip Stark yells as he carries the bucket of fish over to Nate. "Where the hell is everyone?"

"Out looking for Myra," Nate says.

Then Mac hears it, a low, hollow sound coming from the woods: *Myra. Myra. Myra.* The woods are calling for his mother. His legs give out. He sits down on the grass like a puppet whose strings have been cut. Luckily no one sees. They are too busy looking at the howling woods.

Myra awakens to find the sun perched on a low branch of a dead tree, a yellow ball with no warmth, the Cheshire Cat without a smile. Oh, shut up, she thinks, because the sun seems to be saying, "You'd better get moving." She shakes her head; she's not thinking too clearly. It's getting chilly. She should go home.

It would take hours to go back the way she came, and it will be dark soon. She'd get lost in the woods. More lost than she is right now. This creek must be the one that comes out on Old Timber Road, about a mile from where it crosses her own road. If she follows it out to Old Timber, then at least she'd have a road to walk on, even in the dark. Bending over the creek, Myra splashes cold water on her face and drinks out of cupped hands. She's incredibly thirsty. She moves off, following the creek, looking back with longing at the spot where she slept against the tree; she imagines staying there, nourished by nature alone, never going home. She is sick of doing dishes. Feeding people. Making lists and grocery shopping. And it's just beginning. A line from *The Fantasticks* comes to her, and she can't help singing it out: "I want much more than keeping house, much more, much more, mu—ch more." She walks along the bank of the creek, sudden tears streaming down her face like rain.

Less than an hour later, she finds the road and knows where she is. She turns left, in the direction of dishes and laundry. The Girl in *The Fantasticks* learns that love is more important than fame, and suddenly Myra wants to be saved by love, she wants to be in love blindly, without doubt. She wants no choices. *Let me love*, she thinks with each step she takes. And, *Love me*. She feels that unless she falls back in love, just as in those first years, no, *more in love than even then*, she will fall apart, lose herself. She can feel it, a loosening, as if meaning and voice and care were simply things to be left at rest-stop trash cans, to make the load lighter, the car less messy.

Love me, love me. Let me love. She turns the corner onto her road, and a minute later a car drives by, then slows, stops, and backs up. The driver's door opens, and Greg Henry leans out. "Myra?"

Myra wipes quickly at her face with the palm of her hand and says, "Yep, it's me."

"Want a ride?" The sun has gone beneath the horizon, and

the sky casts a gentle pink light on Greg's young handsome face. Myra nods and waits until he leans back into his car so she can wipe her face again and run her fingers through her hair, hoping he won't be able to see that she's been crying.

Once she's in the car, he asks her if she's okay. He looks concerned. Worried. He's a sweet kid.

"Yeah, I'll be okay. Don't worry about it, Greg."

"All right. But if you want to talk . . ."

"No. But thanks for the ride. I think everyone's probably looking for me. We'd better go."

He nods. "Okay." They drive on.

"So you're here to join the greatest rehearsal of them all?" Myra asks.

Greg laughs, his white teeth flashing. "How could I refuse?"

Then they're there. Beth is walking up the lane and spins around as she hears the car. She stops in the middle of the lane, framed in the car lights, squinting at the car. She looks confused. Then her eyes get big, and her look turns to one of horror and disgust, and she turns and runs up the lane.

Oh hell, Myra thinks.

Just as Ben and Will are standing in the field discussing whether to call the police, Ben sees Beth stop, look at the car that has just come up the lane, then turn and run into the house.

Ben nudges Will. "That's Greg Henry's car. And there's two people in it."

In the twilight, it is impossible to tell from this distance who is in the car. Ben wonders if Will is thinking the same thing he is, that Greg may have brought a friend with him, some stagestruck kid Greg wants to impress. Every now and then Greg brings some young, always innocently cute college guy to the theatre to watch a rehearsal. Ben believes that people's choices should not be food for fodder, but the last time Greg pulled a stunt like that, Ben and Will locked eyes, acknowledging the fact they knew what it was all about.

No one gets out of the car, even though the engine has been turned off. The darker-than-twilight shape of Nate crosses the front lawn. Everyone else is out in the woods, yelling for Myra, except Norton, who has forgotten to bring any gym shoes or boots.

Nate walks over to the passenger door and opens it. Out climbs Myra. Ben couldn't be more surprised if Barbra Streisand had stepped out. He and Will both shout, "Myra!" at the same time and run to the car.

Myra stumbles, and Nate grabs her arm. Ben is close enough now to hear her say, "Thanks, but I'm fine." There are pine needles in her disheveled blond hair, and a thin twig. Her eyes are swollen and red, so swollen she seems to be peering out as if blinded by bright sun. Will takes Myra's arm, and she attempts to pull it away from him, but Will's long thin hand fits around Myra's upper arm like a cuff, and he won't let go.

"Myra," Will says, "where were you? Jesus! Look at you! You're drunk!"

Myra looks at Will, and suddenly her eyes are wide, like a child's, and Ben sees something that he's afraid Will is going to miss. That Myra is asking for something. It is the same, exact, wide-eyed question Ben remembers asking his wife when she left him. He couldn't say, *Please love me. I love you.* He'd expected her to know, just by the way he looked at her, that he loved her, that he needed her. She had walked out the door as if he weren't even there—which he hadn't been, many times before, and maybe that was what she had gotten used to seeing: nothing.

But now, Ben watches the hope on Myra's face disappear while Will stares at her with anger and embarrassment.

"I went for a walk. I left a note."

"It's almost ten o'clock at night, Myra. We were just about to call the police, for God's sake. We thought you were lost. Your own son is out there looking for you, imagining you torn in two by a bear. What the hell were you thinking!"

There is a flash of concern in Myra's eyes as she glances toward the woods, then it's gone. "Let go of me, please," she says, with a flat, dull tone that makes Ben wince. Will does, but not before giving a short, quick twist to Myra's arm. She opens her mouth to gasp, and he lets go. Myra heads toward the house, and Will follows. *You stupid fool*, Ben thinks, the thought as quick as the twist of an arm. Maybe she was lost. Maybe she is hurt. For just the briefest of moments, Ben despises Will, but then that goes away, and he is left feeling only sad for both of them.

In the silence that follows, Ben wants to just up and leave. The whole living-the-play idea feels wrong. He's emotionally drained already. The last thing he wants to do is begin a month of delving into the innermost feelings of a needful, slow-witted man.

"Guess we better go get everyone out of the woods," Nate says.

Ben nods. He's not leaving. Who's he kidding?

From the woods there comes a pitiful sound. If Beth didn't know it was only people calling for her mother, she might think it was a herd of sick cows. She watches from her bedroom window as Ben walks out to the pasture to call them all back.

Her door is closed, but she can hear her parents arguing in their bedroom. Beth's eyes are already red from crying—she was so angry when she saw her mom get out of Greg Henry's car that tears just burst from her eyes. Her father says her mom smells like spoiled grapes and looks like she was trampled by a pack of mad pine trees. Her mom says she's put up with him being drunk plenty of times, and it's just her damn turn. Beth can't bear to imagine what the actors must think. Opening her door a crack, she listens to what is going on downstairs. The conversation is muted, not lively, like last night. Her mother has spoiled everything.

M o n d a y

⬥⬥

Beth wakes to sparrows chirping madly just outside her window. Her eyes will hardly open, sticky from dried tears. Her pillow is damp. It will take a long shower to wash away last night. She lets the water run until there is nothing left but cold, then stands with her face turned up, the chilly water tightening her skin, pulling her face back together. In her room, she dries her hair and brushes it until it shines. She will act as if nothing happened at all. A great actress could do this.

There are men asleep all over the living room: on the couch, on all three chairs, and on the floor. Greg Henry is in a tan sleeping bag beneath the front window. His eyelashes are thick, like fur. She imagines them fluttering against her cheek before they kiss. She is breathing in rhythm with him now. She could fall asleep standing here, with her eyes open, just watching him.

She hears footsteps. Her father walks downstairs in his white terrycloth bathrobe and says in a whisper that rattles the windows, "Why is there no hot water?"

"Sorry," Beth says, lowering her head. Without a doubt, she

sides with her father on this stupid mess her mother's made. Imagine embarrassing him when the people he works with are here. Going off and getting drunk all by herself, then having to be rescued by Greg Henry. How pathetic.

"Take short showers from now on." He looks around the room, pointing out the fact that there are people here who will need showers.

Beth makes a face like *Oh, right, I forgot* and nods. Her father goes back upstairs, while she heads for the kitchen. Maybe the smell of coffee and eggs will gently wake some of these people. One in particular.

After she brews the coffee, cracks some eggs, chops green peppers, melts the butter, and pours the mix into the frying pan, Norton Frye walks into the kitchen, wearing a hideous maroon satin robe. He thanks her for making coffee and asks if he could take a bowl of milk upstairs to Betsy. It takes Beth a whole minute of awkward silence before she realizes he means his cat. He's so weird, and his toupee is awful, but at least he doesn't mention last night, and for that she's grateful. She couldn't bear talking to some guy in a maroon satin robe about her crazy mother right now—or ever.

As Norton Frye walks out of the kitchen carrying a bowl of milk, Jimmy McGovern, with red eyes and a red face, stumbles in saying, "Coffee, coffee, my kingdom for a cup of coffee." Beth gives him a slight smile, as if she thinks he's funny, even though he's not, except for the fact that he slept in his mismatched clothes and looks like a rumpled clown. Then Frank Tucker comes in and drifts right past Beth to the coffeepot without even a hello, followed by Nate Johnson, whose kinky salt-and-pepper hair is flattened on the right side of his head and who does say good morning, but not cheerfully at all. A few minutes later Will enters, dressed but not showered or shaved, and Ben, who at least offers to help cook. By this time,

Beth is on her second batch of eggs, and the kitchen is getting crowded. Chip Stark, shorter by a few inches without his boots, arrives, and then Mac, who must have slept in the car and seems to have sweated right through his pajamas. All the eggs are gone now, and Greg Henry is still sound asleep. To top it all off, Myra comes down the stairs, showered and wearing too much makeup. She looks at Will, just a quick, sharp glance, then turns to Beth.

"Beth, is it true what I just heard? You made breakfast for everyone?"

There is something odd about Myra's voice. Pinched and too sweet. Her smile looks really strange.

"Yeah?"

"Oh, that is so wonderful! What a sweet girl you are to have made breakfast!"

"Well, there's nothing left," Beth says, thinking that if her mother expects Beth to make her breakfast after last night, she's way wrong.

"Well, then, we should go to the store and get more food!" her mom says brightly. "There are going to be a lot of hungry men around here!" She glances at Will again. Ben Walton makes a movement with his head toward the living room. One by one the actors file out. Beth wants to die of embarrassment.

"Will you accompany me to the store, Beth? I sure could use your help. Maybe the men will wash the dishes while we're gone. Wouldn't that be nice?"

Before Beth can say there's no way in hell she's going to the store with her mom, who is obviously having some kind of mental breakdown and might drive them both into a tree or something, her dad says, "I'm sure Beth will help you, right, Beth?" His stare dares her to object. "Especially since you're all showered and ready." Then he looks at Myra, who is pulling the sugar-coated knife out of the peanut butter and wiping the ants off with a napkin. "Thank you." In a long silence, her mother and father look at each other, their faces changing expressions like that stupid speechless exercise her dad had them practice. It's like a mime show, and Beth doesn't know what's going on. Finally her mother nods.

"Come on, Beth." This is not said with the same bright cheerfulness, and Beth realizes something is over. She wants to yell, "What? What? Who won?" but the way both of her parents look right now, she better keep quiet.

Just as they are about to leave, her father says, "And honey, could you go to the supermarket in Jamestown this time? Just get a whole lot of everything. Please?"

"Sure," her mom says. "You betcha. Let's go, Beth."

The trip to the store and back takes two and a half hours. Beth doesn't say even two and a half words to her mother the whole time. When they arrive home with eighteen bags of groceries (which includes a half-dozen bottles of wine), there is a long truck pulled up in front of the barn, and a new car in the drive.

"Over there," Will says, trying to fit the familiar set of *Of Mice and Men* into the new dimensions of the barn. He needs to keep the barn door stage left, the bunk beds—not real bunks, just single metal beds with thin mattresses—along the back wall, the heavy wood table a little left of center, and nothing too far right, so there will be room for the hay, and nothing along the front, where the apron would be. Frank Tucker and Jimmy McGovern carry in a bunk, then go back to the truck to get something else. Chip Stark and Ben bring over another bunk. "Right here, next to this one," Will tells them.

Lars Lyman, who plays George, carries a box of props and tries not to trip over Shakes, his dog, who follows Lars so closely, it's like the man has a third foot. Lars found Shakes (short for Shakespeare) at the pound. They didn't need a real dog for *Of Mice and Men*; they could have referred to it as if it were just out of sight, but Will wanted it, and Lars had found this poor feeble mutt moments away from being put to sleep. It was the perfect dog—if you needed a blind, rickety, flea-bitten mongrel that looked like it really ought to be put down. No one even expected it to last the six weeks of rehearsal, or the six weeks of production, but here it is, Lars's best friend. For the most part, Lars carries the dog, figuring Shakes has only so many steps left in him, like a car's starter.

Will had asked Lars to lead the truck here just to make sure it arrived. The truck driver, some guy named Horace or something, will leave as soon as the truck is empty. He doesn't carry anything off the truck. That's not his job. He's a union truck driver.

Will's psyched. The props and furniture are here. The next problem is going to be cash. The executive director of The Mill Street Theatre doesn't even know that the set was shipped out a month early; he's currently in Minneapolis hobnobbing with other executive directors. This whole project of Will's is on the Q.T., until, of course, the invitations go out, inviting all to come see the extraordinary new production of *Of Mice and Men*. So over a bottle or two of bourbon tonight, Will will broach the subject of everyone kicking in for food. The actors are receiving unemployment until the summer season starts; they can afford to pay for some of the food. But still, they'll need more money. He needs to ask Myra to appeal to her parents for a loan, even though they haven't paid off the last two loans. Maybe they should call it a grant.

Almost everyone is here. Victor Peters should arrive sometime today. He'll be the last, except for Melinda, whom Will won't think about right now. Victor, sixty-nine, is slow as molasses, drives like an old lady, and walks like a duck with his feet pointing outward and his knees bent. If he gets here by midnight, it will be a miracle. Melinda is another story, but he won't think about it. He tells Lars Lyman to leave the prop boxes for Beth to check off the master list. Will's dying to open the boxes and set the scene, but he's pretty sure that if he doesn't leave that job for Beth, he's going to regret it.

Will watches Lars nimbly step over Shakes and go back to the truck. The man is so ordinary looking, so average (thirty-five years old, five ten, one hundred and sixty pounds), that he can play almost any role. He's not too tall (like Will himself) or too big and heavy (like Ben) or too old (like Victor Peters) or too short (like Greg Henry, who at five six is going to play young boys until he's playing old men). Lars is so plain American, with his sandy brown hair, sandy brown eyes, and almost featureless face that, if he held up a bank, no one could describe him. Lars Lyman can play the bad guy, the good guy, the fool, or the prince. His only annoying habit, Will thinks, is that he mumbles and doesn't finish sentences. Thank God, when given a script, the man can project with the best of them.

Will directs the traffic of bodies moving crates and metal beds and old mattresses, thinking about the way a simple genetic trait will close options—like Nate Johnson, who simply because of the color of his skin will never get to play George, or Romeo, or Hamlet. Will's also thinking about how to set up Nate's stuff in the small front room of the barn, and wondering when Beth will get back so he can open those boxes, and why Greg Henry had to accompany Norton into town so Norton could get some simple gym shoes, a task Norton could have done all on his own. Then, for the last time, *he swears it will be the last time*, he wonders what happened to Melinda and what he's going to do about her not being here.

"Hi, everyone!" Beth says, coming into the barn. She looks around as if something is missing.

Will waves to her. "The props are over there, Beth. Why

don't you open them up and check them off the list? Lars can help you."

Beth looks around the barn again, frowning. Finally, she walks over to the boxes along the wall and says hi to Lars, and they begin pulling the props out. Well, at least Myra is back with the food, Will thinks. Then he has an idea.

It makes perfect sense. After Myra puts the groceries away, she'll go find her backpack. It's a good backpack, and she can't afford to leave it out in bad weather.

The kitchen is half-cleaned; an attempt was made but probably abandoned when the truck with the scenery pulled up. Maybe she should finish cleaning the kitchen as a sort of apology for yesterday, but damn it, why should she have to apologize? Did Will apologize when he tore off the screen door last year because it got locked and he was so drunk and angry, he didn't even bother going around to the back? No. It just got turned into a good story. And did Jimmy McGovern apologize when, dead drunk, he tried walking around in high heels and fell on the phone table and broke it? No, he did not. Or when—oh, hell, she could go on and on! So screw them, she thinks. How dare they come here and take over the place, expecting her to play the pretty little hostess. The groceries are only partly put away, and Myra is already seething. She slams the can of baked beans down on the counter and decides they can do the rest.

And just to prove she doesn't have to worry about what the actors think, she takes a bottle of wine out of the pantry and puts it in a bag with a can of sardines. Cradling the bag under her arm, Myra walks out of the house. The truck is pulling out of the lane, and Myra stops to watch, feeling as if it is the land pulling away, that she is on a ship that has cast off its ropes and is moving into choppy waters.

Will walks out of the barn. "Myra! Come here. I want to ask you something!" Then, toward the barn, "Okay, okay, I'm coming!" He motions to Myra to follow him.

Myra doesn't want to talk to Will right now, but how can she just walk off into the woods, ignoring him? She hasn't even left a note. Well, she'll tell him she has to go get her backpack. He'll understand. They both believe the world is too materialist, too disposable. He will have to let her get her backpack.

Let her. The words stiffen her spine. She can't believe she thought those words. She will simply tell him what she is doing. She doesn't need his approval. She puts the bag with the wine and sardines next to a peony bush, the stems bending almost to the ground with huge globes of pink flowers. She pushes the bag with her foot, and it slips under the bush. She'll get it after she talks to Will.

As she enters the barn and sees the furniture and props from *Of Mice and Men*, Myra has a funny feeling, a fluttering of longing. She feels as if she might actually want this to be happening—the actors here, the energy of theatre—but she also feels something inside her say, don't you *dare* get excited about this. Still, for a moment, she sees what Will has seen, the possibility. It's not like this could really be the real bunkhouse at a ranch in California forty years ago, but with just a bit of imagination, it would be so easy to pretend.

Will turns from talking with Lars Lyman (who always annoys Myra because the man can't finish a simple sentence) and comes over to Myra. He puts his arm around her shoulder. "See?" Will says. "What do you think?"

"Nice," she says, the word a bit tighter than she meant it to be, but she is holding in a lot right now.

"Listen, Myra, I've been thinking," Will says. He says this not just to her but like an announcement, and Myra wants to roll her eyes. He's so dramatic. He's probably going to tell her he's going to sleep out here with the men, something she's been expecting. He'll be one of the ranch hands—one of the guys.

"Since we can't find Melinda, how would you like to fill in for her? Just for the rehearsal, unless something terrible has really happened to her, then you can decide if you want to go on, or if we should replace you with Sandy. But you might have fun, just rehearsing, no pressure. What do you think?"

I'm going to kill you is what she thinks. How can he ask her this in front of all these people? She doesn't hate him for having the idea but for the ignorance and carelessness of asking it publicly. There is an answer inside her, but it needs to be worked out by talking with someone she can trust—to understand the fumbling this answer will take. Years ago that would have been Will. She and Will on the couch after the kids had gone to bed, discussing the idea of maybe just getting involved in a rehearsal, being an understudy. But this subject, of her on the stage again, has been a closed book, and just the thought of opening it up makes her throat raw. And now, after their fight last night, he throws this at her like a fastball out of the blue. She almost laughs with the absurdity of what she expects of him: consideration. He's done this publicly in order to look benevolent. She wants to spit.

In her silence, he must realize something has gone wrong, like a man asking a woman to marry him in front of his family and suddenly seeing she might say no. He looks so utterly confused. People confuse him. He only understands fictional characters. She remembers his dismay about his own children, so many times. Why did Beth want to go to Debby's instead of to the zoo with him? Or why doesn't Mac want Will to wash his hair anymore? That look of "what happened to the world I knew" has always softened her, and it does again, so that instead of slapping him across the face, she says, "It's something to think about. We'll talk about it later, all right? I have to go turn off the stove."

No one speaks as she leaves the barn and walks right past the peony bush and into the house and up the stairs to her bed, where she curls up on top of the covers and pulls the pillow to her chest and doesn't think about the part of Curley's Wife, the thrill of memorizing lines, the possibility of acting again. She finds, oddly, and thankfully, that she can curl up with her pillow and not think at all.

Will doesn't know what to do. Last night, every time he went upstairs to talk to Myra, it turned out to be a big mistake. Only when she was asleep did he dare crawl into bed, her small curled shape reminding him how scared he'd been that she might have been lost in the woods. He'd wrapped himself around her from behind, and in her sleep she had moved in against him, and they had slept like that the whole night. But what should he do now? Words didn't work last time, and it's too early to climb into bed. Should he follow her out of the barn or let her have her space? Let her have her space sounds best to him.

The actors are suddenly busy studying the walls of the barn. Beth is sitting on the ground holding a bullwhip, her mouth hanging open. She looks like she might cry. What is up with his daughter anyway? Jesus, his family is making him nuts. "Okay, Nate," Will says, a little too loud, which means everyone turns his way, "Let's get you set up in the front room. That bunk's yours, and that nail keg, right? Let's move them in."

Nate shakes his head slowly. "You're serious? I'm sleeping by myself in that little room?"

"Yes, Nate, that's the idea."

Nate shakes his head again. "You and your ideas. Let me tell you, a raccoon comes walking in there, or a skunk, and I'm in your bed and you're in blackface playing my role, got it?"

"Sure, Nate. We'll close the barn door at night. You'll be safe."

But when they carry the bunk into the narrow front room, Will sees a large hole along the bottom of the barn floor. As a matter of fact, there seems to be fur stuck to the wood. Will doesn't point it out.

Nate's trying to get the barn doors to close. They've been left open for years. A good-sized bush grows in front of one of the doors. The other one seems to be moving—when a squeal like a stuck pig is heard, and the door rocks forward and falls to the ground, splitting evenly in half.

Will rolls his eyes and laughs. "Looks like we have some work to do. Let's get the props put away, and then we can build a new door, in character!"

"Which means," Nate says, "you get to watch, Mr. Director."

Will laughs. "You caught me, Nate." Then he thinks about it and gets an idea. "You know what? I'm going to be one of the ranch hands. We'll make up a character, and I'll sleep out here with you guys!"

Nate snorts. "How about you play the part of a crazy old fool, Will? Typecasting if I ever heard it."

But Will is already thinking ahead. There are two extra bunks, just part of the set, so that's no problem, although his feet are going to stick off the end a good foot. He shrugs. You have to suffer for your art. Actually, it might be fun. They'll hang lanterns and play cards all night. By God, Will loves these guys. He will save this company if it's the last thing he does.

Two hours pass as Myra lies in bed, and when she gets up, there is a crease along the side of her face from the edge of the blanket; it doesn't go away for the rest of the day. Now and then she touches her cheek and feels the indentation, but she does this absently, without care. She's numb through and through. Dully, she notes that it is not just the possibility of acting again that has her in this fog; it is because she knows something now that she doesn't want to know, which is: she doesn't love Will anymore. She doesn't know when that happened, and she doesn't know if it's temporary. Will loves her, but it is the kind of love he fits into the cracks, the spaces between acting, the moments between directing. Will's love for her is something he will get to, after this play. He believes she will always be there. Maybe not, she thinks. The thought is heavy, it sinks inside her, from mind, through throat, through lungs, right past her heart, into her stomach, where it sits, fermenting and turning sour.

Downstairs, Ben is putting away the groceries, and Myra thanks him. She fills three glass canisters with water, adds a few tea bags, and sticks them out in the sun. She yawns a lot, as if she can't get enough air. Outside, men are working on a barn door, and Frank Tucker is practicing his golf swing in the backyard without a golf club. Actors come inside for water, and to use the bathroom, and to grab a piece of fruit from the bowl she has set up so nicely in the center of the kitchen table. They speak kindly to her, and she speaks kindly back. She doesn't remember what they said as soon as they're gone, but each time someone takes an apple or a plum, Myra replaces it with another one so the bowl always looks full. Will doesn't come in for anything.

While Myra makes egg salad, Mac comes into the house and says, "Mommy," with an intake of air that makes her look up quickly. He has gotten a splinter from the barn door and needs Myra to get it out. This small action brings her out of the fog that has muted the afternoon so she could move through it, to now, when she is needed by her son. She comforts him and feels comforted. She takes the splinter out carefully and painlessly, then offers him a Popsicle, even has one herself. It's the best Popsicle she's ever had, the lime bright in her mouth. She decides she wants to take the role of Curley's Wife.

When Greg Henry and Norton come back from shopping for sneakers, Beth is ready. She's leaning against the side of the barn, watching her dad, Jimmy McGovern, and Chip Stark fix the door. They're using some old plywood from the basement that had been slung between two sawhorses to store cans of paint. Beth pretends to be absorbed in the study of fixing barn doors, so that when Greg comes up and says, "Hey, hi, Beth," she looks up startled, as if she had no idea he was standing exactly one foot, three inches away.

"Oh, hi, Greg. You finally got here, huh?"

"I got here last night. Where were you?"

"Oh, I was up in my room reading *King Lear*, again. Guess I was pretty absorbed." She can't look right at him, or she'll blush, but she can tell anyone exactly what he's wearing: white T-shirt with a V-neck, cigarettes rolled up in the sleeve, cut-off blue-jean shorts, Birkenstock sandals, and a copper bracelet that gleams across the very tan skin of his wrist. Most of the other actors look like those blind fish that live at the bottom of the ocean. They're inside the concrete building of the theatre all day. Somehow Greg has found time to work on his tan. Beth decides she'd better spend a little more time in the sun herself.

"So you're going to have the gang staying here, huh? Think you can put up with us?" Greg says, poking her in the arm with his finger. She feels flushed all over, just by that one little touch.

"Sure, I guess," she says.

"Hey, it ought to be fun, don't you think? Far out, you know? Guess we'll all get to know each other real well by the time this is over." He winks at her. She is so stunned, she just stands there. Greg laughs. "Well, I guess I better go show these guys how to fix a door."

Beth nods. She can't believe he winked at her, like what he meant was he was going to get to know *her* really well. He was flirting! And she was so stupid, she didn't know what to say! God, is she stupid! Next time she's going to say something smart, keep the conversation going. Jesus, she stood there like an idiot! She watches Greg but pretends she's still interested in fixing a barn door. She doesn't know anything about construction, but it sure seems like there are enough nails in that door by now. Patting Chip Stark on his bald head, Greg says, "Guess you've killed it dead by now."

Chip puts on his heavy southern accent. "Well, big guy, we've just been waitin' for you to mosey on over and carry this door over to the barn. Reckon you can do that?"

"Wouldn't want to hurt my hands," says Greg, his grin wide and perfect.

"Yes!" says Beth's dad. "That's the way to think, Greg!"

Beth knows her dad is happy because Greg is acting in character, referring to Curley's dream of being a pro boxer and not wanting to mess up his hands. And that's when it hits her, the thing she never even *thought* about. If *she* were to play the role of Curley's Wife, she would be playing the *wife* of Greg Henry's character. Please, please, please, let her mom say no.

Victor Peters drives up Will's lane just after sunset. The sky is that violet blue that makes his heart skip. Stars flicker in the distance. If he had been born later, and tons smarter, he'd have been an astronaut.

Victor sits in his car for a moment. He had to stop twice on the way here for a little shut-eye. Doesn't sleep so well at night, but something about the daytime knocks him right out. Just thinking about the next few weeks makes him tired.

He told Will he'd come 'cause he likes Will. Will could hire younger men—makeup can make anyone look old onstage—but Will's never given up on Victor. Always finds a part for him. And Candy's a great role, one of the best. Still, he'll need a vacation after this. On the moon would be nice.

A figure steps out of the house and stands in the doorway. It's got to be Will. No one else in the company's that tall and skinny. With the backlighting, Victor is reminded of that science fiction movie with the tall, spindly aliens. *Okay, Helen*, he says to his dead wife, gone now three years, *I'm going to need your help these next couple of weeks. You stay nearby, you hear?*

No problem, I'm here, she says. She always thought Will was a bit of an odd wicket, but she liked him. That was another reason Victor said yes to coming here. Helen liked Will, and Will liked Helen. That means a lot to Victor.

Helen was his confidante, and his confidence. Not a day goes by he doesn't miss her so bad it hurts. That's why he's so tired. Can't breathe sometimes from the pain. Sometimes he thinks he ought to retire. Sit the last dance out. But Helen would get madder than hell. When he does finally kick the big one, last thing he wants is to face Helen mad. She's a tough one.

Wish me luck, he says. *Luck*, she says.

Victor opens the car door and steps out into the night.

Will has rounded everyone up into the living room, and the edge of the dining room, and the stairs to the second floor, where Beth and Mac sit on the bottom steps and Myra sits halfway up, watching silently. Damned if she's going to hide in her room while everyone else is down here.

It's the goofiest group of men she's ever seen. Jimmy McGovern looks like he's trying out for *Laugh-In* with his Day-Glo clothes, and Norton is dressed as if he's going out to dinner, sitting stiffly next to Lars, who needs a shave and seems soft and out of focus, like the fuzzy dog he's holding in his lap. Victor Peters, who's a very sweet old man, always reminds her of the Wizard in *The Wizard of Oz*, and then there's Frank Tucker, standing in the corner, his posture perfect, chin held high, smoking a pipe as if he were posing for some ad—and Nate Johnson, standing in another corner, dark and distant as ever. Chip Stark sits in one chair, looking cocky, and Greg in another, his legs curled up under him like a little kid at the movies. And, of course, Will, the chief beluga, with one foot on the coffee table, one hand on the back of the high-backed chair, his dark eyes gleaming with the glory of theatre. He's quite charismatic. She can't deny it.

Now Myra doesn't know how she feels about Will. She's mad at him, yes, but he has offered her a chance at acting again, a chance she hasn't even allowed herself. How is she supposed to feel? She used to have a small pocket calendar for just this kind of thing. She charted her fights with Beth to see if the arguments could be related to either's menstrual cycles. She charted Mac's colds to see if they could be connected to high pollen days. She marked the days down when Will came home late without a good excuse. Now she needs to buy another calendar and mark a 0 for the days she doesn't love him and an X for the days she does. Then she can measure her feelings, not make judgments from the heat of the moment. But what about a day like this, when she hated him and wanted to love him; what code can she find to represent that?

Myra decides she will tell Will about her decision to take the part of Curley's Wife when they are in bed tonight: see if he asks her how she came to this decision, how she feels about it. Then she'll decide how to mark this day down.

Will's expounding on the state of resident companies in America, and his voice rises as he gets to the heart of his speech. "So tell me, why isn't theatre as important as rock and roll? We need plays that get the attention of a whole new generation! New York is staging *Hair*! A musical with nudity! What can a small resident company do? We need to put on plays so vivid they make our audiences *gasp*! Let's find those plays and bring them to life. Let's make theatre necessary to their very souls!"

It is a passionate speech, but Myra has heard it before. So have most of the actors, but it is always a good place to get everyone started listing their favorite plays, which is exactly what happens for the next half hour until Norton raises his hand and clears his throat.

"Excuse me, Will, but tell me something."

"Yes?" Will leans over expectantly, ready to answer any question about the theatre ever asked.

"Could you please explain this arrangement you have for allocating showers? You mentioned something about odd-numbered days for everyone under thirty-five and even-numbered days for everyone over thirty-five? Are you quite serious?"

"Okay, okay," Will says, as several other voices pipe in questions about the sleeping arrangements. "That plan for the showers is correct. As for beds, any actor playing a ranch hand sleeps on a bunk in the barn. Nate's going to sleep in the front room, and he's not to go into the main part of the barn, just like in the play. Norton will sleep in Mac's room, since Mac is sleeping in the station wagon. Is that right, Mac?" Mac nods. "And Greg will sleep in Beth's room. Beth and Myra will sleep in our bedroom, since I'm going to cast myself as a ranch hand for the duration of this rehearsal and sleep in the barn myself."

Oh, I was right after all, Myra thinks, then flinches as Greg Henry shouts, "Far out! I get a bed!" and Beth drops her empty Coke bottle on the bare wood floor. Shakes, who had been sitting quietly in Lars's lap, yelps when Greg shouts, and begins to wheeze, spraying mucus in the direction of Norton Frye, who cries, "Oh, Mother Mary!" and jumps up to move away but trips on Victor Peters' leg and falls in his lap. Lars pulls his dog close to his chest and murmurs, "It's okay Shakes, it's okay," and Ben Walton and Jimmy McGovern start laughing so hard they can't stop until Will shouts, "Enough!" Shakes freezes in midwhimper.

Everyone quiets down. Norton has gotten himself out of Victor Peters' lap and stands under the dining room arch with his arms crossed, looking sour.

"Finally," Will says, "there will be no smoking in the barn. It's a fire hazard." Everyone groans. "We'll place cans around the outside of the barn. Please use them. Now, tomorrow at nine we will meet in the barn and make solid plans. Bring your thinking caps. I know that together we can make something important happen, something startling. Oh, Myra, did you decide to fill in for Melinda for us?"

She didn't see it coming. She expected he would ask her in private, that he picked up on her discomfort. She feels like a fool. She marks the day as a big fat 0.

"Yes, I will," she says, because she wants to. She really wants to.

At the same time as Will says, "Great," Beth gasps. Norton announces, "I'm going to bed." People get up. Jimmy McGovern asks where the liquor is kept, and Will points to the kitchen. Several people head in that direction. As Beth goes upstairs, she glares at Myra. Oh, Myra thinks, sleeping in the same bed with Beth is going to be so much fun.

In less than a minute, the living room has cleared out. Myra sits on her step, halfway up and halfway down. It feels like the right place to be, so she just stays there.

Beth feels as if she's fallen off a roller coaster. One minute Greg Henry is sleeping in her bed, an idea full of possibilities, such as tiredly slipping into her own bed in the middle of the night, an understandable mistake. Then, boom, her mother takes the part of Curley's Wife, a young, seductive woman. Are they crazy? *And I have to sleep in the same bed with my mother? Yeah, right.* Beth makes sure there is no underwear on the floor or Tampax on the bureau, gathers up her nightgown, the top quilt, and one pillow (leaving one for Greg), and stomps back downstairs, past her mother who is still on the step, and announces—not to her mother but to anyone else who might be listening, "I'm sleeping on the couch!" There is a hitch here, Beth knows. People will want to sit around the living room and talk late into the night. Well, they will just have to deal with her living right here, on this stupid old couch. Everyone else is making all sorts of decisions; she's making hers. If she had a can of spray paint, she'd write, *This Couch Belongs to Beth*. It's about all that does.

Will returns to the living room, looking for Myra, who is still just sitting on that damn step. Why the hell doesn't she get up? He wants to ask her if she minds him sleeping in the barn. "Myra," he says. That's as far as he gets. For the next ten minutes, a parade of actors file through the house asking for something. Jugs for water. Bowls. A flashlight. A long electrical cord. Is there a shotgun in case a bear comes into the barn? Will is desperate to keep everyone happy, so he answers these questions as if they made sense. How long a cord? To stretch to the barn? No, but write it on the list on the kitchen table. A gun?

No, it's been years since a bear was seen around here. Honest. When Jimmy McGovern asks if there is a generator they can hook up out there, it's getting pretty dark, Will tells him that's what the three lanterns are for, but Jimmy points out those lanterns are just props and there's no kerosene in them. Will says, "Add it to the list." Then Jimmy tells him Greg Henry just drove off to go into town for a while, and God help him if he brings anyone back to the barn tonight, "if you catch my drift." Will says Greg's not that stupid, then suggests Jimmy take out the last bottle of scotch and just try and relax. Finally, when he turns to talk to Myra, she's gone, and he hears the bathroom door close with a solid thud. Will decides to just give up. Timing is everything. He's missed his cue.

Turning around, Will notices Beth on the couch with the quilt pulled over her head, her feet sticking out at the other end. Just as he leaves the living room, he hears a whimpering noise and wonders if Lars's dog is still in the house.

They are grown men sleeping on prop beds in a dark barn for the love of theatre. But that doesn't mean they don't complain. They make complaining an art form. An amusement. A play:

FRANK TUCKER. This is completely ridiculous. Absurd. Who took my pillow?

JIMMY MCGOVERN. I saw a raccoon walk off with it, Frank. He went that-a-way. (*He points toward the smaller room where* NATE *is making up his bed.*)

FRANK TUCKER. Oh, shut up, Jimmy. Seriously, has anyone seen it? It has blue and white strips. It's got down feathers, for God's sake.

CHIP STARK. There's mouse shit everywhere. I'm sleeping with my boots on.

JIMMY McGOVERN. You screw with your boots on, Stark, so what's the big deal?

CHIP STARK. And did you see the *size* of those spider webs?

BEN WALTON. *(He sits on his bed, and it creaks like chalk across the blackboard.)* This bunk won't hold me. *(He bounces up and down lightly. A spring lets loose.)*

CHIP STARK. There's not enough liquor in the world to keep me here. *(He grabs the bottle of scotch from* JIMMY *and takes a slug.)*

VICTOR PETERS. Something smells rotten. Smell it?

FRANK TUCKER. It's the dog. Or Jimmy. Changed your socks this month, McGovern?

LARS LYMAN. *(Quietly, but with strength.)* Leave the dog alone.

BEN WALTON. I'll have to put the mattress on the floor.

(A bat flies through the barn from stage left.)

THREE OR FOUR VOICES. Shit!!!

VICTOR PETERS. Bats eat spiders.

FRANK TUCKER. No they don't, Victor. They eat flying insects.

JIMMY McGOVERN. Who the hell cares what they eat? I'm going back to the house.

BEN WALTON. *(Testing out the mattress, which is now on the ground.)* We can't. Will wants to talk to Myra.

CHIP STARK. Talk? I'll tell you what he ought to do. The woman needs . . .

FRANK TUCKER. Shut up, Chip. We don't need your filthy talk.

CHIP STARK. *(With a big, dramatic shrug.)* Hey, man, I just call it as I see it. She's one unhappy-looking woman, if you ask me.

BEN WALTON. No one's asking you, Stark.

LARS LYMAN. *(Quietly, but everyone hears.)* She does, though . . . look sad.

(After a pause, Jimmy's flashlight flickers, then dies.)

JIMMY McGOVERN. I'm outta here. *(He heads toward barn door but stops when* BEN *speaks.)*

BEN WALTON. How about charades?

CHIP STARK. Are you nuts, Walton?

BEN WALTON. *(Still sitting on the floor.)* I dare you, Stark. You'll be captain of one team. I'll be the captain of the other.

CHIP STARK. You *are* nuts. There aren't fucking captains in charades.

BEN WALTON. *(With a grin, standing up.)* Bet you five bucks my team wins.

CHIP STARK. You and what fucking team?

BEN WALTON. Me, Victor, Lars, and Nate against you, Jimmy, Frank, and Norton.

CHIP STARK. Why do I get Norton? Hell, he's not even here! He's upstairs in a soft bed laughing at us suckers. And where is Nate anyway?

(Everyone looks around.)

(In the narrow extra room between the barn doors and the rest of the barn, NATE JOHNSON *sits on his bunk listening to the sound of men. He was wondering when they would miss him. If they would. Now they only need him to make the teams even. Nothing's ever even, he thinks. Nothing. He wouldn't mind some company right now, but he's drawing the line at playing charades with a bunch of drunken white guys.)*

BEN WALTON. Hey, Nate, get your ass in here and play charades with us!

NATE JOHNSON. *(What the hell, Nate thinks. He's never played charades. And he ought to do his part to keep everyone from going in the house, disturbing Will and Myra. Lars is right. She's looking sad. Will ought to spend some time alone with her.)* Thought I wasn't supposed to be coming in the big room, Mr. Walton. Mr. Will Bartlett be saying—

BEN WALTON. Cut the crap, Nate. Will's just a horse's ass sometimes, and you know it.

WILL BARTLETT. *(Walking into the barn, through Nate's room, carrying a six-pack and a carousel of betting chips.)* Hey, Nate.

(He walks into the main room and holds up the chips.) Poker, anyone?

CHIP STARK and JIMMY McGOVERN. Count me in.

LARS LYMAN. Sure. Okay.

BEN WALTON. Hey! We were going to play charades!

CHIP STARK. In your dreams, big guy.

JIMMY McGOVERN. What's the limit?

CHIP STARK. The sky, my friend, the sky.

(NATE, in his narrow room, stays on his bunk and turns off his flashlight. Limit's much closer than the sky, he thinks. Limit's right here. What the hell was he thinking?)

BEN WALTON. *(He walks over to the opening between the main room and Nate's room.)* Nate! Now it's poker. These sissies can't handle a game of charades. Come on in and join us.

NATE JOHNSON. No thanks. I'm going to bed.

BEN WALTON. You sure? Nickel ante. Stakes won't be that high. Come on.

NATE JOHNSON. *(He shakes his head.)* Too high for me, Ben. But thanks.

BEN WALTON. *(He stands in the doorway for a beat, then raises his hands in surrender.)* You change your mind, you know where to find us. We'll be the group of assholes making too much damn noise in the next room.

NATE JOHNSON. *(With a chuckle.)* You got that right, Ben.

BEN WALTON. Night, Nate. *(He goes back into the main room.)*

NATE JOHNSON. Night.

(The lights fade to the shuffle of cards and the laughter of men.)

FRANK TUCKER. Where the hell is my pillow?

Tuesday

❧ ❧

Under a dreary gray sky, the actors stand outside the barn smoking cigarettes and drinking coffee. "Come on, let's get started," Will says, feeling a rasp in his throat. They'll have to cut back on this late night stuff. "Let's meet in the barn. Put out the cigarettes. Bring in your coffee. Let's go." He takes a last puff of his Viceroy and looks for a can of sand, but there aren't any. On the ground, just outside the doors, there's a pile of butts, like offerings made to the barn god. At least they're not smoking in the barn. Will knocks three times on the door. It doesn't fall down.

Nate Johnson walks over to Will, shaking his head. "Guess I'll just go home."

Will's muscles tighten so quick, he worries he might have pulled something in his back. "What?!"

"You said I'm supposed to stay out of the main part of the barn, but seeing that's where you all are going, I'll just go home. You make up your mind, let me know."

Will counts to five, worried Nate might leave before he gets to ten. He knows Nate didn't sleep well. He said something crawled over him in the middle of the night.

"Okay, Nate, I get your point. Let's just say that you don't come in the main part of the barn when we're rehearsing or doing improvs. How's that sound?"

"You don't want to know how it sounds, Will. Trust me."

Will puts his arm around Nate to lead him into the inner barn. "When this is over, I'll treat you to dinner at the Brown Derby. Promise."

Nate slips out from under Will's arm with a little twist of his shoulder. "If I haven't been eaten alive first."

"Nothing's going to eat you, Nate. You're too tough."

"Quit while you're ahead."

Will does.

In the barn, those who slept on bunks glare at those who slept in beds. Everyone complains about cold feet and long lines for the bathroom. There's not enough food. Will has to promise everyone they can take a shower today just to quiet them down.

Will knows there's a lot to be done, but wasn't that the idea? "Okay, now I've got assignments for chores, which we'll do *in character*. This will be fun!" He notices no one smiles. Well, physical labor will help work out the tension. Maybe that's how the ranch hands survived living together—they were too weary each night to hold on to yesterday's anger. Will imagines himself as a laborer, large tan muscles, sweating in the hot sun. It gives him an extra boost, and he assigns the tasks with vigor.

Chip Stark, Jimmy McGovern, and Frank Tucker will build the outhouse. Victor Peters will find cans and fill them with sand. (Will has given Victor something he can accomplish between naps and do one-handed, since his character has lost a hand in an accident.) Ben will carry the building materials and help the outhouse gang. Nate Johnson is to rake out the barn and putty the holes. Greg Henry will pick up the cigarette butts and mow the lawn. Beth will wash the dishes and clean the kitchen—the dishes are technically props, although this explanation seems to annoy Beth all the more. Norton Frye is to figure out the approximate cost for items on the *"to get"* list (which is so long—blankets, flashlights, lanterns, ashtrays, toilet paper, napkins, matches, cigarettes, garbage bags, toothpaste, pillows, electrical heaters—Will decides to fine-tune it later). They do need blankets. It did get pretty damn cold out here last night. He asks Myra to borrow blankets from the neighbors. For himself, Will has to make phone calls and plan the rehearsal schedule.

Think in character, he tells them. *Move* in character. *Breathe* each breath in character. He is wounded by the eye-rolling. Don't they know art is hard work?

While doing the dishes, Beth watches Greg Henry mow the lawn. Shirtless. Her heartbeat is erratic. It's the way he mows, going all the way around the house in a circle; Greg is in her sight for about two minutes, then out of sight for four minutes. Two minutes of *bam bam bam* against her chest, holding a dish tight in her hand. Then she leans to her left to watch him go around the corner of the house, and then her heartbeat goes back to normal (sort of) as she washes the plate, or bowl, or glass, or pot (there are so many dishes!), then her heart picks up again; hearing the mower (the rumble of the mower!) makes her heart, like that Pavlov's dog thing, start to *bam bam bam*.

She's wrong. He doesn't really look like Kurt Russell all that much. Paul McCartney—that's who he looks like. Paul McCartney with curly hair. Paul McCartney not wearing a shirt. Every time she thinks she's done with the dishes and can go outside, someone brings in a dish from the barn or, worse, takes a just-washed plate from the cupboard, and just-dried knives, forks, and spoons from the drawer, and proceeds to make something to eat. Beth herself is starving, but she won't eat a thing that needs silverware or plates. SpaghettiOs sounds great, but she can vividly imagine the sticky orange mess in the pan and decides to go on a diet. Everyone should, she thinks, glaring at Chip Stark as he opens the cupboard for a plate. Beth's father made it clear that if she didn't do every dish in sight, he would consider hiring another prop girl. Right. Like who? Her mother? Still, if she goes outside, it'll be more obvious that she is watching Greg Henry mow, and from here, well, she *has* to stand in front of the sink. She can't help it that he walks by her window every four minutes.

Mac watches as, after the meeting in the barn, the actors break up like a toy being taken apart, which makes him think of the toys he's lost, like the red metal fire truck. One day it was on his floor at home, the next day, gone. He looked all over for it, and when he couldn't find it anywhere, he began thinking maybe Beth took it. That was when Mac realized Beth was different from him, not just on the outside but on the inside. People were different, each and every one. They might see blue when he sees red, or feel hot when he feels cold. How would he ever know? It's a lot to think about.

His family is like a toy falling apart too. Lately, his mom and dad hardly talk to each other, and they keep forgetting he's around. Even Beth's ignoring him. She hasn't tried to trip him in days.

But Jimmy McGovern is his buddy now. The way Jimmy says *Mac*, it sounds like a tough name. Mac can almost see himself as a construction worker when Jimmy says *Mac*. Big muscles and a hard hat, wearing one of those huge tool belts. Mac says "Mac" out loud, to see if it still sounds tough. Not as tough as when Jimmy says it.

His dad didn't give him a job, so he hangs around the back of the house watching Jimmy McGovern, who's standing with Mr. Tucker (who talks down to Mac as if Mac were standing in a hole) and Chip Stark (the guy in black who walks real slow).

"Hey, Mac!" Jimmy yells. "How the hell are we supposed to build an outhouse without you? Come over here, kid, and grab a shovel!"

Mac knows Jimmy's kidding, that they don't need him to build an outhouse, but he runs over anyway, kind of hoping they do. Jimmy puts his hand out for Mac to slap, and Mac does. He likes the way that slap sounds, and what it means. He stands next to Jimmy as the actors talk about how to build an outhouse.

"Hell," Jimmy says, "let's just dig a hole way back there near the woods, put the dirt to the side, and leave the shovel."

"What am I supposed to sit on?" Mr. Tucker says, petting his mustache. Mac wonders if it is fake, like the ones his dad wears sometimes, and if it might fall off if he plays with it too much. "And what about privacy? What's to keep anyone from watching?"

"Hell, I won't look at you. Honest, Frank. And I'm betting no one else will either." Jimmy says. "Right, Mac?"

Mac grins. "No way!"

"See? So let's do it."

"But Will said we were to build an outhouse."

Chip Stark sticks his hands into his pockets and rocks back and forth in his shiny black boots as if he were standing on a baby teeter-totter. "Hell, Frank, no one's going to use it. Will's smart. He told us to build it just to get us to do something and quit griping. Let's just dig a hole and call it a day."

Mr. Tucker shakes his head. "Fine, fine, whatever you say."

Jimmy hands the shovel to Mac. "Ready, Mac?"

Mac nods. The shovel is pretty heavy, but he picks it up as if it weighs nothing. As they walk across the field, Mac thinks he just might grow up to be a construction worker. He hopes his dad doesn't mind.

Nate Johnson putties the holes in the barn, thinking about his character, Crooks. Here was a guy who had to live separated from everyone, and it made him so bitter he became the kind of man no one wanted to be around anyway. It's easy to understand how that could happen. As a kid, growing up in Harlem, Nate hadn't thought much about bigotry—everyone was black. The war changed all that. He'd been nineteen when he'd enlisted; he needed more than religion and the odd job to satisfy him, and he thought enlisting was the answer. It took a long time to understand his help wasn't wanted. After half-assed training for over a year at Fort Huachuca, Arizona, he was assigned to the Ninety-third Division, one of the few black combat units, and sent to Italy. His white southern commander called him "boy" and refused to let anyone carry live ammo. He saw little combat until the battle in the foothills of the Apennines, outside of Rome. It was a disaster. Their training had been so poor that half the men turned and fled. Dozens were killed. Nate had carried a kid named Mitch, blood oozing from his stomach, seven miles back to base, where he died from lack of Negro blood. They wouldn't give him a white man's blood. That day Nate stopped loving God, who was as much a part of him as Harlem and his own skin. He had carried God with him all through the war—or as his mother would say, God carried him—but watching Mitch die, Nate decided he didn't want anything to do with God. That loss scared him as much as the war. If you couldn't count on God, who could you count on? No one but himself, that's who.

When he came back to New York City, Harlem had changed; it was no longer a place you could hide from prejudice. But he had to stay there. His mother had gotten sick, and he had to support her, so he got a job filling cigarette machines. He took his mother to church each week, but he wouldn't speak to God. God had something to say, he could talk to Nate. He could explain some things. But God wasn't talking.

One day while filling the machine at a theatre, the manager gave Nate a ticket to a play as his Christmas tip. *The Iceman Cometh*. It was a strange, mesmerizing play, and for hours he had forgotten about the war and the world he would return to that night. It was magic, that's all he knew, and he wanted more of it. Not only did he want to see another play, he wanted to be in them.

It took years, but he never quit, and he began getting good parts, the few there were for a black actor. When he heard about an audition for regional theatres, he decided to give it a try. His mother had died a few months before, and he wanted to get out of the city. Nate was the only black man at the audition, but he got offered a job. He'd been smug about that for a while, until he realized he'd been hired simply because he was black. By then it didn't matter. Not much did, but acting.

He still went to church. He did it for his mother, and because he was still waiting for God to notice he was mad at Him. Do something about it. Strike him with lightning or pull him back into grace. Seemed to be at a standstill. Nobody giving an inch.

It had been close to fifteen years since he left New York, and he'd never gone back. He could almost claim he had forgotten about the war—how it made him feel dirty, how it made him turn his back on God. But now, trying to understand his own past to understand Crooks, he has to admit that he turned his back on more than God. His closest friends are the actors, and he doubts if even one of them knows his birthday, or his age.

Nate throws the putty knife against the barn wall, where it wedges into the soft wood. *Enough!* He doesn't have to make himself miserable to play the part of Crooks. He's never been a method actor, and he's done just fine, thank you. And what is this "fix up Will's place and call it acting" malarkey? Maybe it's time to move on.

When Beth is finally finished with the dishes, she decides to take Greg Henry a glass of lemonade. She has to make the lemonade first, which makes her grind her teeth, but she does, then washes off the wooden spoon and wipes up the counter, where sticky lemonade has sloshed over the side of the plastic pitcher. She fills the tallest glass she can find with five ice cubes, pours in the lemonade, and looks out the window to see where Greg is. He is standing by his car with Norton Frye, who's wearing a red scarf around his neck. Her father hands Norton something, and then Norton and Greg get in his car and drive off. She can't believe it!

Mac walks into the kitchen, his shoes two clumps of wet mud. He actually asks her if she'll make him a grilled-cheese sandwich. She tells him he'd better get lost or she'll grill his butt. The little creep actually smiles.

Beth pours the lemonade down the drain and leaves the dirty glass in the sink to rot in hell.

Myra is uncomfortable with asking the neighbors for blankets. Even though she runs into them at the grocery store now and then, she doesn't know them all that well. She passes up their nearest neighbors, the McCrearys, because they are somber people who don't approve of Will and Myra, especially after the outdoor rehearsal of *Midsummer Night's Dream* a few years ago. She decides to try the Griggses first, who have a small dairy farm about a mile down the road. She first met the Griggses when their bull got loose, and Mr. Griggs (Tom, she thinks) came looking for it. Every time he sees her in the store, he asks if she's seen any stray bulls. His wife (Mary?) is a small woman with a gentle smile. Myra drives down the road rehearsing her words. "Hi, I'm Myra, remember me? Your neighbor? I was wondering if . . ."

Pulling into their drive, Myra notices the quiet right off. There are no signs of life, despite the usual array of rusted farm equipment and cars on blocks. But there's no car *with* wheels. There is something more that bothers Myra: an absence of care. The lawn is uncut, and the porch is covered with leaves. On the door of the house is a large white piece of paper. Myra gets out of the car and walks over, feeling like a trespasser. *Auction*, it says. *May 30th*. The county is auctioning off the entire farm. Myra looks around. There are no cattle. No chickens. How could she not have noticed before?

She gets back in the car. Just across the road are the Millers. Myra backs out of the Griggses' drive quickly and turns into the Millers' drive, as if that were where she wanted to go all along.

Mrs. Miller (Pat?) opens the front door as Myra walks up the steps. Mrs. Miller is about seventy, so Myra calls her Mrs. Miller and doesn't have to worry about her first name. "Hi, Mrs. Miller," Myra says. "Remember me? Myra? Your neighbor?"

"Of course I do, sweetheart. How can I help you?"

Myra's ashamed she's never been here before, even though Mrs. Miller brought them an apple pie the first summer Myra and Will moved in, and Mr. Miller was the handyman who'd helped them rebuild the side porch. It's so obvious that Myra isn't here just to say hello that she gets right down to the business of borrowing blankets. "We have a lot of people staying with us for a few weeks, and I was wondering if you might have any blankets we might borrow. I'll get them cleaned afterward. It's just that we don't have enough. We didn't think this through, I guess . . ."

Mrs. Miller laughs. "Oh, don't worry. I have two wool blankets in the cedar chest, not doing anything. Hold on just a minute. I'll go get them." She comes back with two blue wool blankets. "Here you go," she says. "Hope they'll help some."

"Oh, they will. Thank you so much." Then, because Myra knows she can't just walk away, she adds, "So how is Mr. Miller? He did such a great job on our porch."

"Well, since he lost his eye, it's been pretty difficult for him," Mrs. Miller says, so matter-of-factly that Myra is sure she misunderstood. Mrs. Miller notices Myra's confusion and explains. "An accident with the chain saw. A big limb fell and came right through the attic ceiling. Pete climbed up on top of the roof and tried to cut it loose. The chain saw slipped. Cut a huge gash in his forehead, and he lost his eye."

"How awful!" Myra says. "Oh my god. I'm so sorry."

"I'm sorry too. Took me a while not to be just plain furious, since I told him to leave that branch alone for someone younger. I guess I have to be grateful it was just an eye he lost. He came pretty darn near to bleeding to death in the process."

"When did this happen?" Myra asks, holding the blankets in her arms and feeling as if she has stolen something.

"It happened last June. He's doing okay. He's up in Buffalo getting a glass eye right now. He says he's going to have them make it blue. Always wanted blue eyes. He's still a joker, that's all I can say."

"Yes, he is," she says, as if she knows him. "Well, thank you so much for the blankets. I really appreciate this. It's very nice of you. Please give our regards to your husband. And if there is anything we can do . . ."

"There's nothing you can do, sweetheart, but thanks for asking. Just bring the blankets back when you don't need 'em anymore. It does get cold here in the winter. But you won't need them then, will you?"

"No," Myra says. "We'll be gone by then." Somehow these words make her feel like a deserter—as if by leaving Chautauqua each fall, they commit some kind of crime.

Myra's legs tremble. She is sure she saw Mr. Miller in the store last summer. How could she not have noticed?

Another quarter mile up the road live the Horners, in a white house with pretty blue trim. The Horners' daughter is about Beth's age, and during their first summer here, the girl (Netty? Betty?) came over to play with Beth, but they didn't hit it off, and the next summer she came by only once. Mrs. Horner (*Lucy*, she's sure it's Lucy) seemed like a nice lady. *Normal*, Myra tells herself, as if maybe the last two neighbors weren't, and it wasn't really Myra's fault she didn't know them very well. Myra pulls into the Horners' drive feeling a need to talk to someone who is like her. Lucy Horner answers the door and looks just fine to Myra. She says of course she remembers Myra. Myra asks how her daughter is and is relieved to hear that Netty is doing fine. But Mrs. Horner can't lend them any blankets because her sister, who was born crippled, was living in a home that burned down just last month, and Mrs. Horner sent all her spare blankets and towels, along with a bunch of clothes and pots and pans, to the place that took all those people in. She wishes she could help Myra, but they don't have two of anything right now.

Myra's face is hot. She tells Mrs. Horner how sorry she is

about her sister. It sounds awful the way she says it, as if having a crippled sister were the most terrible thing in the world, where what she really meant was she was sorry the home had burned down. Myra backs up and trips on a stone. "See you soon," she says, and Mrs. Horner nods and smiles. When Myra grabs the wheel, her hands are wet with sweat. She drives all the way to Jamestown and buys ten cotton blankets from Woolworth's, writing a check that she hopes won't bounce. She wants to buy ten more blankets and send them to the place that took all those people in, but she can't face going back to the Horners'.

Driving home, Myra is something more than embarrassed, but doesn't know what she really feels until she drives by the Griggses' deserted farm. She and Will didn't know them at all. They have surrounded themselves with theatre people; everyone else is peripheral. If the theatre closes, could Will get a job as a director at another theatre? They may not want someone his age. Then they would be people who are *not* in the theatre, in a world where people work with chain saws and lose their eyes. They might have to sell the summer house, they might be poor. They have been wearing blinders. Today her blinders have slipped. She doesn't like what she sees, but she is glad she sees it all the same. She might be scared, but she knows she wants to be different now. She wants to be someone who would have bought the extra blankets and taken them to the Horners.

She vows she'll throw a big party at the end of the summer and invite everyone on the road. She'll give Mrs. Horner all the blankets she just bought. She'll talk to these people. She'll get to know them. She promises she will do this, no matter what.

But when she gets back to the house, Will starts complaining before she can say a thing. Norton Frye took a shower, even though he wasn't on the list since he had one yesterday, and it's thrown off the whole schedule. The outhouse is just a big hole.

No one is working in character. How difficult can it be to be ranch hands as they work?

Myra drops the blankets on the floor. "How in God's name can you or any of these actors portray people you know nothing about? When was the last time you spent even one moment with someone who isn't involved in the theatre? You live in a world of make-believe. You don't know crap about real life!"

Will looks stunned. Good, she thinks. But then, from the corner of her eye, she sees Beth standing in the doorway. Afraid she is about to cry, Myra runs upstairs. Someone's in the bathroom. "Please hurry," she says. In less than a minute, Ben comes out, his hair dripping, towel around his waist, his large torso like a gigantic pillow. She imagines putting her head on his chest and going to sleep.

"Myra?" he says, obviously concerned. She can't bear his kindness. She can't bear anyone's kindness right now. She slips around him into the bathroom and closes the door.

Beth can't believe what a bitch her mom is. What *is* her problem? She got the role of Curley's Wife. What more does she want?

Beth goes over to where her dad sits at the small phone table that has become his desk. He looks funny sitting there; the table is polished and fragile and small, and he is big, angular, and rumpled. He looks wrong sitting there. Miscast, she thinks. This thought surprises her, because it's the kind of thing her dad would think, and he would be proud of her for thinking the way *he* does, but she can't tell him, because she can't say he doesn't seem to fit into his own home anymore. He already looks pretty upset.

"Can I help you, Daddy?"

"No, honey," he says. "Everything's fine."

"But she—"

"Shhh," he says. "It's nothing. Your mother's tired."

"From what? I just did all the dishes!"

"Beth," he says, his lips tight, "give her a break."

Right, Beth thinks. In a million years. "Fine," she says. She'd stomp up to her room, but it's not her room now. Stomping over to the couch would be just plain stupid. She stomps outside. No one's around except the dog, who's deaf anyway. She wonders how she can feel so crowded-in without a soul in sight.

After a while, Beth comes up with an idea. She waits until her father leaves the house and no one else is inside, then calls her friend, Deb.

"Deb," she says, "I need some LSD. Three or four hits."

"Since when did you start doing acid?" Deb asks.

"I didn't start. It's not for me."

"But then who's it for?"

Beth hears someone come in the kitchen door. "Never mind. Just get some and mail it to me. I'll pay anything."

"I don't get it—"

"Just do it quickly. I'm desperate. 'Bye." Beth hangs up the phone and jumps over the back of the couch, landing on the cushions as if she were taking a nap. It's just her brother.

"Hey, Mac, how you doing?" she says. She's feeling generous. She's going to get back at her mom for treating her dad so bad. And for taking the role of Curley's Wife. And for getting drunk and lost. And for saying Beth can't act. Just about everything.

At ten o'clock at night, Beth's hands are red from hot water, her hair's a mess, her head's pounding, her back's sore from the couch last night, and to top it off, the actors, and her mom, are doing a theatre game out on the lawn, having a great time, and

Beth has been left out, *worse*, ordered to play Monopoly with Mac to keep him out from under Jimmy McGovern's feet. Thank God someone left a full glass of whiskey on the kitchen counter. She almost puked drinking it, but so far it's stayed down.

Beth walks into the living room after drying her last dish, *ever*, and shakes her head. Mac is sitting on the couch, the Monopoly game all set up on the low coffee table.

"Oh, right," she says. "In your dreams." She picks Mac up off the couch and dumps him onto the floor. Just the motion of leaning over to pick him up makes her dizzy. She lies down on the couch and closes her eyes. In minutes she's asleep.

The sun's setting, and Will thinks, *Good, this might work better in dim light.* "Okay, everybody, form a circle and sit down." Will waves an arm in a large circle, hoping to speed things up, but it takes some time for the actors to pick their spots and spread out the blankets on the freshly cut lawn. Frank Tucker has to study the whole group before finding his place, and Jimmy won't stop monkeying around, tugging Chip's blanket away just before he sits down. Will has allowed them each one beer, to help loosen them up for this exercise—they would have brought out alcohol no matter what he said anyway. Not being in the theatre building has diminished his authority. This farm has been the place of too many drunken parties, and no one takes him seriously.

Jimmy McGovern runs around the circle shouting, "Duck, duck, duck, goose!"

"Sit down, Jimmy!" Will shouts. "Right there!" Jimmy falls down, almost into Myra's lap. She seems to have recovered from her funk today. He has no idea what could have set her off like that. He was glad she agreed to join them tonight.

It makes Will nervous, though. He wants her to do great things. He's just afraid to watch her try.

"Okay, now, listen. The characters in this play have very little privacy, day in and day out. The ranch hands live together. Lennie and George travel together. There's no room for secrets between these people. So what's that like? To constantly be exposing yourself? And Jimmy, not one damn wisecrack, do you hear me?" He stares at Jimmy. Jimmy nods, but his freckled face is laughing.

"What I want you to do is, tell us a secret dream. What you have always wanted. See how it feels to be exposed." Again he looks at Jimmy, who grins, making a zipper motion across his lips.

"Absurd," says Frank Tucker.

"You are welcome not to participate, Frank," Will says. "I just assumed that as an actor, you were willing to push yourself, to grow. But if you feel you have hit your pinnacle and have no higher ambitions, you may be excused from what the rest of us are working on to better our art." Will keeps his face straight, even though he's grinning inside. He knew Frank Tucker would protest and had prepared this little speech. He's so glad he got to use it.

"Well," Frank sputters, "I never said I wouldn't join in. I'll go along with it, if the rest agree."

"I'm willing to try anything Will suggests," Ben says. "I'll even go first." He takes a slug of his beer. "I want to act. That's it. Plain and simple."

Will's glad for Ben's support, but he's not going to let him get away with this. "Too easy, Ben. What do you want that you *don't* already have?"

Ben's quiet now for a minute. Will's sure Ben is going to make a joke to break the tension, but then, quietly, he says, "All I need is love." He tries to make a silly face, to cover the seriousness of what he said, but he ends up looking so miserable, Will can't help but look away.

"Hey!" Jimmy shouts. "That's a song! Can we use songs? Then here's mine. 'I want to hold your hand.' " He grabs Norton's hand.

"Keep your paws to yourself, lamebrain," Norton says, pulling his hand away.

"Who you calling lamebrain, Mr. Toupee?"

"Stop!" Will yells. Something in the woods scurries for cover. "Ben has expressed exactly what I was looking for, even though he's hiding his feelings behind a song title." He looks at Ben, who shrugs. "And because he spoke out, because we got to see a little of Ben that we don't normally see, it made us tense. That's what it's like on the ranch in *Of Mice and Men*. These guys don't want their innermost secrets to be known, but they slip out all the same, causing tension. They get in fights, but then they have to work together. See what I'm getting at?"

"Not particularly," Norton says under his breath.

"Well, how about you go next, Norton," Will says. "Help us out."

"Oh, fine." Norton agrees. "And I won't stoop to using song lyrics either." Norton sits up very straight. "It's actually quite simple. I would like to travel. I've lived in the same apartment for fifteen years, and in Pittsburgh for my entire life, except during the war. I'd like to see the rest of America. Experience new places. Meet new people. That would satisfy my soul."

Will had no idea Norton wanted to travel. The man seems so set in his ways. "Thanks, Norton. That's exactly what I mean. Who's next? Greg?"

Greg Henry looks around the circle. "Well, what the heck. I'd like to be . . . well, it sounds stupid." He blushes and looks down at his hands. "Taller."

Everyone's quiet. Everyone's taller than Greg. Will's amazed the kid had the guts to say it. He can't imagine being short. It's one of the few things he can't imagine. "Greg, that's what I'm looking for. Some real honesty. Lars?"

Lars Lyman is silent for so long, Will thinks he's not going to say anything, but just as Will decides to push it, Lars clears his throat, looking sheepish but at the same time a bit desperate. "I don't know. I guess what I want is . . . is to . . . well, this lady once told me she loved babies but didn't want her own. She couldn't handle the scary parts of being a parent. Bad things happening . . . So she wasn't going to take the chance . . . I understood, what she meant. But maybe there's something to not playing it safe. You know? Take a chance, I guess. Try something . . ." He shrugs.

"All right," Will says, not sure what else to say. He's never been sure if Lars's stumbling words mask a brilliant inner thought process, or not, and he's still not sure. "Jimmy?"

"Hell, you're serious, huh? Okay. I want a million dollars. I want to look like Rock Hudson. I want Brigitte Bardot as my personal slave. I want—"

"Jimmy, come on. One thing. One simple honest longing."

"Chip's love life would be good enough for me."

Will grinds his teeth. "Try again."

"World peace?"

"*Jesus Christ, Jimmy!* Be serious, just this one time. You are part of this company. I expect you to be honest or say nothing at all."

"Well, hell," Jimmy says, almost angrily, the cheery, good-natured voice suddenly gone. "How's this? I have eleven sisters and brothers. My mom died having me. One pregnancy too many, I guess. So I wish the pope allowed birth control. My mom could have used it. Good enough?"

Hands holding beers freeze in midmotion on the way to open mouths. This isn't what Will expected from Jimmy, but exactly what he was hoping for—he thinks. The exercise is working, but he bets no one will ask to do it again.

"Good, Jimmy." Will hears how stupid that sounds, considering what the man just told them. "I mean, thank you. That was very brave. Well now, Victor?"

Victor rubs at his face with a hand covered in age spots. "It's too easy, Will," Victor says. "I want Helen back. I know you'll say that that's not a secret dream, but I dream about her every night, and day. If pushed, I'd say I'd like to walk on the moon. So I've got two dreams, both impossible. Take it or leave it."

"All right. We'll take that. I'd like Helen back too. Thanks, Victor. Nate?"

"I'll pass."

Will looks at Nate. Nate looks right back at him. Nate's eyes are a steel gray, and Will wonders why he never noticed that before. "Nothing?"

"Nope, Will, not a thing."

Will knows when to quit. "All right, who's next? Chip?"

Chip stands up and sticks his hands in his pockets. "Well, Will, my dream is to be just like you."

There are a few laughs. Will doesn't know what to say.

"Got you there, huh, pardner?" Chip says, rubbing his hands together. Will recognizes that motion and knows he's being teased. He can feel anger lurking in the background, but how can he be angry with someone who says he wants to be just like him? Chip goes on, now waving his arms around, and once again Will recognizes the imitation and thinks Chip's not doing him justice. "You know. Be a well-respected actor and director, with a lovely wife." He winks at Myra. "Throw great parties. Offer your friends plenty of beer and booze! Hey, and just to be nice, I'll throw in an extra dream. To own a Harley. And I will. Hey! *I Will. You Tarzan, I Will.* Get it?" Everyone moans. Chip bows and plops down on the blanket.

Will finds he is actually flattered, even though Chip's obviously drunk. "Frank, you willing to give this a try now?"

"Not particularly. But . . ." Frank takes a deep breath and looks around the circle. "I have ambitions to act in movies, but you all know that. To play this game fairly, I'm supposed to share a secret dream, and then we will all be better actors. Well, then. I despise my father, and always have. He's a foolish man and has lost more money than I'll ever see in my life. He gambles, bets the horses. He lost our house, our car, my mother's life insurance after she died. And I hate horses. Stupid animals, running around in circles." He pauses, then resumes, his voice low now, not talking so much to the actors as to himself. Will notes this, how people do this when they are being honest—tell themselves, as much as the person they are talking to. It can be used in *Of Mice and Men*, he's sure of it.

"My father," Frank continues, "is a failure. My dream? I wish I could love him all the same. But I can't." Frank looks up. "There. Now you can't blame the demise of the theatre on me, Will. I did my bit for God and country. Happy?"

Will is, but he knows better than to say so. "No, not happy, but grateful. Thank you, Frank." There are plenty of wide eyes around this circle, Will notes. He wonders if they will think differently about Frank now. Oddly, Will doesn't. He still thinks the man is an egotistical asshole, but a sad egotistical asshole. Still, the first person who comes up behind Frank and whinnies like a horse is out of this company for good.

"Myra's turn," Ben says. "How about you Myra?"

"Playing Curley's Wife?" Myra says. To Will, it sounds like she's asking herself if this is what she wants.

"Is that all?" Ben says.

"Not by a long shot, but if you think I'm going to spill all my beans in front of a bunch of guys, you're nuts. We need more women here. I'm outnumbered."

If there were women here, you wouldn't be playing Curley's Wife, Will thinks.

"Well then, my turn," Will says. "Unless you want to try now, Nate? Don't say I didn't give you a chance." Will would like to know Nate's secret dream. Will has imagined himself all sorts of people, kings, fairies, and fools, and believes he could imagine himself being black, but he'd like to hear what Nate has to say. Would he say, if he were honest, that he wishes to have been born white?

Nate is a quiet enigma in this circle of men whom Will considers his friends. Perhaps he has never been much of a friend to any of them; he has never asked these questions of them in friendship, only now, as a lesson in acting. Will's suddenly ashamed. Nate hasn't answered him, and in the quiet Will knows that each man here has trusted him, but Nate doesn't. And Nate may be the smart one. Will wants a drink. A cigarette. Jimmy to make a joke. Something to take away the edge. He does want Nate to answer, but in this moment of honesty, Will knows he wants Nate to answer him as much as a sign of forgiveness as to hear what Nate might say. The exercise has worked, and Will is miserable.

"No, Will," Nate says. "You go on, though."

Will had all sorts of things planned to say. Dreams of beginning his own theatre, of winning awards, even making a movie, but it all seems gaudy now. He'd like to say something simple and true. "I'd like to see Beth act someday, on the stage of The Mill Street Theatre, a well-respected, well-supported resident theatre. That would make me happy."

"Tell her," Myra says, not too loudly, but Will hears her. He nods.

Will pulls back into being a director, not sure of where any other path might lead him. "Now, we should discuss how this exercise has worked to make us aware of how difficult . . ."

"I think enough has been said," Frank says, and gets up and walks off.

"I'm not doing nothing without another beer," Jimmy McGovern says, heading to the house.

"Bring me one," Chip and Greg shout.

"What do you think I am?" Jimmy shouts back. "A waitress?"

Chip and Greg get up. Lars follows them. Shakes follows Lars. "Be right back," someone says.

"I have to use the facilities," Norton says.

"I better check on Mac," Myra says.

Nate stands up and heads to the barn. Will is left sitting in silence with Victor Peters, who is gazing up at the sky, and a bunch of empty blankets. Will waits, but he waits alone.

Will enters the house, thinking he'll talk to Beth about the exercise, tell her what he said. She's asleep on the couch. What are you dreaming? he wonders. She says she wants to act, but he knows he's influenced her. Who would she be, if he weren't her father? Has he suppressed some great talent of her own? Maybe she could have been a math wizard, or a great piano player, if she didn't spend so much time watching rehearsals. Has he pressed her into a mold that doesn't fit? She's not a very good actress yet. Too dramatic. But that's her youth, isn't it? She can learn. He has a lot to offer her. Not for the first time he regrets starting so late in life to have a family. What had he been doing that was so damn important? But he knows. He was living as only he knew how, with a passion that has not ebbed but is fractured, grown dowdy almost, in a world of movies and TV. He wonders if in the future the sum of live theatre will be Broadway shows, while resident theatre is something antique, old-fashioned, a curiosity. Does Beth even want to act on the stage, or is it only movies she's dreaming of? It's her choice, he tells himself. *Her* choice.

Will bends down to give his daughter a kiss on the forehead and thinks he smells the faint odor of whiskey. Is it her breath, or his, reflected against her skin? He doesn't want to know the answer, so he kisses her forehead and moves away.

When he goes back outside, several of the actors are sitting on blankets, and Jimmy's telling a story about a man who built an ark, just like Noah, on the top of a mountain. Ben passes Will an empty glass, then a bottle. There is something sad about this handful of actors sitting on his lawn getting drunk. Is this what we are? Will wonders. Just what we appear to be? What happened to the men and women he has seen on the stage, regal even when playing the most despondent of men? What must they look like to anyone else? Dressing up, wearing makeup. Pretending. Yet it's the pretending he wants back. The gilded vision. The ornamentation of hued lights, the power of a great line. Even the empty space of the rehearsal hall with taped lines on the floor representing walls would be better than this: what is all too real. He shakes his head, trying to clear out the funk he's in. It's been a long day. He deserves a drink or two.

Hours later, on his way into the barn to sleep on his narrow, uncomfortable bed, Will passes Nate reading by flashlight.

"Sorry," Will says. He's a bit drunk, and it's all he can manage.

Nate nods. "Well, that's nice. I appreciate it. Been waiting a while to hear it. Not from you, but it'll do, for now."

Will's not sure what the man means, but he's too tired to figure it out. "Sleep tight, Nate."

"You too, Will."

That should be no problem. He's exhausted. But tomorrow's another day.

Wednesday

❧ ❧

Will has finally gotten everyone into the barn after breakfast. He wanted to get started earlier, but the actors are moving slowly due to several nasty hangovers. All in black, Chip Stark looks like a dead undertaker. Greg Henry's eyes are so heavy-lidded, his thick eyelashes block his vision. And Jimmy McGovern woke with a face so flushed it looks like a third-degree sunburn. Frank Tucker won't meet anyone's glance, while Nate Johnson appears downright smug. Will himself is not feeling all that well.

"Okay, listen up. I appreciate your commitment to physical and mental labor for the sake of art, but I can see you need a break, so I've decided that we'll start today with just a line reading. Refresh ourselves with the script. No dramatics. We need to get rid of what we did in Pittsburgh. Toss it out. Start blank. Create it all over again. It was too easy before. We, and I am including myself in this, just slipped into what works. It's my fault. I cast the show. I picked you because you fit the part. Throw all that away. Forget how you played it before, and remember nothing in this play comes easy to these characters. It shouldn't come easy to us."

"Is that what you want?" Frank Tucker asks. "A hopeless struggle for a better tomorrow that exceeds our grips?"

"Jesus, Frank," Jimmy McGovern says. "Shut up."

"Well, it bears some thought . . ."

"I understand your worry, Frank," Will says, "but let's give this a shot, please. How else are we to know, if we don't try?" He rubs his hands together, but then remembers Chip Stark's imitation, and it takes the pleasure away. He wonders if he'll ever be comfortable with his own gestures again.

"Okay, grab your scripts, and let's pull these bunks into a circle. Beth, you and Mac can listen, but keep quiet." Outside, the sky is turning black. The air has that tangy feel of a summer storm. Looking up, Will notices a few holes in the roof.

That morning Will gave Myra his prompt script, the text taped to yellow legal paper, with illegible notations scribbled in the margins. She highlighted all of Curley's Wife's lines and had almost wept while doing that simple action. She had no idea how badly she missed it. It's amazing how easy it is to fool your heart, she thinks. Right now, sitting in this circle with the other actors, script in hand, Myra has a tight feeling in her stomach; this used to be her life: *Upstage right. Cross left. Pause, then center stage.* It's more amazing that she still cares, that the desire to act isn't dead and buried after all these years. It gives her hope, looking at Will, that what is lost can be reclaimed. She can remember once loving him very much.

Myra doesn't believe Curley's Wife loves Curley. She makes plans to leave him less than a year after they are married. Marrying a man not out of love but out of the need to be loved is what drives Curley's Wife. Myra will have to explore those feelings.

But first she must name the woman. She has no name. She is a possession; she is always referred to as "Curley's Wife," or by Curley as "my wife." It bothers Myra that this woman has no name, that she dies without a name. Myra will discover her name. It feels very important to her.

The first scene is between George and Lennie, at the creek, where they talk about their dreams of owning a farm of their own. Myra listens as Lars Lyman speaks George's lines with a quiet intensity that is riveting. Ben reads Lennie's lines with a simplicity that astounds her. Myra performed in straight drama only a few times and always liked musicals better. But she can do this. She believes she can do this very well, just given the chance.

Scene 2 takes place the next morning, when George and Lennie arrive at the ranch. The ranch hands have already gone out to the fields. Candy, an old man who has lost his hand in an accident, greets George and Lennie and informs them about everyone living at the ranch, including Curley's new wife, who already "got the eye," meaning she's a flirt. Myra's chin goes up. Curley's Wife is not a flirt. She's just lonely. Men simply don't understand.

Myra looks around the barn, wanting to catch the eye of another woman, to share a knowing look of *Men are so dense*, but she is the only woman here. But then she notices Beth and realizes she may be the only *woman*, but not the only female. Myra has watched Beth grow breasts, her hips curve, her legs get shaved, all with a kind of amusement, but right now something feels wrong. Myra wants to get up and drag her daughter out of here and send her back to Pittsburgh to stay with a friend. She knows it sounds silly, but her instinct tells her she's right.

Suddenly there is silence. The actors are staring at her. Myra looks down at her script. No yellow marks on this page. She turns the page. There! She speaks her line, hears her next cue, and says the next line, all the while blushing, embarrassed, devastated at this lapse. But it's a short scene. Only a few lines and it's over, and the actors have gone on. Myra is left shaking, unsure of what happened. What was she thinking to make her lose her place? It almost comes back to her but is lost in a deafening crack of thunder. Soon rain drums on the roof of the barn, and water begins leaking through at least a dozen holes, a few of them directly onto the actors, including Myra. After moving the crates over to the one dry corner of the barn, the reading resumes, but the thunder and drone of rain continue, and everyone has to shout. It sounds like a room full of angry people. Myra sits with her arms wrapped around her chest, still shaking from embarrassment. Her T-shirt is wet; a damp chill runs down her spine. While still reading his lines, Ben Walton gets up and goes over to a bunk and picks up a dry blanket. He drapes it over Myra's shoulder without missing a beat. She nods at him. It is one of the new blankets she has just bought. It doesn't smell of anything familiar.

Mac watches the actors speak, the way they become someone else, their faces falling off and new ones taking their place. He doesn't get theatre. People do bad things in plays. Mac had seen his own dad get stabbed to death onstage. Why would anyone want to see that? He'd been relieved to see his dad come out onstage for the curtain call, but a little nervous when he came home that night. And now Jimmy McGovern, who took him fishing, is acting like a mean person, talking about shooting an old dog. Mac knows it's acting, but, boy, he wants Jimmy McGovern to wink at him, grin—something. Beth told Mac that if you crossed your eyes for too long, they got stuck that way. He's worried the actors could get stuck this way, they could forget who they really are.

The funny thing is that even though he doesn't like the theatre stuff, he stays right in the barn and watches, when he could be somewhere else. He wants to keep his eyes on things. If someone gets stuck in their role, he wants to see it happen. He doesn't like surprises.

They break for lunch, which takes a whole hour because there is such a lot of fussing to fix a simple meal. The kitchen is too small, that's the problem, Will thinks. There has to be some way to set up a food station where people can get at the food easily. The paper plates, though, those were a good idea. Saves time. But it's costing more money than he planned on, and now the barn roof needs to be repaired. They all took shop in college. They should be able to patch a few leaks. Still, he'll have to talk to Myra tonight about money.

Before anyone can wander off, Will raises his voice and announces, "Let's do it one more time, without the rain." The rain has stopped. Will crosses his fingers and heads to the barn; the rest follow—which reminds him of his very first role, back in sixth grade. *The Pied Piper of Hamelin.* He loved that role. He wonders if there's some way to adapt the play, make it an adult production. Something to think about.

The second reading goes better than the first. Myra hits her cues and brings some softness to Curley's Wife that Melinda was missing. (He won't think about her blowing her lines this morning. He just won't.) And Nate puts some backbone into the part of Crooks that wasn't there last year. Even Victor Peters stays awake for the entire two hours. What more could he want?

"Okay," Will says. "That's it! Call it a day! Tomorrow we'll go back to living the play. We'll fix the barn roof in character. Now have a good evening!" For just a moment, he has forgotten that they are staying here and expects them all to just get in cars and drive off. Instead, they head to his house and form a line for the bathroom. Will walks through the tall soggy grass in the back field to the sad, small hole that was supposed to be an outhouse. The shovel stands in a pile of wet dirt like a lone soldier. By the time he gets there, he's lost the urge.

Dinner—hot dogs, potato salad, and beer, which Beth's not allowed to drink, so she sneaks a chug of gin from the bottle someone has left next to the toaster—is loud. Everyone has something to say, although no one's left to listen. Frank Tucker combs back his hair with his fingertips, tilts up his chin to catch the sunlight as if it were a spotlight, and goes on about "the necessity to document the vision of Steinbeck's ranch," while Victor Peters, whom Beth can't stop staring at now that she's noticed how big his ears are, is asking Nate Johnson if black people believe in the space program. Nate shrugs and turns to Will to ask if he can sleep in the house tonight, until the front room of the barn is completely animal-proof. Her dad nods, but he's actually nodding at Frank Tucker's comment. Jimmy McGovern is arguing with Chip Stark about how to fix the barn roof, and Lars Lyman agrees with Jimmy. It's decided that Jimmy McGovern and Greg Henry will be the ones to climb up on the roof, and her dad will go with them into town tomorrow morning to get the supplies and buy some wood to make a big table and benches. Thousands of things they need get suggested, but by that time the conversation has split up again, and words like *hose, coffee, extension cords, sticky fly tape, bug spray, flashlights* (more), and *rodent traps* collide and explode into oblivion. Watching all this, Beth feels dizzy. Maybe she should go get stoned. No one's paying any attention to her anyway.

But then Beth hears Greg Henry say, "I'm going to do the dishes tonight," while her father adds, "Beth will help you."

Greg Henry looks at Beth. Their eyes meet. "Well, Beth?" he says. "Will you help me, pretty please?" He bats his eyelashes at her. Her stomach flips right over. She can feel it.

"Sure," Beth says, hoping there will be a whole lot of dishes tonight.

Dinner ends with Jimmy McGovern telling a story about a six-legged cow that was stolen from the freak show in Indiana by a poor starving family that ate it, then mailed the bones back for posterity—but put their return address on the package. They were fined the going rate, per pound, of beef, plus five hundred dollars a leg.

Ben starts a story about a woman he knew with one leg, but then looks at Mac and stops. He sticks the last half of his hot dog on his nose and pretends to be Pinocchio. Most everyone gets up to find another beer. Beth cups her hand in front of her mouth and checks her breath. Time to do the dishes.

After dinner Will asks Myra if she would like to take a walk down the lane. Jimmy McGovern and Chip Stark overhear and in perfect unison say, "Awww! Ain't that sweet!" Will loves these guys but wishes they could just back off a little, say to Pittsburgh. The thought bothers him; this closeness was his idea. He tosses that worry out and concentrates on what he needs to say to Myra.

He knows better than to bring up money right away, nor does he want to. Mostly he would like some time alone with her, a quiet stroll. He's surprised, when he takes her hand, how much he needs it.

Only when they get to the end of the lane does he speak. "Want to keep going?"

"Yes."

They turn left and walk down the center of the road. The last cloud in the sky reflects the red sunset, like a last hurrah. It's a great lighting effect, and Will stores it in his memory for another play. Will and Myra don't speak again, until the absence of their words becomes too much intentionally unsaid.

"Did you like it? The reading? How did it feel?" Will doesn't add, *after all this time*, but those words are heard by both.

"I liked it. I'm sorry I flubbed the first lines. Something important caught my attention, but I forget what. It seemed important." Then, after a pause, "I liked it."

"I think it went well, considering. The second reading felt very alive. There's an energy you wouldn't expect in a reading of a play they've already performed. I think I'm right, doing this here." He thinks maybe this is the time to say, *Maybe we should invite the whole company*, but then thinks twice. Instead he says, "Maybe it was something about food. What you were trying to think about?"

"No," Myra says. "Not food. It was something *important*." This is said stiffly. Myra walks a bit faster. Will keeps hold of her hand, slows her down. Obviously he said the wrong thing. What is the right thing?

"Your reading was good. Curley's Wife is not a dim bulb, just lost. I think you found that."

"Thank you," Myra says. Her body slows. Will can feel her relax.

"The actors like you. You can see it in the way they look at you."

Oddly, Myra stops walking. She pulls her hand from his and turns at him, not to him. Will can see by the way her eyes get shiny that he has somehow said the most wrong thing possible.

"Are they yours, to offer me their friendship? At this late date? Let me tell you something, Will, they have always liked me. I have been around. I may not be an actor anymore, but I'm no goddamn shadow you have just cast the spotlight on. These are my friends. Of course they fucking like me."

Okay, he sees her point. Now he's afraid to open his mouth, but if he doesn't, he might as well walk to the nearest train station. "You're right," he says. "I'm sorry. I didn't mean it that way. Condescending. I just . . . well, I guess I was feeling proud, of you . . . the way they look at you . . . even Frank Tucker. They want to please you. It makes me proud. That's what I meant. I didn't mean to . . ."

"All right," Myra says. "You weaseled your way out of that one. Stop before you blow it."

"You know I love you, don't you?" Will says.

"Sometimes," Myra says. She takes his hand, but loosely, like a warning that it may not stay. They walk on. A bat swoops low across the road. Something coughs in the woods. A raccoon, probably. Will shot a raccoon as a kid. He's felt bad about it ever since. He actually apologizes to every raccoon he ever sees. "Did I ever tell you about the raccoon I shot?"

"Oh, come on. The kids can recite the story verbatim. What do you really want to talk about?"

Will supposes this is the time to mention the money. If he waits any longer, she's going to be suspicious of everything he's said. "Okay, I'm worried about money. Everyone says they'll chip in some, but it's not enough. We've got five hundred in the checking account, and what I get from unemployment until the summer season starts, and the savings account for the kids—which I know we can't touch. We need money."

They approach the foot of a hill, and not having the energy to walk up, they turn back toward the house.

"So you want to ask my parents?" She says it simply, but he knows she's not happy about it.

"We'll call it a grant. We'll make them a plaque." He crosses his fingers for luck.

"Don't be stupid. Just tell me how much?" she says.

"One thousand."

"We owe them two."

"I know. I appreciate it. You know I do. I think you have the greatest parents alive. The fact that they're rich, that they're generous, that they don't seem to mind being asked as much as we mind asking, makes me the luckiest in-law in the world. I'm not making it a habit, but it's now or never with this theatre, I know it."

"Let's say this plan of yours doesn't work. Let's say they disband the summer theatre, and the Mill Street follows suit. What then?"

"I'll start a new theatre. A small one. We'll find a building to rent. I'll drive a taxi or something. And maybe we'll have to borrow another thousand, in a year. Myra, they said, 'Just ask.' I know you hate to. I'll do it, if you want. But I want to make this work. I believe it will." He says this with emphasis to help make it true.

She's quiet. They keep walking. Will veers over to the side of the road, spotting some purple wildflowers. He tries to tear them off, but they're tough, and he ends up pulling them out by the roots.

"I do love you," he says, bowing as he hands them to her.

"Let's not talk love and money at the same time," she says, but takes the flowers, the long stems like a handful of dirty green shoelaces. "I'll ask them, because I don't see how we can tell everyone to go home after you've invited them here. But this better work."

"It will. This is my chance to do something important."

The way Myra shakes her head, he wonders if he said something wrong again. They are quiet all the way back to the house.

In the kitchen, Beth dries and puts away the dishes that Greg Henry washes, and occasionally they bump into each other, arms brushing arms, hands brushing hands, a foot bumping a foot. It's warm in the kitchen from the hot water. Greg's curls are slightly damp. His shirt, a soft blue, short-sleeved cotton is unbuttoned to the last two buttons. The thick curly hair on his chest peeks out. She's pretty sure he's doing this on purpose.

"So," Greg says, "you want to act, huh?"

"Yeah. I always wanted to act, ever since I saw my first play, *The Tempest*. I wanted to be Ariel. It just seems like there's nothing else worth doing. Nothing else excites me as much as acting. I take lessons at the theatre. You know, the ones for kids on Saturdays. But I'm too old for that now. I'm sixteen now. They should offer classes for the older teenagers. You know? Maybe you could do that? Teach those classes." She takes the glass he has been holding during her whole speech and turns away before he notices how badly she's blushing. Why did she tell him she was sixteen? Maybe he'd think she was older if she didn't say anything at all. She's tall for her age. He might have thought she was eighteen. She turns back to look at him. He's grinning.

"Yeah, that would be cool," he says.

Beth has forgotten what she has said now, except for the sixteen-year-old part. "Yeah, it would be cool."

He hands her a pot. "I wanted to act all my life too. My first-grade teacher, Mrs. Slive, had this thing for plays. I think she was a wannabe actress or something. We put on skits every week. *Little Red Riding Hood* and *The Ginger Bread Man*. I loved first grade. I cried when they told me I had to go to second grade. I thought it was like a punishment. I wasn't too bright, I guess." Greg laughs. Beth laughs too.

"Oh, I bet you're really smart," Beth says, and lightly punches him on his arm.

"Smart enough to get kitchen duty with you." He dips his hand into the soapy water and flings bubbles at her.

Beth squeals and reaches around him to get herself a handful of bubbles. They slide into each other. Greg grabs her wrist and twists her around so she can't get to the sink. "Now, now," he says. "No, you don't. I'm a guest. You can't get me wet."

"Oh, yeah?" she says. She pulls out of his grip and just manages to get a bit of dishwater on her fingers, which she flicks at his face. A few drops of water cling to his cheek, and one little bubble lands on his nose. Greg looks down at it with crossed eyes. He looks so goofy (and so cute) that Beth giggles.

"Hey, Beth," Greg says. "You're in charge of drying. Get this bubble off me." He sticks his face out toward her, eyes still crossed. Beth wants to kiss his nose. Lick the bubble off. She is so high on Greg Henry, she wants to shout and dance. Using one finger, Beth touches the bubble on his nose. It bursts and is gone.

"Back to being good little boys and girls now," Greg says. "There sure are a lot of dirty dishes."

"Oh, well," Beth says. She imagines them living together, making love on the kitchen table each night after the dishes are done, sometimes before the dishes are done. She can't believe what he said about being smart enough to get stuck doing dishes with her. He is so sweet. And so cute. She wonders when he's going to make a move. It's obvious he likes her.

When Myra and Will get back from their walk, everyone except Beth and Greg Henry are sitting in a circle on the front yard, a beer in hand. The stars are brightening in the dark sky like shy children growing bold. Myra can't bear the thought of going inside the house; it's a night to stay outside, the air is warm and fresh against her face, and it's early enough in the year that there are no mosquitos. She'll join *her* friends on the lawn. There is an open spot that she imagines has been saved just for her.

But before she can sit, Will asks her to come around to the back of the house. What now? she thinks. What more can he want?

"The garbage is piling up," he says as they turn the corner. "I was thinking of getting some extra wood tomorrow and building a little shed right here. It'll keep the raccoons out of the garbage until we get it to the dump. What do you think?"

Myra sighs. He can invite nine people to their home for a month without batting an eye, but he can't build a little shed without her approval. "That would be fine, Will." She turns, and through the kitchen window, she sees Beth and Greg Henry laughing. It's completely innocent—probably more innocent than Beth realizes—but it reminds Myra of what she was thinking about in the barn, during the reading.

"I remembered," she says. "I was thinking about Beth. All these men . . ."

"Oh, come on, Myra," Will says, rolling his eyes.

"No, really. It makes me uneasy."

"No one's going to do anything."

"It's not what they might do, Will, it's what she might do. Don't you remember being sixteen? Maybe we should think about sending her back to stay with Debby, just for a while."

"I promised she could be the property assistant, Myra."

"But she won't have anything to do until the season starts. Until then, she's just going to hang out."

"Everything will be fine," he says.

She's not so sure. They walk back around the house. Beth

and Greg are sitting in the circle of actors. The space that was waiting for Myra is gone.

Chip watches Myra and Will go off for their walk, then come back and go behind the house. There is an easy, slow manner to the way they walk, the way they look at each other, and it occurs to Chip that he has never gotten this far in a relationship: to the calm after passion. He wonders if the end of passion leads to something greater, rather than something less. His parents divorced when he was ten, and his mother never remarried. His dad did, though, three times. He married women who were thirty and divorced them before they turned forty. But to be fair, Chip knows his dad loved those women. With each successive wife, his dad had said, "This is the one. God, I love her so bad it hurts." His father needed that hurting-so-bad love more than the women themselves. What would it be like, a one-woman kind of love? Like Myra and Will. There's something warm and fuzzy about that idea. Then again, he's probably just had too many beers.

Chip's only slept with one woman Myra's age, but he can easily remember how great that was. Women are like beer. There are so many different kinds.

Last night Chip dreamt about sex, and it got him hard as a rock. Not much he could do about it in a barn full of men—that is, nothing he'd dare to do. Anyone saw him do something like that, it would be the running joke for the next month. And these guys liked a good running joke. They were still needling Norton Frye about the red velvet shirt he wore six months ago. But it seems Victor Peters' snoring is the joke this week. It's not good enough to last much longer. Everyone's flawless imitation of Victor's nasal wheeze is getting old quick. Chip's not going to be anyone's joke, ever again.

Myra stops just outside the circle of actors as if looking for someone. The flicker of an oil lamp lights the underside of her chin and across her neck. She holds her head so high, Chip thinks, but it's an effort. His mom was like that, after his dad left. Chip moves over, nudging Jimmy to move, too, and waves for Myra to sit down.

Lars watches as the group of actors shifts around to allow Will and Myra in. The actors have, for the most part, worked together for years, buddied up, shared the good times. The worst thing they've had to deal with was Victor's wife dying. They were all there for him, and that was a good feeling and a bad feeling too. But the good times don't make Lars any less nervous; they make him more nervous. He isn't a "glass is half empty" kind of guy, he's a "glass is going to break" kind of guy. Sometimes he wants the bad thing to happen, to get it over with, so he can relax for a few minutes. He has a bad habit of slowing down when he drives by an accident. Accidents are somehow reassuring. He's not so crazy, just careful.

The conversation stops as Will and Myra sit down, until Ben Walton breaks the silence with a bad elephant joke. Everyone laughs except Nate Johnson and Frank Tucker. Even Lars laughs. It's a really bad joke, and it's followed by dozens of really bad elephant jokes, which become really bad dumb blond jokes. Lars tries to tell one but can't remember the punch line. Everyone knows it anyway.

The laughter fills the dark spaces between the actors. It reaches out into the night like a flare of good hope. Lars closes his eyes and feels that, for a moment, everything is all right.

Thursday

❧ ❧

Thursday is cool but clear. The morning is spent getting rid of hangovers, eating breakfast, going to the store. Ben is sure this whole idea of Will's is nuts, until the strangest thing happens: it starts to work.

He can feel it as Greg Henry and Jimmy McGovern fix the roof, laughing and insulting each other, but working hard and in character. He can feel it as Frank Tucker helps Lars Lyman build the new picnic table, as Nate Johnson cleans out the barn, and as Victor Peters and Will assemble the garbage shelter. Even Shakes seems to be acting his part. The dog stinks.

As Ben hauls the heavy stuff, he feels Lennie invade his mind; his thoughts slow, the world grows simple. He picks up heavier and heavier loads, just to make people happy. A voice inside his head says he's going to pay for this, his back will be killing him tomorrow, but he won't listen. Norton Frye walks around inspecting things, just like The Boss would. Myra appears with iced tea. She's not quite the character of Curley's Wife, she's not openly flirting with anyone, but she's there, on the edge of things, soft and feminine. Her smile widens when anyone talks to her, and her laugh is light and carefree. Ben, just as Lennie would, notices just where she is at all times.

Earlier, Myra dropped off Mac and Beth in town for a matinee of *In Search of the Castaways*, Beth protesting loudly. Ben heard that argument, as did anyone else who came near. A private talk was impossible with all these people around. That was when Ben was thinking Will's idea was a disaster. But right now, Ben's carrying a five-gallon bucket of tar over to the ladder, grinning his stupid head off. "Hey, George!" he yells to Lars Lyman, "Look at me! Look at me, George!" He lifts the tar bucket up over his head and prances around. He slips on a patch of wet grass and falls on his ass.

"Hey, Lennie, cut it out!" Lars yells, edgy but still amused, just the way George would sound. Ben puts on his bashful, chagrined look and says, "Sorry, George." He picks up the bucket of tar and carries it with his head lowered. They know who they really are—it's just fun to be someone else. That's why they're actors.

Norton thinks the whole thing is dopier than Donald Duck, but damned if he's not enjoying himself. Each night as he fills his journal, he finds himself grinning. He's written more in the last few days than he would have in a month of Sundays. Road trips to small, quaint towns suddenly sound dowdy, and he wonders if that was really what he was planning to do. His cat, Betsy, sits in the open window, pleased as punch to be looking out at new scenery. Norton's even thinking of letting her out. The road is far enough away, but didn't someone say something about bears? Last night Nate offered him ten bucks for his room, and Norton laughed so hard, his sides hurt.

And all he has to do is walk around and tell people what to do, because he's The Boss. They'll do whatever they darn well please, but the charade is working for now, and it's rather fun. Sometimes he just sits and reads. He's got a lawn chair and a crate for a table set up out behind the house. Betsy can see him from her perch in the window. Getting paid for this isn't such a bad idea.

Beth's going to kill her mother. If it weren't for *her*, her dad would never have sent her to this stupid movie with her stupid brother. Not only is she being sent away from her *own* home, but she's being forced to watch *In Search of the Fucking Castaways*! She would just die if anyone she knew saw her at this little kids' movie, but luckily she doesn't know a goddamn person in the whole town. *Woodstock* is playing right now in Pittsburgh! But not here, you could bet your life on that. Her mother even said she couldn't wear her cut-offs, the ones she had spent hours fraying the ends of and drawing peace signs on the back pockets.

She has already written Deb and asked her to please, *please*, buy some acid and mail it as quick as she can. She knows exactly what she'll do with it: spike her mom's drink right before a rehearsal. She can just see it. Her mother acting like an idiot, no one knowing why. They'd think she was drunk again. If Deb can't get the acid, Beth will have to think of something else.

She leans over to Mac, and just as the giant condor grabs the little kid, she whispers loudly, "There's a big hairy spider on your head." She smacks him, harder than she means to. His pop spills in her lap.

It takes all day to fix the roof, build the table, and make the garbage enclosure. Will couldn't be happier. Everyone's getting into his idea now. He's decided to mix in some rehearsals tomorrow, fit the improvs in between. Equity won't allow the actors to work more than seven hours in an eight-and-a-half-hour time period, five days a week, but who's going to tell?

Beth comes back from the movie like a wraith from hell, smelling like a bucket of warm Coke. She stomps up to the bathroom, and even though it's not her scheduled day, takes a shower. Will shakes his head. The girl is all elbows recently.

Myra and Ben make barbecued chicken and baked potatoes for dinner. Will had no idea Ben liked to cook so much, but he's cracking jokes and singing songs with Myra as he flips chicken on the grill. Learning to cook, that's what happens to single guys, Will thinks. Thank God he's got Myra.

Greg Henry has convinced Will to let him build a bonfire pit between the house and the barn, and Greg and Chip Stark dig up the grass in a large circle. Everyone else (except Frank Tucker, who's reading a *New Yorker* magazine in the living room—although Will imagines he's just looking at the cartoons as most people do) drags dead branches out of the woods. The branches are piled seven feet high before Will can convince them it's big enough. At least there's no wind. Victor Peters says the lack of rain this spring is really hurting the farmers, but Will thinks the weather couldn't be better. He feels blessed. This is meant to be. He knocks three times on the newly built picnic table, which is very sturdy and takes four men to move.

They eat dinner off paper plates while sitting around the raging bonfire (not at the picnic table, which bothers Will just for a moment). Mac roasts marshmallows for everyone, even the dog, who is one helluva a sticky mess. Victor Peters, whose skin has been ruined by forty years of makeup, holds a flashlight to his face and tells ghost stories. Mac scrunches over even closer to Jimmy McGovern. Will tries to convince everyone to be quiet and listen to the sounds of the night, but this lasts less than thirty seconds before Jimmy McGovern lets out a fart that sounds like a broken trumpet, and there's no quieting anyone after that. By midnight, Mac and several actors are asleep in the chairs around the fire. Will carries Mac to the car and eases him into the backseat, making sure the windows are cracked, and then nudges the rest of the sleeping actors until they wake and crawl into bed. Still at the bonfire are Beth, Greg Henry, and Victor Peters, talking about life on other planets. They promise to douse the fire, which is a pile of glowing cinders, when they go to bed. Will mentions they might want to get some sleep before the rehearsal tomorrow, which will start at nine-thirty sharp, and they all say, sure, sure. Heading for the barn, Will changes his mind. Myra went up to bed only a half hour ago. She might still be awake. If not, he'll rouse her gently. She used to like that. She's been acting a bit more like her old self—or he should say, young self—since the reading. Maybe he could push his luck.

Myra moves from sleep to being touched, from a dream of acting class in college to the smell of her husband's flesh. He strokes her back, long waves of pulse and pressure from shoulder to rump, lingering, of course, lower down. She doesn't speak or turn over. She will take whatever caresses she can get first. When she turns over, it will become sex.

Finally, his hand stays on her rear, then curves down between her thighs, and she arches backward. And even though the rest is good, even though she wants him, there is something common about it. They know what works. She does what she should, and does it well, but she's thinking more about it being over, not because it's not good, she thinks again, but because she wants mostly the part that comes after: the holding, the way their bodies press into each other, worn out, warm; when they are past all embarrassment and comfortable with who they are.

"It was a good day," he says softly, after a while, after long enough, and she is grateful he has waited, but she wishes the first thing he said wasn't about the day, or the rehearsal, but about the two of them, as if maybe they are what's important here. She believes, each and every time, during the silence that follows making love, that he can hear her think; she whispers to him with her mind, hoping that he will answer: *I hear you, you are in my mind.* She won't give up this possibility. She has given up other things, but not this.

"It was," she says. "A good day."

"I was worried," Will continues. "I have to admit it. Things got a little crazy, but we're on track now, I can feel it."

She nods against his chest. Why not? What good would disagreeing do?

"I'm tired," he says. "I'll go to sleep here, but I might get up in the night and go into the barn, just to wake up with the guys, keep this thing going. Okay?"

She nods again. A small nod.

"I hope they douse that fire," he says, then gives her a kiss, turns over.

She doesn't fall asleep for a while. She is waiting to be left.

Will has left her in too many ways to count, each one small and forgivable on its own—except the affair he had, which she has sworn to put behind her. But it is the small leavings that hurt most, because they make *her* feel small, easily forgotten, when he runs off to the theatre or loses himself in an idea, a script, a set design. But how can she hold these things against him, when his passion for theatre, his brilliance in directing, are what attracted her in the first place? How can she say *I love who you were, but not who you are to me now*, because, really, he hasn't changed at all?

But oddly, when Will carefully gets out of the bed and leaves the room, thinking she is asleep, Myra doesn't feel alone. She has company. She has another woman inside her, a friend, a companion, a character. Curley's Wife grows inside Myra like a fetus, like the vision of a painting before color is put to canvas. She will name her Lyla. Myra falls asleep, comforted by a role, and looks forward to tomorrow.

F r i d a y

Friday morning brings a cold fog that sticks to skin, dulls sound, quiets color. The actors, stepping out of the barn to piss against the nearest tree and light cigarettes, move slowly, talk softly. Some stay shirtless, the way they slept, because no one wants more of anything touching them, especially their clothes, which are damp and heavy. By nine, seven men sit around in the kitchen and living room thinking about dryers and warm flannel. Beth is sleeping on the couch, her mouth hanging open as if unhinged, her right arm dangling crookedly off the couch, her legs spread open like broken scissors. Ben is the first into the living room and picks up the quilt off the floor to cover her as best he can. Still, she looks like a puppet that fell off its strings, and there is something raw or naked in that look, battered and uncomfortably sexual. The men who come into the living room tend to find something in the kitchen they have forgotten, then stay there, leaning against counters. Will is sound asleep. It is the calm before the storm.

———

Will wakes up groggy, having dreamed all night about staging the rehearsal, his dream so real, he is confused by the idea that it never happened. He's not upset by the idea of doing it all over again; the rehearsal in his dream did not go so well. There was something about actors missing, and lines flubbed, and a flood. Will walks out of the barn and yawns, trying to shake off the dream, only to see Jimmy McGovern, Nate Johnson, and Mac, over by Jimmy's car, looking at a fishing rod. Will turns to Ben, who is walking by. "What exactly is going on?" Will asks.

Before Ben says anything, he hands Will a Viceroy and lights it for him. "Jimmy convinced Nate to go fishing with him, can you believe it? They're not in the scene you said we'd rehearse this morning. They said they'd be back by one."

Even though Will can't think of a single reason to say no, he wants to. There is something about this running off to go fishing that's driving him crazy. Will walks toward the car, just in time to hear Jimmy invite Mac along. Mac says sure so fast, Will does a double take. This is the kid who took ten minutes, just last week, to decide between vanilla and chocolate ice cream, until Will just got him both? For the first time, Will wonders if he may have been had that day.

"We'll bring back some fish for dinner," Jimmy says, then drives off. Will shakes his head, trying to loosen his jaw. The word *fish* makes him grind his teeth. Damned if he'll eat any.

"Everyone in the barn!" Will yells a little too loud, bringing on a headache. Frank Tucker is nowhere in sight. *I'm going to cast him as the rabbit in* Harvey *next year*, Will thinks. If there's a next year. "Go find Frank," he tells Norton.

As they head to the barn, Will asks Myra if she called her parents. With a nod, she says they agreed to send one thousand dollars, no problem. Will watches as she walks into the barn. Her pants are pretty tight, and that T-shirt, isn't it Beth's?

"Okay," Will says, when everyone's inside. "Listen up. No scripts. We did the line reading to get us back into the mood of the play, but I don't want you carrying scripts today. I don't want you tied down to anything. If you feel something come over you, let's see it. Then we'll figure out where it came from, if it's important, and if so, how we can go back to the script, adding what you found—through something physical, or tonal, or maybe in the timing. We'll do it stop and go. Remember what we discussed, the feeling of innocence, the need for something better in life. Beth, you'll have to stay out of the barn today." He almost asks, *Any questions?* but he doesn't want any questions. "Okay, let's go!" He almost cries out as everyone leaves the barn, forgetting that act 1, scene 2, begins with an empty stage.

Beth can't believe her dad has kicked her out of the barn. How is she supposed to be his right-hand man if he keeps telling her to get lost? What *is* lost, she suspects, is the whole idea of being his right-hand whatever. She should have known, but it still hurts.

Outside the barn Greg Henry, Frank Tucker, and Chip Stark are whispering to each other. Last night she and Greg had talked by the bonfire until two in the morning. Once she even moved her leg so it brushed against his, but he moved his leg away. Of course, Victor Peters was there. Greg had to be careful.

Beth keeps waiting for Greg to look her way, so she can walk over and join in, but the actors are bent head to head for the longest time. Finally, when they stop whispering, Greg turns her way and grins. She grins back, but then freezes when he says, "Hey, Myra, come here. We need a woman's viewpoint on this." Beth turns away before anyone can see her eyes start to water. She goes inside the house.

The place is a mess. There are glasses and shoes and sweatshirts and stuff everywhere. She knows it would make her dad happy if she cleaned up. Too damn bad. Sending her out of the barn! Making her do dishes! She should be Curley's Wife! Her mother is *old*. Are they *blind*?

The phone rings. It's the most annoying ring in the whole world, and Beth says, "Oh, shut up," but answers it.

"Hi? Who's this?" the voice on the phone asks.

"Beth. Who's this?"

"It's Melinda. Hi, Beth. Trent Kane said your dad was looking for me. That he's doing a rehearsal, right there, at your farm. Is that true?"

"Yeah," Beth says, her heart beating. "He's rehearsing *Of Mice and Men*. Right now. He called you a million times."

"That's what Trent said! He said your dad was going to *live* the play! That sounds so far out. I'd love to come. I was in New York City for the last week. They're doing all sorts of stuff like that. It's so exciting! Tell your dad I'm leaving now and I'll be there by twelve-thirty. This is so cool! Your dad's a genius, you know?"

"Yeah," Beth says.

"See you soon. Peace!" Melinda hangs up.

Beth's hand is shaking as she hangs up the receiver. She knows just what she's going to do. Nothing. She was told to stay out of the way. So she will.

Myra's nervous about the rehearsal and excuses herself from the group of actors to do relaxation exercises, breathing slowly and letting her shoulders sag. It's so bloody stupid, she thinks. This is a rehearsal of a role she will never get to perform, but her heart takes it seriously: what if she stuns them? What if she has in her a new, mature, intelligent talent she doesn't even know she possesses? What if she is the best damn Curley's

Wife—*Lyla*—anyone ever saw and . . . *Stop it!* she tells herself. *Relax.*

She can hear the actors inside the barn, and she listens for her cue to speak. At this moment, Candy, the oldest ranch hand, is explaining to George and Lennie why Curley was so mean to Lennie, how he's always looking for a fight. Myra wonders if Curley hits his wife. She doesn't think so, but they've only been married a very short time, and she bets he's raised his hand more than once. But it's not being hit that scares Lyla; it's that this marriage has become the end of something, not the beginning. She feels just as if there is a limited amount of air left to breathe, and it's nowhere near enough.

It's almost Myra's cue to walk into the barn when she hears Will speak. "Okay, wait. Let's stop here a minute. Lars, you're playing it very tense, and that's right, but you're pushing it. There's some serious thinking going on in George's anger. Show me that thought process. Do you see what I mean? Let's go back to where Candy exits. And Ben, when George sticks his hands in his pockets, watch him do it, then do the same thing."

Myra rolls her head from shoulder to shoulder. She breathes slowly and thinks, please don't stop again. Please don't let anything get in the way of my dream. They don't. She steps into the barn on cue.

"Hi there. I was wondering . . . have you seen Curley?" she says. She's glad Will has given the actors the freedom to improvise the lines. It makes her so much more comfortable. She wonders if Will thought of that, did it for her. She grins, putting herself back into the character of Curley's Wife. Lyla. Lyla's not really looking for Curley. She's just looking for someone to talk to, and she heard there were new ranch hands in the bunkhouse. One's big and goofy looking, but the other one's nice looking. He tells her Curley's not here.

"You're new, right? You just got here, huh?" she says, feeling bold.

George frowns at her. "So?"

Lyla tilts her head. "Well, I'm just looking for Curley, that's all." She says it too defensively, then shrugs it off.

George snaps at her. "You see him here?"

He's mad at her, but the big guy is staring at her like all get out. She smiles at him. He's kinda sweet looking. "Okay. He ain't here. I can see that."

"I'll tell him you were looking for him, if I see him," George says.

She turns back to the little guy. "You can't blame me for looking."

He holds her gaze. "Depends on what you're looking for."

He's so mean. All she wants is someone to be nice to her. Just talk to her for a minute. From outside the bunkhouse, she hears Slim yell to someone to put the horse in a stall. Then Slim comes into the barn and looks at her disapprovingly. Lyla feels her face get hot.

"Curley's up at the house," he says to her.

"Oh! I gotta go." Curley won't like it if she's not in the house. "Bye!" She turns and runs out of the bunkhouse.

Her heart is still beating hard, but she loved it! Five minutes, and she feels like a new person. She'll have to tell Will it was a good idea, having the rehearsal here.

During lunch—tuna sandwiches and chips, not Norton's idea of a satisfying meal (he wishes he'd added ripe pineapples to the "to get" list)—everyone is talking about how well the rehearsal went, and it certainly did, but something is not quite right. It's the daughter, Beth. She's uncommonly quiet and polite, staying out of the way, bringing out the platter of sandwiches then going back inside, not eating with the rest of them. Norton, sitting next to Greg Henry (whom Norton thinks is turning out to be quite a pleasant fellow), was expecting the child to wedge her way in between them and monopolize the conversation, but all she did was ask if anyone needed anything else, then disappear.

Norton, who's never had children, thinks becoming a parent makes you blind. He's seen it over and over, parents relating glowing tales about their kids, and then, when he finally meets those children, he wonders who in heaven's name the parents were talking about. Norton thinks, although he's smart enough never to say it out loud, that if parents want to know the truth about their child, they should ask a stranger.

So right now, he's wondering what Beth has up her sleeve. If the girl brings out brownies for dessert, Norton will have to pass. As it is, he's not touching his Kool-Aid.

Ben watches Myra all through lunch. He can't help it. It's as if Lennie has stayed in a corner in his brain and keeps whispering, *Look! Pretty!* The conversation that Ben is having with himself is going like this:

LENNIE. She's pretty.
BEN. Shut up. She's Will's wife.
LENNIE. But she's soft and pretty. I like her. She smiles nice.
BEN. She's just happy because she got to act again. And she's good. She's glowing right now. Yeah, she's pretty, but this woman is Will's wife.
LENNIE. I'm not going to hurt her. I just want to touch her cheek. She sure is pretty.
BEN. Oh, shut up.

Ben turns to Frank Tucker, needing a conversation with someone sane. Well, maybe none of them are sane, but at least Frank's isn't a voice in Ben's head trying to get him in a whole lot of trouble. "So Frank, what's your wife doing in Texas again?" He knows full well she's there looking after her mother, but he also knows Frank will talk for the next half hour about his wife, and that's just what Ben needs to hear right now. About loyalty. Spousely love. Because Myra's smile is making things move around inside him that better damn well hold still.

Ben hears a car and turns to look. It's not Jimmy back from fishing. It's a blue and white Volkswagen van. Ben knows whose van it is. Apparently so does everyone else. There is an immediate reaction: everyone turns to someone else and says, "Melinda!" the murmur of her name like the chorus of a Greek play.

At the sight of Melinda's van, Will freezes in midbite. *Melinda? What's she doing here now? Why didn't she call first?* Will looks at Myra, although he keeps the van in view, wanting it to be Melinda, and wanting it not to be Melinda. What the hell's he going to do now? Melinda's the right actress for the part of Curley's Wife. Myra's too old, but it would have been nice for her to have a few more days. A week. Could he ask Melinda just to hang out and watch for the next week? He closes his eyes, knowing he can't do that; she's driven all the way here to play the role she's already been assigned. And she needs to join in immediately, to make his idea work, to live this play, find its heart. He'll have to tell Myra thanks for filling in, but Melinda needs to take over now. It's what he has to do. Myra will understand.

He's lying to himself and knows it. Myra is not going to take this easily.

Will opens his eyes. Melinda is really here. *Why didn't she call?*

As the actors get up and walk over to Melinda's van, Myra

is left sitting at the end of the table, holding up a fork; a nameless spear-holder, a bit player again.

"Myra," Will says. She turns toward him, startled. She shows him, deliberately, a flash of such anger Will feels his face pale, then she stands and walks toward the van. Will stands, too, walking slowly toward the woman he has been calling all week long to come here.

Melinda's wearing a very short orange skirt, a gauzy white peasant blouse, and sandals that have straps wound around her calves all the way to her knees. Her long brown curly hair is loose and wind-whipped. She's laughing at the clamor of questions and holds up a hand giving the peace sign. The girl loves a grand entrance, he thinks, but don't we all?

"Whoa!" she says. "Cool out. Didn't Beth tell you I was coming?"

Beth is nowhere in sight. Everyone turns to Will. He looks at Myra. "I didn't know," he tells her, shaking his head. "Beth didn't tell me." He thinks she believes him, but a coldness in her eyes says it doesn't matter either way. She knows what he will do now. The play must go on. The theatre must be saved. He wonders if he's making a huge mistake. But he needs to be a director now, so he can provide for his family. He has responsibilities. Myra could never support them. What could she do? Sing for their supper? All she has ever done is raise kids. He needs to keep his job. How can she blame him? He's forming a really good argument in his head, when everyone else starts talking.

"Who told you we were here?" Ben asks Melinda.

"Where were you?" Greg asks.

"Are you . . . ?" Lars Lyman asks. "Are you going to . . . ?"

"Are you going to stay for the rehearsal?" Chip asks.

Melinda laughs. "Trent told me you were trying to find me. I was in New York City for the last week. God, it was great! Uta Hagen let me watch her classes, and I sat in on a rehearsal of *Jesus Christ Superstar,* and I went to hear Richard Schechner give a talk on The Living Theatre that was so fantastic. And now you guys are doing this! It's karma! Of course I'm staying! Where should I put my stuff?"

"In my room," Myra says. "I'll show you." She turns and walks toward the house.

Melinda pulls a carpetbag out of the backseat, and Lars Lyman takes it from her. "What have you guys been doing?" Melinda asks Lars as they walk away. Lars says something Will can't hear, and Melinda laughs, her laugh so young and happy, Will wants to hold it in his hand like a lucky rabbit's foot. He needs it to keep him young. And brave enough to face Myra.

"What?" Melinda says. "You did that without me? Oh, cool! We'll have to do it again!" When they go in the house, everyone turns and stares at Will. He notes there is some underlying humor in their supposedly somber looks. They should be able to hide those smiles. He's taught them to act better than this.

"Okay, so Melinda's here," Will says quietly, not moving a muscle. "She'll play Curley's Wife. We'll call the next rehearsal in a half hour. I need to go talk to Beth. And Myra. Everything will be just fine. Clean up the mess from lunch and get ready."

Will heads to the house thinking Beth may be too old to spank, but all the same, his hand itches to smack something. He's glad that stupid dog isn't around right now. He can vividly imagine drop-kicking the old thing; then, because his imagination is so good, he becomes disgusted with himself for committing such a horrible act and promises to be nicer to Shakes from now on. He thinks about the dog as he walks toward his house, in order not to think about Myra.

Even going fishing sounds better than going into that house.

The boat tips to one side as Jimmy McGovern takes a sharp turn, and Nate wonders what prompted him to say he'd come along on this fool's outing. Here he is with a freckled-faced white kid playing James Bond in a boat, and a little kid who won't even look at him. He knows why he came, though. He felt a need to get away from that farm, that narrow room, the feeling that he was becoming a character in a play. Living the play's no great idea if you have to be someone who doesn't like who he is and don't like no one else either. He is even beginning to talk and think like Crooks. Nate was perfectly happy with his life up to a few days ago, so he thought. He must have a death wish now, getting in this boat with this fool. He can't swim neither. *Either. Damn that Crooks.* Then, *sorry.* He shouldn't be damning nobody, specially some poor black guy who's just a fictional character Steinbeck wrote up to represent poor black stable hands gone old and bitter.

"Hey, Nate!" Jimmy yells from the front of the boat to where Nate sits on a hard, wet, metal box. "You can get those rods ready! There's a place about a mile from here we caught a ton of fish last time. I'm heading her there. Hold on!"

Nate's already holding on, and he's not letting go till the boat's not moving again. "Don't know how to get the rods ready, Jimmy!" he shouts back, which is true, since he's never been fishing in his life. All this yelling—Jesus, he thought fishing was supposed to be quiet.

"Woo-ey! A fishing virgin! Why didn't you tell me? Damn! Buddy, you are going to love this! Hey, Mac, you can teach Nate a few things yourself! And look at that sky! What a day for fishing!"

Big white clouds march across the sky. Nate can see their shadows travel across the water like huge gray fish. The wind blows into his eyes, and he's just figuring out how to keep them open by turning his face away, not looking directly ahead. There's something mesmerizing about this, the way the boat rises and falls, the V of waves that follows them, the smell of the lake. Maybe it won't be so bad.

He wants to tell Crooks that. The world ain't so bad. He wants to believe Jimmy asked him to come because they are friends in some way, not just because he is the only other guy not in the scene they're rehearsing back at the farm. Hell, he'd like to believe a whole lot of shit.

What he would have told Will that night they were all sharing their dreams was that he'd like to have a reason to believe again, in God and in people. And a friend, that most of all. But it's not something a man can ask for. Asking for a friend isn't the same thing as just being one.

The sun comes out from behind a cloud, and Nate looks up at the sky. As always, he has the thought, *What you doing up there, God? Hiding?* But this time, his thoughts go one more step. *Just like me, huh?*

The boat slows, and the sound of the engine grows softer, like the murmur of a loud heart. "Hey, Nate!" Jimmy shouts. "This is it. You are about to catch your first fish! Man, I envy you!"

Jimmy turns off the engine. Now there is nothing but silence as the waves lap against the boat. But the silence lasts only a minute. For the next hour, as they fish and drink beer, Jimmy McGovern talks nonstop, and Nate and Mac laugh. No one catches a single fish. Nate says Jimmy's stories are scaring away the fish, and Mac grins and nods. Mac doesn't actually talk to Nate, but they laugh at the same jokes, and every now and then, Mac will look right at him and grin shyly. Nate wonders what they'd do with a fish if they ever caught one, but he doesn't really care if they do.

Beth has been watching the action from her bedroom window—it has the best view of the front yard, and it is her room, technically. She left the door open, thinking it might seem really weird if Greg happened to come up and find her in his room with the door closed. But of course, it's not Greg Henry who comes upstairs.

Her mom walks right by, not even glancing at Beth. A minute later Beth hears Melinda and Lars walking up the steps talking, and the scratchy-nail sound of Shakes trying to climb the stairs. Melinda does look in Beth's room.

"Hey, kid," Melinda says. "Didn't you tell anyone I was coming?"

Beth shrugs.

"They looked pretty surprised out there. You didn't forget about me, did you?"

Beth shakes her head no.

"Oh," Melinda says, giving Beth a wink. "I see. Just wanted to shake things up? Been boring for you? Well, I'm here now." Melinda gives Beth the peace sign and moves on. Then Lars passes by carrying a red suitcase-kind-of-bag, and a minute later the dog scuttles by. Polite conversation is going on in her parents' room about towels, and then Lars goes back downstairs, carrying Shakes. Next, Beth hears slow, steady footsteps coming up the stairs. Knowing who that will be, she dashes to close the door, but she's too late. As her father comes into her room, she backs up and sits down on her bed, instinctively protecting her butt. The grin on her face from ten minutes ago is long forgotten.

Her father has never struck her before, but she saw him punch a kitchen cabinet after getting a phone call from the board canceling the production of *Lysistrata* because it was too political. His hand went right through the cabinet and broke three glasses, so Beth is trying to look as small and fragile as possible. This isn't what she planned. She planned on smirking and saying, "No, I didn't tell you. So what?" But plans change.

"Oh, Daddy, I'm sorry I didn't tell you. I just got so mad. You said I could help you, and then you gave Mom the role and kicked me out of the barn. Can't you think about me sometimes?"

Her father looks at her so coldly, she wants to crawl under the blankets. "You will stay in your room the rest of the day. Tomorrow you will clean the whole house, top to bottom. And you will apologize to your mother. Do you understand?"

"But all I did—"

"We both know exactly what you did and why. You wanted to embarrass your mother. I'm greatly disappointed in you. And ashamed. You should be too. Damn ashamed of yourself." He leaves the room and heads downstairs. Beth feels hit. She feels something broken. She hates everyone, including herself, her father, and especially her mother. Her father was blind sometimes, and that was because he was a great actor and director and got lost in his art, but her mom was her *mom*, who *could* have said no to the role of Curley's Wife, who *knew* how badly Beth wanted to act, who always used to tell her she'd step in front of a speeding train for Beth, if she had to. Cut off her own right arm. Couldn't she have done this one small thing for her? Shouldn't she have? She can remember loving her mom. Can't her mom remember loving her? And what about her dad, really? Maybe the times he seemed to love her were an act, the Dad role. And he's such a good actor, he's just fooled her all this while. Doesn't he know he can make her feel so great, and so bad? Crying, she puts her head down on the pillow. It smells different, and she remembers whose head was on this pillow. If Greg Henry would just hold her, she would be okay. She would be fine.

Will's not sure he understands his own daughter. He could swear she's bubbly, cute, curious, and loving. But these qualities come with an image of a girl much younger, six, he thinks: they are walking down a country road, her small hand in his, and she's asking him where the stars go in the day. Then sometimes when he looks at his daughter now, he is startled and has to think, *Oh, yes, that's my Beth*, the dark eyes, the square shoulders, the long legs. But is she sweet? Is she curious? Is she loving? He doesn't really know. A lot seems to hinge on hope.

A day and a half. She should be able to forget a day and a half. There are whole months that Myra can't recall, vacations she remembers only from the pictures. What's a day and a half? Thirty-six hours. Thirty-six hours of being whole again. Thirty-six hours of believing in herself. She should be able to leave that behind like a paper bag under a hydrangea bush. She had forgotten that bag. So why not just forget today?

Sure, she can tell herself that she can act again. Now that she knows she wants to. But no one will give her that chance. This rehearsal was different—no one will ask her to rehearse a part just for the fun of it again. Not with her history.

She could try community theatres, where no one would know that she once froze in front of an audience, but to Equity actors, those are just people having fun—it would be like an oil painter going back to crayons. Could she enjoy that? If she weren't seeing herself through Will's eyes, then maybe she could. And there's Beth's respect that Myra has to face. It shouldn't matter how harshly her child judges her—Beth will grow up. But Myra is flattened to her core that her own daughter hates her enough to have embarrassed her this way. Myra wonders if Beth's anger, and Mac's quietness, stem from the same fear: of not meeting Will's expectations. A good mother might go to Beth now and tell her she loves her no matter what, that Beth doesn't need to find self-worth in her father's eyes, that kindness will get her further in life than anger. But Myra must not be that very brave and wonderful mother, because she stays in her room. She cannot face the possibility of defeat in a good gesture.

As she skips across the lawn toward the actors who stand smoking by the barn, Melinda hums "Jesus Christ Superstar." Will's farm is such a great place. The air is fresh, and the green trees glow with health and happiness. She loved New York City, still loves New York City, but that doesn't mean she doesn't love the country too. Love shouldn't have limits, she thinks, or restrictions. The more things, or people, one loves, the better. Melinda wants to learn how to love everything, even her enemies—although she doesn't have any enemies, except maybe Nixon, and warmongers, and lawyers, and—well, she should love them too. At this very moment, with the sun on her face, Melinda believes a great love will grow from her very soul and save the world. She's flying high right now. She doesn't do drugs anymore—she has even given up alcohol and caffeine— but yoga exercises, like the ones she performed in that apple orchard before she got here, give her a better rush than any chemical ever could.

Melinda leans over and picks up cigarette butts from the grass, watching herself from the others' eyes, a habit she's had since childhood. She's aware of how she looks arching down without bending her knees, how, as she straightens up, her loose blouse catches a slight breeze and puffs open at the neck, how her unbound hair hides her face until she shakes her head. She must look like a peaches-and-cream peasant girl picking flowers in some beautiful European country, an image that makes her laugh, since she is holding a handful of cigarette butts. The imagination is a wonderful thing. She's so glad she is part of a company directed by Will Bartlett.

Will doesn't talk to Myra. The bedroom door is closed, and he can't face knocking on his own door. He's going to go with his instinct this time, which says, *Stay away.*

Back at the barn, he calls out, "Okay everyone, gather up." He stands framed in the doorway as they cluster on the lawn, smoking.

"We're going to do a read-through. Now that Melinda is *finally* here, it will bring us back together before we move on. But first, we need to get rid of all the excess energy caused by the recent turn of events." They are still acting like a bunch of schoolkids, glancing at each other, winking, whispering. He expects they'll start passing notes if he doesn't do something about it. "Form a circle out here on the lawn. Ben, bring me that rubber ball over by the house. What we're going to do is toss the ball around the circle, like kids do. When you catch the ball, you have to shout out something that your character wants or needs. We've heard what you want, now it's your character's turn. Don't think, just shout. When you can't think of any more words, repeat the one thing that sounded best. Continue until I call a halt. We're miles from anyone. Use your voices. Do you understand?"

"Yes!" Melinda says. The bright, happy look in her eyes makes Will almost forget how much trouble this woman has given him. Her enthusiasm is what he's been looking for all along. He smiles at Melinda, then ushers everyone into a circle.

"Ready?"

Myra listens to the sound of Will walking away, then waits two minutes and gets up off her bed. She goes out the side door, finds the bag under the peony bush, and sneaks into the woods.

Beth sneaks downstairs and makes a phone call. Deb answers on the first ring.

"Hello!"

"Who are you hoping I am? Cliff, right? You're sitting by the phone waiting for Cliff to call. The guy's a jerk, Deb. Give it up."

"Screw you, Beth."

"Listen, I'm going crazy here. Did you find me some LSD? I really need it."

"No. I couldn't score. But I sent you a package with the brush you left at my house and your pink underwear, and I stuck in a box of Jujubes. I put ten of my mom's Valium in the Jujubes box and taped it shut, so don't start eating the candy till you find all the pills. My mom mailed it yesterday. She'll never miss the pills. She's got like a half dozen bottles. Take, like, two, and you'll feel fine. Three will knock you out. I did three last Friday night, and Cliff must have done something to me, 'cause the asshole buttoned up my shirt wrong and hasn't called me since. I had a hickey on my boob. I'm going to kill him."

"Valium? I need acid, Deb. It's not for me, don't you get it? I'm going to spike my mom's drink."

"Well, I couldn't get it. What do you want me to do? If I can't get it, I can't get it." She pauses. "You know, you should be grateful I sent you anything."

"Yeah. Okay. Thanks. But if you get acid, send it to me right away, okay?"

"Sure, but don't hold your breath. Did you hear Cindy Wasserman's pregnant? Can you fucking believe that?"

"How would I hear that? I'm stuck here in the middle of nowhere, Deb. Was it Patterson?"

"Uh-huh. Can you believe it? God, I'd die first."

"Look, Deb, I gotta go. I'm supposed to be grounded in my room."

"What did you do now?"

"Nothing at all. But I gotta hang up."

"Okay. But don't tell anyone what I told you about Cliff, okay?"

"Who am I gonna tell? The goddamn trees?"

"You know what I mean, Beth. Promise."

"Okay. I promise. And thanks for the pills. Three would knock me out, huh?"

"Yeah. So be careful."

"Okay, 'bye."

With any luck, the package will arrive tomorrow, but probably not until Monday. She'll just have to wait till then.

Will's idea to exhaust the actors with this latest exercise has backfired. It started out just fine, but somehow it ended up as a wild game of tag with the ball. And his idea of a read-through is impossible because Jimmy and Nate have not returned from fishing, which is exactly why Will is going to insist that all the actors stay at the farm from now on. He might as well just give up. Ignoring the actors' hoots and hollers with the damn ball, Will goes behind the house to piss on the pine tree. Shakes, who has followed along, goes up to the pine to sniff Will's pee. Will's not angry at the dog anymore, can't even remember why he was, and feels a bond with the poor old dog who is just trying to be a dog, just as Will is just trying to be a director. He bends down and pats the dog on his bristly head, and says, "Sorry, Shakes," thinking, *Did I kick this dog?*

Ben comes around the side of the house, and Will thinks Ben must be looking for him, until Ben unzips and whizzes on the pine, at which point, Shakes, so intent on getting a smell of this, too, gets pissed on.

"Stupid dog," Will says.

"Calm down," Ben says. "Things will turn around."

"When?" Will asks.

"Hell if I know," Ben says, zipping up his pants.

"What should I do?" Will asks.

"Keep trying. We'll catch on. Don't give up on us."

Will sighs. "You know what, Ben? It's not you guys I'm worried about. It's me. Maybe I've lost it. I never knew where it came from, these visions I have. When I saw the barn become the set of *Of Mice and Men,* I felt inspired, but right now, I feel a little crazy. Maybe I've lost it this time."

Ben's face droops, as if the muscles just give up on trying to be cheerful. But then, as always, he grins. "We trust you, Will. You still got it. Don't worry so much." Ben places one big hand on Will's shoulder, and with the weight of that hand, Will remembers all the times Ben has done this, listened to Will talk out his ideas, his questions, his worries. Yet Ben has never once come to Will with his own troubles, even when the man was doing back flips to get his wife back. Ben sent her flowers every day for three months. He never asked Will what he thought, just, "Sent them again today. Maybe she'll see I'm not so bad," then shrugged off any of Will's help, as if the relationship just didn't work that way. Will feels bad about that. He needs Ben, just as he needs Myra. He wonders if they know it.

"Thanks, Ben," Will says. "But there's more than the theatre at stake here. Myra's going to hate me, isn't she?"

Ben doesn't say anything, just looks away.

It's not the answer Will wants. "Well, Ben," he says, "let's get back there before they begin to wonder about us."

"Yes, honey," Ben says in falsetto.

Shakes lifts his leg and, wobbling like an uneven three-legged stool, pisses on the pine, then heads back to the barn.

As Will passes the house, he notes how quiet it seems. He hopes Myra and Beth are having a long mother-daughter talk. He tries to imagine them baking bread together, but he doesn't have enough energy to make this vision work.

"Oh, shit," Jimmy McGovern says from the helm of the boat.

"What?" Nate asks, but as he looks up, he sees immediately what has caught Jimmy's attention. The sky at the west end of the lake looks like a dark wall.

"Damn thing just came out of nowhere." Thunder rumbles ominously. "Fast," Jimmy says. As they watch, the line of black moves inches across the sky. "Reel in, guys. *Now!* Move it!"

Mac turns, obviously frightened by the tone of Jimmy's voice, then sees the storm. He lets go of the rod. It drops into the water.

"Oh, shit!" Jimmy yells, and Nate knows it's because he's scared, but Mac thinks it's because he dropped the rod. He looks at the rod floating away, then back to the sky, then back at the rod, then back at Jimmy. His eyes are filled with tears.

"It's a cheap rod," Jimmy says. "Forget about it. But we gotta get out of here. Nate, hold that kid tight! Goddamn fucking shit!"

Nate pulls Mac into his lap, and Mac doesn't resist in the slightest, just holds on to Nate, trembling. A second before Mac buries his head against Nate's chest, the two of them look at each other, both, Nate thinks, with the very same emotions: fear and gratitude. Nate is scared too, but strengthened just by the weight of this small child in his arms, strengthened in a way he can't quite understand but feels. Suddenly Nate feels deeply protective. He'll hold on to Mac at all costs. See him to safety. It's a second chance, not just to save someone but save himself.

With more candor than he's felt in years, Nate asks God to protect them both. And Jimmy.

Whitecaps break the surface of the lake. The boat's going so fast, the bow crests high above the water, then dips, and spray from the planing boat soaks both Mac and Nate. A bolt of lightning streaks down behind them sharp and bright. The shore is about a mile away, where docks sprout out from the land like fingers.

"Any dock in a storm!" Jimmy shouts above the roar of the boat. "Just be ready to jump out and tie her down."

From the child held against his chest, Nate hears, "Mommy."

Myra tells herself she won't touch the wine until she finds her backpack, but stopping first in the open woods on the ridge, she tries to sing, and, instead, cries. Finally, her legs fold beneath her, and she sits on the ground, opens the wine, and drinks half the bottle in five large gulps. When she's done, she's not crying anymore, so she waits to see how she feels. Still lousy. She stands and begins to hike in the direction of where she must have left the backpack. The air smells like rain.

Myra starts down the other side of the hill and finds herself at the edge of a grove of sumac trees. Above her the sky is growing dark, even though it can't be very late. She'd better crawl under the sumacs, where she'll be protected. Trying to crawl, the wine bottle gets in the way, and she pulls out the cork and finishes the bottle off. Although she is still depressed as hell about Melinda showing up, and mad at Will for just about everything under the sun, she suddenly laughs. "Screw them," she says out loud. Giggling, she pats the thin trunk of a nearby sumac and says, "Sorry."

She hums "On a Clear Day," which it's not, but what the

hell. Myra closes her eyes and thinks she hears drums. "We don't need drums," she says. "No drums please." But a band is marching this way, playing a whole different song than the one Myra is trying to hum.

When Will returns from behind the barn with Ben, only Melinda, Norton Frye, and Greg Henry are left. "Where the hell did everyone go?" Will asks.

"Frank just walked off," Greg says. "Lars and Chip went inside, and Victor's asleep in the barn." Greg flips his cigarette butt on the grass, and Will loses all patience.

"Goddamn it, pick that up! Were you brought up in a barn?"

The absurdity of this statement makes Norton snort, an obnoxious sound if Will ever heard one. Then Greg starts to laugh. Putting a hand on Norton's shoulder, the two snigger away while Melinda reaches down and picks up Greg's cigarette and carries it over to the sand-filled coffee can. "Would you throw a cigarette butt in your mother's hair?" Melinda asks. "The earth is your mother."

This causes the two men to become hysterical, leaning on each other amidst whoops of laughter.

Will puts two fingers into his mouth and whistles. His voice is loud; his whistle is deafening. Greg and Norton jerk backward, covering their ears. "We need to talk. Melinda, will you please fetch the men from the house? Ben, wake Victor. Greg, Norton, in the barn please. No cigarettes."

In five minutes, the cast of *Of Mice and Men*, sans Jimmy McGovern and Nate Johnson, are sitting in the barn. "I'm disgusted with the lot of you," he says in a low tone that he hopes will show just how disgusted he is. "I'm goddamn sick of being the only one committed to—"

"Daddy!" Beth shouts, running into the barn.

"What!" Will snaps. He can't believe his daughter, whom he has grounded to her room, has interrupted him this way.

"Look at the sky!"

The way the actors stare at Beth makes her feel important, but as soon as they are outside and see how quickly the blackness has moved in only a minute, she feels small and scared. Already the wind has picked up so that twigs and last year's leaves rush by, so that voices are carried right past ears, unheard. It's not a tornado, but whatever it is, it's wide and very black. "In the house!" It's her father's voice, the one sure sound besides the howl of wind. They run.

Victor Peters trips and falls. Shakes is blown sideways, and Lars runs to get him, missing him the first time, but finally grabbing the dog by the back of the neck. Ben has gone back to help Victor up. Her father yells something about the barn doors, and Greg Henry turns around to give him a hand. Even though she's scared, Beth runs back to the barn to help them. They pull the doors shut, then run toward the house; the wind pushes them sideways, and they zigzag across the lawn like drunks. Halfway to the house there is a deafening crack of lightning so close by that Beth freezes in midstep, sure the lightning must have struck the ground only feet away. Chip, holding open the kitchen door, shouts and points. As Beth turns to see what he's pointing at, a dead branch, as long as she is tall, flies straight at her, but Greg Henry pushes her aside, and she falls. The branch smacks into Greg's face, and he's knocked to the ground. Beth shrieks, her legs shaking so badly she can't stand up. Her father appears out of nowhere; suddenly it's dark, like night. Or is she blinded by the lightning? Beth wonders, as her dad picks her up and carries her into the house. Coming in behind her, Ben has Greg in his arms. He lays Greg down on the kitchen floor, and the people in the house hold still for a moment, looking at each other and listening to the storm. The walls shake, the rafters creak, and the house is pummeled by branches, lawn chairs, and cans of sand, sounding like gunshots as they hit the house. Greg Henry lies on the kitchen floor, his eyes closed, a gash across his face.

"Oh my god! He's dead!"

Beth's scream makes Greg flinch. His eyes open. He's alive, but bleeding to death!

Greg Henry has saved her, and she must go to him, but he's surrounded. Ben holds Greg's head in his lap, Victor Peters holds his right hand, and Norton Frye presses a dish towel to Greg's face. As Beth tries to get closer, her father says, "Move back, Beth. Move back."

"You poor boy," Norton Frye says, then looks right at Beth. "We should have remained in the barn."

Will looks at Greg's face, horrified. Outside, the wind whips thick sheets of rain against the window. It's impossible to see the barn, but he thinks it's still there. Past the barn, to the north, from the direction of the storm, there seems to be a thin line of clear sky, or at least, less darkness. Will has never seen anything like this before. A tempest, he thinks, in awe of the real thing.

He'll have to drive Greg to the hospital as soon as it's safe to leave the house. Strange that Myra hasn't come downstairs with all of Beth's screaming.

"I worked in a medical unit in the war," Norton tells Lars. "I know what I'm doing. We don't need ice, we need pressure! Right, Will?"

Will hasn't a clue. During the war he was in charge of

morale, stationed in South Africa; he spent most of the war running the movie projector and trying to get entertainers to sing and dance for the wounded soldiers—who were already bandaged. "I think so, Norton," Will says. "Are you okay, Greg?" It's a stupid question; the boy is pale, the dish towel is bloodred. Greg doesn't answer.

"As soon as the storm calms down, I'll get my car and drive up to the door." *Where the hell is Myra?* he wonders. She'd know what to do. "Beth, go upstairs and get your mother!" He doesn't mean to sound angry at his daughter, but her sobbing is getting on his nerves, and she should have thought about fetching her mother already.

As Beth maneuvers around all the people crowded in the kitchen, Melinda tells Ben to move over—something about massage. Is she out of her mind? But she slips Greg's head into her lap while Norton holds the towel to Greg's cheek, rubbing her fingers in circles above his temples. Greg's grimace seems to slacken. Will's out of his depth here. Blood and gore, unless they are stage makeup, make him very nervous. He looks away from Greg and back outside. There's a tree missing.

"Mom's not here!" Beth says, breathless in the kitchen doorway.

Will can't believe what he's just heard. The girl is like the messenger in a Greek tragedy, always foretelling some kind of doom. He forces himself not to yell at her. *"What?"* Apparently he says this a little too harshly. Beth starts to cry again.

"She's not up there, Daddy. She's not anywhere in the house!"

"Well, where the hell is she?" Will says. He looks around the kitchen, half-expecting her to just appear. There are enough people here. Why not Myra? Then it hits him. If she's not here, then she must be outside.

Will looks at Beth. She has just figured this out too. Her

mouth opens. Huge tendrils of mascara roll down her cheeks. They both move as quickly as they can to the window. Will can barely make out the shape of their tan station wagon. "The car's here," Beth says. Her voice is flat and breathy. "Maybe she's in the barn?"

"No. She wasn't in the barn."

Beth puts her hands over her mouth and moans.

"Listen, Beth," Will says. "She's probably gone into the woods. The wind is much stronger out here in the open. She'll be protected." It makes sense. The woods will block much of the wind.

Down on the floor there is a lot of murmuring, like the low buzz of a crowd scene. Will wants to shout, *Cut.* He wants silence so badly he could scream. The wind outside is driving him crazy. And then it stops.

Everyone looks up. There is only the beat of ordinary rain on the windows. The sky begins to clear. The storm has passed.

"It must have come in over the lake," Frank Tucker says. "I've read about these storms. I think they're called vertical bursts. They come down suddenly over lakes and the force spreads outward so that—"

"The lake!" Will says.

"Fishing . . ." someone else says.

"Mac . . ." Beth says.

"What?" Melinda says. "Who?"

"Jimmy took Nate and Mac fishing on the lake," Ben says, his voice hushed.

"They left quite a while ago," Victor Peters says. "They should have been off the lake when this hit, Will."

Will nods. Yes, they had been gone a long time. They would be safely on land by now. Then again, no one has come back from fishing when they said they would.

Greg Henry yells out, a sound that makes Will's blood run cold. He can't help thinking it's the same sound he wanted from Greg once before, in some play; he can't remember what play, but he remembers wanting that effect.

"He's going to die!" Beth moans. Will almost tells her to bring the hysterics down a notch; if he were directing this, he would. She's making him nervous.

"All right," Will says. "Norton and I will take Greg to the hospital now. Lars, will you please drive down to the marina and see if the boat has come back? Victor, see how the barn survived. Ben—you, Frank, and Chip look for Myra. Beth, check to see if the phone is working." She doesn't move. Ben goes into the living room.

"It's out, Will."

"I'm coming to the hospital too," Beth says.

"No, you'll stay here," Will tells her.

"But I want to be with you, and Greg. Greg saved my life."

"Stay here," Will says. "No discussion, do you hear me?" Then to Ben, "You will find Myra, won't you?

Ben nods. "I'll find her, Will."

"What should I do, Will?" Melinda asks from her cross-legged position on the floor. Greg's eyes are closed. Blood oozes out from under the towel.

Will thinks of a few things Melinda could do, including running away with him to Jamaica. He wants to be anywhere but here. "Make dinner?" Will asks, hoping she won't be offended by this request.

Melinda nods. "Can do," she says. "Do you have tofu?"

Is that some kind of fish? Will thinks. "No," he says. "Hot dogs would be fine."

"Oh, I'll do better than hot dogs, Will," Melinda says, and leans over and kisses Greg on the forehead. Beth moans even louder.

She's just afraid, he reminds himself. And so is he. He goes over to where Beth is slumped against the fridge and puts his palm against her wet cheek, discovering that through the dampness, there is heat. "Your mother will be fine. You stay here, where it's safe." He can't even think about Mac. His body won't let him. Move, or think about your son, it says, and Will chooses to move, only because that is the easier choice.

The storm comes so quickly from the other side of the hill that Myra has little time to get scared. One minute she's nodding off, drunker than she realized, and the next she's drenched, but not hurt. The sumac trees are short and flexible; dead leaves rush about the ground and lift off like little brown paper airplanes. She ducks her head between her knees and remembers hiding under her desk in the drills they did almost thirty years ago.

Instinctively, to keep from worrying, she sings. She sings, softly and slowly to the ground, her eyes closed. She sings "Blue Moon," because she loves the sound of it and it fits her range so well. But she doesn't feel blue. She feels alive and glad of it, giddy with it. Being stuck outside alone in a great storm brings a sort of excitement, a wash of adrenaline. She sings "Singin' in the Rain," for the sheer fun of it, then "Soon It's Gonna Rain," because it just slips out, and then "Here Comes the Sun," for hope, and then, just as if the storm has listened to her, it passes, carrying her songs with it. But she has more inside. She may never act again, but she has songs, and she can sing, and you know what? she tells herself, *Will can't sing.* Not a bloody note. Not "Happy Birthday" or the Pledge of Allegiance. He has all this imagination, but he can't make music. He'll never know the pleasure she feels from a simple song coming from nothing but herself. She almost feels sorry for

Will. She giggles at the absurd thought. She's laughing, and it's a wonderful feeling.

Myra crawls out from under the sumac trees, and there, like a gift, is a field of shaggy bush and tall grass, with a regal elm in the middle, everything glistening and dripping. She knows this field. If she walks down the hill, there should be a narrow stream, and she can turn back into the woods where it meets a line of ancient maples that must have been boundary markers at one time, and then she will find herself in the open woods, and then home. But she's not ready yet. She sings "I'm Just a Girl Who Can't Say No." She sings "Somewhere over the Rainbow." She's so full of gratitude, to be alive and singing, that she promises to love everything and everyone from now on. No more poor-old-me. No more melancholy. No more anger. She will kiss the first person she sees, even if it's Norton Frye—or Beth. She is soaking wet, and her shirt, a bright pink polyester, clings to her uncomfortably. Taking it off to squeeze the rain out, she feels the warmth of the sun on her skin, so she steps out of her jeans and underwear and lays them over a bush. There is no hurry to go home. She can dry off first. Naked, Myra sings "High Hopes" to the clear blue sky.

Ben, Frank, and Chip decide to split up. Chip will drive his car around the immediate area, calling out for Myra, while Ben and Frank go into the woods. Ben will follow a deer path that Beth told him leads to a place near the top of the hill where she once saw her mother. Frank will go through the pine forest to the right of the house.

The ground is soggy, and the tall grass is flattened all in the same direction. Ben crosses the field, imagining a steamroller a mile wide. Tree limbs lie scattered like a giant's broken toys. God forbid anything has happened to Myra.

In the woods, he calls her name over and over. After a while, he comes to a spot that looks like the place Beth described, and he hollers, "Myra," turning in all directions. Then he listens. Nothing. Nearby is a huge fallen maple that has brought down more trees in its path. Ben imagines Myra pinned under a tree, unconscious, or worse. He walks as quietly as possible so his footsteps won't mask her cry for help. The deer path leads through a hole in some brambles, and he has to hunch over to get through. The land slopes down, and when he gets through the brambles, he's on the other side of the hill. The damage is noticeably less on this side. On the ground, in the mud, he sees a footprint. Then he hears singing.

Ben is so surprised, he doesn't call out, but follows the voice, which seems to be coming from a place right ahead, a field, maybe. The singing grows louder. He can hear words: "tender bough," "garden wall," "fairies sing." It *is* Myra; he recognizes her voice. He creeps forward quietly. He should call out, but he doesn't.

Mac is so scared, he's crying and can't stop. The boat smashed real hard into the dock sideways, and Jimmy yelled at Mr. Johnson to get out and do something with the rope, but Mac clamped his arms around Mr. Johnson's neck and wouldn't let go. When the boat hit the dock the second time, the dock cracked like a broken pencil. Mr. Johnson jumped out, holding Mac tight, carrying him quickly along the wobbling wet dock. Mac was sure they were going to fall, but Mr. Johnson never even slipped. Jimmy jumped out too, yelling, "Fuck the boat!" and he did fall but grabbed onto the dock and got back up to scramble to the shore. The wind was so strong it pushed them, like a big hand. The rain hurt. They ran as fast as they could to this little white shed, where Jimmy banged his shoulder into the door until the door gave way, and they dove inside. Even now, Mac is still holding Mr. Johnson; he can't let go because he is crying, and shaking, and the shed is shaking too. Mac hears the black man saying, "Shhh, shhh, you'll be okay."

A shrieking noise, louder than the wind, makes Mac bury his head even farther in Mr. Johnson's shoulder, so he can hardly breathe. Rain comes down on them in bucketfuls, and Mac understands that the roof has just been torn off. His whole body goes rigid; he can feel his muscles become bone and his jaw get so tight his teeth hurt. Jimmy is yelling, "Fuckin' shit! Jesus Mother Mary!" and these words scare Mac even more. Mr. Johnson holds the top of Mac's head with the palm of his hand and bends over, keeping some of the rain from landing on Mac, even though Mac is all wet, every bit of him. Mr. Johnson keeps saying, "Shhh, shhh," and it helps Mac breathe again, but then he starts crying louder because he remembers his mother making that same hushing noise when he used to cry, and he wants his mom so bad. He's sure they are going to die, but the *shhh shhh* sound gets louder and the wind gets softer, and pretty soon the loudest sound is his own crying.

"Oh my god," Jimmy says, then says it again a few more times. Rain is coming down, but the shed has stopped shaking. Mac lifts his face up. The roof is gone. He cries out once, takes a big, huge lungful of air to cry again, and chokes on it. He didn't know you could choke on air, but he has. His body is heaving, trying to let the breath in or out. Mr. Johnson thumps Mac's back, and the air rushes out, and he's okay.

"You all right?" Mr. Johnson asks.

"Uh-huh," Mac says, surprised he can talk. "Did we die?" The sudden quiet of the air, the sky being light again, seems suspicious.

"We made it," Mr. Johnson says. "And I think we should say thanks." Then he does something Mac has never seen anybody do, but he knows just the same what it is. Mr. Johnson prays, folding his hands together around Mac's body, lowering his head, and talking to himself in a slow, quiet voice, a voice Mac likes right away.

"Dear God," Mr. Johnson says. "Thank you for sparing our lives today. Thank you especially for making sure Mac was not hurt. And thank you for giving me an extra day on this earth, and whatever time Jimmy might need to learn not to swear so much. Amen."

Jimmy laughs and adds, "Amen to that!" Mac, who has just been prayed for, says amen too. Mr. Johnson rubs Mac's head with his hand and says, "Good boy." He gets up, awkwardly, still holding Mac. They step out of the shed.

The boat is upside down on the land.

"Jesus, was I scared," Jimmy says. "I think I pissed in my pants. How about you, Mac?"

Mac doesn't know. He's so wet, he could have. He shrugs.

"The boat's a goner for sure. I wonder what those papers were I signed before we took her out."

They just stand and look at the boat. Finally Mr. Johnson says, "How about I put you down, Mac?"

Mac nods. It's a bit uncomfortable now anyway. Mr. Johnson lowers Mac so his feet touch the ground, and Mac stands on very shaky legs. Mr. Johnson's hand slips into Mac's, and Mac holds his hand right back. It feels like the most normal thing in the world, even though Mr. Johnson's hand is so dark, Mac can't believe skin can get that color, and he never imagined he'd be holding a black man's hand. But it's all right. They walk over to the upside-down boat.

Beth sits on the wet porch steps, blowing her nose in a napkin. Please let her mother and her brother be all right, she thinks.

What would she do without her mom? It's like looking at this big empty place—she can't even imagine it. And her brother . . . But even as she works up a good scare, she just can't believe anything could really happen to them. They are just too much a part of her life. They can't die. But Greg Henry, now *that* she can imagine. A young man dying from the act of saving a girl he has fallen in love with. And by now he might be dead. Oh my god! Her mother could be badly wounded . . . and her brother might have drowned . . . and her boyfriend's probably dead. It just couldn't get any worse.

While Jimmy McGovern knocks on a door to ask if he can use the phone, Nate stands on the lawn looking at the gingerbread latticework scattered across the green grass. It is our souls that have survived, not the structures, he thinks. He had been sure, out on that lake, that he was a dead man, and he had been afraid, not just for the boy but for himself; he was not ready, and apparently God agreed. This storm was sent for a reason. Nate has never forgiven God for the pain and death he saw in Italy. Nor has he forgiven himself for wanting to go to war, for believing in war. This storm, and this boy whose hand he now holds, is a message, plain and simple. He has been given time not to understand God but understand himself.

Jimmy hops down the front steps shouting, "The phones are out!"

Nate shrugs. "We'll have to walk to the marina."

"It's gotta be miles away," Jimmy says.

"Well, we'd better start now, then," Nate says. He and Mac head east toward the marina, hand in hand. They are on the road that runs around the lake, and the marina is on the lake. They won't get lost. Heck, Nate's been walking about with his eyes closed for so long, it will be a pleasure to be walking with his eyes open. He was scared out there on the lake, scared mostly that he might have died just when he was learning how much he wanted to live.

"Hey, Mac," he says. "You okay?"

"Yeah. How about you, Mr. Johnson?"

"Fine, Mac, just fine."

Norton stays by Greg's side while the doctor finishes stitching his face. Twenty-two stitches so far. Norton has counted each and every one. The local anesthetic must be working; Greg doesn't wince as the needle slides in and out of his skin, although he did complain about having a terrific headache.

But Norton himself is having a difficult time, and it has nothing to do with the blood or raw flesh. (Will has decided to remain in the lobby. The man seems to be rather faint-hearted about this whole thing.) Right now Norton is having trouble with his own feelings. He keeps looking at Greg Henry's face, his thick eyelashes, his whiter-than-white teeth, the soft pink flesh right inside his swollen bottom lip. At first Norton looked at Greg's face because he was concerned about the gash, which he is, certainly, but concern is not the feeling that is most prominent now. Norton can't find the word that best explains his feeling, but his hand desperately wants to brush the dangling brown lock of hair off Greg's forehead. He can imagine doing even more, and closing his eyes doesn't help one bit.

Norton isn't fooling himself. He's a homosexual, just not a *practicing* homosexual. It's a choice he made a long time ago, in college, after a brief affair with a young man who—deciding *he* wasn't a *homo*—went and joined the army. Norton had been so embarrassed by the whole fiasco, he decided there were other things besides sex. Theatre, art, literature, food—the good things in life. So right now, looking down at Greg Henry's face, with those big brown eyes, Norton thinks he should turn and walk away. What he *wants* to do is much more complicated and frightening.

Greg is just a kid. Norton is fifty. There's not a chance in a million Greg Henry would have the slightest interest in Norton, yet . . . Norton remembers seeing Greg at the bar with an older gentleman, and right before the local anesthetic, Greg had reached out to grip Norton's hand, giving a little squeeze, saying, "Hey, Norton, you're the best." That little squeeze made Norton's stomach flutter.

"This is the last stitch," the doctor says, giving the thread a little twist and turn to tie it off.

Twenty-four, Norton thinks. It's silly, but he knows he will remember the number of stitches in Greg Henry's face forever. It will be one of those stupid facts he will go to the grave remembering—a time when Greg Henry most likely won't even remember Norton's name. A harsh thought indeed, which might work to quell some of these unwanted feelings, except that at that very minute, Greg Henry says, "Help me off this table, Norton." Norton reaches over and takes hold of Greg's upper arm.

"Not so fast, my friend," the doctor says, placing a hand on Greg's shoulder to ease him back onto the table. There's an uncomfortable moment before they both let go of Greg that Norton sees as the physical struggle of his very soul.

"You need to take it easy," the doctor tells Greg. "Move slowly, and don't stand or sit up quickly. Use a bag of ice for the swelling, ten minutes every hour for the rest of the day. If there's any seepage, I want you back here pronto. Do you understand?"

"Sure, doc," Greg says, grinning lopsidedly, half his face not responding.

"I'm going to give you a prescription for aspirin with

codeine. Someone should keep their eye on you for the next twenty-four hours for signs of concussion, make sure you don't become unusually sleepy." The doctor turns to Norton. "Could you do that, sir? Will you be around to observe Mr. Henry?"

Norton nods. "Yes, doctor, I could do that."

"Norton will take good care of me, doc. Thanks for sewing me up." Greg slips gently off the table, not needing help from anyone. "I could use that medicine though. My head's killing me."

As the doctor writes out the prescription, Greg looks in the mirror above the sink. His lopsided grin falls, and his eyes widen in horror. "Oh my god! I'm Frankenstein!"

"No, no, Greg. It's not that bad," Norton says, coming up behind Greg and putting a hand on his shoulder, feeling the warmth coming through Greg's thin cotton shirt right into Norton's palm.

"It looks bad now, Mr. Henry," the doctor says, "but it will heal. It wasn't a clean cut, and there will most likely be a thin scar by the corner of your lip. You'll need to come back in a week to get these stitches out, and by then you'll be looking much better."

"You look fine, Greg," Norton says to the back of Greg's head, to the soft curls of brown hair, to the curve of his neck. "A scar will add a mysterious character to your handsome face." Norton can't believe he has said this, it was only a thought. How did it come out of his mouth? Miraculously, Greg smiles slowly and meets Norton's eyes in the mirror.

"Thanks, Norton. A mysterious scar. I like that. Now let's go home."

Norton takes a shallow breath, because he can hardly breathe at all. It's the *let's go home* that floors Norton, the casual, simple words that mean Will's farm but that Norton envisions as meaning so much more. But Norton doesn't suffer fools lightly, and he knows one when he sees one. The fact that the fool is hiding behind his own face makes no difference.

Ben sneaks up close enough to peek out from behind a bush and catch a glimpse of Myra. What he sees bypasses his brain and heads straight to his heart.

Her blond hair glows in the sun. Her arms wave about like wings. She is singing "White Coral Bells." And she is naked. He watches her until he's dizzy with longing, literally weak in the knees. Get a grip, he tells himself. Slowly he backs up, until he can't see her anymore, then steps hard on a few dead branches, coughs loudly, hollers, "Myra! Myra!" and steps on a few more branches, making enough noise to frighten bears. After a few minutes of this, he stops and listens. It doesn't take long.

"Ben! Ben? Is that you?"

"Myra!" he yells. "Are you all right? Where are you?"

"Just stay there!" she yells. "I'm fine. Just give me a minute. I'll find you!"

After a short time (in which he imagines her putting on her clothes, which makes him crazy all over again), she appears from between two thick bushes. The clothes don't matter one bit; he's crazy, but he thinks he's fallen in love with her. Ben feels like a teenager. He wants to ask her to the movies. He wants to walk her home and kiss her on the sidewalk in front of her house. He wants to touch her breast on the second date, ask her to marry him on the third. If he can't touch her, his body will ache. "Myra," he says.

She does something he doesn't expect. She walks toward him, calmly, almost lazily, with a tranquil, sweet look on her face. She stands right in front of him and grins. And then kisses him. Their lips don't match up; her mouth presses against his bottom lip, mostly on the left side. She leans back and laughs.

"Oops!" she says, then kisses him again, right on the mouth, quick but hard. Then it's over, and she's standing in front of him, looking at him.

She's a mess. Wet, tangled hair, scratches on her arms. Why did she kiss him? Has she been hit on the head? Is she delirious? He's thinking these things as his hand reaches out and touches her tangled hair. "Are you hurt?" he asks.

"No." She doesn't move back. She doesn't even shake her head. His hand stays on her hair. "I'm just happy," she says. "I'm happy you found me."

He wants to tell her he heard her singing, that she has a beautiful voice, that he's suddenly crazy about her, even though it's just about the stupidest thing in the world he could do, and the scariest. He's more scared now than when he thought she was hurt. Because he knows this isn't good. The way they are looking at each other tells him that. It's not just him.

"I was worried about you," he says.

"Thank you."

"You're wet," he says.

"I know."

"You have a scratch right here," he says, moving his hand from her hair to touch a red mark near her right eye. As his hand touches her face, Myra closes her eyes, but not in pain. Her face is serene and peaceful. She leaves her eyes closed long enough to let Ben understand. He leans down and kisses her, on the lips. This time it is nothing like a short, quick, friendly kiss.

At the marina, a man wearing a Pete's Marina baseball cap paces back and forth along the edge of the water, swearing loudly. Against the cement wall built along the shore, docks are smashed to pieces by boats that are now piled together like dead fish. Lars tries to interrupt the obviously distracted owner of the marina. "Please, sir. Two men and a young boy rented one of your boats early this morning. Do you know—"

"Gone!" the man says. "Gone to hell in a handbasket! Everything is shot to hell!"

"All right," Lars says. "Thank you." He walks back to his car and leans against the hood. He can't return to the farm without Will's kid. He'd rather play the bearded lady in a freak show for the rest of his life than face Will with no Mac. So he'll wait here. Jimmy's yellow car is in the parking lot. Lars leans against his car and watches the lake. The sound of sirens fills the air.

Myra just meant to kiss Ben out of sheer happiness; she swears she had no idea it would go farther than that. But it was more before she could even think about it. It was so easy to close her eyes and be kissed. It was so easy to kiss back. She knew it was wrong, but not while it was happening, only after. Then it was too late. She is surprised how little guilt she feels right now. How much she wants him. Her hand moves up and down his arm as she says, "We shouldn't."

"I know," Ben says. He begins to step back.

"Please." She doesn't let go of his arm. She's asking him to forgive how she feels, forgive how he feels, to stay right there. He understands. He moves toward her and touches her hair again, as if maybe this is safe. But it isn't. They kiss gently, taking their time.

When they stop kissing, Ben cradles her in his arms. They stand there hugging in the woods while leaves drip, soft seconds on a broken clock. She buries her head against his chest and thinks, *There is no time but this*, but knows she is wrong. She might be drunk, but she isn't stupid.

186 & Sarah Willis

"That was quite a storm," she says, just to say something besides *We shouldn't do this.* "Is the barn still standing?"

Ben tenses. Whatever he suddenly remembers is not good, and it can't be about the barn. She wouldn't care if the barn blew all the way to hell, and he knows that. She braces herself for what he will say.

"Will had to take Greg Henry to the hospital. He got hit by a tree limb."

Myra begins to say, "Oh, no," but Ben shakes his head, and the words stop in her throat. "What?"

"Mac hasn't come back from fishing."

She thought Mac would be back by now. She thought everyone would have been safe in the house, that she was the only one at risk. She turns to run, but Ben holds her hand and stops her. "Lars has gone to the marina. They were probably on land by the time the storm struck." Now he lets her move but keeps hold of her hand. It's hard going, mostly because she keeps seeing a boat capsized and a small body sinking to the bottom of the lake. They move quickly, and Myra knows if not for Ben's grip, she would have tripped and fallen several times. She is glad for a hand to hold. His hand.

Still, as they reach the opening to the field, they both let go at the same time.

Melinda has whipped together three quiches, using all the eggs she can find, some milk, some presliced Swiss (it will have to do), an onion, the hot dogs sliced into small pieces, a bag of flour she found way back behind some canned soups, and a scoop of Crisco. Next she cut up ten pounds of potatoes (unpeeled; the peels contain the vitamins), four onions, and three cloves of garlic (from her van—she has developed a thing for garlic and likes to keep it around), and she is now frying the potatoes in three different-sized frying pans on top of the stove. (She'd bake them, but there's no room in the oven because of the quiche.) An empty pie crust sits on the kitchen table. After turning the potatoes, Melinda begins to peel apples.

She has even cleaned up all the blood off the floor. Everyone else had panicked, but she won't believe anything awful has happened; it's bad karma. She will put her energy into positive thoughts. It can only help. Either way, people will need the comfort of food. She erases that thought. She will not think about alternatives. Everyone will be fine. *Everyone will be fine. Everyone will be fine.* She sends her thoughts out like waves from a calm blue ocean.

When she was ten, she wished her mother would drop dead. She was so mad about something, but she can't remember what. "I hope you drop dead!" she had shouted. Her mother looked so sad. "I wish you hadn't said that. If I get hit by a car, or get killed by a freak of nature, even years from now, you will blame yourself. Be careful what you say. Words can haunt you as strongly as your actions. Let's pretend you never said it, okay?" Melinda had nodded, chagrined at the honest concern in her mother's voice. Her mother had always thought the best of everyone and everything, and when she died, some ten years later from breast cancer, Melinda had vowed she would do the same. Thinking positive thoughts became a habit, and then became her. She carried around the spirit of her mother this way. Melinda doesn't believe in religion—look what horrors it has caused over the centuries—but she does believe that all the atoms are connected to each other, so that she is part of the sun and the stars, and the earth she walks on, and the air she breathes. Just exactly like Tillie's speech in *Gamma Rays*. The fact that Melinda was cast as Tillie, whose very words Melinda believes with all her heart, is enough to convince Melinda that there is more to this world than meets the naked eye.

If she has time, she wants to draw pictures on the white napkins. In her van she has a set of Magic Markers bought at an art store in the East Village. She's really into drawing small intricate designs; then, like the Buddhist monks who make pictures with sand, she destroys her art. It is the process of art that excites and moves her, not the article itself, waiting to be judged, frozen, dead, done becoming what it is. Art should be held only in memory, as emotion, not material wealth. (She hates museums and thinks of them as tombs.) That's why she loves theatre, because it's live, and different each time if done right. True, theatre *has* begun to get stagnant, but there are people out there trying to change that, and Melinda plans to be one of them. Will Bartlett is one of those people. Even though he's old enough to be her father, he has a young and vibrant heart. She loves his oddness, his visions, his devotion to art. She hopes he likes quiche.

Beth is going crazy. People could be dying, and she's stuck here with the Betty Crocker of hippies. She will just have to drive to the hospital. There are plenty of cars out there. Maybe someone left the keys in the ignition. Beth sneaks out the front door, closing it quietly behind her. In the kitchen Melinda is singing "Layla," so badly that Beth actually appreciates her mother's voice. Melinda doesn't even know all the words and puts in "da da dee dee" wherever she feels like it. And Beth once thought Melinda was so cool. It's amazing the mistakes you can make about people.

The first car she checks is Ben Walton's Camaro. The keys are right there on the seat. But it's a fucking stick shift, which she can't drive. She's willing to bet anything that there aren't keys in a single other car, because, as she has just figured out, life stinks!

Beth turns away from the car and trips on something soft and furry. She lets out a scream, thinking *rabid groundhog*, because that would be her luck, but hears a pathetic whimper, high-pitched and miserable. Shakes. Lars has left his dog here while he's off at the marina. The dog's turning in tight little circles, trying to howl, which sounds like a baby crying. Beth isn't big on babies, but it's hard not to feel sorry for this dog. He looks like he's a thousand years old; red weepy skin hangs from under his eyeballs, and there are places where fur is just missing. She really doesn't want to touch him—she could just walk away and not feel too bad about it, but being ignored, that she understands, and it makes her almost cry. So using all her skills of imagination to pretend Shakes has plenty of soft fur, she sits down on the ground and lifts him into her lap. Cradling Shakes against her chest, she looks around at the damage from the storm. The big tree that used to be near the house is lying across the front lawn. "We're not in Kansas anymore, Toto," Beth says. She thinks she has the line right. She's not sure. She's not sure of anything except that she's sitting on wet grass, holding a moldy dog, and she wants her mother.

"I just want my mommy," she tells the dog.

"What?" Victor Peters has just come around the corner of a car and looks down at Beth.

Beth is so embarrassed that she wants to jump off a bridge. If there were a bridge anywhere around, she'd do it, holding the dog, just for dramatic effect.

"I didn't hear you, sweetheart," Victor Peters says. "I'm half-deaf in my right ear. Did they find your mom yet?"

Beth bursts into tears. She cries because she is the worst daughter in the world, the worst sister, doesn't like babies or dogs, is all wet, can't drive a stick shift, is so glad Victor Peters is almost deaf, will never kiss Greg Henry who is probably dead, and because the tree is lying on the lawn, broken, never again to be there, where she expects it. It was a really great tree. She pulls Shakes so tight to her chest, he nips her arm, and Beth jerks, throwing him two feet across the lawn. Now she just sits there, motherless, dogless, treeless, loveless, and cries.

"Oh my god," Beth hears her mother say. "Beth, are you hurt?"

Beth looks up. Her mother and Ben are standing right there, and her mother doesn't look hurt at all, just messy. But she does look scared. She must have been as worried about Beth as Beth was worried about her. Beth's too far into crying to say much, but she shakes her head and manages to blurt out, "I'm fine."

Now a look of absolute horror crosses her mother's face. "Is it Mac? Is he . . . ?" She turns away from Beth and looks to Ben for help and comfort. She doesn't look back at Beth; she has already been completely forgotten. Beth's fear that her mother was hurt turns around inside her chest and becomes something else hard and brittle.

"No one's back yet," Victor Peters says. "And the phone's not working."

"I'll drive you to the marina," Ben says. Myra looks at him gratefully, and they run to his car, without so much as a glance back at Beth.

Beth decides she will sit here forever, or for a very long time, until her mother and Ben have driven away, until Melinda has baked every last thing she can find, until hell freezes over—or until Greg Henry comes back alive.

Chip Stark has been driving around the block for an hour, hollering for Myra until he's hoarse. He doesn't know if it's really a block per se, but it's got four corners, so he figures it must be a block, although he bets Frank Tucker would know what it's called, not that he'd ask him. That's the kind of stupid thing he's thinking while driving around, because there's nothing to see but trees. Everybody keeps saying what a pretty place this is, and maybe he *did* think it was pretty for about ten minutes when he first drove up, but now he thinks he's lived in the country for about as long as he ever wants to in his whole life.

During the summer season, Chip usually stays in an apartment above the Fine Time, the bar in Mayville. He's thinking of finding out if the room's available now. That damn bunk's killing his back, and Will's wife's habit of walking off is getting on his nerves. And now this damn storm. He's still embarrassed that he was the first person in the house. By more than a few strides. The only thing stopping him from splitting is how to tell Will. Chip would give the finger to bikers, if there were a good reason, but he doesn't want to tell Will he'd like to leave.

Chip decides to drive back up the lane and see if Myra has shown up. He did this twice before, but both times Victor Peters told him she wasn't there yet. This time, as he drives up the lane, he sees Beth sitting on the ground. He gets out of the car.

"Hey, Beth, whatcha doing?"

"Sitting," she says.

"All right." He sticks his hands in his pockets. "Any news on your mom?"

"Yeah. She's fine."

"Really? She's back?" Hell, why didn't someone come find him, so he didn't have to keep driving around like he lost a dog or something?

"Yeah, *really*."

This girl's got a problem. He can remember feeling like that, all full of anger and indignation. But she looks good, mad like that, her bottom lip sticking out, arms crossed under her chest. He grins. "You pissed at something?"

"Yeah."

"You look pretty wicked when you're pissed. I wouldn't want you pissed at me, that's for sure." This makes her look up. She might even have smiled for a second. "Anything I can do?" he asks, thinking he can think of a few things to cheer her up.

"Not really," she says. "But thanks anyway."

"All right then. Stay cool." He goes to the house. Maybe he'll stay here after all.

It's almost dusk as Will, coming home from the hospital with Greg and Norton, turns onto the lane and sees a boulder up near the end, on the grass. Jesus, he thinks. That was a hell of a storm. That wasn't there before. Then the boulder stands up. Since he saw a boulder first, he can't get that image out of his mind quickly enough, so what he sees is the boulder turn into his daughter, and for a minute he's overwhelmed. He has told Beth that if she works hard enough, she can be whatever she wants, but for the first time, Will understands that his daughter is capable of miracles: not turning into or out of boulders but of simply growing up and becoming something wonderful. He left the house four hours ago, and she was just a child, whom he loves (he's always loved her, it's just hard to like her some- times), and now, illuminated by his headlights, she's a young woman who will be capable of love, understanding, and pas- sion. Will's used to finding analogies and metaphors in the scripts he reads; they come to him as easily as basic math to a mathematician. He knows Beth hasn't changed, it's simply that he sees her now, like that first star at night, distinct, hopeful, and very beautiful. He honks the car horn and waves.

Beth runs to the car as soon as it stops and opens the pas- senger door. "Daddy! How is he?" She looks in the back of the car, where Greg and Norton sit. "Oh! You're alive! They let you come back! Are you all right, Greg? Is he okay, Daddy? Oh! Look at your face! Are you okay?"

"I'm fine," Greg says, slurring his words.

"Does it hurt? Did they check you for a concussion? Are you sure you're okay?" She helps Greg get out of the car. Norton rushes around the car to get Greg's other arm. They look like they're playing tug-of-war with the boy. Then it hits Will: Beth is stuck on Greg Henry. He can't believe it. Myra will have to do some explaining to Beth, before she makes a fool of herself. Love is so blind, he thinks.

"Beth," Will says loudly enough to get her attention, "is your mother back? Is she all right?" She must be. It's what he's told himself so many times in the last few hours that he has come to believe it. He needs Myra, so he can ask about Mac. Lars's car isn't here. Or Jimmy's. He is having trouble thinking about what that might mean. He's having trouble just thinking. Everything's so out of control, he feels helpless. He'd like to grab something solid—know he had a hold of it, then throw it hard against a brick wall.

"Yeah, she's fine. She went to the marina with Ben." Beth says this tightly. Will doesn't want to know why Beth's mad at her mom again, but it's getting old fast.

"All right. You and Norton get Greg into a bed. I'm going to the marina. Tell everyone to eat." He gets back in the car and drives to the marina, trying not to imagine what might have happened to Mac. The only way to do this is to not think at all. If someone asked him right now what play they were rehearsing at his farm, he wouldn't even understand the question.

There is chaos at the marina. Boaters who survived the storm have come back with no place to dock. Men who rent space from the marina have arrived to check on their boats. The owner of the marina has called in his wife to help, but the two of them immediately began arguing about an insurance policy that may not have been paid. Lars has watched all this from the hood of his car. He's beginning to get hungry.

"Lars!"

He turns to see Myra and Ben running toward him.

"Any sign of their boat?" Ben asks.

"No, I asked the owner, but he hasn't—"

Ben and Myra walk right past Lars, over to the owner, who is being yelled at by a lady in a yellow hat. Something about code violations. Lars doesn't know if he should follow Myra and Ben over there. He's much happier with specific directions. He loves blocking a script. He stays where he is.

When they walk back from talking to the owner, Ben has an arm around Myra's shoulder. Tears are running down her face. They stop ten feet from the car and talk quietly to each other. Lars is used to this. He is somehow inconsequential in the great scheme of things, an observation made by his last girlfriend— her point being that Lars has assumed this inconsequential position himself. Not that it's true, she said; he has value—she just neglected to point out the specifics. She told him this while breaking it off, saying if he ever decided to become part of the living, she would like to hear from him. Lars didn't really believe she wanted to hear from him again; it was merely the kindest thing she could say.

He met her, as he had met every girlfriend he ever had, after she had seen him in a play. Acting in a play, he is alive. He can feel it happen with the first read-through, and that feeling grows stronger with each rehearsal. Onstage, in costume, under lights, the house full, Lars is as solid and whole as he imagines everyone else is all the time. But, someday—and this is a very new thought, brought on by the exercise Will had them do outside in the dark—he'd like to direct. His nerves tingle and twitch at the idea, like walking on a foot that has fallen asleep.

Ben and Myra start running. They run right past Lars, and he turns to see Mac, Jimmy, and Nate walking up the marina drive. Lars is relieved to see them, but he stays on the hood of the car.

Hugs are given all around, more than once. Myra lifts up Mac, crying, then puts him back down on the ground to inspect his face, then makes him turn full circle, then she hugs him again. Now Mac takes Nate's hand and pulls him close to Myra, telling her something. Myra hugs them both. Then she turns to Ben and hugs him. Lars is glad he didn't go over there. Jimmy McGovern, who has gotten the least of the hugs, spots Lars and walks over.

"I don't suppose you brought food, huh, Lars? I'm dying of hunger."

"Ah, no," Lars says. "But I could—"

"Jesus, this place is a fucking mess!" Jimmy says, looking past Lars at the broken docks and piled-up boats. "You should have seen our boat. If we hadn't got out of it when we did, we'd be dead as doornails. Didn't even have Mac wearing a life jacket. I hope Myra doesn't ask about that. Shit. I never thought . . . Not a Twinkie? Anything? Jesus, Lars, you should have seen the boat."

"Pretty bad, huh?" Lars says.

"Fucking upside down on the shore. Hold on. I'm going to tell these guys to get a move on." He goes over to the Myra-Mac-Ben-Nate group hug and comes back. "They say they're going into town to get some iodine. We should just meet them at the farm. What a storm! Jesus, I was scared. I think I upset the kid. Nate was cool, though. Cool as a cucumber. Which reminds me, I'm starving. See you back at the ranch." Jimmy heads over to his car but takes a look back at Mac, who's still holding Nate's hand. There's a pause in Jimmy's step, and his smile fades for just a moment before he gets into his car and takes off.

Lars imagines he directed this scene. Not a play, he thinks. A movie. Something like those independent films John Cassavetes makes. In black and white. He would pan from the up-ended boats in the dark water to the marina owner and his wife, then to Myra and her son. Finally, close-up on Ben's face as he watches Myra. Lars has known Ben as an actor for a long time, and he knows the things Ben does to hide himself onstage and the moments when he can't. And right now, Ben isn't hiding a thing. It makes Lars very, very nervous. He gets into his car and drives off.

Ben drives them to the pharmacy, and Myra sits in the backseat with her arm around Mac. He says Nate Johnson saved his life, and Myra believes him. She looks at Nate and Ben in the front seat, these two men who are so different from each other but are now both so important to her. Inside this car Myra feels warm and safe. She imagines the four of them driving across the country.

Ben pulls up right in front of the drugstore. There are no lights on in the whole town, but the drugstore is open, and there are people inside. "Stay there," Ben says. "I'll get it. Is there anything else you need besides iodine?"

"Band-Aids, maybe." She thinks she might start crying again. She is so grateful that all they need is iodine and Band-Aids, and that Ben knows she needs to stay in the car with Mac.

"If I see something else, I'll get it. Don't worry. I'll be right back."

Myra buries her face in Mac's curly hair and breathes. She

can smell the lake, the wind, and the distant memory of a baby in her arms.

On his way to the marina, Will sees Jimmy's car speed by, with just Jimmy in it. Then Lars's car, with just Lars in it. When he gets to the marina, there's no sign of Ben's car. Will finds the owner and asks him if he's seen Mac. The man says he doesn't know where the hell anyone is. Will had been looking carefully to see if Ben passed him, and he hadn't, so maybe they found Mac, and he was hurt, and they'd gone the other way, to the hospital. Will jumps into his car and drives as fast as he can, swerving back and forth to avoid running over the large branches that lie across the road. Will hasn't shed a tear yet, but his eyes ache, and he is afraid of what is held inside him by nothing more than a thin membrane.

Melinda wants to wait for Will before she serves her meal, but everyone is ravenous, so she cuts a large piece of quiche and takes a big scoop of potatoes, putting them on a plate in the oven to stay warm. She insists that everyone sit down at the picnic table rather than help themselves from the pans in the kitchen. Still, the food is gone in minutes. She's definitely going to hold on to the pie until Will gets back.

Will drives up the lane, as if on cue. Seeing Will's car, right after she has just thought about him, sends a shiver up her spine. Life is so amazing!

Will walks up to the table and puts a hand on Mac's head. "Are you all right?"

Mac nods.

Will turns to Myra. "I went all the way to the hospital, looking for you. I thought Mac was hurt."

"I thought you would turn around and come back. I was just about to ask someone to go look for you."

"Thanks," Will says. "And you're okay too?" His voice is devoid of any inflection. Will uses tone and inflection as an artist uses color, Melinda thinks. The way he speaks to Myra now is like a painter covering over a picture with black paint. It's a statement in itself. From the dead silence at the table, it is not lost on anyone.

"I'm fine," Myra says.

"Good, I'm glad," Will says. "How's the barn, Victor?"

"Barn's fine. No problem with the roof, I can see."

"Good. And Greg? Is he doing okay?"

No one knows who Will is asking, so Frank answers. "He seems fine, Will. Norton took him upstairs."

Melinda stands up. "Would you like some dinner? I saved you some."

Will doesn't answer right away, and Melinda's sure he's going to say no, but then he rubs Mac's head and says, "Sure, Melinda, I'd love some dinner. Scoot over, Mac, and tell me what happened to you in the storm. Were you in the boat? On shore? Were you scared? I want all the details."

Mac's eyes go wide. He has jelly on his chin. "I was fishing. I dropped my rod right in the water when I saw those black clouds. Jimmy says it was a cheap rod, but could you buy him one anyway? Then we started going real fast to get away from the storm, and . . ."

As Melinda goes inside to get the quiche and potatoes for Will, she wonders what it would be like to have kids. It's just a thought. She's not ready to play mom yet.

Will is exhausted. Moments ago he was furious, but he doesn't have the energy for it now. Mac tells the story about the storm with as much detail as Will could ever hope for, but he's just too tired to listen. Mac's safe; the story's just the frosting, and even though Will eats the food Melinda serves him, he's not hungry. He wants to go to sleep. He'd like a comfortable bed tonight, but he's not going to sleep in the same bed as Myra. He knows she must have been upset by Melinda showing up like that, but she walked off, again, without so much as telling him. And look what happened. He'll sleep in the barn.

Mac stops talking. "Wow!" Will says. "What a story! I'm so glad you're safe. Absolutely amazing. You'll have to tell the whole thing again tomorrow, okay? It's a lot to keep straight." Will stands up. "I'm going to bed. We'll start again tomorrow at ten—that is, if you all agree we should go on." The storm has taken something from him, and without their confidence, he's not sure he can go on. He's not sure he wants to.

Chip Stark, sitting next to Beth, says, "Hey, Will, we're here for you. No one's going anywhere," and many of the actors nod. It is not a loud and boisterous vote of approval, but Will's pleased.

"Good night, then," he says, and walks over to the barn. He's too tired to change his clothes or brush his teeth. The ranch hands must have felt the same way after a long day.

Will turns and looks at the large table with the actors and his wife and his children, faces glowing in the lantern's warm light, heads bent in conversation. He sees, too, how they turn to each other, and who they turn to. Something is different now. The storm has changed more than just Greg Henry's face. He'll have to think about what that might mean tomorrow.

Saturday

❧ ❧

The day is quiet, like a pause; it's not hot, or cold. It's a day to ignore the weather, and for that, Will is thankful. He knocks three times against the barn door. The door doesn't fall over. His muscles relax.

The actors are awake and ready to rehearse. The bunks have been made, personal things put away. Everyone's had their coffee. There seems to be a new seriousness about them. Will feels they're ready to let him shape and mold the rehearsal as he sees fit. He sees actors waiting to act. It's taken a week, a lot of confusion, and a tempest. He knows it wasn't a real tempest, but it sure felt like one.

He must admit, Melinda has something to do with all of this. She woke the actors and served breakfast (toast and some kind of strange crunchy cereal). She must have been up early because there's cream for the coffee and new jams with plaid cloth covers. She's the one who made the bunks and asked Beth to set up the props. She's even placed the blue canvas chair he likes right where it should be.

Greg Henry looks awful, worse, if possible, than the day before. Part of his face is purple, part red, part green, all swollen. Greg says he's fine. His eyes are half-masked, and Will figures it must be the pain medication, but the boy is here, and Will thinks he's a real trouper. A cut on his face—or a scar—will not be a problem. Greg's like the poster boy of cute young men with baby-face smiles that pass through the theatre every year or so on their way to Hollywood, and oblivion. The scar will give him some depth, Will thinks. Still, Will's glad the kid didn't break his leg.

Beth and Mac are pulling in chairs, and Will decides to let them stay. He doesn't know where Myra is. He tells himself he doesn't care, but he does. He just can't think about it right now. Later, when things get back in shape.

"All right. Act two, no scripts. Stop and go at my discretion. I want you thinking about who you're talking to. Are they an impediment to your dreams? Can you trust them or not? I don't care about pacing, but I don't want to see any of the old tricks. No southern accents, Chip. No goddamn perfect diction, Norton. Frank, I want your back to the audience at all times. Melinda, Curley's Wife doesn't need to bat her eyes at anyone. And see if you can find some backbone in the woman, all right? And Lars, we know George is Steinbeck's everyman, and you do that well, but goddamn it, who does *George* think he is? No! I don't want answers, I want to see it happen right here in front of my eyes. If I don't, I'll stop you, and we'll do it again and again. I've got all day. Oh, and by the way, no more leaving the property during rehearsals, for anything. After lunch I'll be taking Lars and Ben down to the creek, and I expect you to do whatever you do, right here, in character, for the rest of the day. Ready?"

The actors move into place quietly, and, Will believes, with great expectations.

———

Beth watches the rehearsal from the corner of the barn. She has watched her father direct before, from the wings, and from the red velvet seats in an empty house, but this is different. He's like the bonfire they built: mesmerizing, glowing, radiating heat and light. She wants to hold out her hands, palms out. She wants to feel the heat.

After lunch, Ben quietly follows Will to the creek. He can't stop thinking about Myra. Doing the dishes last night, they'd talked nonstop, telling stories about their childhood, as if they were building a past to stand on in the future, laughing so much they had to cover their mouths. They understood the rules; they couldn't let anyone know how happy they were. Once Myra reached under the soapy water and took his hand in hers. Their wet, entwined fingers were enough to make Ben crazy.

He doesn't understand what is happening to him. Given this scenario, say in a magazine, Ben would have filled in all the spaces that proved he was not the kind of man who would cheat with his best friend's wife, so he's surprised at the feelings he has when he thinks about chilling his heels, taking a step back, and putting the hex on this before it's too late. He gets angry. Angry at Will for ignoring Myra, and angry at the world; this could be his turn at being happy. And Myra's chance, too. If Myra can feel this way about Ben, then she must not love Will. Thinking back, Ben can't remember Myra and Will holding hands, standing arm in arm, whispering in each other's ears. Maybe they haven't been in love for a long time.

But hell, he must be crazy. Misreading the whole thing. She couldn't want him. She's probably back up at the house trying to figure out how to tell him, kindly, that she is just in need of a friend. Thanks anyway . . .

Myra should go grocery shopping, but she wants to stay where she can catch a glimpse of Ben, or talk to him, or touch him. She feels like a kid. She feels loved, and sexy, and young again. And giddy—she has a secret. A big secret. It stuns her. That she would dare . . . She knows that Will had an affair years ago. He thought she didn't know, and she didn't, actually, until it had been over for almost a year. She had found out from the woman herself in a drunken moment of bravado. Myra hadn't mentioned it to Will, what the woman had said. She had been pregnant with Mac. She watched Will carefully for a long time afterward but found no clues that he was straying again. There were good reasons, she tells herself, why she never said anything. It was the right thing, then, to go on with the life she knew. But now, with Ben, she is definitely not doing the right thing.

Then how come it feels so damn good?

Last night, she, Ben, and a few of the actors had sat around the picnic table talking late into the night. They were stirred up from the storm, as if electricity were still in the air, and in the darkness lit by only a few lanterns, she and Ben had grinned at each other brazenly. Melinda had gone to bed earlier, and when, finally, Myra had gone up to her room, Melinda was there, asleep, curled like a small child on Myra's side of the bed. But Myra couldn't find anger, or offense. Here was a woman, sleeping in her bed, who had taken her role—the role she had named Lyla and believed might save her from her own failures—and Myra was so high on Ben's warm smile that as she climbed into bed, she was close to giggling, wanting to wake Melinda and tell her everything, like kids at a sleepover. She had known better, but still, it took forever to fall asleep, and even now, after waking at eight this morning, she has so much energy that scrubbing the bathtub is over and done in no time flat. The house is swept. The laundry is in the washer. Obviously, the dishes are done. She needs to do something to keep moving. When she stands still, she is overwhelmed with fear, but when she moves, her body does the thinking, and her body wants Ben. But no more housework.

The tree. The one that fell. She'll build a bonfire for tonight. The ax is hanging on the wall in the barn, part of the scenery of *Of Mice and Men*.

The rehearsal is the one thing she has to push out of her mind when it comes in. Entering the barn is not the easiest thing she has done all day. Entering the barn is harder, by a lot, than reaching for Ben's hand under the sudsy water while her husband stood right outside. Beginning an affair is much easier than she ever imagined, and for the briefest of moments, she understands what must have happened to Will, and forgives him just a little.

Feeling slightly smug in her generosity toward Will, she looks around the barn for the ax.

Beth's repulsed by the mess of stitches and purplish skin on Greg Henry's face, but he has other body parts to look at. Norton has convinced Greg that warm sunshine will help him heal, and has set Greg up in a lawn chair in the backyard, with an upturned crate for a table. Greg has taken off his shirt—a white shiny material with a wide collar that is now draped on the back of Greg's chair like angel's wings. So she looks at Greg Henry's chest, and shoulders, and upper arms. She stands inside the kitchen door, Windexing the window. There's a big smudge of peanut butter where Greg Henry's left shoulder was, so she decides to clean the glass and look busy.

There's something fishy going on with Greg Henry and Norton Frye. The way Norton fawns all over Greg Henry would drive her crazy, but it doesn't seem to bother Greg at all. Beth wonders if Greg might be the kind of man who wants constant attention, like her uncle Pete. Beth really hopes Greg isn't that kind of guy.

Gazing through the window, she begins to modify her fantasy about Greg, which didn't exactly hang on marriage anyway. It might be okay if they just lived together. She imagines touching his chest, and her hand moving downward . . . She closes her eyes, a little queasy. A lot tingly. She hears a *clip-clip-clip* sound on the linoleum floor. When she opens her eyes and turns around, Chip Stark winks at her. The guy has winked at her so much today, she thought he had something in his eye.

"Hey, Beth, what you doing?" His voice is really low. Kinda sexy.

"Nothing," Beth says.

"You know, neither am I. It's pretty damn slow around here. Do you have a radio? If I don't hear some music soon, I might do something crazy." He flashes her a smile. He's got small, even teeth. Cute teeth.

"Crazy like what?" Beth says.

"Just crazy," Chip says. He sticks his hands in his pockets. They are very tight jeans. They look pretty good on him, tight like that.

"Well, I have a record player, but it's upstairs."

He grins real slow. Beth feels a bit nervous, but she likes the feeling. "And what albums do you have?" he says.

"A lot," Beth says, flipping her hair over her shoulder and combing it with her fingers. "Spirit, Beatles, Black Sabbath . . ."

"I could get into Black Sabbath. The record player's in your bedroom?"

"I could bring it down," Beth says with a shrug.

"You want some help?"

Beth's picking up all sorts of vibes from Chip, and knows this is not a simple offer of carrying a record player. But she's not so fickle that she'd fall for some almost-bald guy, even though he's got a pretty cool ponytail and really blue eyes. Still, music would be nice. "That's okay," she says. "I'll be right back."

"I'll be waiting," he says.

Beth can't help grinning as she runs up the stairs.

"Now," Will tells Ben and Lars, "I want you two to spend the next couple hours here, just being Lennie and George. Make a campfire, spread out your blanket rolls. You can eat those cans of beans, we can get more. Then, when you're ready, do the scene as written. Do it a few times. I'll come back for you in, say, three hours. Okay?"

"Sure, Will," Lars says.

Ben just shrugs and ducks his head. Will's noticed how Ben's been acting more and more like Lennie recently. At least someone's going along with Will, trying to help him make a go of this. He pats Ben on the arm. "Good luck."

"I've got some ideas, Ben," Lars says. "How about we . . ."

Will figures Lars has just run out of whatever he was going to say, but then he notices Lars looking at him, nodding, with a tight smile. Will knows when he's not wanted. As he walks away, Lars begins talking in a low voice. Will finds it annoying. The man should speak up.

Will doesn't head back to the house. He's stuck between wanting to ignore Myra and wanting to throw her down on the ground and screw her royally. He doesn't know what to expect from her anymore. Myra's been his backbone, his rock of Gibraltar, his—his *wife*. But she's been acting so strangely. Today she was singing, right in front of everyone. She never did that before. He doesn't really mind the singing, he's just worried where it might lead. He has this feeling she might do anything—dye her hair black or join the Hare Krishna. He shudders, imagining her bald, passing out flowers at the Pittsburgh airport. If she dyed her hair black, now that wouldn't be so bad.

Will has wandered into a patch of pines. Some kind of birds chirp from the branches, little black and white birds that remind him of Christmas cards. Aside from these birds, he's alone. He's always wishing he could have a moment alone, but now he feels awkward. He doesn't understand what Myra sees in the woods. He looks around, trying to see things through her eyes. He starts by imagining himself as a woman, his body softer, curved, and much shorter. He squats down a foot, but that's so obviously stupid, he stands back up. Now, he thinks, what else? How is Myra different from him? Besides physically, which shouldn't matter anyway. She moves more slowly. He slows down, shortens his steps, lets his gaze linger on the sharp green needles and the thin bumpy branches of the pines. What he sees are the gnats that hover just in front of his face like those little fish that swim with sharks. He tries to swat them away, but they come right back. Damn things. Now, what else? She's stubborn, he thinks, but gracious. People like her. Do people like him? He stops walking. Yes, he thinks they like him, but do they like him because they want a good role? Directorial wisdom? A job?

Will looks around the woods, depressed now. He doesn't like the way the pines stand there, so damn patient and quiet, flaunting the fact that they will outlive him in the long run. The whole place is too quiet. He's getting antsy standing here alone, with just his own thoughts rolling around in his head. What Myra sees in the woods is beyond him. He turns around and walks back the way he came.

When he gets close to the creek where he left Ben and Lars, he begins to creep quietly forward, sneaking from tree to tree, until he's standing behind a thick pine. He peeks around the tree to watch the rehearsal. He feels much better.

Melinda makes dinner again. She has actually broken Will's commandment about not leaving the farm, but she believes that what you don't know can't hurt you, just as strongly as she believes what you *do* know can hurt you. She bets no one will tell Will that the theater exercise of living the play this afternoon lasted less than fifteen minutes. Half the actors are sleeping in the sun. In character, if anyone asks.

This meal will be vegetarian. Brown rice with sautéed mushrooms, onions, green peppers, and of course garlic. There was absolutely no tofu to be found anywhere—or even anyone who knew what she was talking about. This revelation brought up a question she needs to consider: is living in the country actually healthier? The potbellies on the men she sees around here astound her. Haven't they heard about high blood pressure?

Along with the rice and vegetables, Melinda has made a fruit salad. (The skin on fruit is great fiber, but possibly the worst part due to chemical insecticides. She's decided to not peel the fruit but has spent a good deal of time scrubbing the apples, pears, and peaches with the hopefully pure well water, although she just read somewhere about chemical companies dumping their wastes in country creeks.) If anyone asks why there are no grapes in this fruit salad, she's prepared to give a stern lecture about the treatment of migrant workers. You would think artists portraying field hands would have done a little research, but they are merely actors at a small resident company, and if they read anything besides *Playbill*, she would be very surprised.

She has also made steamed broccoli with cheese sauce and without, for anyone who might be lactose intolerant—not that she believes anyone here knows if they are lactose intolerant, but Melinda's planning on explaining lactose intolerance before dinner. A little information on this subject might possibly stop some of those long waits for the bathroom.

Myra has offered to help, but Melinda can see the woman's in another world altogether. Possibly because of that work-out with the ax. Exercise can bring on a high-like experience. Melinda told Myra that everything was almost ready, but if she wanted, she could pick some flowers and set the picnic table. Myra left the house singing "White Coral Bells," the lilting notes sounding demented against Black Sabbath blasting from the living room.

Will, Ben, and Lars return from their rehearsal beaming. They were at the creek for several hours. Melinda slaps Will's hand as he reaches into her fruit salad. "Just wait," she says. "Go wash your hands. Use the green soap I left on the sink up-stairs. You don't want to know what toxins are in the soap you were using."

The oatmeal raisin cookies are all done and it's almost time to eat, so Melinda decides she will personally go round every-one up. First, into the barn, where Victor Peters snores on his bunk. She needs to give him plenty of time to come back to this reality. There's a transition between sleep and wakefulness that should not be jarred or rushed. She firmly believes that alarm clocks should be outlawed. People can train themselves to wake when they need to. The mind controls the body. It's so obvious.

After gently waking Victor and explaining that it's time for dinner, Melinda goes out to the backyard, where Greg Henry and Norton Frye are relaxing in lawn chairs, each reading a book. On closer inspection, Greg Henry's holding a book but is sound asleep. She gently wakes him up. His groggy response is not that of natural sleep. After dinner Melinda will have a talk with Greg to explain how the pills he's taking are throwing off his natural clock, along with other things. Norton says he'll make sure Greg gets to the table.

Mac and Nate Johnson sit on the grassy strip that runs down the lane, doing something with pebbles. "Dinner," she calls to them. They wave back. Mac gets up first and offers a hand to help Nate up. Melinda thinks that if she were a photographer for *Life* magazine, this moment would have made the cover. Too bad her camera's upstairs in the bedroom. No, a photograph would have frozen the moment. Now it can grow inside her. She will give away her camera at the first opportunity. Maybe Beth would like it.

Melinda doesn't see Frank Tucker anywhere, but as she walks back to the barn to check on Victor—in case he needs another brush with a soft voice to get him moving—she hears Frank. He's practicing a monologue from *Hamlet* behind the barn. There are no plans to produce *Hamlet* that she knows about, and to Melinda it's a dead play, overdone and usually overacted, but she does admire Frank's determination. She waits until the speech is over, then turns the corner of the barn and says, "Your presence at our evening meal is requested, prince, if you would so oblige us."

"Certainly, my fair woman," Frank replies. "It would be my pleasure." They walk back to the house arm in arm. Inside, Melinda asks Beth if she wouldn't mind putting on Crosby, Stills, Nash, and Young for dinner, then opens the front window. Lars, Ben, and Will come downstairs, followed by Jimmy McGovern, who's complaining about being kicked out of the bathroom just when he was about to take his shower.

"Argue with her," Will says, pointing to Melinda.

"Food now, shower later," Melinda says. "I'll even scrub your back, if you like."

For once Jimmy is speechless, and Melinda laughs.

"I'll take that back scrub if he doesn't want it," Chip Stark says with a wink.

There's something very cute about Chip that she's never noticed before. Maybe living in the country has allowed him to free his inner spirit from the trappings of his macho egotism. "Anytime, handsome," she says, grinning back. A screeching sound comes from the speakers. Beth has dropped the needle on the record, and it skids across the album. A long scratch defaces the vinyl.

Melinda reconsiders giving her camera to Beth. Maybe Mac would like it. She tells everyone to go out to the picnic table. Chip turns and looks over his shoulder at her before he leaves the room. Very nice eyes, Melinda thinks. The eyes are the window to the soul. Melinda turns over the record, pleased to find the song "Our House" on the unspoiled side. She turns the volume up, heads back to the kitchen, and picks up the bowl of brown rice.

Outside, the scene around the picnic table looks like one big happy family. Melinda takes a picture of this moment, in her mind, to save—and grow—for all time.

Ben can't sit still. He wants to do the dishes. "Well," he says, standing, "guess we better get things started here. There'll be a lot of dishes tonight." Melinda wouldn't let them use the paper plates, citing the number of trees cut down each day for the sake of lazy Americans. (Ben had immediately agreed with the wisdom of this.) He picks up Victor Peters' plate. There's some food left on it, but considering that Victor's eyes are shut and he's snoring, Ben figures he's finished for now. There's always dessert. "I'll do the dishes tonight," he says, rubbing his stomach with his free hand. "I need the exercise."

"Oh, Ben," Myra says. "That's so kind of you. But I'll help, really. I'll dry and put away, since I know where everything goes, and I'm finished eating anyway." There's a big pile of rice on her plate, but Ben's not going to point it out. They go into the kitchen.

Melinda watches Myra skip into the house carrying dishes. She's still on that high—if anything, it's getting worse (or better, depending on how you look at it). Myra's obviously very happy. Melinda's slightly jealous. Myra has Will, and all these wonderful people staying at their farm, and two great—well, nice—well, slightly odd kids. This morning at sunrise, when Melinda rose to get an early start on her first day here, she noticed how peacefully Myra slept and how very lovely she is. Although jealousy's an emotion Melinda disdains, emotions are not something that should be policed, and she allows herself this feeling, but then counters it by turning to Chip, who sits next to her. "Care for a walk in the woods later?" she whispers in his ear. Good emotions, such as an attraction to another human being, always outweigh the less desirable ones. Love conquers hate. Melinda's proud she is part of the generation that will bring an end to war.

Beth can't believe how Melinda's flirting with Chip Stark. She's so obvious! She's been whispering in his ear all dinner and keeps touching him all over. Who does she think she is? She's sticky sweet to all the guys, even playing up to old Victor Peters, but when Melinda fed the peach to Greg Henry, Beth almost went nuts. Greg nibbled it from her fingers, taking little baby bites because his mouth couldn't open very wide, and then he licked her fingers! Everyone laughed and made stupid catcalls. Well, Beth didn't think it was funny at all. Pretty immature, if you ask her.

Norton's chest aches. It's such an unusual feeling, he thinks maybe he's having a heart attack, then wonders if it might be some lung disease—or maybe he *is* lactose intolerant. But he knows better. When Greg Henry licked the peach juice off Melinda's fingers, Norton almost fainted right over his plate of brown rice. He's begun to have the most ridiculous fantasies, like passing Greg Henry love notes under the picnic table. Norton blames Will for all this, bringing all these people together, saying, *Open up your hearts, feel your emotions.* That was easy for him to say, he's happily married. But damn if it isn't wreaking havoc on Norton's normally calm, collected demeanor. He actually offered Greg a bite of his own broccoli, using a fork, of course, but Greg said he was too full. He said it with a grin, but then again, Greg has been grinning a lot tonight. All the attention, Norton supposes, is going to his head. That and the codeine.

Lars has been thinking about this "living the play" idea and feels Will's got it all wrong. After four beers, he has the courage to say something. Maybe he can get Will away for a few minutes. He takes another slug of his beer and gets up.

"Excuse me," Lars says, tapping Will on the shoulder. Will doesn't hear him. Jimmy McGovern's balancing a beer can on the sleeping Victor Peters' bent-over head, and everyone's laughing. "Hey, Will," Lars says, a bit louder. "Can I talk to you alone for a minute? I have an idea about this rehearsal."

"All right! Everybody, listen up! Lars has something to say," Will says, clapping his hands together for attention.

Victor Peters straightens up, and the beer can topples, spilling beer all over him. "What? I heard thunder. Is it raining?" He looks at his wet clothes and scratches his white hair. Jimmy and Chip hoot. Greg Henry starts giggling and can't stop.

Will clears his throat. Everyone turns his way. "Lars has an idea about the rehearsal. Let's get serious here for a minute. Someone call Ben out here."

Eight people shout, "Ben!!!"

"I could have done that," Will says.

Still, they have to wait more than a few minutes before Ben appears.

Will stands and looks around the table. "Now, what do you have to say, Lars? We're all listening."

Well, no backing down now. "I wonder if we're not on the wrong track here." If they weren't quiet enough before, this sure does the trick. Lars wants to go sit down. He swallows and takes a deep breath. "Look at the stage directions . . . The creek is, at most, a lighting effect. The hayloft scene is a bare stage, a suggestion of hay. Steinbeck says don't get a real dog. He's not asking for reality. I think he wants to keep it simple, universal, so the audience can accept the characters' problems as their own, not something that happens only to particular people on a particular ranch. I think we need to trust Steinbeck, not the trappings of a real bunkhouse, or busying ourselves building picnic tables. If we stick to the script and keep it honest, our work will be accomplished for us. What we're doing is getting in the way . . ." He ducks his head, feels his face blush. He can't believe he's said all this. The way people are staring at him, they can't either. "I mean, it's something to think about . . ."

Will's arms drop. He shakes his head. "Then everything we've been trying here has been for naught?"

"No!" Melinda shouts, standing up. "Lars has a point, but you guys have to face the truth. Who cares about us? Nobody. Without theatre, life goes on, people die, lawsuits get filed, roads get paved, presidents get elected. We're not necessary. We're lucky enough to have a theatre and an audience—but if you haven't noticed, that audience is getting smaller. If we don't change, we will go the way of dinosaurs!"

Now Melinda looks directly at Will. "I sat in on classes at Circle in the Square that tore away the masks and fears we act with. I saw a rehearsal of a script by an unknown writer, performed by unknown actors, that had the audience on the edge of their seats. The one-act was unpolished, raw, and so honest, we wept without relief. We need to learn to act naked. And I don't mean this as a metaphor. There are classes in New York City where you do monologues completely naked. At first you try to hide, then you find you can't. I think we should try it here."

Jimmy McGovern breaks the dead silence that follows Melinda's speech by shouting, "Oh boy! I could go for that."

"That's what we're up against?" Will asks. Even in the dusk of night, Lars sees Will has lost all the color in his face.

"I think so," Melinda says. "It is the seventies now. It's a whole new world."

"I don't think I could act naked," Will says.

"You could try," Melinda says.

"I don't think so," he says.

Lars feels terrible. "Will, I didn't mean . . . Maybe we shouldn't . . . you know, *live* the play. Maybe we should let the play live . . ." He shrugs. Next time he has a great idea, he's going to keep his mouth shut.

Will sighs. "I must admit, I'm speechless. My instinct here is to go on with the rehearsal tomorrow as planned. Concentrate on its honesty, which we *were*, and throw in the improvs for those willing to try them. Is that okay with you all?"

"No, sir," Nate says. Everyone turns his way. Lars takes the opportunity to go sit back down.

"What?" Will says, squinting at Nate. The lines on his forehead scrunch together. It looks painful to Lars.

"It's Sunday tomorrow, Will. I won't be rehearsing on a Sunday."

Will puts one hand to his head. "Seriously?"

"Seriously."

"Well then, we'll rehearse the scenes that don't include you, Nate. Is *that* okay?"

"Fine by me, but I may not be the only one wants to go to church. Any takers?"

Victor Peters raises his hand and nods. Frank Tucker says he's coming.

"Care to join me, Mac?" Nate asks.

"Sure," Mac says.

"I might come too," Myra says. "Maybe it's time I try church." She looks at Will.

Lars watches as Will and Myra stare at each other. It takes only a few seconds before Will turns away, shaking his head again. Lars wonders what would have happened if Will had asked Myra *why*. He's intrigued by the idea that one word can make such a difference.

"I could use a drink," Will says, "I've got a bottle of Jack Daniel's inside. Any takers?"

As the actors stand and head inside, Lars thinks that Will could have brought that bottle back out here. He simply wants to change the scene, be in charge. Sometimes in a production, Will will turn a spotlight on a minor character, even when the action is someplace else. It can have a dramatic effect, lessening, or reinforcing, a particular moment. Lars sits at the table in the dark, wondering if there are two different kinds of directors. The ones who control the show, and the ones who follow wherever it may lead them. A play directed by Will Bartlett always has Will's handprint on it. Is that a good thing, or not?

Melinda feels terrible for Will. She was only trying to inspire him, but instead she upset him. She sees now that Will has a lot of trouble facing change, as much as he pretends to be looking for it. The seventies may be hard on Will Bartlett, Melinda thinks. She wishes she had known him twenty years ago. In his prime. Right now he needs a long massage, and someone to explain that there's no growth without change. She's sure Will can understand this, if put the right way. At the right time. Which would definitely not be now.

Melinda takes Chip's hand before he can go into the house. "A walk?" By the grin on his face, Melinda knows she's won one small war against alcohol for the moment.

As they head in the direction of the woods behind the house, Melinda hears a door slam. Beth. That girl was in a bad mood all night. A massage wouldn't be enough for her, Melinda thinks. Acupuncture, maybe. Holding Chip's hand, Melinda pictures Beth with a thousand pins sticking from her skin, a human porcupine. She laughs, then, appalled at her own streak of cruelty, vows she will give the camera to Beth as a penance.

"Something tickling your fancy, ma'am?" Chip says.

"As a matter of fact, I hope so," Melinda says, stopping in the middle of the field. Why go all the way into the woods? It's dark enough right here.

Ben watches Will get drunk, the sloppy, fall-down drunk, the drunk of obliteration. Will does it quickly, without pleasure, rants for a few minutes about the lousy support art receives, then staggers out to the barn. Greg Henry's passed out in his bed, and Norton's up there watching over him. Chip and Melinda haven't come back yet from their walk, and Nate Johnson and Mac are playing dominoes at the kitchen table. Ben's had two glasses of Jack Daniel's, but he doesn't feel them at all. Frank Tucker and Jimmy McGovern have had more than a few glasses and are arguing about Catholic ideology, Frank using all the big words and philosophies he can espouse and Jimmy McGovern shouting "Crap! You're so full of it," until Ben thinks of Jimmy as the chorus of a long song and begins to sing along. It's simple fun to tell Frank he's full of crap, and it passes the time. Lars Lyman sits on an uncomfortable dining-room chair, watching them as if they are performing a play. Myra nurses a glass of something, sitting on the stairs. Every now and then she looks directly at Ben. He is terrified, and thrilled, at how long she holds his gaze.

Beth is camped on the couch. She has refused to let anyone sit next to her—that is, until Victor Peters comes downstairs from his long stay in the bathroom and, oblivious to Beth's bad mood, asks to sit next to her. Beth swings her legs down off the cushions and says, "Fine." Victor pats her knee, and Beth just smiles at the craggy-faced older man, as the drinking and arguing resume.

But Ben's not arguing with himself anymore. The voices inside his head have all quieted. They know a brick wall when they see it.

As they cleaned the dinner dishes a few hours ago, Myra told him she wants to go to church tomorrow to see what she is capable of becoming. Could she be a born-again Christian? Why should she be afraid of such a thing? Why should she be afraid of being different than she is? She is going to face her fears and give in to her desires. All this was said in reference to going to church, but they both knew what she was really talking about. Most people don't blush when they're talking about church.

Ben loves listening to Myra talk. He swears she grows prettier by the minute. He told her so as they washed the dishes. She smiled, and he said, "See, I'm right." She had kissed his hand, right there, in the kitchen. Just at that moment someone had yelled his name. If he was ever going to have a heart attack, it would have been then. He's sure now that a weak heart is the least of his problems, although a strong heart might be the killer.

"Oh, blow it out your ear, Frank," Jimmy says. "I'm going to bed." Frank follows Jimmy, saying something about pagan rites. Myra excuses herself and heads upstairs, giving Ben a little wave of her fingers that makes his knees weak. Victor asks Beth if she would like to play gin rummy.

"Sure," Beth says.

"Well, good night, Victor. Good night, Beth," Ben says.

Beth won't look at him. Ben gets a queasy feeling. His self-worth comes from the friendships he has formed. If something becomes of Myra and him, well, it may end up being just the two of them, alone. These people, they would not forgive him. During the moments Myra looks at him, or touches him, it seems that the two of them will be enough, but right now Ben worries that maybe he needs a company of love, a love of many rather than a great love of one. At least that is what he thinks as he walks through the dark night to the barn, but that's because Myra is not with him. If she were, he would be thinking differently. He is too easily swayed, bound by nothing but the moment.

In the barn, Will snores loudly. His blanket has fallen to the dirt floor. Ben picks it up and covers Will. *Love her just a little more than I do,* he thinks, *and I'll leave you both alone. Love her less, and I will not be able to help myself.*

For the next hour, Beth plays gin rummy with Victor Peters. Hoping for another seven is about all she's capable of doing right now. She's lived with a group of actors for more than a week, fallen in love twice (there was a moment while listening to music with Chip Stark that she fell in love with him, a decision reversed the minute Chip walked off with Melinda, but still, being in love with Chip Stark for an hour has caused all the same pain of falling in love for a week, or a month), been alone only in the shower, seen the way her mother looks at Ben Walton, watched her father be a god and then get reprimanded by the want-to-be earth mother, Melinda, then seen her father get drunk and spit fly from his mouth as he put down the world Beth is looking forward to. Gin rummy seems to be the best way to get through another hour of her life without having to deal with all sorts of conflicting emotions.

Victor Peters talks to fill the silences. He's kind of nice, even though his face is so old and pockmarked. He talks about his wife with this look in his eyes like she's sitting next to him. "Helen and I went to Vegas once, thinking we were such hot blackjack players. Lost two hundred dollars before we realized that what we liked about playing blackjack was beating each other so we could kid about it the next morning. Losing to the blackjack dealer just made the game kind of ugly. We hardly played it after that. Gin rummy's my game now. Stay away from Vegas is my advice."

His talking makes her feel tired, but since the couch is her bed, she can't excuse herself to go to bed. He just keeps dealing out hands. Beth imagines them playing cards for the rest of their lives. It's that kind of night. *Twilight Zone* time.

Just as Beth gets dealt a winning hand, around one o'clock in the morning, Melinda walks into the house with most of the field still stuck to her damp clothes, carrying her sandals, her curly brown hair a mess, her lips swollen, her cheeks rosy. Beth's fist tightens around the cards, and they bend and crumple. She hates Chip Stark from such a deep, dark spot in her chest that her heart hurts. The anger she has let drain from her for the past hour engulfs her. And it feels right. It's her due. She has every right to be royally pissed. Just try and stop her.

Victor Peters looks at the bent cards as they drop on the floor. "Guess it's getting late," he says. "I enjoyed our evening together. Thank you, Beth, and good night." He gets up, using the arm of the couch to push against. He has the kind of arms her grampa had, with the skin hanging down in loose, soft folds.

"Good night, Mr. Peters," she says. "It was fun."

"Sleep tight," he says. Beth can't remember the last time anyone said that to her. Then she remembers about being mad at everyone. She yanks the blanket over her head and lies down. God knows she won't get any rest tonight. She's too mad to sleep.

Sunday

❧ ❧

Will stands in the last row of the house: the seats and stage are empty. Where's the audience? Where's the set? Myra walks on-stage. She's dressed in a white toga. He expects her to give a speech of some sort, an oration. She just stands there. "Go on!" he says. She doesn't seem to hear him. She cups a hand above her eyes and looks out into the audience. "Do something!" Will yells. She rises into the air and flies around the stage in a circle, then flies offstage left. Peter Pan? Will thinks. I'm directing Peter Pan?

Myra dreams she is on the stage, wearing a loose white dress, singing loud and wonderfully. The house is full, but Will is nowhere to be seen. She wants him to be there. When the audience rises to its feet in applause, she looks around for Will. She sees Ben.

Ben sees Myra in a large open field, wearing a white sheet that she lifts up into the air like the wings of an angel. He tries to go to her, but with every step he takes, the space between them doubles. Through the woods he can see a house. It takes forever to get there, but when he does, Will opens the door.

Victor Peters is in his house. Helen's in the kitchen wearing a white apron. Pots clank, cans get opened, a spoon clinks. He can smell pot roast cooking. Once, as she walks by the opening of the archway, she wiggles her finger at him from behind her back, right at butt level, and he knows that means he's going to be lucky tonight. And he's not talking about food.

Chip's making love to a woman. He can't make out her face, but it feels to him that they are meant to be together. They lie naked on a fresh white sheet. He kisses her breasts, her stomach, the inside of her thighs, her lips. He's overwhelmed with sweetness. Even though he knows it's a dream, he pretends it's real.

Lars Lyman is the director of a movie he watches play on a big white screen. He is in control of everything. Nothing can go wrong. Nothing is real. The movie has no end. It's the greatest feeling in the world.

Frank Tucker accepts an Oscar from a beautiful woman in a white dress, who just happens to be his wife. "I am the luckiest man in the world," he says. His wife kisses him. The audience bursts into applause.

Beth kisses a stranger in a white shirt. Their lips are locked in an unending embrace of complete, utter passion. The kiss is the whole dream, except she wonders if she is really a close-up in a movie. She wonders if the passion's real, or if she's acting, and she wonders if sometimes there is no difference.

Melinda dreams of white doves flying, of baking pies, of kissing Will, of standing on a stage and speaking to the world about love and understanding. The world applauds, and all wars end. She's elected president.

Greg Henry's leg is broken, and he's wearing a white cast covered with names. "Love you" is written all over his cast. His leg is broken because . . . he can't quite remember. Something about a movie he's in. Or was? Or is this it?

Norton is in his college dorm room. Theatre posters cover

the white walls. Greg Henry is asleep next to him. The whole dream is Norton lying in bed, knowing Greg is inches away.

In the car, the window cracked, Mac dreams of his mother. She's running through the woods wearing white clothes that are getting snagged on branches. Mac follows her. He wants her to stop running. He passes by a tent in the middle of nowhere.

Nate Johnson dreams of war, which is a dream that comes in summer with the first hot nights. He's in a tent, alone. Outside is the war, and as soon as he opens the tent flap, he will be killed. He wishes there was someone in the tent with him, someone he could talk to before going outside. That would help make it easier to die. He waits for the courage to open the flap.

Jimmy McGovern dreams he's in a boat with Nate and Mac. A wall of storm clouds races toward them as whitecaps swell in the water. "Put on a life jacket, Mac! You too, Nate!" Thanks, he says to someone—whoever gave him the chance to do it right this time.

Rain falls into dreams, comforting some, frightening others. Mac wakes shouting—the rain on the car roof sounds like gunshots. Nate hears a young boy's scream and wakes. He hears Mac yell again, and he runs through the rain to the car. Melinda dreams that with a wave of her hand she opens the roof of the Capitol. "The rain is the earth's tears. Listen to it!" Beth wakes up and decides she will kiss Greg Henry today or die. Will hears the sound of rain and decides all his problems are caused by the weather, and he rolls back over. Some make the choice to keep dreaming, others, to wake up.

After breakfast (oatmeal, cantaloupe, and fresh-squeezed orange juice, although Mac just made a peanut butter and jelly sandwich), Mac, Nate, Myra, Ben, Victor, Frank, and Jimmy

McGovern drive off to church. (Jimmy is going to church just to prove something to Frank Tucker that Mac doesn't understand.) Mac has never been to church except to go to his cousin Sylvia's wedding and Grampa Bartlett's funeral. He knows about God—God has the power to do anything, if he's real. If he's not, then things just happen. Both ideas are kind of scary.

Mac's going because Nate wants him to, and Mac is willing to do whatever Nate asks. There is something about Nate (Mac calls him Nate now, because Nate asked him to) that Mac trusts, even more than his mom or dad right now, which makes Mac feel bad, but it's true, and Mac can't do anything about things that are true; it's not like you can just change them. His dad keeps forgetting about him. He bumped right into Mac last night and didn't even know it. Mac's mom, even though she doesn't bump into him, is acting funny; sometimes she's all huggy and weepy, and the next, she's singing and laughing.

This whole week has been pretty weird, and it's kind of nice to have Nate to talk to, who sat with him in the lane, finding pebbles that were really neat looking. Some had bands of color running through them, and some were pure white or pink, like jelly beans. Nate showed Mac how to wet the stones in the gully on the side of the lane so they shined. They carried them into the house and put them in a bowl of water. Nate says a bowl of stones will never die and get moldy. The idea of those stones staying the same forever is neat, especially since everything else around him keeps changing so fast, he doesn't know what to expect. Mac's decided that he's going to eat peanut butter and jelly sandwiches for every meal, until the theatre people go, and with that decision, he feels a little better. Nate says that Mac's pretty smart to figure out a way to control his own environment. Mac's not exactly sure what Nate means, but he's memorized the words. *Control his own environment.* He likes the idea of controlling something; it's better than the idea of

God, or no God. Mac wonders if he goes to church when there isn't a wedding or a funeral, if that's when you meet God.

They drive to church in two cars and park on the street. No one says anything as they go inside the church, where they sit in the back row. There's no stage. That's okay with Mac.

Myra feels nervous and slightly embarrassed. She is going to church for the first time in more than a dozen years for the purpose of testing Pandora's box. If God speaks to her, she will turn her life around, become religious, and devote herself to the church. If God doesn't speak to her, then she will take it as a sign to go on with her own plan, which is to have an affair with Ben. She knows she has stacked the deck in Ben's favor, so she vows she will listen very closely, in case God whispers.

She's not sure if she believes in God, but she'd like to. Someone who will save her if she says she loves him. How much easier could life be? But on the other hand, she wants to be touched by Ben. He's sweet and kind and could lift her up and carry her away. He listens to her. He looks at her. She has forgotten the lure of being looked at deeply. It's exciting. She's excited. She blushes. Opening the hymnal, she begins to sing. She realizes she is singing too loudly to hear God. He will have to speak up.

Ben wants to make love to Myra. He wants one day with her, a separate day from all the other days, a day without consequences. Even sitting here in church, Ben can think of nothing else. *Sorry*, he says to God, like a kid who says sorry to his dad so Dad will forgive him and let him go back out and play. Ben figures God knows this. He hopes God is just a little bit too busy with the war in Vietnam to pay much attention to a middle-aged man lusting after his best friend's wife. Ben's embarrassed by how little the war affects his life and how much this one woman does.

Nate sings and prays, just as he has for hundreds of Sundays, but for the first time in years, he means what he says, and knows God is listening—he understands that all along God has been listening. It's up to Nate to do the things he's asked God to do. The people on this earth are God's hands. Must be hard, Nate thinks, to have your hands doing what they like all on their own, good and bad. Must be frustrating as hell. It's not a job he'd ever want, being God. Being a good actor and a good person is what Nate's got to concentrate on now.

Nate watches Mac, who probably doesn't understand much of what he's hearing, but still, Nate's glad to be the one to introduce God to this child. Someday Mac might need God, and it will be a welcoming back, not something foreign or frightening. Nate has quite a few questions he wants to ask God, but they can wait. He's in no hurry to be face to face with God. Right now he's content just to sing "Nearer My God to Thee." In the row ahead of them, a lady in a pink dress sings off key, and Nate wonders why God didn't give everyone a nice singing voice. Now, that wouldn't have been so hard, would it? Just another question to put on the list.

Jimmy McGovern has come to church just to prove Frank Tucker wrong, but he's never been in a non-Catholic church, and he's so surprised by its simplicity that he forgets what they were arguing about. It's nice in here. He remembers going to mass with his own family, praying to the saints for his mother's soul, how his dad held them together all those years after she was gone. He was a good man, and funny, could make every-one laugh. What kind of guy can laugh after losing his wife? Jimmy wonders. Someone who still loved his kids. A good man. *I'm going to go visit him, soon,* Jimmy thinks. *Just show up at the door. It'll surprise the hell out of his old man.* Jimmy grins, then thinks about what Frank Tucker said about hating his old man. Sad as shit, that story. Jimmy's going to be nicer to Frank, and just to make it stick, he tells God. *I'll be nice to Frank Tucker,* he says. *And watch over my old man,* he adds.

Jimmy looks at the people he came here with. He's just a bit player in this play. Will told him once he'd get better parts when he got older, that he was going to be a very good charac-ter actor someday, like Victor Peters. It didn't sound all that good to Jimmy then, but now he knows it was a compliment. He just needs time, and more parts. It's funny, thinking ahead, trying to have patience. But look at old Victor, his head held high, singing out "Nearer My God to Thee" in his craggy voice. Hell, if Jimmy could play the part of Candy someday with half the talent Victor has, he'd be pretty damn proud of himself.

He's glad he came to church with these guys. He's looking forward to the rest of the month. He has to admit he kind of likes arguing with Frank. Egging him on. He bets Frank likes a good argument too. But what the hell was he going to prove by coming to church again anyway?

Mac didn't see God, and he wonders if God was at another church today. He'd ask Nate, but everyone's so quiet on the car ride back that Mac is afraid you're not supposed to talk for a while after going to church, like not swimming for an hour after you eat. There's a lot of stuff he doesn't know, but Mac doesn't mind having a lot of questions. Questions are fun things. It's the answers that are hard. You have to do something with the answers, like fix the world or make tests for schoolkids. Mac really doesn't want to have to be an adult. Except for driving a car, he doesn't see what being an adult is good for. Beth says when he becomes an adult, he has to go to war and he'll probably get killed. Even spiders don't sound bad next to that.

It's so quiet, Mac wonders if everyone is thinking about something, as he is, or if sometimes people can just *not* think, if right now everyone has a big blank piece of whiteness in them with no sounds becoming words. He tries to do that, make no words inside his head, but he can't. Mac wonders if watching plays and movies, and even going to church, is a way to let other words fill you up and give your own thoughts a break. Sometimes counting things can do that for Mac—like back in Pittsburgh, he counts how many cars drive by his house when he's in bed looking out his window; how many red and how many blue and how many white. It takes away the words that make him worry and helps him fall asleep. He can see how church might do that too. It was pretty hard to keep his eyes open sometimes.

Beth has done the most amazing thing, and she can't believe she did it. She's so nervous, her legs twitch and her hands shake. She had better find something to do, like running around the world, before her whole body just flies off in pieces. She went into her room—Greg Henry's room—knocking softly at first, then knocking louder. When she opened the door a crack, Greg was asleep on her bed, completely out. Creeping in, barefoot and on her toes, Beth went right up to where he lay, his mouth slightly open, his wound covered with a fresh bandage, and she touched his shoulder. He didn't move or make a sound. She said his name maybe five times, and then, without thought, leaned over and kissed him on the mouth. Seeing that he didn't even flutter his eyes, she leaned back over and kissed him again, then, absolutely flying, she left the room, came downstairs, and began picking up things, like a fork on the floor, and old napkins, and someone's pants. In just a few minutes, the room was clean. She could paint the house right now and still have enough energy to mow the lawn. She kissed Greg Henry, and his lips were as soft as silk. Satin. Rose petals. Kittens. Butter.

Oh my god, she kissed Greg Henry while he was sleeping! She can't believe it.

"Beth!" It's Melinda, calling from the kitchen.

"Yes?" Beth doesn't really want to talk to Melinda. She's still mad at Melinda for that thing with Chip Stark, but Beth is so hyper right now, she'd talk to a tree.

Melinda comes into the living room. She's wearing some kind of white cotton short-sleeved dress with bright embroidery across the top. Her hair is in two loose braids with dandelions woven into it. No makeup. Not even mascara. Beth can't imagine being caught dead without mascara and some blush, but it takes all kinds. What Chip Stark sees in her, Beth can't imagine.

"Hey, Beth," Melinda says. "I have a present for you." She holds something behind her back. Beth thinks, if it's a bran muffin, she'll puke. She'd also like to know who ate all her chocolate éclairs, but she's guessing it wasn't Melinda. Beth would die for a chocolate éclair right now.

Melinda hands her a camera. It's black and bulky and really heavy. "It's a Nikkormat FT," Melinda says. "There's film in it, and I have another roll for you. I'll show you how it works."

Beth stands there dumb. Melinda's giving her a camera? Like, lending it to her? So she can take a picture or two? She can't be *giving* Beth this camera. It must be worth a hundred dollars. "I don't get it," Beth says. "I'm sorry. What do you

mean? Why would you give me your camera?" Beth's so sure
there's a catch, she's waiting to hear what the terms are. Some
kind of bribe to stay away from Chip? What?

"I have no use for it anymore," Melinda says. "I figured you
might like it. Pass it on when you outgrow it. Maybe you
won't. Maybe cameras will be your thing. That's cool too. But
it's hard to use. You have to focus and get the meter just right.
I'll have to show you how to set the film speed. Would you like
it?"

Chip hasn't been mentioned. Or washing dishes for the next
month. Beth's still confused. "You mean you're giving it to me?
Really?"

"Yes. Really. It's a gift. You understand what a gift is,
right?"

"Yeah. Yeah. It's just . . . Well, thanks. It's really neat. I
mean, I like it a lot. It just feels weird, taking your camera. My
mom probably won't want me to just take your camera, you
know . . ."

"Don't you worry about that. Let's go outside so I can show
you about the meter. Come on." They go outside, and for the
next half hour Melinda shows Beth how to use all the rings that
turn, how to judge backlighting, how to bring things into sharp
focus. Beth loves it. She points it at a pink peony, finding out
how close she can get before she loses focus. Without the tangle
of the branches and green leaves, or the distraction of the house
behind it, the flower, framed, alone and clear, takes on a whole
new beauty. Or maybe it has always been this beautiful, but she
just never knew it, and using a camera is a way of looking at
something a little more carefully than she normally would. This
is the kind of thing Beth usually thinks about after smoking
pot, and it makes her feel high. She thanks Melinda, even gives
her a hug. Melinda's okay. Chip Stark's still a jerk.

"Use up that roll of film today, then tonight I'll show you

how to take it out and put in a new roll. Have fun!" Melinda goes back into the house, probably to bake bread or something. Beth is way off in the back field when her mom and the others come back from church. She points the camera at everyone crossing the yard, but they're too far away and won't make a very interesting picture. When she has only one more picture left, Beth heads back to the house. Victor Peters comes out of the barn, and she asks him to stand against the old pitted wood. She focuses on the wrinkles that radiate from his eyes. She never noticed before how wonderful wrinkles are.

"Watch out, I'll break your camera," Victor Peters says.

"No, no, you look beautiful," Beth says. She means it. He grins like he just won a million bucks, and she presses the button. He has huge teeth that stick out of his gums like leaning gravestones. His face is as pockmarked as the gray wood behind him. His ears are big and droopy. He's her first portrait, and she will never forget this moment.

After a lunch of fresh-squeezed lemonade and a large colorful salad—with poppyseed dressing on the side (Melinda recommended eating the salad without dressing but was prepared for objections)—Will asks Ben and Lars if they are ready to go back to the creek in the pine forest to rehearse the last scene of the play. This scene is the hardest to rehearse, and perform, since it requires a depth of emotion that can leave most actors drained and depressed. Lars agrees immediately, but Ben hesitates. Melinda can understand. It's a beautiful sunny day, and Will's asking Ben to go into the dark pines and be killed a few dozen times. It's a wonderful moment in theatre, but being a character that gets killed herself, she understands Ben's feelings.

"I'll give you a long massage when you get back," Melinda offers.

Ben looks toward the house, then back at Melinda. "That's okay. You don't have to bother." Will, Ben, and Lars go off to the barn to get their props, including the gun. Shakes follows them but halfway to the barn gives up and, circling a few times, lies down, looking like a well-worn coonskin hat. Melinda decides she will cook him up something special.

When Will comes out of the barn, he hollers to the actors at the picnic table. "I expect you all to go do some improvs in the bunkhouse! Let Melinda give you some ideas. No strip poker!" He heads down to the creek, Lars and Ben in tow.

"I'll do the dishes," Nate says. "Want to help me, Mac?"

"Sure."

"If I go into the barn, someone needs to check in on Greg," Norton says. "He didn't sleep well last night, so I'm letting him rest, but someone should check on him every fifteen minutes to see if he's breathing normally."

"I will," Beth says.

"Well . . . all right," Norton says with obvious hesitation. "But don't disturb him. If he wakes up or his breathing gets labored, come get me. And don't let my cat out."

"No problem," Beth says.

Melinda notices Myra, who is listening to all this from the porch steps. "Myra, would you like to join us in an improv?"

"No thanks. I'm going for a walk."

There are some odd looks from the actors at the table, which Melinda doesn't understand. What could be the matter with Myra taking a walk?

"Okay, kid," Nate says. "Time for KP."

"What's KP?" Mac asks.

"I'll tell you while we wash the dishes."

"Okay."

Melinda heads to the barn. Just before she goes inside, she looks around. Lying on the lawn like a dead giant is the old tree. Nearby, the picnic table, large enough for two dozen people, is covered with the remains of leftover salad that look like leaves from the fallen tree. Ten cars are parked on the lawn that borders the lane. One woman wearing a Mexican wedding dress is standing by the barn. A seemingly dead dog lies in the sun. What would someone driving by think? Melinda wants to know the stories they might invent. As she walks into the barn to play theatre games, she can't help gloating. There are people working in factories, cleaning sewers, stuffed into suits at board meetings. It takes all kinds; she's just so lucky she is her kind.

Beth carries a dining-room chair upstairs and places it by Greg's bed. While waiting for Greg to wake up, she imagines her life as it will be. She'll get a small role next year in her father's theatre, perhaps in *The Prime of Miss Jean Brodie*. Her father will direct her and be amazed at what she can do. He'll ask her to join The Mill Street Theatre, where she'll act for three or four years, cutting her teeth on some good roles, then she'll move to Hollywood. Being in movies is what she's really interested in. Not TV. She knows how shallow TV roles are. Her father has told her that a thousand times.

Greg's eyes open, then close. "Hey, Greg," she says.

"Hey, Beth," Greg says, with his eyes still closed. His face is purple and bruised.

"Can I get you something?" Beth asks.

"A new face." He opens his eyes, and they twinkle. One corner of his lip curls.

"Your face is perfect," Beth says. She blushes, but he doesn't notice because his eyes are closed again. It's easier this way, she thinks. She imagines them both lying in bed, side by side, their eyes closed, sharing their deepest secrets.

"A perfect mess," Greg says. "Maybe some water."

"Okay. Just a second. I'll go get some." When she gets back, he's asleep.

For the next two hours she sits by his bed—her bed—and has short but sweet conversations with Greg Henry as he wakes and falls back asleep. Each time he wakes up, he seems surprised that she's there and doesn't remember what was said before. It's like rehearsing the same scene, and each time she does it better. She hardly blushes at all. She has the water waiting.

Myra walks up the hill to sing but changes her mind and sneaks back through the woods to watch the rehearsal. Ben and Lars are crouched at the edge of the creek. Will stands a dozen yards or so behind but interrupts every now and then. Kneeling behind a tree, she keeps her eyes on Ben. She stares at him as she has sometimes stared at the setting sun, knowing she shouldn't. She is out of control, tumbling head over heels. She has the instinct to reach out and brace herself but doesn't. She wants to fall.

She is smitten. With a big, burly, not-really-handsome man who is warm and kind and sweet and wants her and is her husband's best friend. She imagines she's in a Shakespearean comedy, where the characters have all been drugged with fairy dust, all falling in love with the wrong people. She used to think those plays were so funny, but she's not so sure now.

When the rehearsal's over, she watches the three men walk away. She has been married to Will for seventeen years. At this moment, she can't feel anything for him. Not anger, or hope, or love. The shape of Ben's large body moving through the woods makes her heart flutter.

Shit, she thinks. I'm in trouble. She heads back up to the hill, then down to the house. When she gets there, Ben comes out.

"I snuck out to watch you," she says.

"I know," he says.

She looks around. "Did you see me?"

"No. I just knew you were there."

She holds perfectly still, to savor this moment of believing him. She wants to touch his face. "I better go," she says. As she walks into the house, and he walks out, Ben runs a hand down her thigh. She closes the door behind her and sings out, " 'Come out, come out, wherever you are, and meet the young lady who fell from a star.' "

"Jesus, Mom," Beth says. "Keep it down. Greg Henry's sleeping."

Myra stands with her hands on her hips and stares at Beth, who is wearing orange lipstick, thinking she is the Queen of Sheba. Myra bursts out laughing. Big mistake. Beth's face reddens, and her lips get tight. She gives Myra that *I hate you* stare and turns and walks out, heading back upstairs. Well, her motherly instincts are shot to hell right now, right along with her wifely duties. What she's got left is just a whole lot of love, for Ben Walton. Myra rolls her eyes and—very quietly—sings a refrain from "Love Me Tender." God forbid she wake up Greg Henry.

Beth and Greg Henry come downstairs for dinner: hamburgers, baked potatoes, canned corn, and leftover salad. After dinner Will lights the bonfire Myra built, and everyone plays charades in the firelight. Melinda shows Beth how to load the camera, and she takes a dozen pictures of the fire and the shadowy shapes of the actors sitting around it, then she sits next to Greg. Every now and then she touches him on the shoulder to get his attention or wake him up. Norton sits on the other side of Greg, doing the same thing. Melinda and Chip sneak off after charades and make love in the flattened grass behind the barn. Victor Peters, going into the barn to bring out a blanket, hears them and grins, remembering a night he and Helen had done something just like that. Everyone drinks, except Melinda and Mac. (Beth takes a beer out of the cooler, and no one even notices.) Frank Tucker goes into the house and calls his wife long distance and talks to her for an hour, leaving a dollar under the phone when he's done. No one gets too drunk except Jimmy McGovern, who does an impression of Mae West and staggers into the bonfire but is caught by Will, who has been standing by the fire all night as the master of ceremonies, a title Melinda has bestowed on him, which includes a paper crown she made from a cereal box. Myra kisses Ben out behind the house. Shakes is fed pieces of hamburger until he wanders off and throws up, coming back to beg for marshmallows. Melinda, on impulse, lets out Norton's cat, who wanders into the barn, catches a mouse, eats its head, then comes to the fire and curls up next to Norton, who, drunk on the nearness of Greg Henry, doesn't mind at all that she has been let out. From the open window, music drifts into the yard. Nate Johnson looks up at the stars and thanks God for this life.

M o n d a y

※ ※

Will wakes Monday morning before anyone else and eases his stiff legs out and over the bunk, slowly unbending them. He has lain curled on his side on the short bed, and his body protests even these minor movements he must make to put his feet on the ground. His age and his doubts combined have made him feel feeble; he wants both to take it easy and to shout profanity into the damp, gray morning. He's fighting more than the board of directors. Here, on this farm, this summer, he's fighting to be part of the future. That he's had honor in the past for his talent is not enough; he needs to know that he possesses something *now*. He needs to show Melinda, and the world, that he is not old yet.

Standing in the opening between the barn doors, Will looks out at the morning and this place he can call his own. The pebbled lane, the fields of tall grass, his house. Lying across the front yard is the old tree, its branches roughly hewn off and burned to cinders in a bonfire. It's too much symbolism, even for him. Will closes his eyes and rubs his face, bringing back circulation and warmth. He's not old; he just needs to sleep in a regular bed, next to his wife. He's hardly spoken to Myra in two days—but he has been proving a point; the point is vague, and Will decides it must have been made. He will sleep with Myra in his own bed tonight. Will knocks three times on the barn door before heading into the house.

The house is oddly clean for the number of people using it. The dishes are washed and put away. Something about the clean dishes nags at Will, something he can't exactly put his finger on. He discards his worry. He will not worry today. Neither will he act naked.

Pouring coffee from the pot, Will imagines Melinda acting naked. There's no way he would allow such a thing, but his mind begins to list several reasons he could give it a try.

Will walks into the living room where Beth sleeps on the couch. She's curled up tightly, and there's just enough room to sit on the end of the couch near her feet. Will sits there, drinking his coffee, smelling the warm, sleepy scent of his daughter. He places his coffee cup on the side table and picks up Beth's feet, sliding them into his lap. Gently he rubs a foot, pressing with his thumb against the soft arch underneath.

"Hi, Daddy," Beth says, her voice husky from sleep.

"Hi, Pumpkin," Will says. "Good morning."

"What's happening?" Beth asks.

"Nothing. Just rubbing your feet. You don't mind?"

"No."

Will switches feet. Beth tucks the already-rubbed foot back under her blanket. No one talks for a while. It's the moment when people don't speak that tells us what their hearts say, Will thinks. He wonders how often he has used the love he feels for his children, and his wife, while acting. Is it possible that his distance from Myra is more poignant because he sees its theatrical possibilities?

"I love you, honey," Will says to Beth. He's already thinking, In what play might love be shown by the simple act of rubbing a foot?

"I love you too, Daddy," Beth says.

"You want to act, don't you?"

"Yes. I've asked you a lot. When can I?"

"Soon," Will says. "I'll look for a small part for you next year. If we're still together." He pauses. "The theatre, I mean. I just worry about you. It's not all fun. It's hard work and disappointments. It's playing small roles and wanting the big ones. It's patience, and taking chances, and failing. And talent. It's not for everyone."

Before Beth can answer, someone can be heard coming down the steps. They both turn to look. It's Myra.

Myra stops about halfway down the stairs and just stands there looking at the two of them on the couch. Something about the way her mother looks at her father makes Beth uneasy, and then her mind goes *Oh!* Beth knows, with some female instinct, that her mother doesn't feel the same love for her father that she did only weeks ago. Looking at her dad, Beth thinks that her father doesn't know what he's lost. Or maybe he does. Maybe that's why he's sitting here right now. Maybe her dad is lonely and sad and has turned to Beth for some comfort. Which makes her feel really weird, and mad. Shouldn't her dad care for her all the time, not just when he's sad and needs comfort?

And who does her mom think she is, standing up on the steps looking down at them? She's the one who's been smiling at Ben Walton, trying to look all young and flirty. What's her problem? Beth thinks both her parents are a little fucked up right now, which makes her feel older, and alone.

Myra walks down the steps and goes into the kitchen. Will

doesn't say anything, like he's scared of her or something. Beth has this strange thought. Right now her dad is like Superman exposed to kryptonite, and her mom is the kryptonite. Beth feels like she should protect him. The thought doesn't make her feel all warm and caring, just angry. She pulls her foot back under the cover. Her dad doesn't seem to notice. He stopped rubbing her foot when her mom came downstairs anyway.

Myra stands in the kitchen watching Mac make a peanut butter and jelly sandwich for breakfast. Beth and Will sit on the couch. Suddenly she wishes all the actors, including Ben, would disappear, *poof!* and her memory of the past week with them. She knows it won't happen. She knows the actors will wake and come into her house, that today she will make love to Ben. She has balanced this idea, of making love with Ben, against everything else—God, family, honesty, self-respect, and duty— and she knows there is not one single argument that outweighs the simple fact that she will make love to Ben. She doesn't understand it, she just feels it. Last night, by the fire, Ben had whispered to her, *just once*, and she had known exactly what he meant. Her heart races as she thinks about it. Maybe, she thinks, it is her heart racing that compels her. Maybe she is just afraid to let it stop. What then?

One by one the actors stumble in. When Melinda kisses Chip good morning, right there in the kitchen, Myra notices a flash of jealousy on Will's face. How dare he? Ben walks in. Myra looks at him and thinks, *Yes, today.*

After everyone has had some coffee, Will rounds the actors up on the front lawn. "Okay," he says, "I think we need a run-through. We need some congruity here. I want to see what needs work, and set a schedule. If you're not in the scene, stay out of sight. Anyone who wants can come down to the creek for the final scene. I think Ben and Lars hit it on the head yesterday, and I'd like you to see what they found. Sit on the top of the small hill by the pines. Okay? All right. Let's get moving."

As the actors walk over to the barn, Myra feels left behind. Knowing Beth must feel the same way, she turns to her daughter. Beth glares at Myra as if this, too, is all her fault, and walks out of the kitchen and up the stairs. Myra turns the other way just in time to watch Mac walk out the kitchen door and head down the lane. Her children have abandoned her, and she feels an odd satisfaction in this. A justification. A permission to do as she pleases.

She spends the rest of the morning thinking about making love to Ben. There is not an inch of her skin that doesn't think about it. She even thinks about the fact that these thoughts she has now might be the most exciting part. Ben is a large man. How will he look without clothes? Will it bother her? But then she thinks about being touched by hands that have never touched her breasts. His mouth sucking her nipples. His thick fingers going inside her. Myra burns three pieces of toast trying to make something to calm her stomach, then gives up and eats the burned bread, taking little bites with her front teeth, wandering around the house. She begins to notice small things, the red roses in the hooked rug her grandfather made, the book on gardening she has always meant to read, the way the sunlight falls on the brass vase she picked up at a garage sale: the small things that make this house her home, the one she may be leaving behind. They tug at her, they say, *Stay*. But I need this, she tells them. Can't you see that? She expects the couch and the chairs she has brought to this place, the pillow she has sewn, the curtain she has hung, the things she has touched, to understand, to say, *Go ahead, it's your turn to shine*. They don't. They accuse her in silence. She walks out the kitchen door and sits on the side porch, her back to her house.

Lars, Ben, and Will hike into the woods for the first scene. Lars, like Will, is anxious to begin the play at the beginning and keep going; doing the improvs has just whet his taste for *Of Mice and Men*, and he feels like a man who wants to drink the whole bottle. Lars also wants to immerse himself in the play because living here at the farm *and* rehearsing *Of Mice and Men* is like being in two different plays; he's uncomfortable with the one that is happening outside of Will's direction. Even though Lars is oddly fascinated by whatever is going on with Ben and Myra and wishes he could secretly film them, he knows the difference between film and reality, and he does not want to be around when Will figures out what's happening.

Will doesn't say a word, just sits down by a pine, his thin body becoming part of the tree, so when they look that way, they see pine, and not Will. Lars and Ben kneel down by the creek, in the flat, dry spot they found the day before. They spread out the props, and together they take a moment to imagine themselves alone. A minute of silence. Then the curtain rises.

Lars falls into George's role as easily as breathing. He's frustrated. Lennie has lumbered behind all day, looking behind him every goddamn second hoping to see a rabbit hop out onto the dirt road they have been walking down, and hell, when one does, they're stuck there, staring at the stupid rabbit forever, until, of course, Lennie has to try to creep up on it. The damn rabbit stays all hunkered down till the last minute, just when Lennie's hopes are high, and then it scampers off, and George has to cheer Lennie up by telling him the story about them getting their own farm. And right now the big hunk has got a dead mouse in his pocket, which George knew about but was letting pass, just to keep him walking, but no way in hell is Lennie going to sleep with a dead mouse in his pocket. George tells him to take the goddamn mouse out of his pocket, and Lennie's moaning and begging start all over again. When George tells the farm story this time, he gets excited himself. Maybe it will really happen this time, maybe they can make some money at this job and put a deposit down on that farm he heard about. When George lays his head down to sleep, he imagines himself waking up in his own bed, walking out his own door, a cup of coffee in his hands, thinking about the work that needs to be done, his own boss. It's a nice dream.

Then the scene is over, and they pack up their stuff. No one speaks. No one wants to break the spell. They walk into the bunkhouse, all empty—the rest of the ranch hands are off in the field. A chill runs through Lars, first because it's all so real, and then because he's George, and George is worried. They are back again among men, and the hopes he had last night hitch in his throat. Something always goes wrong. He warns Lennie again not to say a goddamn word, let him do the talking. But don't you know it, as soon as this old guy Candy walks in, Lennie goes and opens up his big mouth. Jesus Christ, the guy can't remember nothing. And sure enough, there's a woman here. She walks in smelling of perfume, and George can see Lennie's eyes get all big. Damn it. Just let that woman stay away from them. Let them earn a little cash, and they'll be out of here in a few months.

The rest of the play moves forward easily. Lars remembers something Will said, and he builds a house of cards during the card scene, the house being the farm he dreams of. At the end of the scene, he scatters the cards and they fall to the dirt floor. He wonders if someone in the audience will notice that, the subtle meaning in a small action. He has to believe they will.

Everyone goes down to the creek for the last scene, silently finding places by trees where they won't be so obvious. When

George kills Lennie, the air is as still as a held breath. Lennie
lies on the ground, face against the dirt. From up on the rise,
Lars hears Melinda begin to cry.

Ben tries to sit up. His face is pale. Sweat trickles down his
forehead. "I feel shot," Ben says. "Damn if I don't feel shot."
Lars reaches out and helps him up. Above them on the ridge,
the trees applaud.

The rehearsal's over, but some of George stays in Lars, as if
he has soaked too long in a warm lake. Lars is happy to have
George linger on. Better George than many of the other characters Lars has played. George is a good man who has worked
hard, made hard decisions, and followed through with his
choices. He'd like to think that maybe George has stayed with
him because he has always been there; that by finding George,
Lars has found Lars. A decent man, not loud or pushy, but one
of the guys. Someone with a dream, someone he can be proud
to be. Lars stands and bows. The audience on the ridge stands,
still applauding. A bluejay shrieks. The breeze picks up and
whispers bravo through the boughs, and a pinecone falls by
Lars's feet. He picks it up and holds it in his hand, as happy
with it as if it were an Oscar.

It was a great rehearsal. It's only one-thirty, and even Lars
feels full of acting.

The other actors, Will, and his family come down to the
creek.

"You were acting naked," Melinda says, the excitement raw
in her voice. "My heart aches."

"Hey, lady," Ben says, "aren't you dead?"

"I am so alive it hurts," Melinda says, and she kisses Ben,
then kisses Lars.

"How about lunch now?" Jimmy McGovern says. On cue,
his stomach growls. The actors laugh. Together, almost, they
walk back to the house.

Lars notices that Ben and Myra trail a short distance behind. He also sees Beth turn and look back at her mother and
Ben. If Jimmy goes fishing today, Lars will ask to go along with
him.

Mac watched the end of the play. He knew what was going to
happen since he saw it before: the big guy got killed, and the
dog, and the girl. One death would have been enough for him.
And not the dog, for sure. After he saw this play back in Pittsburgh, he didn't want to see plays anymore and had told his
mom. She promised him that in the next one, something about
flowers, no one would die, but then some girl skinned a cat
and brought the skeleton onstage to show everyone, and he
wouldn't go to the next play, no matter what his mom promised.

He had watched the end of this play again, hoping that
maybe it would end good this time, since his father kept talking
about making this play better. So why not let the big guy get
away in the end? He might mention that idea to his dad tonight. Maybe he just hadn't thought about it yet. Maybe his
dad would be real proud of him to think of it, when he's already asked everyone else for ideas and nobody thought about
making the end not so sad. Mac is pretty sure if he ever becomes an actor, which he doubts 'cause he doesn't want to talk
that loud, but if he did, he'd only want to play the good guys.
He's not too sure who the good guys are in this play. Maybe the
big guy, but he killed a puppy, and a girl, so he can't be all that
good. Mac is glad it's over now and time for lunch.

On the way back to the house, Mac wonders if his dad
wouldn't mind if he became a construction worker, or maybe
a fireman. He could tell his dad the costumes were pretty
good.

While Mac eats his sandwich, Nate asks him all kinds of questions, like what sports he likes and who his friends are. Mac tells Nate about his friend Stephen Nickelson, imagining how he will tell Stephen about Nate Johnson. He will have to tell Stephen how cool Nate is before he mentions that Nate is an old black man, 'cause Stephen wouldn't listen the right way if he told that part first.

There's very little food, so lunch is a hodgepodge of leftovers laid across the table like an absurdist's painting. Three cold hamburgers. A sliced green pepper next to a container of plain yogurt. A bag of cheese corn found in the back of Ben's car. A box of Froot Loops. Ritz crackers. A bowl of hash browns from three days ago. A large bowl of heavy-syrup cling peaches. Green olives. Peanut butter and jelly, and seven slices of white bread. Oatmeal raisin cookies. Bruised apples. An orange. A quickly made pot of Campbell's vegetable soup (two cans with a bit more water than the directions called for). A large bowl of baked beans swimming in ketchup. A variety of beers, half a pitcher of lemonade, a large can of V8. (No one knows how old this last is, or remembers buying it.) A hot dog.

Nothing is left uneaten.

"Someone needs to go to the grocery store," Will says, looking around the table as if casting his next lead.

"I'll go," Frank Tucker says. "I'd like to get the newspaper."

"In that case, I'm going too," Jimmy McGovern says. "Someone will need to get real food."

"Like more baked beans, McGovern?" Frank says. "Please spare us."

"Hey, Tucker, eat this," Jimmy says, giving him the finger.

"I'll come too," Lars says quickly. "You two will need a referee." This is followed by suggestions for a number of different food items. Beer is mentioned several times. Everything gets written down on a napkin.

"And what will we be using for cash?" Frank asks.

Silence.

"There may be a check in the mail today," Will says. "It should be here by now. I'll go look."

Beth jumps up. "No, Dad, I'll go." She takes off running down the lane. When she comes back, she's holding a small brown box.

"No check, Dad. Just my brush Deb mailed me." She runs into the house.

"I'll get the tab on this one, Will. But you'll owe me," Frank says, wagging his finger at Will.

"Thank you, Frank," Will says, not very graciously.

Lars, Jimmy, and Frank make their exit and drive off.

In the bathroom, Beth opens the brown box and finds her brush, underwear, and a box of Jujubes. Carefully she pours the contents of the Jujubes box onto a white towel that she has laid on the floor. Eating one green Jujube, she puts the rest back into the box, leaving the yellow Valium just as they fell. She counts them. Ten. She almost picks one up to place in her mouth; she can feel the pull of the White Rabbit calling her. No. These are for a purpose. She has to make some decisions.

Can she do this? Should she? She's suddenly glad that Deb didn't get the acid. She would never really have the nerve to spike her mom's drink with acid. It's kind of scary, what she's just thinking about doing with the Valium. She's all tingly and nervous, and her heart is beating fast. It's exciting, and kind of powerful. And this way she can get back at her mom for doing whatever she's doing with Ben Walton, and get Greg Henry a little loose . . . And really, Valium's just going to make them tired or silly. No one's going to really know it was her.

Okay, she's convinced herself. Now to get on with it. Beth sets three pills aside and labels them "Mom" in her head.

Next, Beth wants to get Greg Henry relaxed enough to go into the woods with her. She puts two aside for him. Finally, she needs to knock Norton out. Norton's so stuck on playing nurse, she won't be able to get Greg into the woods alone without getting rid of Norton. Four go in his pile. Which leaves one. She picks it up, sticks it into her mouth, and drinks it down with some water from the faucet. She really needs to calm her nerves. She's pretty shaky right now.

Now, how to get the pills into these people? And when? Her dad's given everyone the rest of the afternoon off. It'll have to be now. She'd never dare to do this during a rehearsal.

Greg will be easy. He's been taking pills for days now. She can just hand them to him and say "Here," and he'll down them. Norton will be trickier. Especially since there's no food in the house to slip them into. She will have to grind them up and pour them into his drink. She could do the same for her mother, but her mother doesn't drink much between meals—except, it seems, when she goes off into the woods. Then Beth remembers seeing an oatmeal raisin cookie on the ground under the picnic table. If Shakes hasn't eaten it . . .

Beth sticks the Jujubes into the cupboard and pockets the Valium. As she leaves the bathroom, Nate Johnson's standing outside, waiting. "Oh, sorry," she says.

"Nothing to be sorry about," he replies, then slips into the bathroom and closes the door. A moment of panic grips Beth, and she reaches into her pocket and pulls out the yellow pills, counting them. Nine? Oh, right, she took one. Okay. Now she's ready.

Outside, under the table, there's no cookie. Not even crumbs. Damn that dog, Beth thinks. Now what? She goes inside the house and opens the fridge. There's nothing but jars of jelly, some butter, and ketchup.

Mac walks into the kitchen. He's chewing something.

"What are *you* eating?" Beth says.

"Taffy," Mac says, stepping back like she might take it right out of his mouth.

"Where did you find taffy?"

Mac takes another step back. "In the car."

She should have thought about looking in the car. "Great!" There are about a dozen pieces in an old plastic bag from God knows when. She takes them out of the bag and sticks them into her other pocket. Her shorts are tight, and it looks like she's got some funky growth on her hip. Back inside the house, she finds a spoon, a bowl, and some tin foil. Ben walks into the kitchen.

"Hey, Beth, what's happening?"

Beth holds the stuff behind her back. "Nothing much." She backs up toward the living room. "Just need to go upstairs," she says. "Bye." She walks backward until he's out of sight, then turns and runs up the stairs. The bathroom door is shut.

"Anyone in there?" Beth says.

"I am." It's Nate's voice. *He's* still in there?

"Are you going to take a shower?" Beth says.

"I was considering doing just that," Nate says through the door. "Any problem?"

"Ahh, no, that's okay."

Beth looks at her room. The door's open and Greg's not there, but he could come upstairs at any moment to lie down. Norton's door is closed, but she knows he's not in there because she just saw him in the backyard setting up two lawn chairs. But he could come back up, too, and how would she explain being in his room? Maybe her parents' room? The door is shut. She knocks.

"Yes?" It's Melinda's voice. Damn.

"Never mind," Beth says.

"Beth?" Melinda says. "Is that you? Come in. I want to show you something."

Shit. "Okay." She has to be nice to Melinda now, because of the camera.

"Hey, Beth," Melinda says.

Beth stops, the door half open, the doorknob tight in her hand. Melinda's sitting on the bed, her dress pulled up around her waist. She's not wearing underwear and her legs are spread partway open. A bush of curly brown pubic hair is right there, between her legs, like an animal taking a nap. In the split-second that Beth looks at the apparition before she lowers her eyes, she's sure that Melinda has more pubic hair than anyone in the world.

"Come here, Beth," Melinda says. "Sit down."

"Ahhh, thanks, but I better go," Beth says to the carpet.

"No, really, it's important, and I don't think your mom's going to teach you this. They *should* teach it in junior high, but I don't think we'll break that barrier for a while. Sit down."

Beth inches over to the bed, hoping someone will call her name before she gets there. No such luck. She sits as far away from Melinda as possible, right on her mom's pillow. Melinda produces a white plastic case and opens it up.

"This is a diaphragm."

Beth thinks she will die. The only reason she doesn't is because the Valium must be coming on. Beth sticks her hand into her pocket and pinches a pill between her fingers, thinking, *I might need another one.* She looks at Melinda but not right at her.

"Oh, yeah?" Beth says, trying to sound casual, like she's

sat on dozens of beds with half-naked ladies showing her diaphragms.

"I was just about to put it in. Let me explain how it works." Out of a little homemade denim bag, Melinda pulls a white tube. Beth doesn't look close enough to see what the tube says. She's trying pretty hard to blur her vision. "You have to spread the spermicide around the edge of the cup, and put some all over the inside. You don't want to miss any spots. Sperms are tricky little guys. They're determined to reproduce." Melinda squirts the goo into the diaphragm, which is a flesh-colored rubber-cup thing, then uses a finger to rub it all around. Beth knows her mouth is hanging open and shuts it.

"It folds up. See?" Melinda bends the diaphragm, and it kind of snaps closed. "This way you can fit it in, and when you get it in the right place, it opens up and covers your cervix. That's the thing inside you that feels like the end of your nose. You should feel for it first, so you know where it is."

Beth must have made some kind of noise, because Melinda stops talking for a second and looks right at Beth and nods. "I know. It sounds pretty strange, but you mustn't be afraid of your body. There are IUDs and the Pill, but personally I think they're too invasive. The diaphragm's not hard to use. It just takes some practice, which is why you should try it before you need it. Condoms break. A condom and a diaphragm are best. I carry condoms too. You can't count on a guy. Would you like to see how I insert it?"

Beth stands. "No thanks." She inches back to the door, which is still open. If Nate Johnson comes out of the bathroom and looks in here, Beth will die, Valium or no Valium.

"Well, I wanted to offer, you know. You're getting to that age. Just keep your mind open, Beth. Don't make judgments. And remember, you're responsible for your actions. A baby is a wonderful gift, if you're ready, but until then, protect yourself."

"Okay. Thanks, Melinda. Bye. Really, thanks, but I gotta go now. Bye." Beth steps out of her mom's room and closes the door. She makes sure it clicks shut. If she had a key, she'd lock it.

The bathroom door is still shut. The shower is running. She has to grind up these pills. She can't very well do it on the kitchen table. She'll have to chance Norton's room. She knocks on his door. No answer. She opens it a crack. The cat dashes out, brushing by Beth's leg. Beth gasps. Her own house is like the funhouse at the fair. God knows what she'll find behind the next door. She peeks into Norton's room. No one. Quickly she closes the door behind her, sitting on the floor with her back against the door. She spreads out the tin foil, puts the four Valiums for Norton in the bowl, and presses against them with the back of the spoon. They crumble into pieces, then into powder. With the spoon she scrapes the yellow powder onto the tin foil, then folds it so she can easily open it. There's some residue on the bowl, so she wipes it off with her finger and licks her finger clean. It tastes terrible. Beth hopes Norton is drinking something besides water. Vodka would be nice.

On the stairs, Beth hears Ben and her mom talking in the kitchen, which reminds Beth that she forgot to put the Valium in the taffy. She tiptoes down the steps, so she can listen. Her mother says something about the woods. Beth steps on a squeaky step, and the voices stop. The kitchen door opens and shuts. By the time Beth gets to the kitchen, they're gone.

She puts the bowl and spoon in the sink, then walks out the door and around to the back of the house. Norton and Greg are in the lawn chairs. On a crate between them are two open beer cans. Greg's eyes are shut.

"Shhh!" Norton says as Beth gets closer. "Greg's sleeping."

"Oh, okay," Beth whispers. "But by mistake I let your cat

out of your room when I went to get Mac something. She's in the living room, I think."

"Oh," Norton whispers. "I guess that's all right. Don't worry about it."

"But she might get outside," Beth says a little more loudly.

Norton frowns at her. "Well, she was all right last night. Came right up to the door and meowed to get back in."

"Oh, okay," Beth says with a shrug, then, "You know, the McCrearys' cat got carried away by an owl just last summer. Mrs. McCreary said she could hear her cat howling from two hundred feet up, until the owl broke its neck."

Norton gets up out of the lawn chair. "I better get Betsy back in the room. Thank you." He goes into the house.

Beth looks over at Greg. He's asleep with his mouth hanging open. She unfolds the tin foil, pouring the powder into Norton's beer. Some sticks to the foil. She licks it off. Picking up the beer, Beth swivels it around to mix it up. It's about half full. She takes a small sip to see how it tastes. Awful, like beer.

Looking at Greg, Beth thinks getting him relaxed might not be a problem. Just waking him up might be the difficult part. She'll save his two Valiums for an emergency.

Now for her mom. Beth goes back into the house to get a sharp knife to split open the taffy, then goes out behind the barn. Voices come from inside—her father, Chip, and Victor Peters—but she can't make out the words. She sits down on the ground, takes out a piece of pink taffy, carefully peels open the wrapper, sticks the knife in the taffy, takes one Valium out of her pocket and shoves it into the slit, then squeezes it shut. You can hardly tell. She repeats this with two more pieces of taffy, both pink, and lays them down on the ground when she's done. Then she pulls all the taffy out of her pocket and, finding only one more pink piece, eats it. She doesn't know how she's going to get her mom to eat three pieces of pink taffy, but she'll figure that out later. She's kind of tired right now. She'll rest a few minutes, then go find her mother. By then, Norton will be asleep, and she'll wake Greg Henry. She hopes he has a condom. Maybe she should have asked Melinda for one.

Will asks Chip and Victor for their opinion about his idea of inviting the rest of the actors to come up here for the last two weeks before the season starts, to do theatre games and rehearse some one-acts. Chip says it sounds good. Victor doesn't. Will's already imagined it happening and finds it hard to let go of the idea. He decides to ask Myra and get the ball rolling. He heads for the house.

Ben's in the kitchen.

"Hey, Ben," Will says. "Where's Myra?" As soon as he says this, it bothers him. Why would Ben know?

"She said she was going for a walk."

"Jesus Christ, you're kidding!" A vein begins to throb in his left temple.

"No. She left maybe ten minutes ago. Everything all right?"

"Yes, yes. Fine." What the hell. Why even *ask* Myra, if she's not going to be around anyway? "I'm going to make some phone calls."

"Need me for anything, Will?"

"No. I'm fine." He walks out of the kitchen and into the living room, but before he picks up the phone, he hesitates. He has this speech all worked out, to convince Myra. He needs to say it, have it agreed to. He turns back to Ben. "Where's Melinda?"

"Upstairs, I think," Ben says. "You sure you don't need me for something?"

"Yes, I'm sure, Ben." He doesn't want Ben's view on this one. Some part of Will tells him Ben might disagree. That same part tells him Ben hasn't been a team player recently, or a good friend. That part of him says all this so quietly, Will can ignore it for now. He scratches his ear where a bug must have bit him and goes upstairs.

Ben gives himself one more chance to back out but fails. He tried. Will doesn't need him. If Will had said, *Yes, help me on something here, Ben*, Ben might have stayed in the house. Then again, that too is debatable.

Ben goes out the kitchen door and walks around the front of the house, past the fallen tree and across the lawn, the shortest distance to the woods. It's not the same direction Myra went, but he knows where she will be, and in the cover of the trees, he follows the curve of the field and heads toward the open woods on the hill. She took a blanket. He carries nothing but doubts overshadowed by desire. With each step he tosses his worries out behind him like pebbles in his pocket until they're mostly gone. What's left is a whisper, a *Sorry, Will*.

Beth opens her eyes. Her nap has taken only a few minutes, but she feels better. As she walks around the side of the barn, ready to find her mom and offer her the taffy, she sees Ben Walton by the edge of the woods. He looks back at the house—obviously to see if anyone has noticed him. Quickly she steps behind the barn, before he sees her. When she peeks around the corner, he's just disappearing into the woods. As soon as he is out of sight, Beth runs to the house. She's got a better idea.

Myra tries to sing as she walks through the woods, but her voice breaks. She's singing from her throat; the rest of her body, lower down, is too nervous to draw a deep breath.

She made love in the woods once before, in a national park, near the top of a mountain, in a flat area that was hidden from fellow hikers by large jutting rocks. It had been warm and sunny, and she believed she was in love. She told him so. He didn't say anything. Nothing at all. The rest of the camping trip was very awkward. Only one man had told her he loved her. Will. He said it full of drama and meaning. (He was currently playing Romeo, and that may have had something to do with his exquisite presentation.) She had said it back, *I love you too.* Neither of them said it often after that. He did, though, say *I love you* more during the time he had his affair than anytime before or since.

At the top of the ridge, Myra finds the place where she first kissed Ben. She spreads out the blanket and sits down, facing the direction he will come from, hoping he will say he loves her, and so afraid that he might.

For days, Norton has hemmed and hawed, back and forth, from fantasy to reality, from impossible to possible, his whole body reaching out, only to be called back in with a mental *whoa!* firm enough to stop a bolting team of horses. But now, after placing Betsy back in his room and drinking a second beer, Norton gives up his internal battle. So what if he makes a move and gets brushed off? No one will know. Greg Henry is a good person, not one that would be cruel enough to talk about it. It's the sweet Greg that attracts Norton, the happy-go-lucky smile, the good-natured brown eyes. So if Greg says no thanks, it won't be the end of the world. Norton will still be an actor, and alone, and Greg Henry will move on and forget him, having brushed off many other men in his day. (Hopefully the boy is not completely indiscriminate.)

Norton just can't seem to find the energy to worry about being turned down. All Norton knows is, the moment has come.

He grins. A week on this farm has changed him. He's very calm. Actually, he could sit here all day, not even reading a book, just watching the grass in the field sway in the breeze. Is there a breeze? He looks at Greg to ask him, but then remembers Greg is asleep. But then, like fate, Greg Henry opens his eyes.

"Hey, Norton, what you looking at?"

"You." It is the slowest word Norton has ever said. He watches as it slips out of his mouth and hangs in the air to be heard by Greg, to be reheard by Norton, to be pondered in all its implication. Greg takes it more simply than it was meant.

"Well, I'm quite a sight, I guess. I never knew skin could turn green. I feel like one of those lizards that change color. What are they?"

"Chameleons." Greg answers his own question just as Norton says the word. They grin at each other. "Jinx!" Greg says.

"Excuse me?" Norton says.

"We said the same word at the same time! I called 'Jinx' first. You can't talk till someone says your name three times."

Norton is unsure of what to do. He thinks he should laugh it off, but there is something exciting about Greg telling him not to speak. He looks right at Greg, trying to say something with his eyes, like *Let me touch you.* Greg laughs.

"Hey, Norton, you look like a baby bear about to cry. Don't worry. Norton, Norton, Norton. There now, I've saved you from being mute the rest of your life. You owe me." Greg Henry grins. Norton feels his legs go weak.

"I'd like to clean those sutures," Norton says. "Bugs could have been crawling on your wound while you slept. The gnats are bad in this heat. Let's go upstairs."

"Okay, Boss," Greg says.

When Norton stands, he finds his legs *are* indeed weak, and he wobbles.

"Hey, bud," Greg says. "Steady. Guess you melted in the sun."

Norton nods, accepting Greg's hand on his arm to steady him. The touch of Greg's hand makes Norton's legs feel even weaker. He finds it strange that just two beers have affected him like this, and he's suddenly afraid that he's not well, but that fear goes away like rain off a duck. Usually he has to consider all the alternatives before dismissing a possible illness, but this time it just disappears into some empty void. Norton tests this new ability by trying for a moment to work up some worry about what he's about to do, and that, too, just slips away, unformed, like a half-realized thought. Greg lets go of Norton's arm, and they both enter the house.

"I'll need some warm water," Norton says. He reaches for a bowl and turns on the tap. They wait. There is no warm water. Nate Johnson walks into the kitchen rubbing his head with a towel.

"I think I used up the hot water, Norton, if that's what you're trying for."

Norton can't work up any indignation and just stands there looking at Nate.

"We'll heat some on the stove," Greg says. "No problem."

Nate leaves the kitchen, and Norton stands at the sink staring at the pot in his hand. "Here," Greg says, nudging Norton over and filling the pot with water. "This'll do it." Norton imagines kissing Greg's cheek, working his way to his lips, but the excitement of fifteen minutes ago seems diminished. He wonders if he's in shock, if his decision to pursue this desire has caused some part of his brain to shut down. Is that the only way he can make love to Greg, by closing off his emotions? He's sure that the last time he had sex—although that was a long time ago—he felt passion, excitement, fear, love, and hurt, and so maybe it is the water as Melinda insists, or pesticides on fruit, or . . . The entire thought vanishes, and Norton's mind is left with a space filled with the word *what?* Greg looks at him.

"What are you looking at, Greg?" Norton says, a smile spreading across his face.

"You," Greg says.

They both laugh. Greg pours the hot water into the bowl and carries it upstairs. Norton follows, holding on to the banister. They go into Greg's room. Norton closes the door behind him.

In the barn, Chip and Victor Peters talk about Will's idea. It's a conversation to fill time. Chip is waiting for Melinda, for something special she had planned. Victor and Chip have already said everything twice, they're just finding new ways to say it, like rewriting a line until it reads well.

"We could use the extra stimulus of the other actors," Chip offers, thinking this sounds worse than the way he phrased it last time. Hell, where is Melinda? She's been in the house at least an hour. Is she taking a shower? "I mean, that last rehearsal was so great, we should give the other actors a chance, or they'll resent us." Shit, his first try, "Will's idea is pretty good," was better than all this mumbo jumbo. Chip's about to go into the house to look for Melinda when Nate Johnson walks into the barn carrying a towel, obviously just out of the shower. Mac follows him, carrying a board game. Checkers.

"You were in the shower!" Chip says.

"Yes sir, Mr. Stark. I'm hoping that was all right with you," Nate says, bobbing his head.

Chip realizes he asked his question with a bit of an attitude. "I didn't mean it that way, Nate, so cut out the act. I thought Melinda was in the shower."

"Well, it was only me in there all by myself, I can tell you that for sure. I'm old, but I would have noticed a naked lady."

"Well, what's she doing?" Chip says, standing up.

Victor Peters chuckles. "I can't tell you the specifics, Chip, but let me tell you two things. One, you don't want to interrupt her, and two, I imagine it will be worth the wait. Sit down and relax. Give the woman some time to fuss."

Chip's not so sure Melinda's the type to fuss, but what the hell; if she is, it could be fun. "Guess I'll wait a little longer then." He sits back down on the bunk.

"Mac and I are going to play some checkers," Nate says, placing the game on the heavy wooden table. "I'll let you play him first, Chip, take your mind off your wait. I'll play the winner."

"But I thought I was going to play with you, Nate," Mac says.

"Oh, you will, Mac. You're just going to win this game first."

"Oh, yeah?" Chip says.

"I'm betting on it," Nate says.

"How much?" Chip says.

"Two bucks."

Chip sticks out his hand, and they shake.

"You're betting money on me?" Mac asks.

"Yes, sir," Nate replies. "It'll be like taking candy from a baby."

Victor Peters reaches into his back pocket. "I'm putting two bucks on Mac too."

"Well, I'll be damned," Chip says. "You're on."

Mac's face breaks out into a big smile. "You're both betting money on me?"

"We are," Victor says.

Chip carries a chair over to the table. "You guys are going to lose two bucks each," Chip says, getting into the game of playing the game, knowing full well he won't win, even if he can. "Okay, kid, show me your stuff." They set up the checkers. Chip looks at the barn door. *Give me ten minutes for this game, then you better walk in that door.*

Two games later, Chip is down twelve bucks and actually trying to win. Melinda is still in the house.

"You play poker too?" Chip asks, just trying to ease the tension that has spread from his groin to his fingers.

"Would you teach me?" Mac asks, his eyes big.

"Oh, jeez—I didn't really mean . . . I can't play you for money, Mac. Your dad would kill me."

"Pebbles!" Mac says. "We could play for pebbles! Please? I'll get a bunch of pebbles, okay?"

Mac's looking up at Chip with those large little-boy eyes. "Well, I guess—"

"Great!" Mac jumps up and grabs a tin can off the floor that has a few cigarette butts in it, then dumps the butts into a pail over by Ben's bunk. The "no smoking in the barn" rule lasted only one night. "I'll get the pebbles and rinse them off. How many do we need?"

"Oh, a whole lot, kid. A can full." Maybe by the time he has gotten all those pebbles, something else will have come up—like Melinda walking through that barn doorway wearing red lipstick. "Fill it up, pardner, and make sure they're clean, okay?"

"Sure!" Mac says, running out.

Shakes, who has been sleeping under the table, stands, shudders once, then wanders out. From where Chip sits, he can see Shakes follow Mac down the lane. Just like Dorothy and Toto, Chip thinks. Except Mac's a boy, and he's carrying an ashcan. Still, with a little imagination . . .

Through the sparse trees on the hill, Ben sees Myra waiting for him on a blanket. It's like a dream. There's definitely the feeling of not being in the real world anymore. He grins stupidly as he walks over and sits down next to her. The ground is bumpy. He can feel sticks and stones hidden under the blanket. She hasn't said a word, but they need to talk.

He wants to tell her she's beautiful, that he's crazy about her, but that's not what he really needs to say. "We should talk about this," he says. He wants her to go first. Break the spell, so he can laugh when she says it's all a mistake. Turn it into a joke.

"Really?" she says. They aren't touching, not a knee or a foot or a hand.

"I think we should. I don't want you to regret this. I don't want you to feel pressured."

Myra smiles and laughs, just a small breath of a laugh, but Ben can feel it on his arm. "Ben, I'm not dumb. I know how— nuts this is. But if anyone's pressuring anyone, I think it's me. I'm just as scared as you. But I want this. I want to make love to you." She touches his thigh. "Is that enough?"

Oh, that's enough. Nothing could stop him now. He runs one finger down her nose, then touches her lips. She kisses the tip of his finger and then takes his hand and presses it to her chest, above her breasts. She's wearing a blue tank top and white shorts. Her shoes are off. Her skin is warm. He leans over and kisses her. He feels her hand against the back of his head. They kiss for a very long time. *I won't hurt you, Myra*, he thinks. *I only want to love you.*

When they stop to breathe, Ben begins to lie down.

"Wait," she says. She pulls the tank top over her head and folds it loosely, placing it on the edge of the blanket. Then she stands up and removes her shorts and underwear, all the time looking him in the eye. He doesn't look at her body, just in her eyes. She smiles at him, then sits down. He undresses more awkwardly than she, conscious of the wrinkles on his legs, the way his stomach sags, how his penis, getting hard, bobs about like a fat metronome. He has on long pants, socks, and shoes. It takes some time, but finally he's back on the blanket, naked, lying on his side, facing Myra. She takes his hand again, pressing it to that same spot, not breast or crotch, just the flat area below her neck that offers him no padding between them. He can feel her bones, her warmth, the beat of her heart. He knows now that he loves her. That he is in grave danger.

"Why do I think you have already seen me naked?"

"I did. When you were singing. After the storm."

"That's why you want to make love to me? Because you saw me naked?"

"No. Because I heard you sing."

Myra's hand tightens around Ben's. She takes a breath he can feel through her chest. The bottom rims of her eyes fill with tears, but they don't run down her face. He kisses each eye, tasting salt. Gnats begin to cluster about them. He can feel them land on his back. Something crawls up his left foot. He shakes it off.

With one arm pinned underneath, he has only one hand to touch Myra, and she holds it, so he uses his mouth. He kisses her chin, her neck, her shoulder, her breast. His mouth finds her nipple and she moans. He takes his time, his tongue pulling her nipple into his mouth. From somewhere behind him, he hears a branch snap.

"Jesus Fucking Christ!" Beth shouts.

Myra twists out of their embrace and yells, "Oh, no!" Ben turns around. Beth stands ten yards away, pointing a camera at them.

Beth thought she might find her mother and Ben together, thought something was going on, but she had not imagined fully what she would find, not believed for one minute that her mother would really cheat on her father. When she saw two naked bodies through the trees, she actually told herself they must be some other couple, an odd coincidence. They could not be her mother and Ben.

But with each step forward, they had come into focus, until the vision was so sharp that it hurt her eyes, and she had to stop and close them. But even with her eyes closed, Beth could see the curve of her mother's waist, the way her hair fell loose across her shoulder, the sheer mass of Ben's back. Almost against her will—because what her heart wanted was to walk away and forget what she saw—she crept out from behind the tree, aimed the camera, and walked slowly forward. Just before pushing the button, she stepped on a branch, the snap shocking her. She yelled, "Jesus Fucking Christ," the words coming from her in a push of air like the shout before a karate kick, an attempt to shatter the picture she saw, shatter it into a million tiny pieces that would fall on the forest floor like glass breaking into sand, not a shard left to hurt anyone, not even memory.

But her shout doesn't make anything go away, and she pushes the button on the camera, so frightened that her hand grips the camera as if she and it are now one, as if she will constantly carry around with her the proof of her mother's infidelity. Her mother is shouting, and crying, and grabbing her clothes. Ben's trying to put on his underwear. Beth begins to cry. She paces around in a circle as if she is trapped in a space of three feet, not able to go forward or back.

"How could you!" Beth yells. "What's the matter with you? Do you know how disgusting you are? You're pathetic! You're a slut!"

"Beth," Myra says. "Wait. Listen, Beth. You don't understand. You're too young. I love you. Beth. Please." Some words are shouts. Some are said on an intake of breath so painful, Beth can hear the gasp of air through her mother's throat. Her mother's face is pale, her eyes pleading. For a moment Beth imagines they are mirror images. Except her mother is naked.

"You disgust me," Beth says, trying *not* to look at her mother and Ben. "You're a loser. A big loser." And suddenly Beth understands something. "Daddy won't let me act because he's afraid I'll embarrass him like you did! He's afraid I'm like you. A loser!"

Beth's mom stops moving. She stands there with tears running down her face. "Beth, this has nothing to do with you. Don't hate yourself. I'm so sorry. Please let me get dressed. Let's talk. Please."

"I'll never, ever forgive you. Do you know that? Do you?" Beth yells, the words tearing her throat. "But you know what I'm going to do? I'm going to go sleep with Greg Henry right now, and you better stay away. You better not ruin this. I have the picture. Right here." She waves the camera. "You just stay here in the woods and fuck Ben all you want, because I'm going to be doing the same thing. Like mother, like daughter. Except I can act. I can fucking act. Just you watch me!"

"Beth. Please don't. Don't do this to yourself!"

"Just stay away from me," Beth says. She turns and runs back toward the house. From behind, she hears her mother calling out her name.

The woods waver as if they have lost their solidity, as if the world has come unhinged and forgotten its shape. Nothing will ever be the same, Beth thinks. The forest will never be made of trees again; they will always hold the image of her mother and Ben. She will never be able to look at her mother and not see her naked and weeping. Beth runs faster. She wants Greg Henry. Now she needs him too.

Norton cleans Greg's face slowly, finding in the motions an art; taking care of Greg's face is not a quick fix but a step toward a well-healed wound. He imagines the doctor telling him he did a good job. He smiles, but his face isn't working right, and the smile just hangs there all dopey. He must look like an idiot, but he just doesn't care. Everything is fine. He giggles, then lays the gauze on the bedside table and kisses Greg on the forehead.

"Norton," Greg says. He doesn't say more. He doesn't pull away.

"I've never done this before," Norton says. "Well, once, a lifetime ago, and it was different. I didn't even know what I wanted then. I do now. Well, somewhat. I suspect these things are not so clear-cut. But I want to—"

"Norton," Greg says again, but Norton raises his hand and stops him from saying more.

"Please. Somehow, saying this is just as important as . . . doing it. Maybe not. I'm a little lost here, but please listen. You're so very sweet, and I've become more than fond of you. I want to make you happy, and make myself happy, and I'm not asking for anything more than that. I swear to you, I won't ask again. I might hope, but I'll never bother you. Please." Norton sits down on the bed next to Greg, not wanting to seem pushy, but his legs won't hold him up. His arms feel like they belong to someone else. His lips work. That he knows. He can still feel Greg's forehead on them. His lips feel like sponges, as if they could absorb smell and taste and touch and hold them indefinitely. He puts a hand on Greg's thigh. He wants Greg to know he's real.

"Norton, you're a nice guy, and I'm not saying I don't like you. I mean, maybe in the right place, the right time, I would feel better about this. But it's too weird, you know. I mean, there are people all around. You really want to . . . ?"

Norton has to understand what has been said. He hasn't been turned down. It's the situation. Maybe in a different place? "I understand. I guess it's just that suddenly I have found the temerity to ask, and I'm afraid if I don't do something right now, I might not ever. But I do understand, although I don't think anyone would walk in. Still, if you're agreeable to consider another time. Is it possible you might? But couldn't we maybe, just a bit—something?"

Greg shakes his head, but he's smiling. "You're making me blush, man. I can't resist a come-on like this. But Norton, I'll break your heart. I never said that to anyone before, and it goes to show I respect you, but I'm not in this for the long run. It's me. It's just the way I am. If you can handle that—"

"I don't have a clue. But I'm willing to find out. Thank you."

"Well." Greg shrugs.

They both just sit there.

"Could I kiss you?" Norton says. "Would you kiss me? I could get up then. I could go wash out this bowl."

"Sure, Norton," Greg says. "That's cool."

Norton leans over, expecting Greg to just sit there, to let himself be kissed, but then Greg moves toward Norton, putting a hand on his shoulder. They meet together, in the middle.

"Yes," Will says. "I'm not disagreeing with that, but Artaud's ideas wouldn't play in America. Artaud's Theatre of Cruelty, no matter how you define it, is simply too bizarre for people in this country to accept. No one would come as soon as word of mouth got out that it made people uncomfortable."

Will paces back and forth across the length of the bed.

Melinda sits on it cross-legged, leaning forward on her elbows. He knows he's waving his arms around like a madman in this small room—he's already hit the bureau on the upswing twice and can feel the bruise growing on the back of his hand—but he can't help it. Melinda's got him all worked up. She's too bright to dismiss. She's making him sweat.

"They came to see Godot," she says simply.

"But that's only a step in the direction you're talking about, Melinda. You're talking about performing plays without scripts, with shouts and cries and music and motion. It will confuse an audience. It will offend them."

"Artaud is not saying *no scripts*, but to move beyond our dependence on simple literary translations. Theatre is more than words, it *is* movement and cries and shouts, but we're afraid to go there, yet Greek theatre, which we admire, is closer to the New Theatre than what we have right now. The time for our dependence on realism is at an end. Why are you afraid?"

"People just won't get it."

"No, Will, your generation won't. Give us a chance."

Will's about to explain what there is about the classics that her generation should look to, when he hears a scream. Beth's scream.

"Oh, my, god! Oh, my, god!" There's a thud in the hallway outside the door, something heavy falling on the wood floor. Not a body, not that kind of thud. Will thinks of the prop gun. It would make exactly that sound. He opens the bedroom door to see Beth running down the steps and a camera on the hallway floor. As he runs after her, Will notices Greg and Norton standing in Beth's room. He has a pretty good idea what might have made Beth scream. He's angry at Greg and Norton, but just as annoyed at Beth for causing such a commotion. He shouts her name as he chases her. She's screaming obscenities.

Where has she learned such language? He'll ground her for a year, after he catches her.

Beth spots the keys to the car on the kitchen counter, lying right there, like a ticket. *She's got a ticket to ride*, she hears in her head, but turns it off. Songs are her mother's thing. Not hers. Beth will never sing another damn song in her life! She grabs the keys and keeps running. She can't believe it. Greg Henry and Norton Frye! She tries to tell herself maybe they were rehearsing some weird play, but even her confused mind isn't buying that. Bells go off in her head. Huge loud bells, badly tuned. She has to get away. She has to get away from here. "Damn them," she shouts. "Damn them!" With each shout she's spitting out the images of Greg and Norton, of her mother and Ben. It's a lot to get rid of. She would vomit, but it would hold her back. She tells herself she can vomit all she wants along the roadside somewhere. First, she has to get out of here.

Her father runs out of the house, yelling her name. Beth thinks she'll change her name, once she gets away. She can't stand the sound of it anymore. Greg Henry and Norton Frye stumble out of the house. Others emerge from the barn. The actors must have known about Greg and Norton. Everyone knew but her. They must have had a pretty good laugh watching her eye Greg. They must have talked about her in the barn at night. That poor, stupid girl. Beth opens the car door and yells, "Fuck all of you!" then jumps into the driver's seat and slams the door. She's causing a scene. The idea makes her laugh, a bark that sounds like it came from someone else. She's in a scene! Finally! *How am I doing, Daddy? Pretty damn good, huh?*

Beth has the foresight to lock the doors before doing anything else. By the time she has crawled back behind the wheel, her father is outside the car. The windows are already rolled up.

She's going to drive away and never see any of these people again. As her father bangs on the window, she starts the car.

Victor Peters is trying to say something through the window on the passenger side. Inanely, Beth waves to him, and steps on the gas. The car jerks and takes off, slaying pebbles under the tires. Glancing in the rearview mirror, Beth sees her father running behind the car, yelling at her. Beth turns away, driving as fast as she can down the lane that will lead her to someplace where love isn't as fucked up as it is here. It's hard to see clearly because her eyes are full of tears, but she can't stop to wipe them away. She blinks, then yells, "Oh, shit!" Shakes is sitting in the center of the lane, looking the other way. She swerves to the right, just in time to miss Shakes, but now she sees Mac, straight ahead of her, standing in the ditch. *What?* she thinks. *What is he doing there?* She yanks the steering wheel the other way. Much too hard. She can't see Shakes. She must have run right over him. The car goes off the left side of the drive as she hits the brakes. It nosedives into the ditch, and she smacks her head on the steering wheel. When the car comes to a stop, it's angled across the lane, the front tires stuck in the ditch and her father only a few steps from her window. He kicks the door. "Roll down that window. Roll down that goddamn window right now!"

Beth doesn't know what else to do, so she rolls it down. She's so scared that she's killed the dog, and damaged the car, that it takes a second to realize that now she can't get away, and all the people who thought she was stupid are standing in the lane watching her, thinking she *is* stupid *and* a really bad driver. She's not stupid. She just liked Greg Henry. And she wants to be an actress, and she doesn't want her mom to be screwing her dad's best friend. Or anyone! And she wants her dad to love her, and . . .

He reaches into the window and grabs her upper arm, squeezing it so hard she can't move. She wants to collapse, fold up, disappear. Her forehead hurts, but her father's grip on her arm hurts more.

He turns to Melinda, who's cradling Shakes in her arms. "Goddamn it! Is the dog dead?" he says. "Did she kill the dog?" Beth breathes through her mouth. She's too afraid to cry out. She closes her eyes against the pain.

"The dog is fine," Beth hears Melinda say. "Just fine."

"Well, thank God for small favors," Beth's father says. Then he pulls her arm, and her eyes open. "Get out of the car," he says. He steps back to allow her room to open the door, but not far enough. Maybe the door won't open, Beth thinks. But it does. She gets out and closes it gently behind her, like an apology.

"Jesus Christ, Beth," her father says, his face contorted, actually twisted with anger. "What the hell were you doing? You could have killed your brother, or the dog. What the hell were you thinking?"

That no one loves me, she thinks. "It's not my fault," she says.

"Who the hell's fault is it?" he yells.

He hates her. She can see it in his eyes. But he should love her. She's been loyal to him all along. She can prove it—and get herself out of trouble.

"It's Mom's fault! She was screwing Ben Walton in the woods! I took their picture. Just get the film developed if you don't believe me!" She wishes right away she hadn't said it, and her hand covers her mouth. She wants to tell him she didn't mean it, but she can't. She's shaking so badly, she can't speak. *What did I do?* she thinks. She doesn't want him to know. Her father looks at her as if she hit him.

This will change everything.

Will doesn't believe what he's heard. How could his daughter say such a thing? Then, just as something in his gut begins to answer, he sees Myra and Ben running across the yard, coming from the field, not the house, not from somewhere they could have been doing the dishes. Ben slows, stopping well behind all the actors, who have run down the lane but now stand about looking embarrassed by what they have witnessed. They all watch as Myra runs up to the car. Will thinks, *The actors are now the audience.* He's queasy. Everything is wrong.

"Are you hurt?" Myra asks Beth, reaching out to touch her cheek. Beth, whose forehead now has a pink lump the size of a walnut, jerks away from her mother's touch, and in that one motion, Will knows that Beth has told the truth.

There's movement now from the actors, who silently turn and walk away, each one separately, as if they are afraid of being too close to one another. Melinda carries Shakes. Nate speaks to Mac in a low tone, and with his arm around Will's son, he leads Mac away. They pass Ben, who just stands there, where he is, as if it doesn't matter where he goes now, as if there is nowhere he can go. Unable to help himself, Will realizes the blocking is spectacular. His stomach turns and he's afraid he will be sick, but then that feeling goes away and he feels nothing. His anger at Beth is all gone, and anger at Myra hasn't come. He has been other people in his life, characters that have been betrayed by their wives, and he has imagined their rage, their pain, but never this complete emptiness. He raises his hands which were lying limply at his side, and looks at them as if he has never seen them before. He can't shake the feeling that this is not really happening to him.

He looks up at Ben, who still stands there—it has been only a minute since Myra asked if Beth was hurt, although that's just

as impossible as everything else—and he catches Ben's eyes for
a brief moment before Ben looks back down at the ground. *It's
the last time I'll look in his eyes*, Will thinks, and it's a loss he
thinks he can't bear.

The reality he was searching for has struck him in the face
and left him blind.

Myra saw the accident. She saw the car swerve toward Mac,
then veer away and plow into the ditch. All this as she ran
across the field. She shouted, but there were other cries, and no
one heard her, except Ben.

As the car careened toward Mac, she imagined the impact,
felt her heart stop. Then she heard, in a split-second, the snap
of her daughter's neck. Myra is so relieved her children are not
hurt that she thinks everything is all right. But with relief comes
room to remember the rest: her love for Ben almost killed her
children.

Beth must have told Will what happened. Why else would
the actors walk away like that? Why else would Will not look
at her? Couldn't Beth have kept her mouth shut? It's an awful
thought, but she can't help it.

"What am I supposed to do?" Will asks, looking at the car.
"What am I supposed to do?"

Pretend it never happened, Myra thinks. She pretended he
didn't have an affair. Why can't he pretend she didn't?

Because the car is in the ditch, and everyone knows what
she has done.

"I don't know," she says.

"I can't talk to you right now, Myra," Will says. "You
might want to go somewhere."

"Where?"

"Away. Just away. I have to get the car out of the ditch. I

have to go back into the house and ask those people to help me. I can't look at you right now. Do you mind?"

Myra can't breathe from the hurt in her chest. "I'll go to our room" she says. "I'll wait for you." She won't leave this place. There are things she has to say. Nothing that she can think of right now, but she won't walk away from her family.

"All right," Will says. "Fine. But tell Ben to leave. Will you do that?" There is an absence of all feeling in his voice, and Myra knows exactly how badly she has hurt him. She knows him so well. He must know her too. Why didn't he see what was happening to her? Why didn't he stop her?

"Yes," she says. She's ready right now, after almost losing her son, and possibly her marriage, to forget Ben completely. But even as she thinks that, she can feel Ben's hand cup her breast. Bile runs up her throat like a live thing trying to escape. She wants to ask, once again, if Beth's okay, if she has been hurt by the accident, but she can't; she has lost that place in her daughter's life.

Ben knows Myra is walking toward him, even though he's still looking at the ground. He thinks he should stay and say something to Will, but he can't, and he can't walk away and not say something. So he waits. If he could move backward in time, that's what he'd do. Other than that, there are no choices he can see.

"He says you should leave," Myra says quietly, passing him.

"Okay," he agrees. He's relieved to know what to do, and to not have to face Will. Although he wants to defend himself. He wants Will to hit him. He wants Will to forgive him. And he still wants Myra.

Ben turns away and goes to the barn. Victor Peters is inside, with Chip and Melinda. They have been talking but stop when he comes in. They avoid looking his way. He is packed in a few minutes. His toothbrush and razor are in the house, but he won't go and get them. Myra will throw them away. Myra. How could he have done this to her? Give me another chance, he thinks. He wants to rewrite the whole week. He's ashamed even by that thought, because given the chance, he'd fall in love with her all over again. *I wouldn't let her know*, he tells himself. The thought doesn't give him the solace he had hoped for.

When he walks out of the barn, he realizes the station wagon is blocking the drive. He can't go back in the barn. He can't go in the house. Ben sits in his car and waits to leave.

He has failed terribly. Failed Will. Failed Myra. And himself. He will go home and pack up. He's going to move to New York City, where the disappointments are expected. He should be able to get some parts. He's a decent actor. Shit for a friend and a lover, but a good actor.

One minute he was bending over to wash off a pebble, and the next, everyone was screaming and Beth was driving the car right at him. He was pretty sure he was going to be dead, but the car turned away from him and ran over the dog and into the ditch. Nate came up and put his arm around Mac's shoulder, and Mac was real glad Nate was there, 'cause he had been pretty scared. Mac isn't exactly sure what happened, but he thinks his mom did something bad, even though it was Beth who messed up the car. His dad looks angry and sad. His mom just looks sad.

"Come on, kid," Nate says, turning Mac with a bit of pressure on his shoulder as they head up the lane.

"What happened, Mr. Johnson?" Mac asks. He doesn't call him Nate, mostly because he's worried about so much right now, it doesn't seem right. The way his mom and dad were looking at each other, it was like somebody had died.

"Not sure, Mac," Nate says. "But it's not our business. Not right now, and we ought to stay away, okay? Give them some time to figure it out themselves. Didn't you tell me about catching crayfish in the creek? I never even saw a crayfish in my life. Think you could show me one?"

"Well, I think so," Mac says.

"Good. Then let's go do that."

"Well, okay," Mac says. His chest moves in and out as he breathes, as if his lungs were taking in more air than they usually do, and his heart beats right there in his chest, hard and fluttery. It's like when he's looking for spiders and sure he's going to find one. The bad thing, though, is that what makes him feel this way now is thinking about his mom and dad.

They cross the backyard and head through the field to the creek. "How come you never saw a crayfish before?" Mac asks.

"Because no one ever showed me how to find one," Nate says. "But you will, right?"

"Sure. It's not too hard."

"That's easy for you to say. You can do a lot of things I can't."

Mac looks up to see if Nate is joking, but his face is soft and thoughtful, and Mac can tell he's not kidding.

"What did you do when you were a kid?"

"Oh, nothing much. I lived in an apartment in the city. Played marbles and stickball, that kind of stuff."

"I don't know how to play marbles," Mac says.

"I'll teach you sometime."

Mac can tell, just by the slow, careful way they're talking, that they are talking about marbles so they won't be talking about what just happened. Mac kind of wants to know what just happened, and he kind of doesn't.

They bend down to walk under the apple trees near the creek. "This is the place where they sleep under the rocks, Nate," Mac says, glad he remembered to call him Nate. They are both quiet for a minute, just listening to the sound of running water. There are different shades of green all around them, and some browns. The soft colors make it easier to breathe, and Mac can't feel his heart doing that fluttery thing anymore.

"I don't see any crayfish, Mac."

"They're hiding," Mac says.

"I used to do that too," Nate says, rubbing a hand through Mac's hair. "So let's find them."

Slowly, Mac moves a hand out over the water, holding it there so the crayfish will think it's just a shadow of a leaf. Then he reaches down quickly and flips over a piece of shale. A crayfish scuttles backward in a puff of muddy water.

Nate feels so bad for Will's family, it almost breaks his heart. He's glad he's here right now, that God put him in this place to be with Mac. It's a small gift of time for the both of them, and Nate closes his eyes and says thanks to God, grateful that between laughter and tears, love and sheer pain, there are moments of grace.

"You know," Mac says, "if you put your hand right there in the water behind that rock, it might work better than if I do it by myself. Okay?"

"Sounds good to me, Mac." Nate dips his hand in the water. It's very cool, and that surprises him, it being such a warm day. Here he is, fifty-three years old, and he's just put his hand in a creek for the first time. He wonders what else God might have in store for him.

Beth's legs just give out. They've been shaking the whole time, and as her mother walks up the lane and goes into the house, Beth collapses against the side of the car and slides to the ground. She almost killed her brother. She really almost killed him. She loves her brother. How could she have lived this long and not known that? She starts crying again, scared about what almost happened, and about what she has done. Will her dad leave them, because of what she said?

She wants to be little again. She wants her dad to protect her from everything bad. She wants to say, "Daddy, Greg was kissing Norton Frye," and for him to make everything better, like when he would kiss her cuts and scrapes. But it had all gone beyond that now.

"We'll have to get this car out of the ditch," her father says. He kicks the back tire. Then he smashes his hand onto the trunk. He doesn't say anything else.

Beth's arm hurts from where her father was squeezing it. Her eyes ache from crying. She wants to ask her dad if he'll take her mom back. She wants to know if they will still be a family. "Daddy?" she says.

"Don't say anything right now." He hits the car again with his fist, the sound flat and dull. "Goddamn it to hell!" Then after a minute he looks at her. "I'm sorry," he says. His eyes are all bloodshot, as if he has been crying, but she hasn't seen him shed a tear. She tries to smile, but her smile turns into something else.

"I'm sorry too," she says.

"We have to get the car out of the ditch." He pauses, breathing heavily. "Go get Chip and Melinda."

She thinks she can't, her legs won't support her, but they do. She's very shaky, and now she's got the hiccups. She's glad her father didn't tell her to get Greg Henry. She couldn't do that. She will never be able to face Greg again.

Before she goes, she says, "Daddy, I love you, I really do."

He looks at her and nods. She turns away and walks up the lane.

It takes a lot of rocking the car, and pushing and shoving, to get it out of the ditch. Beth steps on the accelerator as her father shouts, "Go, go on now! Hit it! Now!" She feels sick to her stomach, being behind the wheel. She takes her father's shouts personally. When it is finally back up on the drive, her dad tells her to get out of the car, he'll take it from here. He drives the car up the lane and parks it in front of the Theatre Parking sign. Then he pulls the sign out of the ground and tosses it as far as he can into the tall grassy field.

Beth wants to walk away, down the lane, but she needs her family now more than ever. Still, she can't go home. What could she do in her house? She doesn't even have a bedroom she can hide in.

Coming down the stairs carrying his suitcase and Betsy's cage, Norton sees Greg Henry in the living room.

"Let me carry that," Greg says, indicating Norton's bag. Norton is terrified he might cry and hands it over without a word. Outside, Will's car is back in its place, with tufts of grass and mud stuck in its front fender. Ben's car is gone. The only sound is that of Norton and Greg's footsteps on the pebbled lane, like a sad, soft-shoe dance. After putting Norton's bag in the backseat, Greg Henry says, "Don't worry. I won't tell anyone. No one knows." Norton gets into his car. He's terribly grateful for these kind words, but he's older than this boy. He knows that everyone in the company will know he kissed Greg before the week is out, although that news will be small fodder compared to the things that will be said about Myra and Ben. As mortified as he is about what they have done, he's shamefully relieved to be upstaged this time. Driving down the lane, not looking back at Greg or the house, Norton thinks of quitting The Mill Street Theatre. There's a lot of work to be found in dinner theatres across the country. He could travel. Write in his notebooks. Although he hasn't missed a day of writing in three years, he will not write one word about today. He will try hard to forget it, pretend it never happened.

Chip is confused. *Damn, things went to hell awful fast there.* He heard what Beth said, but he's having a hard time believing it. Ben and Myra? Shit. *Ben?* No way! But Ben drove off pretty damn fast, soon as they moved Will's car. Melinda went into the house after Ben left, and everyone seems to be packing up, even though no one said they should leave. Chip wonders if Melinda might like to go somewhere with him. He'll just wait for her to come out. She's kind of funky at times, but he likes her. And someone ought to find Jimmy and Frank and Lars. Tell them the whole thing just blew up. It shouldn't have to be Will or Myra.

Chip zips up his duffel bag, thinking about Beth. If he had been fooling around with her when all this happened, he sure wouldn't want to be the one to have to help her figure it all out. He's having enough trouble with that all by himself. How the hell could Myra go for a guy like Ben? It makes no sense. Ben is, well, big, and goofy. She never even looked in Chip's direction.

Shit, if this can happen to Will and Myra, what chance does *he* have of sticking with a girl? Maybe Chip had it right in the first place. Enjoy the ride as long as it lasts, 'cause it ain't going to last.

———

It takes Victor a little longer than the rest to pack up. He moves more slowly than usual because he's distressed by everything he's just seen. He wishes he could do something to help, but what? Helen would have gone right up there to Myra's room and said something that might start the healing process. She wouldn't be afraid. But he is. He's going to slink away like all the rest and feel awful about it for a long time.

On his way out of the barn, he sees Greg Henry drive off. Ben's long gone, and Norton's car isn't here anymore either. Chip's duffel bag is next to his car, where he stands smoking a cigarette, looking like a cowboy waiting for his horse. The absence of cars seems like a desertion, rats leaving a sinking ship, and Victor feels that sinking feeling right in his stomach. He has to do something, and he knows what it is. He puts his bags in his car and asks Chip if he saw where Beth went.

"I think she's behind the house, Victor. I saw her go back there after we moved the car."

"Thanks," Victor says.

Beth is there, curled up into herself, and crying. He sits down next to her and puts an arm around her shoulder. He can feel her whole body tense, but he doesn't take his arm away. Helen tells him not to.

"Beth," he says. He speaks her name softly and gently, but now she flinches. "Beth, I know this is all pretty awful, I'm not going to say it isn't, but your dad loves you, and your mom loves you. And they're going to need you."

Beth shakes her head back and forth. "They hate me now."

"No, they don't, Beth. They still love you. Believe me, they do."

She looks at him, eyes bloodshot and puffy. "I don't believe in love. How could my mom do that if she loved my dad? If she loved Ben, she would have left with him. She's staying here 'cause she's embarrassed, that's all. I thought I was in love, but I was just being stupid. And I won't be that stupid again."

"Love is real, Beth. I loved my wife. I loved her very much, and she loved me."

"Well, good for you," Beth says. Then, "I'm sorry, I didn't mean that." She puts her head into her hands and starts crying all over again.

Victor sits there, waiting for Helen to tell him what to say next, but she's silent. Behind the house is a field, blooming with tall grass and early wildflowers, fully recovered from the storm a few days ago. A breeze has just picked up, and everything seems to shimmer in the afternoon sunlight. Beyond the field are the trees, peaceful and quiet. What a beautiful place this is, Victor thinks. He wonders if Will and Myra will ever be able to love this place again, even if they learn to love each other. It's a shame how love can hurt you, he thinks, remembering too vividly Helen's funeral and the months that followed. He carries that pain with him always, even here, but it's been filtered by time and memory to become part and parcel of Helen herself, so it's important to him to remember it all the same. He wishes he could ease this girl's burden, but he suspects he can't. Still, he finds it helps *him* to sit here with his arm around Beth, even with nothing left to say. He closes his eyes. There's no hurry to go anywhere yet.

Melinda has to get her things from out of Myra's room, but Myra's in there. Standing outside the closed door, Melinda thinks that normally she would side with the woman, but she can't this time; she just can't imagine how anyone could do this to Will. That poor man. To be betrayed like this, in front of everyone. Myra needs time to search her soul. That is something best done alone.

But Melinda's uncomfortable with just walking away from a woman in pain. Maybe she should talk to her—maybe there are thoughts Melinda can share with Myra that will help her understand what has happened. Hesitating, she lifts her hand to the door and knocks softly.

"Yes?"

"It's me, Melinda," she answers. "Would you like me to come in, to talk?"

"No," Myra says. Quickly. Without much thought, Melinda thinks. Well, she tried. She'll just leave her things here; they can be replaced. Her money and driver's license are in the van. The diaphragm is in her. There's probably a thrift shop not far away. She'll leave Myra a note. Tell her she'll see her when she comes back for the summer season.

But what will happen to the summer season? What will happen to *Of Mice and Men*? If Myra has ruined their art . . . It's a thought Melinda can't complete, because anger almost invades her heart, and she is quick to stop it from blossoming. She shakes her head at her own folly. She must wish everyone peace, and leave. She'll send them good vibes from wherever she goes. They'll need them.

Outside, Chip waits by his car. "Where's your stuff?" he says. "I thought you were going to get your stuff?"

"What an awful sentiment," Melinda says. "*Your stuff*. Besides, I have everything I need right here." She grins as he looks around for her luggage, and then his blue eyes twinkle.

"I get it," he says. "Cool. But maybe you might want something?"

She tilts her head, curious. "Like what?"

"Me."

"You?"

"Well, let's just say, a friend. Tell you the truth, I could use one."

"Me too," she says. "So where to?"

"Well, I was thinking we should drive into town. Find Jimmy and Frank and Lars. Tell them what happened. Then we go get a cabin by the lake."

She thinks about that. Some human warmth would be very nice. "All right. But shouldn't we say something to Will?"

Chip shrugs, then stubs out his cigarette on the sole of his boot. "The man is pretty tense. Tell you the truth, I think we should just go."

"Where is he anyway?"

"In the barn. No one's in there but him. Gives me the shudders."

Melinda can't just leave Will behind like the things she has left in the bedroom. He has been a father to her, and her muse. "Hold on, Chip," she says. "I'll be right back."

The barn is dusky, and it takes a minute for her eyes to adjust. Will sits on a bunk, his knees bent, his head in his hands. All around are the props from *Of Mice and Men*. The crates and playing cards, the ropes and tackle, lanterns and old metal beds. His thin, hunched-over body fits into this set so well, Melinda feels as if she's watching the curtain open on a play. An old man sits alone in a bunkhouse. Something has happened. Who is he? Why is he alone? It's a drama, not a comedy. You can tell by the lighting and the dusty set, the silence. Will has found the only place he can be comfortable now. In the stuff of his dreams. She hopes he will find the dream again. That it's not too badly broken.

"Good-bye, Will. You're in my heart," she says, just loudly enough to be heard. He looks up at her, startled, then so sad and lost she almost runs over to embrace him, to hold him in her arms. She's surprised that she doesn't, that her body seems to know that this instinct is false, that she can't be a part of what Will needs to find himself. He must understand this too because he nods once to her and lowers his head back into his hands, closing his eyes. She blows him a kiss, even though he can't see her anymore, and then she turns and leaves.

Outside, the sky is so blue.

Myra listens from her bedroom. Four cars have driven off. Each time, as the engines come to life, she feels it in her stomach: a turning over, a tearing away, each leaving a condemnation, an ending, a door closing. She knows the actors are as embarrassed as she, and that makes it worse. She has been a wife and a hostess for too many years not to feel guilty at being the cause of their flight. She doesn't blame them for leaving; even Ben—she doesn't blame him at all. The details of her tryst in the woods with Ben seem oddly distant, as if there were a barrier between her and that moment. And she can't go forward, she can't see the future, even an hour from now. She is stuck here now, and there is no hiding. As frightened as she is, she senses a strange strength; she feels terribly alive, as if she will never be able to sleep again. She is alone in this bedroom, but she is all the company she can stand.

When she first came up here, she huddled on the bed and shook as if she had a high temperature, wanting Will to come running in, to hold her and say he loved her, forgave her, everything was going to be all right. Her thoughts were all single words, with nothing between them but shame. *Will. Ben. Sorry. Help. Listen. Please. Listen. Help.*

These heartbeats of words were trying to get her attention; slowly, they began to take shape. It is not Will she is asking for help. It is not Will she needs to listen to. Not yet, at least.

In the last week she has tried to believe in Will, in his love, in his concern for her. She has tried to believe in God, and Ben, and the role of an unnamed woman. She needs to believe in herself, but what should she believe? Perhaps that Ben was only the key, a key, to the Pandora's box she was so afraid to open up herself. It's open now, and there's no going back, and maybe that's for the best. She needs to be very careful now, to see what else is in it, not to close it back up.

She sits on her bed with her back against the wall, looking at her legs, her arms, her hands, and this calms her, because whoever she is, is still here. She may have destroyed her marriage—she hopes not, even though there is that possibility—but she must go on, wants to go on. She has lived a life that has been good in many ways, and lonesome in others, and not honest, recently, but all this time she has been standing in the wings, waiting for a cue from someone else. And Will, he has put off dealing with what they both have known was a faded relationship for too many years, put off life with her until the next play is over, and of course there is always another play. He has filled the holes in his life with theatre, bringing fictional characters to life, while she has filled the holes in her life with hope of something better, the something always vague and impossible, too far to reach, so why bother? No more. She wants to act again, and sing, but not in Will's theatre. She wants to love Will again, and he to love her, but not in the gaps of their lives.

Will has been struggling with the fact that theatre changes, with trying to stay on top of it, even though that means trying something new, taking chances. He needs to understand love is just the same. That she took a chance at love again. That she would like to take a chance at loving Will again, and hopes he will do the same. She will not beg for his forgiveness; she will meet him as an equal.

Myra lays her hands on her thighs and feels the warmth. She looks at the wall across from her, the wallpaper of plain pale flowers that was here when they bought this place. It's a good house. The room holds her in quiet thought. She no longer wants Will to rush up and save her from herself. She hopes he takes his time, with whatever thinking he is doing now, because she needs it, this time alone. She has things to say, and they are just now forming. She wants time to practice the words she will say, before she shares them with Will. There is a lot at stake. She closes her eyes and sees Beth and Mac. She hopes they will understand.

Listen. Please. It is her own voice. And she does.

Acknowledgments

I grew up in the theatre, spending much of my youth watching rehearsals and performances from my specially allotted spot in the wings, just behind the red velvet curtain. My father was an actor and director at The Cleveland Play House, and the actors and techs were my family. I'd like to thank each and every person who worked at The Cleveland Play House from 1954 to 1972 for their kindness, their friendship, and their gift of grand and miraculous theatre. I would like to especially thank Evie McElroy, not only for the joy of watching her perform but for sharing with me her observations about *Of Mice and Men*, which she directed.

I would also like to thank my friends, family, and fellow writers in The East Side Writers Group, who read the first drafts of this book and whose comments were thoughtful, sincere, and of great value. And a very special thank you to John Glusman and Christy Fletcher, for their inspiration and hard work. I am honored and grateful to have all these wonderful people in my life.